The English Harem

Anthony McCarten's debut novel, *Spinners* (1998), was internationally acclaimed and has since been translated into four languages. His collection of short stories, *A Modest Apocalypse*, was shortlisted in the Heinemann-Reed Fiction Award in 1991. He has also written twelve stage plays, including co-writing the world-wide success *Ladies Night*, which won France's prestigious Molière prize, the Meilleure Pièce Comique, in 2001. McCarten has also adapted another of his plays, *Via Satellite*, into a feature film which he directed, and which had its world premiere at the 1998 Cannes Film Festival.

Born in 1961, Anthony McCarten grew up in New Plymouth, New Zealand, and currently divides his time between Wellington, London and Los Angeles.

ANTHONY McCARTEN

The English Harem

PICADOR

First published 2001 as a Vintage Book by Random House, New Zealand, Auckland

This edition published 2002 by Picador
an imprint of Pan Macmillan Ltd
Pan Macmillan, 20 New Wharf Road, London N1 9RR
Basingstoke and Oxford
Associated companies throughout the world
www.panmacmillan.com

ISBN 0 330 48855 4

1 3 5 7 9 8 6 4 2

A CIP catalogue record for this book is available from
the British Library.

Printed and bound in Great Britain by
Mackays of Chatham plc, Chatham, Kent

ACKNOWLEDGMENTS

I wish to thank Firouzeh Afsharnia and Sassan Saatchi
for letting me borrow their names for two of the characters in the
book and for also sharing their ideas and uniquely Persian stories.
Lastly, and as ever, I wish to thank Petra, without whom.

In pious times, ere priesthood did begin,
Before polygamy was made a sin;
When man on many multiplied his kind,
Ere one to one was cursedly confin'd;
                              John Dryden, 1631–1700

Ah Love! could thou and I with Fate conspire
To grasp this sorry Scheme of Things entire,
Would not we shatter it to bits — and then
Re-mould it nearer to the Heart's Desire!
                              Omar Khayyam, 1048–1122

1

The Scheme of Things

To cope with the tedium of her work, Tracy often let the beat of the scanner lull her into daydreams.

As she swiped groceries over the laser beam, *blip . . . blip . . . blip . . . blip . . . blip . . . blip*, she let her fancies take many forms, but her usual game had begun to spin out of control.

Her daily entertainment involved, by a small act of imagination, substituting the sullen, depressed, suburbanite customers at the Tooting branch of Sainsbury's for famous personages from history, from television and films, and from books. Already that morning she had served Joan of Arc, Lawrence of Arabia, Princess Leia and Omar Sharif. Interspersed between the run-of-the-mill shoppers, these phantoms came out of nowhere, glorious in their courtly regalia, in perfect lace or pantaloons or Saharan burnous, drawing from their antique wallets, pinch-purses and *porte-monnaie* their sovereigns, ducats, doubloons and denarii, and forcing Tracy, when it all got too much, to shut her checkout — apologising first to some Shahrazad of *The Thousand and One Nights* — and rush to the water fountain to gulp mouthfuls from her cupped hand. When she returned to her till, however, the mad roll-call would simply start all over again. The truth was that she didn't even have to summon these ghosts any more. They now came of their own volition: Lord Byron from the Albanian portrait where he looked Albanian, Julia Roberts in several different outfits, Cat Stevens — her favourite singer — exactly as he appeared on the *Matthew and Son* album cover in 1966, Laurence Olivier's Heathcliff and Johnny Weissmüller's Tarzan: these last two in their original black and white, of course.

In the middle of such a procession, actually while laser-swiping the groceries of Elizabeth I, *blip . . . blip . . . blip*, the inevitable happened: she confused fantasy and reality. When Her Majesty Regina popped a packet of Mr Kipling's Bakewell Tarts into her handbag without paying, Tracy chose to look the other way. Store detectives apprehended the old woman on her way out. They led her to the back of the supermarket so she could empty her bag, give her address, and weep.

At Tracy's dismissal interview the video evidence clearly showed a bent-over pensioner ineptly thrusting the tarts into a bamboo-handled carpetbag with Tracy doing nothing to stop her. But how could she begin to explain herself, when she felt she was extending to a monarch the courtesy of turning a blind eye?

'You were dreaming again, just admit it,' her supervisor demanded from the edge of his desk, looming above her with the pretence of concern on his face. 'I can't help you if you won't help yourself, Trace. What in Jesus' name were you thinking about?'

Under his aggressive gaze she withered as usual. She offered nothing in defence. He sighed heavily. He liked her, he said, but what could he do? His hands were tied. 'You know how I feel about you.' His foot grazed her naked calf. An accident? She had to look away.

She was a good worker, he continued, with a great head for prices, the best he had ever seen, some kind of genius. But if she couldn't explain herself he'd have to let her go.

But Tracy couldn't open her mouth. With no stomach for a reply she let her thoughts stray instead.

'Tracy? I'm waiting. Trace? Are you even listening?'

But it was too late: she was beyond his reach already.

'Tracy!'

She didn't even remember leaving the supermarket. She rode the bus home. Then, as she turned east, unemployed for the fourth time in two years, a scrap of sunlight fell onto her shoulder. Craning her head, she orientated her face. Warmth flooded into her. As she stirred from an elaborate daydream, in which she played the heroine, she returned to her senses and began to feel irrationally excited about the future.

The washing machine clicked onto full spin and sent a tremendous vibra-tion across the flat, rattling teacups and ashtrays as well as Eric's box of rusty motorcycle parts on the balcony outside. God knew the number of floors below which were also affected by his unstable machine. As the block's unofficial maintenance man he knew all too well that, at twenty-three floors, the building resonated like a tuning fork.

That afternoon it had been his plan to try taming the washer once and for all but his mind had wandered.

A manual of operating instructions for another washing machine, thrown out three years before, had ensnared him and he was still studying its faded pages when the front door opened.

'Got the bloody sack, didn't I,' his daughter announced theatrically, throwing down her backpack, as if in a rage. 'Personality conflict.'

But he didn't lift his head from his reading. 'Oh no,' he muttered.

It was clear to Tracy that he hadn't heard. Such an overprotective parent would definitely have more to say than this.

'Unbe*lievable* actually. Dad? Did you hear me? Dad? I got the sack. I said I got the push.'

'Who did?' He lifted his head.

'Personality clash. But it's okay. I was sick of it anyway.'

Concern at last reached his features, filling his motorcyclist's face, ruddied by decades of speed without a visor, years of craning around juggernauts, buffeted by headwinds. 'They don't have personalities. How can there be a conflict?'

'Anyway. They still fired me.'

In the course of Eric Pringle's life, two things were dominant: his own happiness and that of his daughter, but in reverse order.

Tracy came first with Eric, that is to say, his pleasure was a corollary of hers. In recent years this unnatural level of stewardship, a by-product perhaps of his own unemployment, too much free time on his hands, had drawn adverse comment. Some friends told him that his devotion was an excuse for not engaging himself. He could not live life through another, especially not a child. Meanwhile he had let his own life slide, let it rust like his motorbikes.

'How did it happen?'

'I don't know. They sacked me. Bam. Like that.'

'Why? What did you do?'

She shaped her reply. 'I did nothing.' This was strictly true, and she didn't want to further alarm her father. She knew how brittle he could be. 'Doesn't matter, though. Best thing. I'll find something else, don't worry. I'm actually going to go and look for something else this afternoon.'

It was important she tell her father not to worry. After all, here was a man who had all his daughter's milk teeth stored like trophies in a special container; a man who showed off the small accidental scars she'd given him as a child with the pride of a war veteran; a man who was unable to sleep at night unless tranquillised by the home-again click of her bedroom door. 'How can they sack you for nothing?'

She shrugged then looked over his shoulder. 'Are we getting a new washing machine then?'

'Forget about the fucking washing machine. That's my problem. What the hell are you gonna do for a job?'

'I'll be fine, Dad. I'll get something else. Got an idea already, actually.'

'Like what?'

'Tell you if I get it, okay?'

She left him with just this morsel and went to her room and shut the door.

He stared at the familiar back of the bedroom door, pondering what his daughter might have in mind now. Two misfits around the house was two too many.

Closing the manual, he went back to the washing machine. He would fix it tomorrow. Wrapping his arms around it, he set his feet, squeezed it hard, felt its weight and then waltzed it backward, his cheek flat against his hulking partner, staggering one-two-three one-two-three back into its cubby space where its four left-footed feet found their original dents in the linoleum. No sense in having eight dents in the floor, unseen or not: such were the ruminations of an unemployed man.

When he plugged it back in he took some satisfaction from thinking he had repaired something in it, even if it wasn't the actual problem: a slow leakage of water about which he had done nothing.

When his wife came in from work, puffing heavily, Eric was still standing by the machine, a wash in mid-cycle, waiting to see if all the heavy moving had accidentally cured the leakage problem. Such luck would raise him in her esteem.

'Oh good,' she said, surprised to see the much-delayed job being addressed. 'Miracles.'

'No leaks yet.'

'Repairman finally tinkering with the lift as well. Hell must have frozen over.' Their flat was on the twenty-third floor. They relied heavily on the lift.

'She got the sack,' he reported, eyes peeled for the first hint of a puddle.

'She didn't!'

'Personality clash she said.' The puddles that formed were incredibly viscous.

'Oh no. Where is she now?'

'Fort Knox.' He nodded to the hallway, towards the locked door.

Seven years before they had both given consent for Tracy to have a lock put on her door. They could never have foreseen the consequences. Since then they had not once been allowed back inside their daughter's bedroom. *Not once, in seven years!* Not to vacuum — Tracy did this herself — not to talk to her — she'd come out, closing the door quickly behind her; not to bring her a single cup of tea — this would be left on the carpet, like a pagan offering, a snake of a hand later drawing it inside. They had learnt the hard way the subtle determination of their only child, and also something of the geo-political carve-up of a house containing a teenager: the patrolled borders, the annexed territories, the delicately negotiated ceasefires, policies of *détente* and *rapprochement*. Realising it was farcical, all the same Eric had a comic image he repeated like a mantra: 'The balloon went up with us holding onto it. We just always meant to let go.'

'Yoohoo!' It was Emily Powell, Emily the next-door neighbour, Emily yoo-hooing and finger waving, Emily freshly widowed, life unwinding, coming over, as usual, to cry.

In her early fifties, just like the Pringles, she had a daughter, Christina, who had been a lifelong classmate of Tracy's. This one detail had flung the Powells and the Pringles onto parallel tracks: achievements in one family read as criticisms in the other. Where Christina had won a scholarship, triumphed over expectations and gone to Oxford, Tracy had dropped out and gone to 'assist Lord Sainsbury', as Eric put it. On the negative side, Graeme Powell had died, and Eric was still alive. It sort of evened itself out, Monica supposed.

'She's been sacked,' Monica informed Emily, before she had even processed the fact herself.

'No! Who? Tracy? No!' Emily also knew who 'she' was. 'I'm sure she'll be fine. She's so clever. She'll be fine. Just fine. How terrible. Poor thing.'

Monica turned back to her husband. 'Why?'

Eric gave the answer he had heard from Tracy. 'Conflict of personalities.'

Monica turned back to Emily for sympathy, putting her hand to her mouth, as though suppressing a welling anguish. 'Conflict of personalities.'

Emily nodded. 'That happens. She'll find something.' But it was hard to sympathise. She had her own worries. She took a seat as soon as one was offered.

The long wait for Tracy to emerge from her room and provide them with more details allowed Emily to deliver, in a low voice, the next instalment of her grief about the death of her husband, taken by non-Hodgkin's lymphoma two months earlier, a withering, miserable exit. Today she had found the courage to drop a bombshell: he had not been faithful.

The quake drew Monica to the kitchen door, and Eric from his thoughts about the washing machine manual.

Together: 'No! Emily? *No!* No!'

Emily collapsed in tears as she told, with waxen pallor, and between sobs, that Graeme had divulged all on his deathbed, saving it for his last energies, the 'now or never' testimony of a coward. Emily had been too stupefied, until now, to let anyone else know about it. The confession almost constituted the man's last words. Even so, Emily had not released her grip on his frail hand, she said, after all, he was dying — this tough detail sent Monica's hand again to her mouth — until, Emily continued, he slipped away, destroying her twice, all inside five minutes. Nice work.

'Oh Emily. That . . . that's . . . just . . . ' But there were no words for such life-lessons in pain. Monica could only try to guess at the place where such an experience left you.

'Jesus,' gasped Eric, anger being the male response; anger, and *I knew something was going on.*

Emily had brought her own box of tissues.

Comparatively irrelevant details now followed. The woman had been a florist, at Harrods, 'nice for some', a simple and generous woman as Graeme told it; he had confessed for the record a mistress of six years standing, six years, six, six, six! 'I could stab her'; and the affair had not even been called off. Death had to do what human willpower had been incapable of.

The ghastly revelation now out, it fully explained to Monica and Eric's minds Emily's constantly blood-drained looks since the funeral, her near-agoraphobia.

In the middle of Emily's tale of woe, Tracy emerged from her room, hands defiantly on hips, pleased as punch about how she looked, which was exactly like a hooker, and excitedly pronounced her bright, new and happy ambitions.

'So how do I look? I'm going out to get a new job.'

Tracy naturally assumed that she was the cause of everyone's obvious distress.

Behind her locked door in the preceding thirty minutes, she had emptied her wardrobe onto her bed and sifted through her clothes. The resulting 'look' was no mishap, but more the result of careful judgement calls. She would need to look sexy tonight for what she had in mind. This was the real world that she was entering, not some supermarket, and she knew how it worked. Cleavage, legs, a come-on smile, a tart's formula; as with any safe-cracker, the right combination was all you needed: click, clack, you're in.

She was excited but very nervous. Her hand shook as she emphasised her eyes and lips in front of the mirror. Within hours she could be counting out the cash from her inaugural night right there on her bed.

As she put on extra make-up, running a pencil along her eyebrows with added pressure, she began to realise what a person loses when they lose a job. After all, the checkout position had not been without its advantages. It had never asked anything that she had not been happy to give. Her time was not particularly precious to her, no great sacrifice was involved. Her brain didn't fret about being underused; she had no illusions about herself: she was good with numbers but no great brain. She was destined to spend her life serving others. And lastly, the job possessed what all jobs must: the ability to swallow hours that would otherwise have to be spent convincing yourself you are happy, liked, fascinating, valid, captivating, talented, going places, sexy, funny, worthy of love, complex. She had seen a character in a book described as 'complex'; it seemed the highest goal of all.

She put down her eyebrow pencil and licked the base of her finger to work loose her gold heart ring. She then held it between thumb and forefinger and glided it back and forth across the lower rim of her eye where a throbbing sty was forming. This grandmother's cure never failed. If her relationship with the doting Ricky Innes, apprenticed in his father's morbid family practice over in Tooting, didn't work out or solve anything, then the ring he had given her, her only golden possession, would always be useful for containing these nascent sties.

'Hi,' he had said, when they met as strangers in a pulsing nightclub.

'Hi.'

'Whatchoodo den?'

'Checkout. Sainsbury's. How about you?'

'Mason.'

'What, like . . . Freemason?'

'Nah, nah. Nuffin' like that.'

'MmKay. So, what, like a bricky then or what?'

'Nah, nah. Monumental mason, yeah.'

'Oh, so like . . . monuments then?'

'Nah, nah. Gravestones.'

'Gravestones?'

'Simple as that.'

'You're joking! You never make gravestones?'

'Dead serious. Joke. Top'a da line. Whatsa matter?'

The monumental mason, her very own master's apprentice in the art of gravestone-making, had given her a ring to cement his intentions, if not his love, and which she now, blinking and clearing her eye of accidental tears and tucking her brown hair behind her ears, slid back onto her finger.

She was ready.

'Like a slut,' her father finally answered, accurately summarising the feelings of all the adults.

Their shared expressions, however, were less of disapproval than of wonder, a wonder about whether all of later-life screw-ups, just like the one they had just been discussing, started way back here, at Tracy's age, with a young person dressing up to go out.

The outfit was clearly unacceptable. The skirt barely descended to cover the pudenda, the high heels and piled hair were wildly provocative, as was the make-up. The lycra halter-neck, which squeezed into existence a previously unseen cleavage, created a body that no one in the room associated with Tracy.

'I'm going out job hunting,' she explained.

'Job hunting?' Eric shouted. 'At this time of night?'

'I'm late. See ya.'

Monica looked at her husband with a *Who goes out to look for work at this hour?* look.

Eric took this up: 'Looking like that? It's after . . . it's five, five-thirty!', he said, consulting his wristwatch.

'I know. I'm just going to look for restaurant work.'

'Don't make me laugh. Now sit down and forget that for now. Tell your mother what happened today.'

'Sorry. I'm serious. It's the only time managers are in. Bye. '

Before anyone could stop her she was gone. Eric shouted after her from the doorway but her pace quickened down the corridor and she was soon gone, down the stairs, forgoing the lift, her heels audible, the image of her swinging derriere and upper thighs loitering in his mind.

'I'm serious. Maybe she's gonna go on the game.'

Emily had gone. He and Monica sat side by side on the tall, new kitchenette bar-stools. Monica laughed and tried to fit a new word into her cryptic crossword. 'Don't be ridiculous.' She was trying to complete the clue: H, I, J, K, L, M, N, O. Five letters.

Eric monitored developments over her shoulder. 'I'm not joking either.'

'Not in a million years.'

'Often from normal backgrounds.'

'Not this normal.'

He pressed an elbow into her ribs. 'Be serious, will ya?'

'Not the type.' She chewed her pen. 'Five letters.'

'That's the point. There *is* no type, is there. They come from all walks of life, and the parents *never* know. Most prostitutes — '

'Oh shut up!'

' . . . most pros are ordinary girls just like Tracy. Not the ones strung out on drugs, not the deadbeats. It's the ordinary ones that make all the money, do all the trade.'

'Seem to know a lot about this.'

'That's what all the blokes want. Ordinary girls. Daughters of people like us, who never even fucking know a thing. We kiss 'em on the cheek, say seeya, they move out, seem to be doing well, buy a car, a house, good girl, then two houses, then two cars, hang on, something a bit funny, a boat! . . . Jesus Christ, ten years later they write a book: "Why I Became A Whore", know what I mean?' He rubbed his forehead feverishly. He had worked himself into a state. Flushed, still grimy from moving the washing machine, he felt his protective shackles rise. There was still a part of the jungle inside Eric Pringle, still the man of action, the vital force, to be reckoned with.

'She's not sexy, Eric. Her mind doesn't work that way. Doesn't even think like that. Not a sexy girl.'

'Coulda fooled me. And if she can do it with that Richard geezer she's seeing then she could do it with anyone.'

'It wouldn't come into her head.'

Eric did not say so, but the source of his anxiety was an article in the very newspaper that Monica was about to write on.

'Water,' she said.

'How d'ya get that?'

'See?' She filled in the blanks.

'What?'

'That's clever, innit? H . . . to . . . O.'

This is more like it, Tracy thought. Taste of Persia? Even the sound of it is promising. I'm on the right track now.

The Chinese, Thai and Italian places she had just tried, and been turned away from, had lacked atmosphere and the requisite glamour. But this was different. All the mysteries she required of life could be imagined with relative ease in a place like this. This was what she was looking for: not a mere job, but a turn in the road, an imaginative departure.

Its dim interior was filled with eastern ornaments; tapestries on the walls depicted ancient battles or tranquil forest scenes; small low tables were set in intimate clusters amid pools of amber light leaking from camphor-smelling lanterns.

The man who stepped forward from behind a fretted screen was fiftyish, balding, compact, with the forlorn air of someone whose life had been spent in the study of human nature. Reaching behind his back he attempted to unlace a flour-dusted apron that flowed all the way to his ankles. His face was lined by the activity of laughter muscles. The sheen of his skin gave it a polished finish. They looked at each other in the dim light with the calm solemnity of people who instantly realise they are from entirely different worlds. 'Yes please?'

He stepped forward. In full light he was better able to appraise her. She noted the look of alarm on his face as his eyes drifted down to her cleavage, her naked legs. But fortunately, she also witnessed the look's disappearance as his eyes clinically moved back up again. He looked startled. *Click clack*, she thought.

'Can I help you?'

'I was wondering about the job in the window.'

'Job? Oh, I see.' He laughed and seemed at once relieved.

'What?'

'Nothing.'

'What?' She became confused again.

'Well, this is a *Persian* restaurant.'

'I know. I can read.'

'Good. Well that's something.'

Bastard, she thought. *If this isn't humiliating enough.*

'I mean, we have no jobs, I am sorry.'

'You have no jobs?'

'Nothing. Thank you.' He scrutinised the scantily clad young lady before him: he hadn't been gone from Iran so long that he didn't find such displays of ostentation disconcerting. To him she was the picture of delinquent English youth, dressed up for Allah knew what, everything but a ring in her nose, a head full of pop charts, everything he detested. He shook his head. 'Sorry.'

'Then why have you got a sign in the window? It's a little bit misleading, don't you think?'

He turned to look towards the door. 'There's a sign in the window? I don't know what it is doing there. You are absolutely right. I will take it down right now. Thank you for pointing it out.' Tracy didn't move. She watched him as he went to the door, untaped the card and removed it. 'I apologise. Thank you for coming in.'

'Or is it just me?'

'No.' He sighed, clearly wearied by this now. 'No, it's not just you. Someone here must have thought we needed someone when I'm afraid that is simply not the case. It won't happen again.'

'Fine,' she said. 'But it's a bit misleading, that's all.'

'I'm sorry.' He opened the door for her.

'Nice place.'

'Oh. Thank you.'

11

She passed under his arm, and he followed her out onto the street where he watched her walk away, shaking his head until a faint smile appeared.

2

Meat

In one way or another, Saaman Sahar, owner of Taste of Persia, had had his life shaped by meat.

The talkative son of one Mostafa Sahar, a well-known Tehran butcher, Saaman had grown up in the shadow of a falling cleaver. The thump of steel into giant wood-block was his first and strongest memory, and the boy fixed like a splint to his father's leg in the torrid open-air market of *Meidan-e-tareh-bar* of the late fifties.

Always short — as an adult he never grew over five foot nine — he could never see much of the actual butchery process, but this did not prevent the relentless thump of the cleaver from transmitting itself into his being, ordering his atoms, sealing his destiny.

By the mid-seventies, his father now prosperous — with a chain of stores and the old market stall a distant memory — Saaman like many others of his generation, was sent for a western university education, to be groomed at great expense in the baffling calculus of Keynesian economics. It was always intended that, upon graduation, he would return and take up the family reins, capitalise, expand and then modernise the family firm and so enter the social life of modern Tehran as an engine for progress.

But it was in England that two things happened.

The first was that he became an Anglophile. With his mind vivified by the cool air of Oxford, this country appeared to be the best possible haven for his energies and his money. It was the home of all civility, the crucible of common sense, the most progressive and charismatic culture the west had to offer. With the irrefutable logic of youth he let the sight of a sunset over rolling Cotswold hills decide his lasting aesthetic, an English forest after a rain shower set his olfactory standards, and a warm English beer after a long walk render all other tastes inferior. He idealised England out of all proportion. With the sentimental eyes of John Constable he accepted it as his soul's landscape.

When he described this antiterra to his mother she wrote back: 'Stay where you are then. If that is your attitude then good riddance.'

Proud of her son, bragging at every opportunity about the fact the Sahars were of an income now to educate their eldest at the 'greatest university in the world', even idealising in her own mind the cultural superiority of the west, she didn't want to lose him to a degenerate, depraved lifestyle. The west cared nothing for the soul. It had nothing to teach in that regard. What she revered she also feared. Her son could love England for now, but soon he must come home, and without regret.

The second event to shake his life occurred after a game of cricket at Christ Church College.

While drinking Earl Grey tea after an indolent game of ten-a-side, in which he and a few classmates had orchestrated a languid draw, the unimaginable happened.

On the afternoon in question, with twenty-five runs on the board against SAHAR S., he drew the short straw to buy lunch for everyone: meat pies. How was he to know what lay in store when he hungrily wolfed down that steak-and-kidney stew fermenting between layers of pastry? And how was he to know the changes that would domino through his life as a result of a summer's day picnic?

The effect was immediate. The resulting bout of salmonella laid him waste for three weeks. Vomiting and explosive diarrhoea so dehydrated him that he required hospitalisation and close observation. Reports reached his parents. He shed two stone as if it was ballast that could be cut loose. He fought fever. And somewhere in his delirium the concept of meat became unbearable. Thereafter it was impossible for him even to contemplate it without a bubble of gas surging up from his duodenum. Henceforward, even the thought of returning to his father's side, to those steaming shops with their incessant thump-thump-thumps, and with the yawning of maw and flesh and bone, was enough to drive his meals of lightly steamed vegetables and crudités upward from the pit of his stomach to a point in his throat where a conscious effort was required to subdue it.

What a failure he was deemed back home! His postcards were burnt. A Sahar vegetarian? An unpardonable shame.

Upon his return to Tehran, Saaman, by then favouring the more English Sam and flourishing a perverse degree in English literature, told his father that he would really rather prefer to open and then run a vegetarian restaurant.

Knives, wooden blocks and knife-sharpeners clattered out onto the street from the latest butcher's shop. It took hours for the shouting to die down. That Saaman did not experience the sharpness of a cleaver that day was due less to the old man's restraint than to his declining energies. His father turned his back and walked away, crestfallen in a baggy pin-striped suit, leaving a trail of bloody shoe-prints on the grey cement floor. Sam glanced at them: each print fainter than the last, a rubber stamp needing to revisit its ink-pad, a reflection of his family's fading powers, a portent of the old man's demise.

Mostafa withered from that day onwards. He suffered a small stroke barely a month later and remained mystified for the rest of his life by his son's quixotic zeal for vegetables. With retirement looming, he faced an even greater problem: he lacked an obvious heir. Sam's two younger brothers were not of an age to take over the empire. He had no choice.

'A thousand years of patriarchy flushed down the *khala* because of an English pie,' he proclaimed.

The shops were individually sold off, offered quickly at auction. The bids soared above their reserve prices, nothing being more financially certain in Tehran than another millennium of passionate meat consumption. This sudden liquidity was cold comfort for Mostafa, however, a devout man for whom meat was life, and vice versa. This could not simply be repudiated. In their final argument on the matter the old man attempted to warn his son of divine repercussions.

'You are dead already without some meat in you. Listen to the voice of your ancestors. You were not created to eat vegetables. Such a man is a zero!'

While his father slipped into the backwaters of retirement, and his mother became a creature of unlit rooms, Sam's restaurant prospered far beyond his first spreadsheet calculations. He raised capital in a buoyant market. By opening a second and a third restaurant he appealed to the western-crazy climate of the last Shah. His take-home fried-vegetable burgers became *de rigueur* in a thousand fashionable Tehrani homes. He

15

introduced his generation to English chips and ketchup. His crowning glory was the purchase of a legendary establishment in the heart of Tehran, where Stalin, Churchill and Roosevelt had lunched in 1943 to plan the re-occupation of Europe. His popularity earnt him the undeserved reputation of a playboy.

But the first time he saw the exiled Ayatollah Khomeini on television he knew the party was over. As he listened to the charismatic call for a return to religious principles and an end to corruption by the élite, he saw the writing on the wall. The face of Iran would change overnight, and caught between two contradictory worlds — he would sometimes read the Koran before making a sizeable decision, but also sang madrigals in an Anglican church when in England — his country was no longer a place for him. He decided, if he could get his money out, to go.

As for his father before him, the auctioneer's hammer fell quickly on each of his restaurants. He was briefly rich. The new owners, young entrepreneurs sniffing quick rewards but blind to social change, thought the murmurs of civil dissent the predictable complaints of the underclass. Sam was to learn, years afterwards, that each had lost their shirts in the crackdown.

His best friends, just as oblivious to the times, continued to drive their Italian cars far above the speed limit, contemptuous of any law, and even intensified their lavish Parisian shopping trips, their commissions of nose-jobs. Against his two younger brothers' pleas for him to stay, he spirited his money into accounts in Switzerland. On the day of the Shah's overthrow and the popular installation of the new Imam, he was on the first plane out. Sipping a spritzer, he shared a first-class row with one of the Shah's nieces.

A day later, on English soil, jet-lagged and giddy from a noon aperitif, he was playing tennis at the fashionable Wimbledon club, calling 'good shot', a regular *bon vivant* in his white shorts.

And so began his years in London, which, for two decades, served as a quiet and commodious base. He lived securely within the parameters of English life, speculating with restraint on the stock market and opening a token restaurant, running it first-hand as little more than a hobby. But like other chameleons he was soon in emotional trouble. The contradiction with the past was unsettling at a deep level. He kept up elements of tradition, links with his family, a few friends, but the hidden strain got to him, made him angry at his homeland for its retrograde steps. He spanned east and west but belonged fully to neither. His response was to sink his energies even more into his adopted country, become a hyper-patriot and weaken his ties with the old. Not for him the whining sentimentality of the émigré!

His restaurant operations in England were modest. His money, converted into pounds, did not go far. Also, the entrepreneurial wind had gone out of his sails. The Taste of Persia, with its vegetarian menu and inventive dishes, was distinctive enough in a city that barely knew what a salad looked like until the mid-nineties. He turned a workable profit without trying too hard. He still had a few stocks to fall back on after buying a nice, detached house, which was a London luxury. His mange-tout tofu shish-kebab was a word-of-mouth hit. The superb aubergine kashk bademjan was a coup lifted straight out of his old Tehran menu. His cooks worked miracles with dolmas, with hot beets and stuffed cabbage. He talked endlessly of opening a second London restaurant and even had plans in draft form, but ever the great Oxford brain, always said he was awaiting the perfect market indicators.

At the age of fifty-two he had prematurely become a melancholic foreigner, an overfed shadow on the margins of a culture he revered.

Tracy returned the next morning at ten.

When Sam Sahar crossed the street from his parked Mercedes she was already there to greet him. Her outfit was so much less outrageous that he had to come close to recognise her.

'Hi,' she said, somewhat triumphantly.

'You? Again?'

'Sign in the window,' she said, pointing to the card reinstated overnight.

He rubbed his chin, blushed, looked away. 'Oh yes, yes, well, change of plans it seems.'

'So? Do you still not have a vacancy?'

'Yes, well . . . perhaps . . . you might as well come in and . . . at least . . . leave your number.' He fiddled with the lock. 'Come in, please . . . let's go inside.' He seemed to want to get her off the street.

It was not necessary for Sam to take down her details. She had made the extra effort of hand-writing a CV overnight. At a table which he cleared of chairs, she forced him, with an intense look of hopefulness, to survey the half-page of achievements. 'Fine. Checkout? Good. Education. Mmhmm. Well, this looks fine. But no restaurant experience.' The phone in the kitchen rang. 'Oh, one moment.'

The aura of the empty restaurant, with its chairs on the tables and cave-like calm, the hanging diptychs with their imperial scenes of Mogul murder and betrayal, pastoral leisure and lust, plus its residual odours of wax and charcoal smoke from the brick oven, gave Tracy the exciting sensation of having stepped inside one of her own daydreams.

To work here would be a paid holiday, she thought.

She went to examine the battle scene close up: warriors with drawn scimitars, a broken lute half-buried in the sand, fallen heroes cupping their pierced sides, making their final peace in the laps of weeping, disconsolate maidens.

Almost unseen, a woman entered the restaurant and crossed the room. She was tall and slender, her hair was pulled up into a chignon. When Tracy turned she received a smile. The woman crouched, appeared to fiddle with a mechanism, and then emerged with a bundle of cash which she put into a handbag. Then, like a spirit, she was gone.

'I really love your place,' Tracy told him when he returned.

He wasn't immune to compliments. 'Thank you.' He stopped at the desk and looked, seeming momentarily puzzled. He grumbled.

'Oh, a woman came in and emptied it.'

'I know. I know. Thank you. It's okay. She always cleans me out.' He grinned for the first time. 'My wife. She is also the one who keeps putting "Waitress Wanted" in the window behind my back. Putting me in the embarrassing position of talking to hopeful young women whom I have . . . no intention of hiring.'

'None?' Tracy looked shocked.

'I am sorry. We are a very traditional establishment in many ways, except the food. Yes, we do need more waitresses. We are very busy right now, which is why Yvette goes behind my back.' He muttered something in his native tongue. 'But we have a big Persian clientele who speak little or no English. The menus are also in Farsi. Also, I want to give the spotlight to the food, not to my waitresses.' Here, he bowed: his first comment to remotely pass as a compliment.

'I'm a quick learner,' she said. 'At Sainsbury's — '

'And tenacious. Extremely tenacious.'

'If you say so. Look, give us a chance. Please.'

He sighed, assessed in his head the damage she could do and concluded that his need for temporary assistance outweighed her destructive potential. 'All right. One week. A trial. I will try you for one week. But I do not want arguments if we both decide it is a terrible mistake, something which will very quickly become apparent.'

'That's fine.' Tracy nodded, trying to keep back the explosion of relief and gratitude for the street, when, unwatched, she could scream and jump up and down. Here she was still attempting to prove beyond any doubt that she was capable of the same level of grace, restraint and decorum which, a few minutes before, she had seen exhibited by this man's wife. 'Yeah, of course,' she said. 'That would be . . . most . . . '

'Most . . . ?' He arched his eyebrows, awaiting a word which, by its omission gained undue importance.

' . . . convenient,' she said.

Tracy pushed the stop button and got off the bus on Rycroft Street, almost leaving her bottle of Tesco's champagne on the seat. She arrived at her boyfriend's house unexpectedly, and frightened the cat.

Her plan was to surprise him with her news, drain the bottle in his front room, and then open herself up to new possibilities. Their relationship wasn't based on spontaneity but tonight she was optimistic and felt hopeful about everything.

He lived in a one-bedroom flat on the ground floor of a modern block so ugly and barren that its disrepair was an embellishment. He kept a goldfish barely alive in a punch-bowl on the windowsill, maintained a satellite TV subscription — its dish outside blotted out all natural light — and he eschewed all housework. But his red car, parked on the street, was spotless. Under its wiper sat a small hand-written cardboard statement: 'Wet'. Freshly sprayed, the car looked brand-new.

She could not resist testing the paint job. Her fingertip left its faint negative on the sticky surface: he would probably discover this, he was finicky about his vehicles, use the forensic evidence to track her down. But tonight there remained a definite romance in leaving her mark. A heart carved upon a tree, an inscription in a book, this tiny secret rose would endure for years.

How had they been drawn together? After their first meeting she had forgotten him, utterly, but during arrangements for her grandmother's funeral they had met again.

She could see on first meeting him that he was a ladies' man and that he possessed the rough charm of the sexually confident, which at once repelled and intrigued her. She had not understood, however, that by walking away, as she had in that nightclub, she would arouse his will to conquer and thereby create, momentarily, a love-sick monster.

When he saw her again a few months later it seemed to the mason that she was even more beautiful and ethereal than he had remembered, her eyes more luminous and her manner more appealing than those of any woman he had craved in years.

Agreeing with him that it was indeed a very small world, Tracy stood at her mother's side as Monica submitted to Ricky's father the text for the inscription, to be cut into the blank remainder of the double headstone. Love. Forever. The great words.

Around the shoulders of their parents their eyes met, the apprentice smiling at her all the time. Being sad helped: it made her vulnerable to the tradesman's looks, to his nods and winks, and it also gave her a falsely magnified sense of the importance of his job. With her sights lowered by tragedy she vastly exaggerated the value of grave-making. She saw it at the centre of life. It suddenly seemed the most fundamental, vital and romantic vocation on the face of the earth.

Richard had decided. He must have this girl, and not because he was capable of loving her more than any of his numerous other conquests, but because he now saw in her surrender the potential for the sweetest victory of his life.

When the stone had to be entirely redone, owing to an error in the grandmother's date of birth which would have made her 180 years old, he saw his chance.

On his second visit the apprentice came alone.

In this assignment the young man sensed a better opportunity to impress the still-grieving granddaughter. To ingratiate himself he reconceived the stone entirely. He unveiled his overblown plans on the table, pointed this way and that like a Napoleon over his charts.

Almost doubling the size of the headstone he proposed curlicues and seraphs, cupidon, bas-relief vegetation and falcons in the bloated style of a Grinling Gibbons, so off the wall in fact that the Pringles entirely failed to see its inappropriateness. He even assured them that it wouldn't cost them a penny more, being the very least he could do to compensate for the inconvenience of the error. At the end of his visit no one was shocked when he quite openly asked Tracy if she would like to pop out for a pint some time.

Convinced that the young man was an artist, a poet of the cemeteries, Tracy allowed herself to daydream that she was falling in love. She drifted into one of a dozen romantic scenarios.

But the young man's real-life attempts to achieve his amorous goals would take more than a few bas-reliefs and full-quivered cupidon.

For three full weeks, when he dropped her back home after a date, she was able to slip from his grasp before he could switch off the ignition. When the act finally did occur, in the back of his grubby van, with the upholstery sparkled with schist, chips of obsidian, tickles of quartz, feldspar and mica, she didn't make a single noise. She seemed to be in some other place, and her lack of involvement in his conquest left him feeling criticised. 'Are you all right?' he asked as he moved. How could she reply? The metronomic beat of the man's movements had sent her straight back to Sainsbury's, to the rhythmic beat of produce passing over a laser beam.

Also, she not only made him wear a contraceptive rubber of the glow-in-the-dark variety — which, as he moved in and out, made him feel as though he were in a nightclub — but also forced him to apply an excess of spermicidal cream.

'It was all they had,' she had told him unapologetically about the condom. These had been her only words to him that night.

He dropped her off at her tower block. She walked away without a kiss. He thought it went well.

With the certainty that a serious relationship had been set in motion, Richard soon overlooked his own doubts and made the journey to Finklestein's, the local jeweller. In front of the assorted collections he directed the myopic old man's hand towards a gold heart ring. 'How much is that one?' Two hours later it was on Tracy's finger: love, Tooting-style.

She accepted it as a matter of politeness, and that night a green phosphorescent glow once again flashed on-off-on-off-on inside his van in the lee of Albert Bridge.

'A friendship ring is whatya call it,' he told her in the dark, watching the heart glister on her finger as he tried to impress her then with a new repertoire of kisses.

It was the first ring she had ever owned.

His front door was ajar, and she went inside. Hearing the door slam he called out, 'I'm in here.' She found Richard in the lounge eating cold fish and chips in front of the television.

'Nice colour,' she said, jerking her thumb toward the road.

'Tracy!' His face drained of colour.

'Your car,' she said.

'Oh. Right. Gave me a fright. Jesus. What are you doing here? You should have phoned. How did you get in?'

'Thought I'd surprise you.'

'Oh great. That's great.'

When she moved to the couch she saw he was watching a pornographic video, one he'd hired for a week, he quickly said, for the two of them. He was merely previewing it. 'So what's up?'

She told him that she had no intention of telling him her news while he watched two naked women kiss, and she set the champagne on the coffee table with a thump, making no move to open it.

'Champagne? What's been happening?'

'Nothing. Absolutely nothing.'

'Then what's the champers for?'

'I got a new job, that's all.'

He finally looked at her: 'Great. That's fucking great, Tracy. I'd love to celebrate with ya, but, what a bummer, I'm . . . I'm just on my way out. Shit. Bad timing. Got a snooker game at ten, y'see. Shit, is that the time? What a bugger, eh?' He hit the rewind button and sent the video images flying backwards. 'But tomorrow night, definitely. We'll go out. Shit, gotta go.'

In the hallway, he pulled on his coat, but when he turned to reach for her she slid out of his embrace and limited his kiss to a peck on the cheek. 'Forget it. I'll see you around sometime, okay? And don't ever rent any of those things again.'

'Hey — don't be like that.' But her heels were already clacking down the path. 'Trace?' He watched the swing of her hips as long as he could before she turned the corner and vanished.

He should have looked disappointed but he did not. His sigh was one of relief. He checked his watch, shut the door, hung up his coat again and returned to the lounge where he swung into action.

He pulled two glasses from a cabinet, polished them on his sleeve, set them beside the champagne, removed the foil from the bottle and clapped his hands once at his good fortune. 'Sorted.' His eyes floated to the television where the action ran backwards at high speed: hyperactive lesbians eased each other into magical clothes which flew into their hands from all corners of the room. Their former passion mutated into embarrassment, until they were eventually no more than strangers. He would make it up to Tracy tomorrow, with flowers, the proper florist shop variety, but right now he needed to hurry. He returned to the front door, and looked up and down the street.

As though the world now obeyed his remote control, the distant slam of a car door was followed a few seconds later by the click-click-click of a new set of heels making their way towards him. Tracy's replacement, a shapely figure, head hooded with a scarf and scuttling at high speed, raced into his arms and then engaged him in a rapid restaging of the doorway kiss which had earlier left so much to be desired.

'Get in here you,' he said to his hurtling understudy as he knocked shut the frosted-glass door with his foot. The hyperventilating couple then fell hard against it.

In the tornado of her cut-price perfume he proceeded to undress her where she stood.

Their Saturday night lust didn't go beyond the hallway. She shrieked her banshee delight as her coat was discarded, her dress hoisted, her knickers tugged to the ground and the bare cheeks of her behind pressed against the cold glass. Anyone on the street could have witnessed it: the full moons of this woman's buttocks waxing and waning with every thrusting assault of her promiscuous lover.

Tracy waited for her bus, the exact change in her hand. She liked catching buses long after the rush hour. Besides being empty, they didn't usually make all the stops. She saw them as huge limousines, exclusively taking her wherever she wanted to go. The drivers screeched round corners as if by prior arrangement, hurrying to get her home before her evening bath drawn by the maid grew tepid. She might even stop off at Cartier's on the way for a private, late-night adjustment to her ring.

She played with the fixture on her finger. One jeweller had adjusted it already but it was now too tight to remove easily, irritating her, especially when she felt like she did now. The more she played with it, the more her finger swelled, and now it was trapped.

She tugged at it, regardless. She blamed herself. She was linked to someone she didn't even like. How could that be? He certainly wasn't the artist she'd thought at first. The gravestone was a royal con. If she wasn't careful she'd drift into marrying him. One thing was for certain: you had to be very careful to whom you said 'Yes' in this life, especially if you suspected that your only motive was to experience the drama of the moment more than the reality that would follow.

3

The Diversity of Wives

Determined to find out whether his daughter had fallen into a life of desperate prostitution, as he suspected, Eric Pringle abandoned his watching of the six o'clock news to follow her. 'Leave it to me,' he told his wife. 'I'll take care of this.'

'Eric, no —'

'Leave it to me.'

As his only daughter boarded a bus, bound for 'work', he pressed his key into the ignition of his car. He had surreptitiously pulled up across the road from the bus-stop and in shadow had seen her pace, then smoke two cigarettes — a habit he couldn't criticise — and impatiently kick pebbles into the road. He felt like a policeman, but one spying on his own life.

When the bus pulled into traffic he eased his car into gear. His aim was to try and keep a respectable distance between them of about twenty metres.

He looked at it this way: parents raised a daughter with strong hopes, instilling in her core beliefs around which they could only hope her life, like a planet, would revolve. Eric and Monica had only one child; perhaps they expected too much of her, it was possible, but it was too late to change that now. Their best dreams, their aspirations, philosophies, ideals, traits, their resources, their time, thoughts, advice, fears — most unflaggingly their fears — had long ago been invested in her. She was now, to their mind, the entire by-product of their lives, the living advertisement of their values and genes in today's world and their sole representative in tomorrow's.

But so what? There was never a guarantee that she, or any child, would stay locked into their pre-ordained orbit. There were no absolutes here, no identical journeys. As science had failed to predict the universe, so Eric Pringle could not rule out the nauseating possibility that, huddled behind the wheel of his car, he might already be the unwitting father of someone else's twenty-quid whore. His mind recoiled. He could not live with such a plunge in expectations. He told himself it couldn't be true, and retraced the events of that week for a new interpretation.

After his suspicions had been awakened he had watched her like a hawk. She had toned down the raunchy clothes but this didn't allay his fears. Perhaps she'd been taken on by a classier whorehouse. He had thought about breaking into her room, going through her stuff, but had come to his senses. Her room was sacrosanct, and any violation would do irreparable damage. No, he would have to bide his time. Watch and wait.

Throughout an early supper in front of the TV, Eric had fantasised about violently upturning his daughter's handbag on the coffee table, scattering its contents and shouting 'Hooker!' when he discovered the tools of her new trade: God knew what creams, devices, equipment they carried. But he couldn't face the possibility of finding such evidence. Instead, he grilled her on the absence of a waitress uniform as she nibbled on a piece of toast while informing them that she'd probably eat at the restaurant. He asked what kind of waitress didn't have a uniform.

'I should get one tonight actually.'

Then, when she turned down his offer for a lift, grabbing her coat and going out, he had become truly suspicious.

'You see what I mean?' he said, pulling on his own coat. 'Since when did she turn down a ride?'

'Don't you dare follow her. You're making a fool of yourself.'

'Just stay out of this. No uniform? If I'm wrong, I'll be delighted. If I'm right, then you'll thank me.'

'Eric!' Monica shouted as he reached for the door.

'Ssshh.' He pointed upward. 'Mrs Wilson.'

'She's twenty years old! Let her go!'

The door closed.

Mrs Wilson was the old pensioner confined to bed in the flat above. Her hearing aid was of such powerful sensitivity that she was a virtual intelligence agency. She was deprived of further information, however, for the remainder of the night.

Tracy got off the bus on Larchmont Street and walked east at a clipped pace. Eric held eye contact with the bus until he dropped into a carpark and followed on foot, already hating his new role. A few times before, when she was much younger, he'd followed her like this, by car, tailing her when she'd been vague about her plans and he'd suspected a rendezvous with some filthy youth with a head full of pornography, but this was the first time he'd gone to the length of shadowing her on foot.

When she slipped into a darkened restaurant, he stopped and lit a cigarette. Taste of Persia, indeed. This address, with its Arabic writing on the glass, could easily be a cover for a knocking shop. His heart quickened again. What was it he had read, a sex network, or something like that? Kidnap of young girls? Yes, he remembered, they took them hostage, that was it. Boats to Corfu, Turkey, Istanbul. He'd read it in the *Sun*: 'Enslaved!' That was the headline.

On tiptoes Eric tried to peer inside but with his left foot still in pain from an old injury, he could not see much above the curtain-rail. His daughter was still inside doing God knew what and he was three inches too short to do anything about it! He could even hear steamy music. That was a bad sign. At this hour music was halfway to debauchery. He backed away, looked around, spied a police cone, dragged it up to the window. On one foot he stepped up, pirouetting badly, and clapped a hand to the side of his face to see past his reflection. In this position, squinting heavily and trying to isolate his daughter in the indistinct shadows within, he completely failed to note the arrival of Sam Sahar, who stood for some time and watched him with considerable fascination.

'Can I help at all?' the restaurateur finally enquired.

Eric looked down. 'Oh. Right. Hi. How are you? Just um . . . just having a look.'

'Something particular you are looking for?'

He jumped down off the traffic cone with as much dignity as possible. 'Sorry. No, mate. Nothing much. Nice place. Just having a, y'know . . . but looks nice.' He jabbed his thumb at the restaurant while smiling amicably at the well-tailored and refined gentleman, an obvious man of means, Arab-looking certainly, but not to Eric's mind a slave-trader.

'Thank you. I am glad you like it.' An amused smile appeared on Sam's face. He regarded this curious stranger, scruffy with bushy cumulus sideburns, with a mixture of amusement and bewilderment. This was London, after all, full of madmen. He knew it well enough by now. Perverts like this had tried to meddle with his waitresses before, but this was his first peeping Tom.

Eric went on the offensive. 'Thinking about bringing some friends in, actually. That's all. Just checking it out. So . . . Arab, is it?' Eric asked.

'No. We are a wholly Persian affair.'

'Persian, yeah? Nice food is it? Persian?'

'Very nice, yes,' Sam replied, with the patience of Job.

'Good. Sounds good then. Brilliant.'

Sam presumed this was the end of the conversation, but the stranger made no move, continuing to smile inanely.

'So . . . so . . . um . . . this restaurant of yours . . . do you have, like, just wondering . . . dancers and stuff?'

Sam held the man in his level gaze.

'You know.' Eric fluttered his fingers, jogged his shoulders once and winked provocatively.

'I am sorry?'

'Like Persian . . . y'know . . . dancers n' that?'

'*Dancers?*'

Another wink. 'You know. Yeah, like . . . ' Eric raised his eyebrows, wiggled his hips and simultaneously suggested ample breasts with his hands. 'You know,' he said, 'like this,' his arms drifting up to become swaying reeds in the breeze. 'Belly-dancers?'

Sam watched him a second longer, then concluded the stranger was indulging some kind of indecent reverie. He clapped his hands. 'Okay. That's enough. I don't have anything like that, but if you're interested, you've just got the job. Now, be gone. Hop it.'

Eric laughed. 'Me? No. No. I was just wondering that's all.'

'We're just a simple restaurant. Nothing for the perverted. Now if you wouldn't mind. You are putting off my customers.'

'Course. Yeah, sorry. Thanksverymuch.' Eric laughed again. 'Sorry about this.' And with that, he shook Sam's hand, returned the cone to the street and retreated into darkness.

Sam shook his head and muttered something in his native tongue as he watched the stranger limp away.

Inside he informed his new waitress: 'Trouble on the street. I'm terribly sorry. This area is getting worse and worse. Now then, let me introduce somebody.'

So light was Yvette's handshake that Tracy had to look down to make sure that they'd actually made contact. It was less a handshake than a caress, a feathery stroke.

'My wife, Yvette.'

It gave Tracy goose-pimples. This was the woman she had seen before, a mysterious beauty: scooped-back hair emphasised fine, perfect features, dark wide-set eyes, full pink lips, lightly tanned skin and a smile that genuinely warmed the heart.

Tracy could hardly believe that her new boss was married to this stunner.

''Ello,' Yvette smiled.

'Yvette,' Tracy replied.

'Stick with me. I will show you everysing. Sank goodness he finally hires someone.' Yvette grinned mischievously. Such a smile fully complemented the soft vowels that rose and fell with the sing-song inverted sibilance of the French.

Her full-length vermilion dress, a pot-pourri of cultures, descended from a closed neckline to a hem of gold brocade. The Chinese sleeves, with their sudden volume, gave her movements a drama she didn't at all require.

'Very beautiful dress,' Tracy said.

'It's our uniform. I am happy that you like it.'

'Really?' She said it too loudly. Her enthusiasm made the husband and wife laugh.

'I sink we have one that will fit you. I hope so,' Yvette chuckled, turning to Sam. 'Don't worry. It's okay.'

'We still have a lot of work to do,' Sam replied.

Whether this comment pertained to the heavily booked night ahead or to Tracy herself was not at all obvious, but with this they went to work, Yvette chiming 'C'est bon', then leading Tracy towards the kitchen.

First the tables had to be laid, and then Tracy had to groom herself in a manner appropriate to the elegant style of the restaurant. Her long loose hair was inappropriate, and Yvette suggested a neat braid. For fifteen valuable minutes, when she should have been setting napkins and cutlery, she struggled to plait her hair tidily at the back, but failed to achieve even a measure of neatness, so that Yvette, taking pity on her, offered to help. With expert speed, and at least half the time looking elsewhere to respond to Sam's questions, she plaited her hair into a makeshift braid.

'This will do,' Yvette said. 'Better off your face, yes?'

Tracy nodded, seeing the immediate difference in the small mirror. She straightened her shoulders to imitate Yvette's bearing.

Next, Yvette told Tracy to familiarise herself with the menu and gave her a crash course in the pronunciation of the Persian dishes. By then the chef had arrived, a jolly and fecund fellow of preposterous good humour called Abdullah. In a cloud of rapidly heated spices, Tracy practised her thick new language in the back of her throat, heavy glottal words, exhausting to say. No parachutist falling into a strange country could have had a faster immersion in a culture. And by the time she stepped through the kitchen doors balancing two hot plates of food in her hands, she was as dizzy as a traveller.

'Has she ever waitressed before?' Yvette asked.

Sam shook his head, shrugged, said 'Of course not', then returned to his corner, immersing himself in receipts.

An elderly couple from Bradford fancied something 'not too spicy'. They hadn't been able to get in at 'the Indian' down the road. Tracy served them solo. Her small fundamental mistakes didn't upset them — she forgot the bread for their table and to light their candle, they had to ask three times for water and then she bought them sparkling instead of still — and when they left they still gave her a healthy tip. The thrill at this achievement was immense but she had no time to celebrate.

In the kitchen she reconsulted the menu and drove the difficult sounds more fully into her memory. Yvette found her talking to herself when she passed. 'Relax,' she said. 'The first night is worst.'

Soon the room was full of people bowed over plates of steaming vegetables à la Persia.

Trying to balance two plates on her right forearm was difficult, and Sam stepped up to adjust them. 'No, no, like this, you see, overlap, they will support each other, you see? A good waiter carries four on each arm. But stick with two. All right?'

'Fine,' she said, and backed cautiously through the swing door, determined to do much better.

An hour later, when Sam spied a lull in the evening, he told her to take a five-minute break. Tracy found an old wooden crate in the alley outside the kitchen and lit a cigarette, relieved to take in some cool air. The work was hard on her underused feet.

Yvette popped her head out to say she was doing very well and not to worry.

'Thanks.' Tracy smiled and offered her a cigarette but she didn't smoke.

'Don't be afraid of him,' said Yvette.

'No. No, I'm not.'

'He's a pussycat. You will get to like him. There is no one like Sam.'

Tracy nodded. It was an intriguing remark, but she felt slightly confused as he seemed relatively ordinary.

The second half of the night was much more difficult. Several parties spoke very little English and Sam came to assist her each time, causing her slight embarrassment until, on the third occasion, she refused to relinquish her order pad, insisting that she was fine and could manage. 'I can do it.'

She turned back to her customers and smiled. 'Salaam, the specials tonight are the . . . are . . . ' Sam at her shoulder looked concerned. She had no menu to consult, the specials board nearby was in Farsi script.

' . . . the *mosto mousir,* which is popular, also a very nice *haleem bodemjune,* that's if you like aubergine. Plus we have a *haleem khoresht ghimeh* for those of you who are very hungry, and to finish a choice of . . . . of either *zulbia* or *faloudeh,* or both. Thank you. *Motshakkeram.* Take your time.' She nodded, smiled and retreated. Sam turned and looked with slightly new eyes at his departing employee. It seemed that the girl had imitated him, even in her gestures, particularly the way she tapped her pad twice with the pen at the end, his own signature. She had lampooned him. He shook his head at this impertinence and returned to his work.

Tracy's next customer asked for camel meat. Tracy was sure it wasn't available but said that she'd check anyway. Abdullah's laughter sent her back to the table with the bad news.

She marvelled at the consumption of bread. Replenishing the nan on every table had fallen to her. A demijohn of black olives was half-emptied over the course of that first night. By midnight, when the last customers were gone, she was ready to drop.

Grabbing her packet of cigarettes, she took the first chance to step

31

outside again. In the half-darkness she fumbled for her lighter. As her eyes adjusted to the darkness she saw that this time she wasn't alone out there. 'Oh, sorry.'

Sam, already smoking, was sitting on her vegetable box. 'No, take a seat. Come out. Rest your feet. I own the restaurant, but not the stars.'

She came out and cautiously sat on the step, feeling nervous. 'Thanks.' She didn't dare to look at him.

'Although,' he said, 'that would be something I wouldn't mind having a slice in.'

She smiled. 'I know what you mean.'

They sat there and smoked in silence, until Sam finally rose, ground out his cigarette with his shoe, muttered 'Right then', and went back inside.

Thank goodness, she thought.

Tracy took a cab home, went up in the lift and found her father pretending that insomnia had kept him up. She deposited two foil containers of leftover food on the kitchen table and said goodnight.

Alone in the kitchen, Eric discreetly opened out the foil flanges with his thumb and lifted both lids. He peered into the containers at the easternised vegetables and after a time even allowed himself a small taste of the cuisine. Not bad at all. The place was bona fide. He went to the drawer and got out a fork.

The next evening, Tracy was early. When Sam came to open the doors she was already waiting. And when the restaurant filled up, she took the opportunity to increase her workload. 'I can do that table as well,' she told Yvette.

'No. You have more than me already!'

'Actually, I've already taken their orders, so . . . really.'

Yvette shrugged. She knew that it was important to impress in a new job and she wouldn't stand in the way. But when customers at one of her own tables asked about champagne prices, and Tracy stepped up to provide the complete list by heart, it was almost too much. Yvette corralled the younger girl in the kitchen at the next opportunity. 'Slow down, slow down. At this rate you are going to get me fired.'

Tracy laughed. 'Really? I mean, okay. But I just wanted to be helpful. I can slow down.'

'And do you really know the whole menu from z'heart now? Sam said you knew it already.'

'I took it home with me last night, that's all.'

Yvette shook her head, marvelling at the application. 'And the prices? The prices as well?'

Tracy nodded, but somewhat ashamedly now.

'My God, but not the ingredients. Not the ingredients.'

'Not all, no,' Tracy admitted. 'Not all of them.'

Midnight came again. As she smoked with Sam out the back, he maintained another marathon silence. She boldly risked a question.

'So . . . so . . . do you miss Iran?'

He looked at her, somewhat surprised, as though a rule had been broken. 'Me?'

'Mmm.'

'Iran?'

She blushed. 'I just thought you might.'

'You just thought I might?'

'Yes.'

'You just thought I might.' He nodded and looked away. She began to think that was the end of the conversation when he said, 'Sometimes, yes. Yes I do.' Whether he was talking to her or himself wasn't quite clear. 'Very much actually. Sometimes I'm a . . . very frustrated exile, even if it is . . . what is the word . . . self-imposed.' His eye followed a plume of smoke upward. She glanced at him. *What an unhappy man,* she thought. 'Sometimes I wonder what I'm doing here. I have family there, but . . . I am a strange fellow. Really very strange, like two people. Full of contra-dictions. A wreck actually.' He sighed. 'But if I moved back there I would just have the same recriminations and have to go again. So here I stay, one foot in two countries.' He stamped two feet on either side of a crack in the concrete, as if it defined some twisted border.

She had entered her own thoughts as she listened. 'I want to live somewhere else for a while.'

He was pleasantly surprised, and faced her. 'You should. Go. Then you must. Do it. Helps you question things. Things you otherwise would take for granted. Very necessary. Good for you.'

In unison now they blew two long plumes into empty space then watched them dissipate.

'So how was I?' she asked cheekily.

'Very good. You? Well done. Very pleasant surprise. Oh yes, before I forget, your tips.' From the front pocket of his apron he drew out twenty pounds. To this he added an extra twenty. 'A bonus.' He pressed the money into her hand. 'But the trial still continues. Any numbskull can try hard until they get their foot in the door.'

Tracy beamed, took the cash and folded it with a reverence he didn't observe.

'Thanks,' she said after some consideration.

'You are welcome.'

Two more long plumes of smoke each.

At the end of the third night, the conversation picked up where the previous one had left off.

'I should be a better person, really,' he said. 'I am not at all sure why I'm not.'

Her brows crossed. Was he talking to her, or was she meant to have left him alone to make some private confession?

'Do you have a steady boyfriend?' he asked her.

She coughed, unprepared, pretended it was smoke. 'Umm . . . yeah. Yeah. I do.'

'So what does he do, this boy?'

After a delay: 'Gravestones.'

'Gravestones? Really?'

'I know. Bit weird really. Engraves them.'

'A lapidary?' He nodded his approval, then looked back up at the clouded night sky.

She studied her employer, put him at forty-five tonight. His age ebbed and flowed, depending on his mood. Anger put ten years on him; a smile performed the work of a time machine. 'Will you ever go back home then?'

'Me? I don't know. There is much that I miss about it. Someday I think so. One is always drawn back to one's tribe eventually.'

'So you have a big family then?'

'My mother and father, my youngest brother. But Seyyed, the in-between one, the handsomest one, he died.'

'Oh, I'm sorry.'

'Yes, a car-bomb. He was just going out to get a newspaper. This was during the civilian unrest. Dreadful. I won't read an Iranian newspaper now. Out of respect for his memory. Irrational, I know. But certain things we pay to the dead.'

Her imagination veered from market bazaars to Muslim minarets, skylines like fields of asparagus, to car explosions and a very handsome young man who had died. 'I don't know much about the Arab thing at all. But that's awful.'

'Actually Iran is Persia, not Arab.'

'Oh.'

'Different language, history, people, not Arab at all.'

'Oh, I see. Really?' Persia sounded much more exotic. 'What religion are you then?'

'Muslim. Originally. But I haven't practised for a very long while. Oh, and I sing in a choir at an Anglican cathedral, but the Anglicans won't take me in officially as I refuse to sign up for the whole package.'

She nodded.

'And now I expect you're worried,' he said. 'Now I've mentioned Islam.'

'No, not really.'

'Because most British people get nervous about it now.'

'Well, it's a bit terrifying, I s'pose.'

'Terrifying, you see? What does it make you think of? When I say Islam? Be honest.'

'Guns. Women in veils.'

'Guns?' he frowned. 'Really? Anything else?'

'Young men. With beards n'stuff. Waving guns, things like that.'

He shrugged. 'Well, that's understandable, if all you do is watch the news reports. But actually, the religion is terribly benign. Demanding, yes, but it is also generous, accommodating, when you get past the western preconceptions.'

'What's it about, then?'

'Islam? It is not easy to say.'

'Isn't it?'

He looked thoughtful. 'If you believe there is only one God, then, actually, there is no more straightforward faith. If you want to talk to the person in charge, then why phone the secretary, like the Catholics?' He regarded his cigarette, now a stub. 'You are merely referring to certain political events, but don't be too judgemental. Many Islamic peoples were traditionally nomads. Now they struggle for national borders, self-determination and so on, but an army is not the face of a religion. If you say "Jesus Christ" to me I hope I will not say "the US Marines".' He extinguished the cigarette. 'But as I say, I'm a fine one to talk, I'm a religious United Nations. Most faiths get a seat at the table.'

35

A second later, a small boy burst through the kitchen door. Grinning, he bounded straight into Sam's lap.

'Mostafa? No, no. Naughty. Up at this hour!' he yelled. 'What has Mummy been doing with you?'

Through the same door came Yvette, pulling on her coat. Behind her — dark-haired, bejewelled, stoled in a soft pashmina — came another woman, slightly older.

'What's been going on?' Sam addressed both of them.

'Earache again,' reported Yvette.

'Earache,' the new woman repeated. She had something of Sam's ethnicity, perhaps she was family, the beautiful side of it.

'Oh, Tracy, this is Firouzeh,' Sam chimed.

Tracy felt intimidated by their combined female glamour. Where Yvette was graceful, birdlike, fun-loving, her friend was opulent, full-bodied, heavily perfumed with rich, kinky black hair, a warm smile but more earnest. Her voice was low and eastern, even more of the desert than Sam's. 'Yvette tells me what a success you were tonight.'

Tracy blushed at the compliment.

'Firouzeh, this is the new waitress,' Sam introduced as he wrestled with the child who squirmed in his father's arms. 'And this one is my monkey. No, a puppy. No, a piglet, Mostafa.' The child beat his father's chest with soft, impotent blows.

'Just the one?' Tracy asked Sam, before glancing at Yvette.

'The one? No, no. The fourth! He is four years old.'

'Wow.' Tracy raised her eyebrows to Yvette. 'He's gorgeous.'

'Oh, he's not mine,' Yvette replied, shaking her head, laughing and turning to her friend. 'All four are Firouzeh's.'

Firouzeh beamed. 'Oh,' said Tracy, also turning to look at the dark beauty, no longer able to disguise her confusion, her mind racing to make the necessary connections. 'Oh. Sorry. I thought . . . that you and Sam . . . were . . . you know — ' Tracy stopped, horrified she might just have let some kind of terrible cat out of the bag. That would be all she needed: to betray a long-running adultery on her third day. The calm looks on all faces refuted this, however. There were no secrets here, only smiles.

' . . . that we were married?' finished Sam. 'Yes. We are.'

'Oh yes,' confirmed Yvette, touching Sam's shoulder.

'All of us,' added Firouzeh. 'We are all married. Nobody told you Sam has two wives?'

Tracy could not speak.

Sam explained: 'I was waiting. Not the sort of thing you do on a first day.'

Tracy stared between the serenely satisfied faces: wife, husband and *second wife?* There was a name for this: she couldn't remember it, only that it was illegal. 'Great,' she said. But not even her private fantasies could embrace this scenario.

Sam took the hands of both women. Not typical in Battersea, or even, to be honest, in Tehran much any more, but it's the truth. I am married.' He grinned impishly. 'Twice over.'

polygamy (pəˈlɪgəmi) *n.* the state or practice of having several wives at the same time; *(zool.)* the condition of bearing male, female or herma-phroditic flowers on the same plant *(fr Gk polu, many + gune, woman).*

Persia (ˈpɜːʒə) *n.* the ancient, and (since 1949) the official alternative name of Iran. The Iranian plateau saw the growth of an early civilisation at Elam (c.4000 BC). The Persians, an Aryan people, settled in S. Persia (2nd millennium BC) while the Mendes, also Aryans, settled in N.W. Persia. (1st millennium BC). At its height, under Achaemenids (late 6th c. BC) the vast empire extended from Egypt to the Punjab and from the Dardanelles to Samarkand.

Aryan (ˈɛəriən) 1. *adj.* (formerly) of the Caucasian race, from which sprang the Indo-European peoples. 2. *n.* a member of the so-called Nordic races of N. Europe, esp. Scandinavia, characterised by tall stature, fair hair and blue eyes.

lapidary (ˈlæpədəri) *n.* someone who cuts, polishes or engraves gems or stones; *adj.* (of literary style) tersely elegant, refined and pithy.

Sitting up in her bed Tracy flipped open the family dictionary, a hardly opened book used only for crosswords and Scrabble. She squinted in the bedside light as she looked up word after word.

After an hour her head was buzzing with a stockpile of meanings, but each was bound to be forgotten by the morning unless she quickly committed it to memory. She didn't let herself sleep. She turned off the light to concentrate in the darkness, enjoying being a temporary intellectual, amazed by the whirl of facts but not in love with the sensation. If this was what it was like to be clever then she didn't think much of it.

In an attempt to impose some mental order she chose a system derived from her supermarket days, allocating each word to an aisle, as if it were a can of beans, and even to a shelf if she needed to be more specific, so that she would be able to find something if she needed to.

Only when she was satisfied did she allow herself to sleep. She carried the data down with her: The capital of Iran is . . . is Tehran. It was founded in 17 . . . 88? She'd check in the morning. Tehran and Iran were in a section called Persia in an aisle called 'Aryan Peoples'. Arabs were in the next aisle, called 'Southern Semitic Peoples'. The Jews were in the third: 'Northern Semitic Peoples'. The Aryans in Aisle One came from the same place as Norwegians and Swedes. That surprised her. What else? Sam had two wives: Firouzeh and Yvette. That surprised her as well. Yvette was from Paris; Firouzeh from Tehran. They were both stacked together in another aisle, far removed, this one called Polygamy.

On the other side of the thin bedroom wall, Monica stealthily asked her husband for a report on their daughter.

'She took the dictionary in there.'

In the dark they both meditated on what this could mean.

4

Beautiful Infidels

Three years earlier, a man had been struck by a car. As he and his wife were walking along a well-lit street hand in hand he was literally torn from her grasp by the cataclysm. This man, who only a second before had been laughing at her side, tugging gently upon her hand and suggesting that they cross the road, now lay a dozen metres from her, immobile, dead on the asphalt.

She could not recognise the twisted body as that of her husband; it was a ridiculous abstraction. Her hand, still shaped to fit his, was holding onto the previous moment.

Life's changes could be quick, light, fleeting, they could be indiscernible, or they could be physical, overwhelming, a full-blooded avalanche. This was the latter, a moment that had erased in a flash a lifetime of hope, plans, talents, struggles, of memory and of love.

While the dead man lay there, she kept her 'real' husband at her side. They were both just watching some terrible accident, one which they'd discuss later at dinner and with light empathetic sadness before passing on to a brighter subject.

Holding onto the past, and so holding back the all-destroying avalanche, the wife stood at the kerb full of expectations which, unlike a life, could not be easily erased. There was the restaurant for which they had a booking and towards which they would soon resume walking; also, they were in love, they wanted kids, had marked pages in a baby catalogue for bedroom furniture; and of the holiday destinations they were weighing up Tenerife looked the likely choice; he was also worried about money, especially being in a foreign country, where work offers were only ever in the wind, but she was optimistic enough for both of them.

At the roadside a swirl of activity and lights built around her. Faces placed themselves in her view. But she looked past them, ignored them, treated them as just so many *noises off.* She did have one thing to say however: '*Non, non.*' She lifted both hands and fluttered them at the wrists in a light gesture of refusal, one she often used when she went out to dinner with Guillaume in response to an offer of a dessert or liqueur.

'*Non, non, non, non,*' the unknown woman on the side of the street murmured to nobody.

Yvette was in the ladies' toilet applying the finishing touches to her make-up when Tracy came in.

In the mirror, Tracy observed the stark contrast in their appearance. Her hair hung drably from a centre parting. The mousy untamed style had undergone no real changes since she was twelve, apart from the occasional impact of a hair-dryer. Before then she had worn it short like a boy.

Her good breasts and long legs were a secret from the world. Even Ricky, who seldom gained sufficient distance from her to gauge her qualities, said nothing about this side of her. What was the point of making an effort when, in total darkness and with shards of schist prickling her backside, no one would notice anyway?

Oddly, Sam had been one of the few people ever to have looked her up and down properly, in a solid manly way, in a lingering and appreciative way. She remembered the sensation exactly when, with most of herself on display, his eyes had ascended and descended like an elevator, pausing on two or three floors.

'I've been practising with my hair but I can't do it properly,' Tracy admitted. 'Could you show me how you put it up?'

'But of course.' With her eyes on the mirror, Yvette experimented with Tracy's hair from behind. 'What style do you prefer? Like ziss? There is much possibility. Or perhaps . . . like . . . ziss? Each say different sing, *non*? Totally different. Each is different statement. It's up to you. Loud? Quiet? Or like ziss . . . *très dramatique?*' She hoisted the hair into a tower. Tracy laughed.

'I'd like it just like yours.'

'Like mine? *Non.* You want it . . . like mine? Okay?'

Yvette pulled Tracy's hair into a vague chignon. Tracy admired her own reflection. 'That's gonna look good.'

'Ziss will be very quick but it will do for now.' Looking at Tracy's pale face she also offered one of her lipsticks. 'Perhaps this colour would suit you. And maybe a little rouge would bring out your cheekbones.'

'I'm not very good with make-up. It's all or nothing with me.'

'You know what? I used to be a beautician. Maybe I could show a few tricks if you want.'

'Would you?' Yvette being a beautician made absolute sense.

'But not now. Perhaps you could come over to our place some time, we could do a little make-over.'

'Are you sure? When?'

'Oh. Don't know. I check with Firouzeh.'

Yvette pushed hairpins quickly into Tracy's hair, and the similar styles made the two women appear a little more alike.

'Love your rings,' Tracy noted.

'Sank you, you have a nice one too. You are engaged?'

'Umm. No. Not at all.'

'*Non?*'

'No. My grandmother's. I just wear it for fun.'

'Oh.'

Tracy tucked her ring finger under her leg and held it out of sight. She would try, when she was next on her own, to prise it off for good.

Sam stepped from the kitchen to survey his customers, his tie tossed over his shoulder so it couldn't dangle in the bamieh sauce he was helping to prepare. He saw his east-west dishes being noisily consumed around the room, and felt a blast of complete satisfaction.

Two Kuwaitis had ordered the all-new broad-bean *ya mahi*. The geyser of steam from their hotplate made it difficult for him to confirm if they were pleasantly surprised.

'Yvette,' he whispered, beckoning his wife with his forefinger as she collected dishes off a nearby table. She turned to face him and he was stunned by his own faux pas. 'Oh! Tracy, I'm sorry. I looked . . . you looked . . . I mistook . . . Your hair, sorry.' He spun round and went back into the kitchen.

Tracy smiled at what she took as a high compliment and, catching her reflection in the mirror, looked to establish how much she had come to resemble her gorgeous colleague. She then returned to work, the smile remaining a while longer.

At a small table in the corner of the kitchen, his secondary office but the one Sam much preferred, out of Abdullah's way but still close to his operation, he kept his books, drafts of new menus, his accounts, his favourite Cuban panatelas, an ashtray, a sugar-bowl of outlawed *zoolbeya bamieh* ruinous to his heart, and a Zippo lighter bearing the Swedish royal family crest, left one night by a drunk diplomat and never reclaimed. He lit a cigar with it, drew back therapeutically on the smoke and sent out a stream over the bobbing saucepan lids. Good cigar smoke, he always believed, the expensive kind, benefited the food, and he happily smoked his cigars in the kitchen.

When business was good, like now, he smoked leisurely. He looked down. His eyes passed from his latest profit forecast to a certificate confirming his purchase of a new commercial property in upmarket Fulham. This would be his legacy to his children. His health had been suspect for years: arrhythmia coupled with an above-average cholesterol count had taken its toll; with blood pressure like his you never knew when your number was up. If his heart gave up the ghost — and stress ate away at it as if the blood carried piranhas — then he wanted his children to be well provided for. 'For your children,' his father back in Iran would tirelessly opine, with a conviction of terrifying intensity reserved only for insoluble truths. 'That is why you are here. That, and only that. ' The fingers of the old man's clenched fist would be white as he spoke. And the edict was not intended for Sam alone but also for the generations yet to come, for him to pass down with the same conviction to his own descendants. He was nothing; Sam was nothing; the individual was nothing.

But Sam hadn't come to this yet: his children were too young for such desert teachings. If he were struck down by a car tomorrow the philosophy would just have to end with him.

The old guilt rose in him again. It always did when he thought of his father. He drew back gratefully on his expensive cigar. What unbearable shame to have slighted and prematurely aged your own father with a near-fatal dose of disappointment. As the eldest child, and the sacred preserver of tradition, his flight from Iran and his shirking of the family business had a thousand years of implications; for didn't vegetarians beget even more vegetarians? Who knew this better than his father? An unbroken filial line extending back into silent antiquity had been severed. And in quiet moments like this how imperiously Sam's ancestors bore down on him for his failures, attacking his conscience as he smoked, even making him cough. His heart rattled in its calcium cage, anxiety scenting his thin blood, his fears simple ground-bait for the piranhas, proving yet again — *you are wrong, Father* — that the enemies of life are all carnivores.

Tracy came into the kitchen to get the next order. Sam lowered his head over profit and loss figures, acted busy, made gratuitous additions with his pen. *A fool to have mistaken her.* If she smiled at him he refused to see it. When he looked up she was trying to balance three plates on one forearm, and one in the other, creeping ambitiously toward the swing-door. She was trying to prove something. The damage would come out of her wages. He waited for disaster, ducked back to his book and secretly prepared to reproach her. He held his breath, and when the crash came he leapt to his feet. The first words were already out of his mouth — 'What do you think you're doing?' — when he found the kitchen empty but for Abdullah, one of the chef's pot lids rolling to a halt on the floor.

The evening passed without further incident. On such nights the restaurant ran like a tight ship, Abdullah at the helm.

At the till Sam totalled his receipts. The figure astounded him! The quantity of wine guzzled by his western customers, more every year, allowing him phenomenal mark-ups, was making him a rich man all over again. His vegetables were only the lure, the bauble: the real key was the inexhaustible human need to be drunk, and he had turned this to his benefit. He was despondency's banker, a war profiteer to match Alfred Krupp, the Cannon King of Essen. And though he didn't forbid himself a glass or two — Oxford had crushed many taboos — his measly heart, and not his past religion, ruled out alcoholism as a viable answer to life's troubles.

'Allah forgive me,' he said to himself, as he rang off the last bills. But he also felt a surge of well-being. There was so much for him to be grateful for. His luck, on all fronts, was the envy of his friends. Allah, the most merciful and compassionate God, be praised: two wives, four beautiful, healthy children finding their feet in a new land, it was almost too much. He brightened; sometimes he could be a miserable wretch.

At the end of the night he pulled his cigarettes from the table drawer and went out to check on the stars. When he saw Tracy already out there, he tried to retreat but she had seen him.

'Hi,' she said.

'Oh. Hello.' Again he blushed. He came out but sat only on the step. Behind him in the kitchen, Yvette and Abdullah ate unsold desserts, off-limits to him now. 'The worst time for me,' he told Tracy. 'Dessert time. My saliva ducts run like a tap. Even the clink of their dessert spoons is purgatory.' He drew out a handkerchief. She expected him to dab the corners of his mouth, but he only wiped his brow of sudden perspiration.

'It's interesting, isn't it,' she said, 'how the Norwegians . . . the Norse I mean . . . ended up in Iran, to become Persians.'

Sam looked at her. 'The who?'

She repeated it.

'Who told you that?'

'Isn't it right?'

'I don't know what you're talking about.'

'Oh,' said Tracy. She had presumed dictionaries to be infallible. 'I looked it up.'

'Well,' said Sam. 'The Persian people were . . . well, nobody knows actually, but we are an Indo-European mix, way back whenever.'

'That's what I mean.'

'What do you mean?'

'Indo is who was there, and the Europeans were the Aryan people, which originally were the Norse. And they mixed. Didn't they?'

'The Norse? What, with blonde hair and blue eyes and with snow-shoes on?'

'Well, they were called the Nordic tribes, and then they moved down.' Tracy believed she had profoundly stirred her employer's interest because he didn't speak for some time. She added. 'But it was in prehistoric times. So they might not've had snowshoes.'

He mumbled, and then nodded. 'You could be right. I'll look into it and . . . yes, I'll give you a definitive answer tomorrow.'

'That's what the Longman's Dictionary said anyway,' Tracy added.

'Really?' He regarded her. 'I think we have a scholar in our midst, Abdullah.'

'That makes two of us then,' said Abdullah, appearing in the doorway. 'Company for me at last.'

When the restaurant had been secured for closing, Firouzeh arrived to collect her family, resplendent as ever. They were to dine late at a private club. Tracy meanwhile released her partial chignon, raked her hair into its old loose hanging style, pulled on her polar-fleece jacket and glanced sideways as Yvette, with the donning of a cashmere coat, transformed herself into a diva.

'I must keep them happy,' Sam joked to Tracy, putting his arms around both women. 'A tough job, but someone has to do it.' He grew in stature in their presence. Tracy noticed how by an expansion of his chest he seemed to grow physically larger, as if to appear capable of twice the emotional workload of a normal man. They all went out onto the street.

'Can we give you a ride?' Yvette asked her.

'No thanks, the bus goes nearly to my door. Really.' At this time of night this was a lie. There were two changes of bus, plus a fifteen minute walk.

The night was cold. She blew her breath into her hands, watched with envy as the Mercedes pulled away, then walked in the opposite direction, to break the news to Ricky Innes.

Even at this hour he had to be told: she'd been in love with a lapidary: *someone who cuts, polishes or engraves gems or stones; [of literary style] tersely elegant, witty and pithy*; but never with a stonemason. What was it again?

A chiseller.

She realised she hadn't had a single daydream in days.

'Let's do it in my room,' Ricky Innes suggested.

'No. I wanna do it right here or not at all.'

Suzy Ballantine dropped onto the new Turkish rug and stretched out. Tracy had bought the rug to brighten Ricky's flat. He had no idea it would possess such aphrodisiacal qualities. 'It's exotic,' she said.

'What's exotic about it?'

'It's eastern and everything. Come on. I feel like it now.' Suzy beckoned him with her arm, a Cleopatra on her hides, a Salome in her tent, tempting him from her rug. The filthy flat, which had turned her off and made sex banal, had been transformed by the exotic carpet.

'All right then,' he said, capitulating with a smile, dropping onto all fours and advancing on her in a bestial state. 'Here I come.'

Tracy let herself in with her own key. When she opened the living room door, she found Ricky already half-naked, and, as a further insult, already using her fake Turkish rug as an instrument of betrayal.

Beneath him, and loudly issuing royal commands to her slave, Suzy Ballantine showed herself, her legs radiusing the carpet at ten and two o'clock.

A ferocious stab of pain drove Tracy backwards. Only the wall kept her from collapsing and buckling at the knees. She clapped her hand over her mouth, horrified by this head-on collision with sexual betrayal — one of life's hardest tests.

Ricky's head twisted over his shoulder to speak, his breath was short, his face was ugly with compression. 'Trace?' His buttocks were exposed: imbedded in them were Suzy Ballantine's fingernails. Tracy averted her eyes, turned and faced the wall, collecting herself.

'Oh God,' she repeated, before adding: 'You bastard.'

The room was humid with panting. Ricky struggled to his feet, reeling as if from a tackle, hoisting his pants up in jolts.

Staring at the bamboo patterns of the wallpaper Tracy tugged at the ring on her engorged finger. 'Suzy Ballantine, Suzy Ballantine, Suzy fucking Ballantine . . .', she repeated as if it would promote clarity. The fact that she had come here tonight to break up with Ricky didn't make this double betrayal any easier.

Ricky now attempted to be angry. 'What ya doing here? This wasn't *meant* to happen! You never fucking phone. This isn't my fault!' He was angry at Tracy for wrecking both their plans. 'What did you have to sneak in for? You see what happens?'

She turned to face him, still trying to wrench the ring free. 'And don't try to crawl back, okay? Just don't try to. And obviously . . . ' and here she let her eyes drop to see Suzy's inelegant attempts to rise to her feet, one ankle manacled by her knickers, 'you can forget totally about this.' She held up the finger which still refused to relinquish the ring, then in furious desperation plunged it into a tray of his left-over chicken korma, using the greasy curry to finally rid herself of the golden tourniquet. She sent it spinning to a far corner of the filthy love-nest, then walked out.

Outside she looked down at her copy of his door keys. The surface of his just-resprayed Toyota was the ideal writing tablet, being one of the two principal settings for so many faked climaxes and emotions — much of it my fault too. Into its brand-new paint, and in large capitals, she scratched the word bastard, right across the driver's door, retracing each letter several times for added legibility so that it would be visible from a significant distance, a definite concern for any good stonemason.

Triumphant, she tossed the keys into the grass. What would have taken an hour took only five minutes. No question about it, if you're gonna break up, she thought, infidelity is hard to beat.

5

A House Leaning in Four Directions

She rejected everything her father offered at breakfast a week later. To his questions about her movements she gave only answers calculated to mystify.

For her trip to the Sahar home in Barnes she plundered her wardrobe and in an attempt to dress appropriately and so ingratiate herself to all parties at once she settled on a disastrous combination of mini-skirt, knee-length boots and cardigan, augmented with a shawl and headscarf, to give her, in the end, the look of an Amish prostitute.

Consulting her *A to Z* she was relieved to see that of the many missing pages the one containing Burton Street was still there: it was both a miracle, and a good sign. The neighbourhood improved radically as her bus drew closer.

On foot she paused in front of the house and drew breath. Before her stood a two-storeyed detached townhouse with a high-angling pantiled roof, set well back from the road with a formal garden in between: to Tracy's eyes a mansion.

'Ber-luddy hell,' she muttered to herself. She looked down: the map confirmed that she was at the right address.

She was about to knock when she saw the doorbell. 'Fucking hell,' she said, as she heard the deep, cathedral-strength *ding dong.* Yvette soon opened the door. *'Bonjour.'* She cheerily greeted Tracy with the two-cheek French minuet which Tracy clumsily tried to reciprocate.

'You found us.'

'Hi. *Bonjour.*'

Inside it was another world.

The children ran to meet her from four directions at once. They were quickly introduced.

Mostafa, the youngest, she had already met. A big-eared Aladdin, he had rooster-tailed hair that defied both gravity and his mother's repeated applications of saliva.

Next was Ali, who, in a single sentence, owned up to being seven, very, very strong and 'happy to meet you'.

Third was Haman, stepping up, silent, shy on first appearances but with a devilish nine-year-old *doppelgänger* evident in the slingshot clutched in a dirty fist: where had the pebble landed?

And finally, the eldest, Aisha, already a replica of her mother, an incipient beauty of eleven, but in whose ethereal grace could also be seen the influence of Yvette. Because this was a house of two mothers, of double influences, and no matter how much Yvette and Firouzeh worked in concert, or how much the former demurred to the latter, the children would inevitably be beneficiaries of both France and Iran.

Aisha took the back of Tracy's hand and pressed it to her forehead.

'Come and have some tea,' Firouzeh said. 'Come through.'

Part sultan's tent, part Harrods, the lounge was a fusion of international personalities: flowing organza curtains complemented many dozen Middle Eastern cushions; a huge racquet-shaped rattan armchair sat beside a chaise-longe; the upright piano upheld numerous antique hookahs. It was a parlour, arranged for deep discussions, or scented relaxation. And romance? She spied scrolls in the bookcase. Were they scrolls? Though modest in its overall effect, the room was still Tracy's idea of worldly luxury.

So who sat where, she wondered. Who did what? Did they watch TV with their dinner on their knees like her family? She could not see a TV. What use did they have for a TV?

Her curiosity was hard to control. She imagined the scenes played out in this room: Yvette lying decorously on the chaise-longe, leafing through a French *Vogue*, Firouzeh reclined on one elbow on the floor watching her children playing non-violent games of make-believe, while Sam, cross-legged on a cushion, read — or wrote? — his Farsi love poems and idly put his lips, every few seconds, to one of his pipe's long siphons.

49

'It's lovely in here. Really nice.'

'With so many people in the house we need to keep it simple.'

'Yeah, really nice.'

'Glad you like it.'

'Really lovely, yeah. It's nice.'

'Have some tea.'

'Yes, please.'

As she sipped piping hot tea from a glass with a silver handle the children crowded round to present small crayon pictures they had just dedicated to her: *was this real?* Presenting his latest smudge, Mostafa jumped into her lap, nestling into a place that looked comfortably permanent.

'Mostafa, let Tracy drink her tea. Hop down now.'

'No, I love kids. Really. I really do.' She gave the child a squeeze.

'No,' the child repeated to his mother.

'Actually, if you ever need a babysitter some time, I'd love to look after them. You can call me any time if I'm not working.'

'Really? That might be quite good actually.'

'Done lots of it, yeah. But don't know many people with kids any more.'

'Well you do now.' Firouzeh pulled Mostafa's hand away from the hot glass. 'Too hot, Mostafa! Too hot.'

'Very hot,' endorsed Tracy, taking over the lesson as well as the boy's hand.

The boy's eyes tested Tracy. 'No, it's not,' he said.

'Very, very hot.'

All the women nodded together.

Eric opened the cubby-door on the twenty-second floor at the top of the stairwell to check how many mice he had killed that day. He was instantly disappointed.

As self-appointed caretaker and unofficial fixer of Melksham Towers he had developed a complex system for the mass electrocution of the estate's vermin population involving a trip-wire, a six-holed feeder primed with peanut butter and a hefty car battery. But all his pest-control efforts had come to nothing now that the mice and rats had learnt to eat the peanut butter, set off the trap and drain the battery without being exterminated. His modifications had not yet been perfected and the rodents ran amok, invigorated by their unexpected shock therapy.

He went back to his flat empty-handed, his morale low, stopping on the landing en route to take his latest spirit-level reading. He had been doing this assiduously for some months, originally as a by-product of his handyman's zest for checking levels — poor carpentry infuriated him — but latterly he wished to shore up his wife's arguments that the building was unsafe and even 'on the move'. Her suspicions were spectacularly borne out in his findings.

Over the course of these months his amateur log showed that the building was not only on the move, but was moving in four different directions at once. On the eastern side, the golden bubble in his level informed him, the building was clearly leaning east but if he walked over to the south face and laid his device on the floor it gave back south-inclining results. While the north tipped northward, the west tended west.

He reported this regularly to Monica, who logged the information in a journal of complaints with a growing sense of outrage. They were living in a death trap.

Clearly, Eric concluded, the tower block was flaring at the top like a vase, a sort of super-Pisa leaning, not in one direction, but in four. When he told this to his mates over a pint at the pub it gave rise to tradesman's humour. Privately, however, he shook his head. He had begun to share his wife's belief that the place was falling apart at the seams.

On the small north-facing balcony in his apartment he pushed open the sliding doors and sat with a cigarette, idly tipping ash over a box of corroded motorcycle parts left over from an epoch of bargain-buying two years before. Here was another project that awaited his energies.

He had hoped to make a small fortune by buying things cheap from the trades and 'doing them up'. Two years later all the other second-hand purchases had been junked, and only the bike remained. The complete ingredients for a Ducati 750 TX, its rusting tank perched on the railing, now deprived him and Monica of the space to enjoy a simple outdoor breakfast. She had allowed him to store it here on his promise of dreamy weekend motorbike rides to the country, as well as a sexy continental getaway for the two of them once a year. Monica had eventually warmed to the illusion of putting some wind through her hair, of whizzing through Toulouse and Dusseldorf clinging to Eric's hips, holding him fast with her thighs. But now, in six heaped ziggurats, rusting away, fused by weather into a single *objet d'art*, the parts were a reminder to both of them that they weren't, in fact, going anywhere.

His crisis of inertia would be resolved however, he promised himself. He'd take care of the backlog of rubbish, both real and symbolic, right now. He rose at once, put out his cigarette and went to take the bins down to the street.

As he rode the lift down, bulging black plastic bags at his feet, he reflected on the good fortune that Monica still earned enough at her pre-school to support them both. Since his disability — a broken-down ankle allowing only a sixty-degree extension and only thirty-degree rotation — he had got by on a piddling disability pension and the small amount of work provided by the tower block. Its gradual disintegration offered the closest thing to job security he had known.

On any given day he might be asked to replace a hinge, reglaze a window or fix a leak in a ceiling. His reputation for reliability had spread quickly. He was up to most small tasks. With toolbox in hand, he was able to limp to the rescue of a distressed resident, descend or ascend by lift towards the minor emergency at a moment's notice and, as his reputation grew, keep himself and his family in pin money. He did anything but wash windows — he was no navvy — and by drinking the cups of tea everyone offered him, and by listening to their tedious stories with interest, he was adopted into a hundred identical homes with the same interior geography as his own; he knew where to find the teacups himself.

If the tower block had been a city, he would have been elected its mayor.

He winced as he jettisoned the bags into the skips at the back of the building. His foot still gave him problems, and would probably never completely heal, or so his physio had told him. Sometimes he was unable to find the forgiveness in his heart to sanctify the dead man who had done this to him. To rob a man of his mobility, in the middle of his life, was an unforgivable crime. But what was this compared with the destruction of his power to earn, the chance to raise his family out of this swamp! How could he ever do that now?

It had been Monica who had suggested they conduct the annual social gathering out of doors in the barren wasteland behind the estate, but the diesel drums had all been Graeme Powell's idea. Eric had just been the sucker who said he'd help out. He turned now and looked out over the barren ground. The drum that had landed on his foot still lay out there on its side amid the weeds. He should never have listened to them.

It was typical of Monica to suggest that all the people of the estate should come together and get to know each other. It was an example of her desire to build on the collective potential she felt was lying dormant in the building. It appealed to her soft left-wing point of view to buy some biscuits, a few pastries, rent a tea-urn and invite everybody out onto the empty lot.

But it was Graeme who had argued for a barbecue, arriving in a van with two forty-gallon drums to prop up the grill, too late by then for anyone to order a proper gas barbecue. Even then, it would have all worked out fine if the drums had been properly drained of diesel or if the screw-caps had been left off. As it was — and for this Eric could never forgive the dead man — when the heat came up in the controlled bonfire, one of the drums overheated and exploded. It launched itself high into the air and in the brief confusion, Eric, who had not seen even what had happened, made towards the fallen patties and sausages, hoping to rescue what remained of the feast. By the time he got there, however, the drum came crashing down. His metatarsal bones were crushed out of recognition and his pulverised ankle was ruined forever. That was four years ago; the limp was still to disappear.

When Graeme Powell had died two months ago, irony of ironies, Eric had to join five others to bear the coffin. Midway down the chapel, hobbling badly and wincing from the pain in his ankle, he thought that at least the poor bastard had lost some weight.

Eric ascended in the lift, watching the illuminated numbers of each floor. To live this way was madness. Monica was right. These places were built for mice, not human beings. He would stop fighting it and instead devote himself, with new energies, to supporting his wife's campaign to have the building demolished. He put the key to the lock and as he pushed open his door was surprised by a voice over his shoulder.

'Mr Pringle? Hi. Is Tracy in?'

He turned. It was Tracy's boyfriend. The name didn't come, only 'the undertaker'. The kid looked nervous. Good God, as if he'd let his daughter get serious about someone in the cemetery business! Morbid bastards. Where did these young men come from, all drooling for his daughter. *Beat them back! . . . back! . . . back!* Before he could speak

Monica had come to the door. 'Oh hello, Richard. Tracy's not in right now.'

'Oh.' The young man was bereft.

'Come on in.'

'Ah . . . no thanks. Shit. It's just . . . I really need to talk to her. Can you tell me where I can find her. *Please*.'

'She just went out, I'm sorry. She didn't say.'

'Come on Mrs Pringle, Mr Pringle. You were young once.'

This shock assessment took both Eric and Monica by surprise. 'You what?' said Eric: this crack had stung him.

'You know what I mean. You must remember.'

Eric raised his voice. 'She's not here, all right? She isn't here.'

'Can you tell her I called at least?'

'We'll tell her,' Monica said.

'Okay. Well, thanks anyway. See ya. Don't forget, okay?'

The Pringles watched Richard Innes go, relieved he'd passed on the offer of tea. They had not steered their daughter through all the jagged rocks of life to see her shipwrecked on the shores of some juvenile delinquent's libido. Let him run his yeasty hands up someone else's skirt; let him drag someone else's daughter through the sump-tray of his lust. The Pringles had in mind a better man for their daughter. If not a king, then one of princely virtues. But where was such a one in SW17? Eric had indeed been young once, and had himself been viewed badly by Monica's father.

'Now don't be like my dad was to you,' Monica told him. 'You know how you felt.'

'Hey, I was being *polite* compared to how your old man treated me!' He remembered well how the old bugger had assumed at first sight that if allowed to get his hands on Monica, Eric would drag her down into impoverishment and a welfare lifestyle, which was in fact exactly what had happened. But the fact that Monica's father had been absolutely right didn't mitigate the unfairness of his presumption. *I should have been chased off just like this.* Eric silenced the word repeating in his head: *failure, failure, failure . . .*

'Come on,' she said. They went together back into their home, and shut the door.

Following Yvette, Tracy passed through rooms which in their general opulence reminded her of a music box; mirrors repeating to infinity richly lustred crimsons and golds. She absorbed all the details that would give her an insight into these people's lives.

Trailing her guide, she climbed the stairs and proceeded down an upper hallway that gave way to numerous rooms. Tracy's neck twisted left and right as she went, seeing past cracks in the half-open doors, and wishing to see through the closed ones, conjecturing wildly. 'Very nice.' She tried to adopt something of her hostess's nonchalance, her gift for understatement.

In a spare room, in front of a mirror, Yvette soon educated Tracy in the tricky art of the French chignon. The real thing suited her even more than the makeshift one, and within an hour she was unrecognisable. Subtle make-up tones enhanced her natural beauty. Her back straightened, she lifted her head and metamorphosed in front of her reflection. 'Yeah, I quite like it.' She changed even the register of her voice.

'You look a different person.'

'So why do you and Firouzeh wear your hair in the same way? Is it for Sam?'

'Sam? *Non, non.* Sam has no idea on such sings. Virtually no interest. And we do not function just to please *him, non certes! Mon Dieu, non.*' She laughed. 'Actually, Firouzeh showed me the hairstyle. At this same mirror. I suppose I just got to like it.'

'How long ago was that?'

'How long? Since I came into this house? Nearly four years. Four, since I marry.'

Why, how, where? 'Oh I see. Four?'

'And Firouzeh, I suppose I have modelled myself on her in some ways. My life has much in common with hers. We have had so many experiences the same.

More, wished Tracy.

The woman in question arrived with a tray bearing two glasses of wine. 'I should charge a royalty on that hairstyle, it suits you too.'

They toasted and clinked glasses before Firouzeh opened double doors and revealed a hidden room, as big as a small bedroom, a vast closet of dresses of all colours and for all occasions. She selected a simple cardigan.

'Wow, that's the biggest walk-in wardrobe I've ever seen.'

'Well, it is for both of us,' Firouzeh said. 'All this stuff isn't all mine.'

She closed the doors again. 'I will leave you to finish. Call me when you're done. I want to see.'

When she had gone, Tracy risked a question. 'So Firouzeh's been with Sam since the beginning, then, has she? Since Iran? Did they come to England together?'

'Oh no. Oh no. Much later. Sam was already here. For years by then. A big-time bachelor, but not a Dodi Fayed, *non, non*, more like a monk, with his vegetables and his books. Swore he would never marry. And Firouzeh, well she was already married at that time.'

'Already married?'

'Oh yes. Yes, she was already married. To his brother.'

'To *Sam's* brother?'

'To Seyyed, yes, the younger brother. Very happily.'

Tracy recalled her talk with Sam: 'The one who was . . . '

'Killed. Yes.' Yvette looked instantly sad.

'Oh.'

'It is very common for a wife to move into the care of her brother-in-law in Iran, especially in a case like this. Sam behaved very nobly.' She waved her hand. 'As he always does. Not everyone would take on his brother's wife and his four children.'

'The children . . . they aren't his either?'

'*Non, non* . . . his brother's, well, of course they are now.'

Tracy nodded

'Does your father have a brother?' Yvette asked. 'Then try to imagine your father taking responsibility for his wife and family. A huge thing.'

Tracy tried. It was impossible. Her aunt was a dragon, spiritually mean, the kids were petty criminals and the families didn't mix at all. Her father would sooner fly over the moon. 'I can't. You're right.'

'A quite exceptional man. You will understand as you get to know him.' Then, quite casually, she changed the subject. 'Now, let's take your hair down and this time . . . this time I leave it to you to put it back up. See how you do.'

With the removal of four hairclips, Tracy Pringle was returned to earth.

As usual Sam had to be physically dragged from his adding machine. He had reconciled his chequebooks and was annoyed by a discrepancy.

Firouzeh instructed him to come down and take a look at something that might make him laugh.

Dutifully, he took his appointed place on the couch, stretched both arms along the seat-back and asked politely, 'So what's this about? Some kind of new game?'

'Just wait,' Firouzeh laughed, the empty champagne bottle in her hand revealing an afternoon of nefarious drinking. She motioned into the hall. 'Now, now, come on. Show Sam.'

Yvette came in, giggling as well, and gave a theatrical bow.

'Well?' Sam asked. 'What's going on? Bloody pissed, both of you.'

'Come on,' Yvette called to someone out in the hall, but had to go out and physically drag her in.

'There!' said Firouzeh.

Sam's face fell.

Paraded before him, dressed like a princess from the *Arabian Nights*, veiled and gowned and reeking of jasmine — an amethyst even pressed into her belly button — was Tracy Pringle, the new waitress. 'Oh my God,' Sam said. 'What have you done to the poor girl? Tracy, you shouldn't let them push you around like this.'

'Just having some fun,' Firouzeh answered. 'Doesn't she look *good*?'

Tracy looked ill at ease, regretting the whole idea. It had seemed a good idea at the time, between the glasses of wine and champagne. But now she froze in front of him and his stern reaction. 'I'll get changed again.'

'Doesn't she look great?' Yvette added.

'Yes . . . of course . . . but . . . ' Sam began to cough. 'Excuse me, I think I need some air. You all go on with what you are doing. Very good.' He rose, tugging his collar, crossed the room and opened a set of french doors which led into a walled garden which was populated largely by Grecian figurines and wisteria.

6

The Capital of Baghdad

During a cigarette break before the start of the Monday night shift Tracy learnt how a Muslim had come to be in the ranks of a Christian choir.

The answer dated back to his first time in England, he told her, puffing away. As a student at Christ Church College he had taken an interest in the singing of western liturgical cantata. Friends had invited him on a 'give-it-a-go' basis but when rain had forced a cancellation of a cricket game his barrel chest was revealed as an excellent echo-chamber for the baritone parts.

His decision to take it up on a regular basis, however, had more to do with the complex nature of his beliefs, which saw no contradiction in one minute celebrating Ashura — the Muslim day of celebration for the creation of the seven heavens, the land and sea, the birth of Adam, the day that Noah left the ark after the flood, also the day Allah saved Moses, the day even that Jesus was born and the day on which the Day of Final Judgement is expected — and the next moment singing the lower fifth part of 'Angels We Have Heard On High'.

The world was presided over by a single God and Sam, by dint of his open-minded nature, and a Muslim's equal reverence for the prophets of Abraham and Moses and Jesus Christ, viewed all the ancient divisions, the age-old arguments, the theological hair-splitting as superficial squabbles compared with the truth of God's universal oneness.

He was no great thinker, he admitted as they smoked: but on one level, life was too short to spend it arguing.

She didn't take her eyes off him. He had begun to lose an employer's thorny edge. He didn't intimidate her any longer, and her opinion of him as an unhappy man had changed in the light of his sense of humour, however small, and with her knowledge of his — what would she call it now? — his general goodness. He had a good character. More than that. How many people would take in their brother's family as their own?

Yvette was right about him. A woman and her children, even a woman like Firouzeh and kids like those, were a huge mouthful to bite off. And yet he had handled it so well that she hadn't known, and still couldn't tell that he wasn't the children's natural father or that Firouzeh wasn't his first choice of wife.

'Do you know what I am saying?' he asked.

She had drifted off. 'Mmm. Definitely.'

'Good. Not many do.'

'So what happened then?'

Surprised at this invitation, he took off into a new explanation of his theories, and this time she did a better job of following his ideas into the wilderness, which was where they always wanted to head.

But she didn't mind it. It was flattering. Apart from her parents she didn't know anybody who spoke more than a couple of sentences before drying up or needing a prompt or feedback. And even when he spoke in speeches of such amazing complexity that she couldn't believe they weren't recitations of something he'd prepared earlier, they still had the power to excite and transport her in ways she had never experienced. As his unbroken sentences unravelled, in all their quite phenomenal glory, they were like some carnival parade that was always capable of producing one last spectacle just when you thought the last float had gone by.

But why me? How come he talks like this to me? If I didn't know better, she told herself, I would have said he was lonely.

Tracy lifted her eyes from her hymnal as the congregation began an antiphonal alleluia. She looked for Sam in the choir. He had told her that he would be singing this Sunday in St Andrews Cathedral and she had come up on the bus to see first-hand what she had not been able to imagine.

Gowned and saintly, Sam was by far the shortest baritone of this Ash Wednesday service and had difficulty in seeing the conductor over the shoulders of the boy choristers. He was red-faced, his hair slicked back on his head like kelp drawn over a rock, his mouth forming a vast O.

Tracy giggled and lowered her eyes to her hymnal, tunelessly joining the crowd, which did not seem to contain his family. By the second verse she gambled another peek at her boss.

The best view she got of him was when the congregation and choir sat in unison and Sam delayed, smoothing his white surplice and closing his missal from which an overlarge vermilion marker silk hung like the tongue on an exhausted Alsatian. He looked like an overgrown child. She, too, remained on her feet a moment too long. She thought it would be fun if he noticed her. She waited, her stomach in a knot of surprising anxiety. He looked her way finally, as he sat, and she thought she saw him wink.

After the service she made a quick getaway.

That night she waited for him to say something but he didn't. He breezed through the kitchen and hardly looked at her. If he had seen her he kept it to himself.

Seated with his three drunken friends at the restaurant's worst table, Richard Innes waited until the owner had walked away before cursing him under his breath. He looked around for Tracy, but didn't fail to appreciate the figure of the waitress with the French accent working a nearby table. He couldn't see his own woman anywhere.

He didn't doubt, though, that she'd show up. He'd followed her here the night before. Peeking through the front window he'd seen her hang up her coat and waltz into the kitchen and he was relieved to learn that she was innocently waitressing. For days he'd burned with the thought that she was seeing someone else, presuming she was out to hurt him now, filling up her calendar with cruel revenge fucks, ready to wage a big-time psychological war. His head held previews of this. He saw her clearly: fingernails deep in another's back; her every gesture a yes. No question, women had it all over men in the revenge stakes.

She would definitely wound him for Suzy Ballantine, very badly, when she found a way. The only question in his mind was when, how, with who and how many times?

The thumb of his left hand throbbed in sympathy with his mind. His hammer had missed the chisel repeatedly this last week. This separation was ruining him: he had almost sliced off his hand with an electric adze. *She wants to castrate me*, he thought. *She won't stop until she does.* They're attracted by your virility, but before they'll trust you they need to bring you to your knees.

The second waitress disappointingly gave out menus then took drink orders — 'beer, beer, beer, beer'.

Where the hell is she? thought Ricky Innes.

Through the kitchen door, Tracy peeked at his table with growing annoyance. It was the worst thing that could have happened. He was a loose cannon at the best of times and he could well ruin everything.

She had heard Ricky's drunken voice make a fuss when he'd argued over tables. She was still watching him, but pretending to polish a coffee pot, when Sam came through the door, almost knocking her over.

'Table three, Tracy, what are you doing? Leave that. Ready to order now. Go, go.'

'Three? But Yvette — '

'Take over, please.'

Tracy tried to approach the table as she would any other.

Ricky's friends fell silent as she arrived and quickly turned to Ricky, who gaped in awe at Tracy, in her uniform, while she, in turn, made every attempt to avoid the gravestone-maker's eyes.

'Hi Tracy,' ventured Robbie Foster, as an ice-breaker. 'Wow! Very cool.'

Simon Treadwell: 'Tracy. Bloody hell, you look a bit different.'

'What can I get you?' she mumbled.

'Tracy.'

'Hello Brian.'

Ricky spoke last. 'Trace?' But she would not look at him, even then. She prepared to write. 'What will it be?'

'What kind of outfit y'call that then?' He reached with his good thumb to feel her fabric, but she recoiled.

'Uh oh,' said Robbie Foster with a snicker and sank behind his menu.

'Are you ready to place your orders or shall I come back?' she asked, her tone level, her attention confined to her pad.

Three of the four young men realised that their appetite for food outweighed that for an incident and so bent to their menus, issuing a string of requests for meat dishes which didn't exist anywhere in the world, let alone on the menu.

'Very funny,' Tracy replied. 'Last chance.'

'No meat at all?!' asked Simon Treadwell.

'No. It's a vegetarian restaurant.'

Now Ricky tried to hijack the moment: 'Anything you suggest actually, darling. I don't care, Trace. Hey, I mean it.' She glanced at him. 'It's up to you, anything you say.' He spoke with drunken volume. 'My life's shit anyway. Over to you. I'm all yours. I'll do anything.'

Not even encoded, this message froze his friends. It was clear that Ricky had just asked her to take him back, and such a moment deserved their respect.

Tracy shook her head in amazement, and then gave a short laugh. Some offer, she thought to herself. In a daydream she'd long ago foreseen their future: the TV not turned off till close-down; so much build-up on the spout of the HP sauce bottle that the lid wouldn't go on any more; an answerphone forever repeating 'Tracy and Rick aren't in right now'; a box of tissues going brown in the back window of the crippled family car; fridge magnets holding up unpaid bills. She looked down at him, and saw that her laugh had surprised him.

What Richard Innes couldn't have realised, sitting sideways in his chair and with his back to the restaurant wall, was that from where she stood he appeared to be completely subsumed into the narrative of the tapestry behind him. On a bloody Persian battlefield, he became the unsaddled and last surviving member of a butchered army, slumped between a fallen horse with a broken neck, its wounds issuing rivers of scarlet threadwork, and an abandoned chest of jewels spilt worthless into the sand. Behind him rose a swirl of dust, signifying the next charge of the vengeful sword-wielding enemy, in which Ricky, clearly doomed, would lose his head. So when Tracy finally gave him her reply — 'Not a chance' — it was redolent with connotations that only she could know.

The fatalism of the answer wasn't lost on his friends, however.

'Ouch,' said Robbie Foster.

Shamed, with his allies present, Ricky rose to have this out once and for all. 'Hey!' he called, but she had turned and moved away.

'Leave it, Rick.' 'Siddown, mate.' 'Go on, man.' 'Be cool.' 'Siddown.'

'Bitch,' Richard Innes muttered, 'bitch,' as his napkin flew off the table in a mysterious breeze and as a thunderous clamour rose in his ears. Momentarily worried, he turned to find that the front door had merely been pulled open. A sudden wind had come up and a huge street-cleaning truck was just passing by.

In the kitchen Sam quizzed his waitress. 'Who the hell are they then?'

'I just know them, that's all,' she told him.

'And so? Who are they?'

'From school, that's all. Morons.'

'Well, I know these types too,' he warned. 'Punks from the pubs. When they close, nowhere else to go — usually end up down the road at the Taj, cause a riot down there. But because we won't sell them a steak and chips or a chicken curry we're usually spared their presence. I don't want these kind of people in my place.'

She went back out and he replaced her at the crack in the kitchen door.

From there he saw the young man lose control, throw a menu aside and pull Tracy into his lap. 'Bastard,' Sam shouted and left the kitchen.

At the table he raised his voice. 'That's enough.' He turned to Tracy. 'Leave this to me now.'

'He was my boyfriend,' Tracy admitted, red-faced.

'What? *This* . . . this fellow, *here*?' Sam scrutinised the young man: an unshaven chin, putty features, the square inexpressive face of a policeman. 'Was your boyfriend?'

'Was?' objected Ricky. 'Thanks a lot.'

'We're cool, we're cool,' said one of the friends. 'Ricky, siddown. I'm hungry.'

Sam looked at Tracy, who straightened her dress and hair, then back to the young men. 'Anyway, that is irrelevant. We closed five minutes ago. And we don't have what you want here. And please don't come here again. My girls do not like being insulted or manhandled.'

'*Your* girls?' chortled Ricky.

'That's right. They work for me.'

'Well, for your information, Saddam Hussein,' Ricky replied, remaining insolently on his feet, 'Tracy's *mine*, okay? Not yours, so why don't you . . . piss off back to Baghdad, awright,' Ricky moved to stand nose to nose with Sam as reinforcements sprang up around him.

Sam looked unfazed. 'If you think I'm going to back down you're mistaken.' He showed no outward signs of fear as he bent forward and smoothed the tablecloth. 'And you're mistaken in another thing,' he said. 'I am from Tehran. An entirely different country altogether.'

'Just bugger off. And I don't care where to.'

Sam shook his head in disgust, met the young man's eyes. 'You

British youth. With all the chances you have at your fingertips, look what you let yourselves become.'

Ricky contemplated violence at this point and the muscles of his face tightened as he moved back far enough to allow himself a good swing.

'Come on Ricky, leave it,' said Brian.

This was endorsed by the others. 'Ricky!' They had decided to leave that instant and pushed arms quickly into coats.

'I must warn you,' Sam added, 'that if you hit me, the satisfaction will be brief, but the repercussions, they will be ongoing.'

'Ongoing? Oh, ongoing?'

'Yes. Ongoing. But feel free. If you are going to hit me, then hit me.'

Tracy was amazed at Sam's gall, just as she was appalled and ashamed of her connection with someone like Ricky Innes. Already he'd done irreparable damage to her standing in her employer's eyes. All her hard work had been sabotaged.

Ricky was itching to lash out but no longer had a constituency in his friends. 'You . . . you bloody . . . ' Ricky groped for a damaging term, something to leave on, which would score as heavily as a punch.

Sam came to his rescue. 'Towel head, perhaps? Something like that?'

' . . . bloody . . . '

'Camel jockey? Please — '

'Huh?'

'Kofta cruncher?'

Their noses almost touched. Ricky didn't like this game. He was too drunk to compete, and all he was certain of was that he was being humiliated. He looked around to where his friends held the door open for him and called his name. 'You're lucky,' he told Sam.

'Please, go on. Tanker trash? Sahara surfie? Bastard refugee? How about one of them?'

'This is your lucky day, mate.' He blindly picked up his own jacket.

'Good,' said Sam, 'then bugger off.'

Tracy found her voice again and quietly pleaded: 'Just go, okay? Please!' She put her hand in Ricky's chest and pushed him. 'You're such an arsehole,' she hissed.

Ricky looked at her before leaving and saw his defeat in her pale, oval face creased with concern. He shot a last look over her under-attainable body, hidden from him under exotic robes. 'Fucking foreigners,' he said, addressing her as well, then turned and walked out.

'Fucking idiot,' countered Sam under his breath, before turning to console the other customers. 'Please, continue your meal. There is no further need for concern. And of course a glass of wine is available for each of you, compliments of the house. Our apologies once again.'

Slowly, the other diners resumed eating, their silence turning into mumbles and then avid conversation once again.

He turned back to Tracy. 'Right. Tracy. Kitchen.'

She obeyed and he followed her out of the restaurant.

Over a medicinal port at the end of the shift and around a cleared table, Sam confided to his wife and Tracy that he had been shaking like a leaf during the fracas but hadn't been at all impressed by Ricky's attempt to intimidate.

'I have been verbally assaulted all over the world, and by experts, real professionals and thugs, but there is nothing quite like the English lout for sheer incomprehensibility. They barely possess the vocabulary to insult.'

He half-drained his glass. 'He was your boyfriend? This guy? I don't believe that. You are far too intelligent.'

'No I'm not.'

'Don't be ridiculous.' Sam lowered his chin, looked at her under his eyebrows. 'Yvette, ask her the price of . . . of a bottle of Pouilly-Fumé. Ask her.'

Yvette smiled. 'Of course she knows. She memorised everything on the first day.'

'Then ask her the name of the first party tonight at the window table.'

This test was more interesting. Yvette faced Tracy. 'Do you know?'

Tracy nodded reluctantly. 'So what? Having a head for stupid things doesn't make you intelligent.'

'And how big was their party? Ask her that,' Sam insisted. 'Ask her what the wife had for a starter. Ask what she had for a starter, a main, a dessert. This girl is an absolute phenomenon. As her what this wife at the window table at the start of the night ordered for a dessert.' Sam grinned triumphantly.

'She didn't have one,' Tracy conceded. 'She had coffee.'

'Cappuccino?'

'Double espresso.'

'And her husband?'

'*Zulbia.*'

'There! You see? An Einstein of waitresses, she is a complete genius, and yet she is going out with . . . with Cheddar Man! That is what I cannot work out.'

Tracy denied it. 'It was years ago. It was nothing. It wasn't serious either. Not at *all*.'

'I also had boyfriends like that,' Yvette nodded, rising. '*Immonde! Gueule de guenon*,' she said, mimicking a simian profile, jutting her lower lip, shuddering at the memory, before walking off.

Tracy laughed, then turned to look at the restaurateur. She squirmed. She didn't want to be left alone with Sam right now, fearing that in the first silence she would be fired. Right now this seemed like the only restaurant in the world. 'I might go and have a smoke actually.'

'Smoke here. Tonight is an exception. In every way.'

She nodded, lit her cigarette nervously into her hands. When she looked up Sam was smiling at her.

Yvette came back to replenish Tracy's glass before leaving with the bottle. 'Restore yourself,' she said, winking at Tracy.

'Hey,' Sam protested.

'No, no. Driving.'

Odd, thought Tracy. Not even once had Yvette shown the slightest jealousy in leaving Sam and her to their tobacco talks, even when they had gone on longer than a single cigarette. After all, a womaniser like this one — she glanced at the extruded brown eyes, the dreamy look — and alone with a much younger woman, his employee, presumably eager to protect her job at all costs, some wives wouldn't let such a husband out of their sight for a second. Class, concluded Tracy. This was how classy women behaved. She suddenly thought. 'I didn't know Muslims were allowed to drink?'

'Why do you think I live in England? Cheers.'

She laughed. They banged glasses. 'You were great. Really great,' she said. 'And I'm so sorry. I feel terrible, I really do. But I didn't ask them to come here.'

'It's over. Please don't mention it. I've never felt so good actually. Ten years younger. In fact, let's get that boyfriend of yours in here every night.'

'Stop it.' She hit his arm playfully.

'Suddenly everyone wants to attack me!'

Yvette passed by with a clutch of empty candle-holders. 'No one feels happier than the mouse who finds he can roar.'

Tracy defended quickly. 'He was fantastic.'

Sam raised his chin. 'Thank you, Tracy. At least someone takes me seriously. We'll finish this and then I will drive you home.'

'No, it's okay.'

'Drink that, then we'll go.'

Tracy wondered for the first time if she was being flirtatious, sitting around like this, grilling him about the details of his exotic life. Was her interest misleading? That would be terrible: a very married man. But certain things about him made her feel very comfortable. She knew that if she dropped a napkin he would stoop to pick it up in a second. If she asked him to drive her home he would scurry to rearrange his schedule. If she was in trouble he was the kind of man who could avert a disaster. Obstacles would disappear as soon as he picked up the phone. Problems would dissolve. If she was becoming ever so slightly captivated by this man it was no wonder: her every action caused such big and complimentary reactions.

And he seemed to like her too. *For some bizarre reason.* His eyes sparkled, his mood improved. It was so easy to make him happy: she just had to listen to him talk. Whenever she did this he exploded with sentiment like a man just released from a long vow of silence. Her father was a little like this too.

'Here.' With his thumb he flipped open the lid on his Zippo, producing a flame, the second her cigarette went out.

'Thanks. But I should really catch a bus.'

A blowfly landed on the table between them. Almost pleased, Sam picked up an empty wine glass and with quick precision, trapped the insect under the upturned glass. 'May I borrow your cigarette for one second? Thank you.'

Quizzically, Tracy passed it to him. 'Thank you.' He put it between his lips and regarded his captive imperiously. 'I am the son of a butcher in a hot climate. We were at war with these creatures. Excuse me if there is no love lost.'

He drew the glass carefully to the table's edge and slipped his hand beneath it. Then, raising it to eye level, he inspected the jailed pest at close range: 'A huge one. My God. The back door must be wide open. A half dozen spores from one like this could close down a restaurant. Excuse me.'

Tracy watched attentively as he drew back on the cigarette, raised the glass to his lips and then filled it with a cloud of asphyxiating smoke. He set the glass back down on the table, the blowfly imprisoned in a chamber of death.

'That's awful,' Tracy shouted.

'Oh, don't worry, I'm not gassing it. All life is sacred. The smoke merely stupefies it. Fresh air will revive it later. Pity I couldn't have done this with your young man tonight.'

'Not mine.'

'Yes. I'm sorry. Now then, what were you saying?'

But Tracy was too distracted, her eyes on the swirling vortex inside the glass. She would have to revise what she'd thought of him. There was nothing predictable about him at all.

Yvette overruled them both with her insistence that Sam drive Tracy home at once: 'After what she has been through it is the least we can do for her. I will wait for the taxi.' She pecked Sam on both cheeks and told him she'd see him at home. 'Go. Go.'

It was a most beautiful car.

Tracy ran her hands discreetly over the upholstery as he drove, dreaming of other destinations than Melksham Towers. She was a little tipsy by then.

'So I presume Yvette has told you about us by now,' Sam asked.

She shrugged, opting for caution. 'Only a little.'

'But did she tell you about Firouzeh and me?'

'She told me . . . about your brother, yeah. I thought that was quite amazing actually. Pretty . . . phenomenal actually.'

'Why is that?'

'Taking them in. You don't hear about people doing that much around here. People are not that close, usually. Or . . . '

'Or?'

'. . . or that nice.'

He thought about this. 'Nice doesn't have anything to do with it. It was a practical problem. It needed solving. We solved it. And it has allowed us to build a wonderful home. And raise four beautiful children. And love has even grown. So there is something to be said for the surprise package.'

'I suppose so.'

'A friend of mine was in the same boat once, but under much more frightening circumstances: an arranged marriage. He had not even been able to see his bride until the door of the bridal suite was closed behind them, not even a photograph. Can you imagine his trepidation as he stood toe to toe in their bridal chamber and looked into her face that first time, only her eyes visible through her *hijab*, wondering what else lay beneath the veil? Beautiful or ugly? Grotesque or divine? Happiness, or profound misery for eternity? Anyway, that is what happened: he lifted the veil. Unmasked his wife.' He sighed, looked beyond the hood of his car at the pedestrians moving along the wet London footpaths. 'I can't tell you how powerful it is actually. A westerner might not understand this, but when the eyes are all you are given, how dazzling it is to have to extrapolate from them the entire face, the entire person.'

But Tracy was ahead of him. 'But what happened? When he lifted her veil?'

Sam shrugged. This was incidental to his main point. 'A gorgon. He was out of luck. A complete gorgon.'

Tracy burst into a fit of laughter.

'What's so funny?' he asked, outraged and appalled that such a gloomy fate could provoke hilarity.

'Sorry . . . I'm sorry, it's just the way you said . . . ' More laughter. 'Sorry, I just thought you were going to say she was beautiful.'

'Beautiful? No. She had a face that could stop a clock. But it's impolite to laugh at someone's misfortune. It ruined him. These are monumental things.'

'I know, sorry. But what about him? Was he handsome?'

'Not much better actually. So it was probably what he deserved. But who is ever happy only with what they deserve?'

After a silence, Tracy repeated, 'Gorgon,' and laughed again more privately.

'There you go again. What has got into you?'

'Sorry . . . just . . . drinking on an empty stomach.'

'You had nothing to eat?'

She shook her head and he turned to look at her.

With near-religious concentration, Sam transferred the coffees and a double cheese burger with fries from the counter to the little formica table by the window. He was concerned that the liquid might spill onto his five hundred-pound suit and he was parsimonious about money — not tight: he believed that money wasted was just more money that had to be earned, thereby elevating the prominence of money in one's life. Thrift, on the other hand, freed you for higher things.

She unwrapped the burger. 'Thanks. You didn't get anything? You said you were peckish as well. That's not fair. Feel stupid eating on my own.'

'You actually like this kind of food?'

'It's okay. Not really. If you're hungry.'

'Forget I'm here. Coffee is all I need.'

Wiping his hands with a paper napkin, he crossed his legs and watched her unveil her meal, a western culinary perversion. The ground beef oozed fat. His stomach turned. 'Actually, I might . . . I might even go and get some air.'

'Sure?'

'In a second I will,' he said. Still on a high, he hid very well his nervousness at being alone with her, covering it up with a cascade of words. He dreaded his awkwardness with attractive young women, but it was hardly new, and he knew its source: it was that same tentative, under-graduate desire to prove himself superior to anyone new, particularly anyone British, whom he suspected of disliking him for his origins. He cringed at the memory of his speech only a half-hour earlier on the subject of love and marriage. Love, of all things! *Saaman Sahar, what are you up to?* Was he trying to impress this young girl, get her into the sack, bed her? Fine, then do it, but not this drivel about love.

He had vowed many times to stop himself from lobbying the English for approval, but he had suffered dirty wounds. If he thought of all the luncheons he had thrown, at huge expense, only for the *Streatham, Clapham and Dulwich Guardian* to print that story about his family, a bombshell honoured by him every August 23 with a migraine, it made his blood boil. The piece had blown the doors open on his marital arrangement. How could he have been so stupid? Anticipating a profile of him and his restaurant, he had invited the amateur columnist into his home. In twenty paragraphs the finished article had detailed his 'plural marriage', all under a sensational headline — 'The Sultan of Swing'. It was a hatchet job, and attracted the kind of attention he would have paid anything to avoid. The article cited an 'inclement air of secrecy', plus an 'overfed tomcat' (a cruel allusion?), a cupboard containing a thousand hats — a damn lie! Then, with 'a bed big enough for three', it had finished him off. His old neighbours turned on him as if he were O.J. Simpson. Even his fellow choristers suddenly gave him the cold shoulder, allotting him the tricky tenor parts at their Thursday night rehearsals, a clearly aggressive act.

After that, he moved house twice but never recovered his civic confidence. Even in the new house in Barnes, a petition was drafted against him, his foreign status underlined. Only a dirty old man, a lecher, a British Hugh Hefner, could have ensnared such beauties, they said. He must have disorientated these women with money, confused them with degradations and now held them captive by some darker pathology. When a card saying 'Sex Fiend Out — Pervert Go Home' was dropped through his letter box for his children to find he pledged to make no further effort to ingratiate himself in this country. No Englishman would have suffered such rebuffs.

And yet, here he was, once again questioning his motives like a child.

Seated on cold plastic under harsh lights, he watched Tracy as she ate in this glorified Wendy-house. She was a straightforward, big-hearted girl, with a sharp mind too. And she was certainly a change from the rest, honouring him with a simple enthusiastic curiosity. He was not strong enough to resist talking to her, and even — admit it — becoming a little flustered, though he already had two wives. 'How does it taste?'

'Fine. Like a burger. I think they do a vegetarian one as well, but you'd be living dangerously.'

He smiled and shook his head.

To win over an English woman: he'd spent years on the project! When he gave up seeking male approval early on, women became his last recourse. As a student, tormented by a desire for feminine acceptance, he'd often try to hit a six off an unpromising delivery, inevitably going out for a duck.

Isolation drove him to London. In the nightclubs of his twenties the shallow girls who might have given him more — real shark-toothed gold-diggers — provided, instead, ten cold minutes.

Dear God, he'd never forget those droning clubs, sitting night after night amid alienating music, longing to engage with someone to whom he could simply talk. He had never been so lonely as when he'd ordered his whiskey-sours in those dim, twenty-pound booths in 1975. Pummelled by noise, impervious to the charms of Sloane Square belles with their blonde-streaked hair, lost in the dazzle of the disco ball and the blitzkrieg of the relentless beat. Unheard, he became a 'wog' in the shadows, a dumb supplier of drinks, an easy touch, a sleazy Arab presumed to have only sex on his mind. In great despondency he once resorted to a prostitute, and found himself selecting a pair: the girls had held hands in the salon and he hadn't the heart to break them up. Anyway, he suspected they were lesbians, and if they were witless then he could just watch. But they were delightful and he delivered a seminar. He laid them waste with his pent-up feelings, sad stories about the daily injustices he faced, drained them dry of any sympathy, and before an hour was up had them beating on the door, demanding to be released.

Sam never took another prostitute after that. His confidence couldn't withstand such blows to his self-esteem.

He thought such experiences would have made him ripe for marriage, but in truth, his wives, when they materialised, literally out of the blue, and in many ways coming to *his* rescue, provided him no great outlet. He was still lonely at heart, at the deepest level.

What an ingrate he was to feel this, what a chauvinist, a world-class bore! How could he have such complaints when he was living in paradise, in an Arcadia of delights, flanked on both sides by true vestal beauties, and in turn cleaved to by four adoring children. He was living in a painting by Caspar David Friedrich and was still sour-faced. But when had a homely restaurateur ever been so indulged? Would he never have enough? His tough-guy father, who had had nothing until late in life, neither money nor options nor ideas, would have beaten him to a pulp, left him bleeding in a corner of his butcher's shop like an off-cut, were he to hear of such complaints. There were few sins more decadent than ingratitude.

But I know what the problem is, he thought. His wives, for all their beauty, had virtually no interest, *and zero tolerance*, for his morose speeches. *At least Tracy here has an open mind,* but with a Parisian wave, Yvette would flee into another room if she smelt a litany coming, and Firouzeh, with manners modelled on three centuries of stoic matriarchs, didn't even have to move from the sedan chair to cut him down, annihilating him by raising her hand in a stop gesture. They were smarter than he was, this was the unspoken truth of it, and what's more all the players secretly knew it. What was fascinating and rich to him was either tedious and self-evident to his wives or else too obscure to profit anybody. He was outclassed in the area he most valued, by people with greater natural gifts but who didn't value them at all.

Compare one chat with Tracy with all that, he thought: lapping up his ideas like a fresher on the first day of term, innocent and interested in everything, willing him to go on, hanging on his every word and allowing him to think for a second that his wives might be wrong, and that he might after all be interesting. He barely knew a single thing about this girl, but didn't need to: just an ordinary creature, another waitress who might move on in a month, but still she was in his league, in the best sense. Let other people decide whether this level was a higher or lower form of the great debate.

'Surprise,' Tracy said.

He returned from his thoughts and looked at her. In his mental absence she had quietly concertinaed a paper napkin, then torn two diamonds into it and opened out the napkin again, multiplying the diamonds. She held this sheet up to her face and looked through two of the holes, her eyes fixed on him. His heart leapt at the illusion of *hijab* in the mini-America of the takeaway bar.

'A gorgon,' she said and whipped the sheet aside, revealing a set of french-fry fangs sprouting from her mouth.

'I really need some air,' he said.

Outside he looked back in at her. He berated himself: his thoughts were haywire, exaggerated. He glanced at his watch and regretted having stopped at all. Still, he felt excited, revved up by the near fisticuffs, and now by his resistance to the fully fledged attraction he was feeling towards this girl. He would never drive her home again. It was a bad error. How had he let Firouzeh and Yvette put him up to this? What were they up to anyway? What kind of wives threw their husbands into the paths of gorgeous young women?

He went back inside with his coffee.

'Anyway,' she said, 'keep talking. Go on. I'm really interested.'

He gaped at her, and waited for the rush of adrenaline to subside. 'Talk?' To his hermetically sealed heart such a word was a virtual *open sesame*.

'So tell me how you came to have two wives. Cos I was wondering. Can't they lock you up for that sort of thing? You know, for polygamy?'

'Polygamy?'

'Cos it's illegal, isn't it?'

'I suppose they could lock me up, yes.' He loosened his tie. He was even starting to sweat. 'If we were polygamous, that is. Which we are not.'

'You're not?'

'Not at all.'

She wrinkled her brow. 'Cos in my dictionary you guys kinda fit with polygamy. One guy, a bunch of wives.'

'Slow down. My God, since when was two a bunch? And we're not legally married. You have to be legally married to get into trouble under British law.'

Tracy nodded her understanding.

He looked at her closely. 'Okay, you ought to know this, I suppose. Firouzeh and Yvette are only my *common-law* wives. We have exchanged rings and we have celebrated two Persian-type ceremonies and as such we consider ourselves married in every other way. There are no legal consequences.'

'Great, so you — '

He cut her off. 'We are bound for life. That's all. That's it. No snip-snip. I will never divorce them unless they divorce me first.'

'Oh, okay. So you — '

'And if they want to do that, to go off, if they wish this, well then,' and he snipped in the air twice his twice-ringed fingers, 'they can go.'

But Tracy's curiosity hadn't finished with him. 'So . . . so they don't they mind sharing you then? Cos that's the bit I can't quite get. How two women could share a man, and a house and all the rest of it, without driving each other mental. Cos for me it would . . . I dunno, do my head in on day one. Seriously. Having a man I was married to, for a start, like, *being* with someone else and all the rest. No way.'

His thick eyebrows arched. 'You can't understand that? Why not?'

'No way. I just don't get how your wives don't mind. It's freaky to me. I bet you hate talking about this.'

He had relaxed again. 'No, no, not at all, go on. You have questions, fine.'

'Cos we're all kinda built to *mind* that sort of stuff. The whole point of . . . well, love 'n everything is to have someone you like to yourself. Like underwear, we want our own, right? That's sort of the favour we pay each other, right? Saying, you-and-me-together-always, that kind of thing; and not, hey-you-and-me-and-one-other let's go for it whoopee.'

'Good,' he said with a grin. So much for underestimating her. She was a much greater challenge than he'd thought.

'Like I mean, I had this boyfriend once, okay, and I kind of crashed in on him and found him on the floor shagging the smithereens out of someone I knew, right there on this rug I'd lent him, this really nice rug, know what I mean?'

'Extremely disagreeable.'

'And I wanted to murder them both. And I wasn't even into him, but I wanted to murder them both. Especially her. See what I mean?'

He nodded, amused. 'Of course you did. A breach of trust. Murder is the first thought. Naturally. But these were clearly third-rate people. And this should help you see my point, actually, that some people, perhaps even most of us if we are honest, would rather share a first-rate lover than have a third-rate one all to ourselves.'

She pondered this only briefly. 'I don't believe that. Sorry. No. Everybody gets jealous. They just do. Your wives have to get jealous. All there is to it.'

He shook his head, increasingly delighted by this conversation. 'No.'

'Then they hide it from you. Maybe even from each other. Cos women are women. End of story.'

He laughed, puffed out his chest, pleased to have been baited. 'So that is what you've been thinking as you work? You're shocked, shocked at what you think is our life together. Your imagination has filled in the gaps in your understanding. But you have tarred us with your brush, so to speak. So let me disabuse you of one thing. First off, you're assuming that to share a partner is a major problem for my wives. But have you considered that it might be the chief attraction?'

'The attraction?'

'I'm just asking. Have you considered that? It's possible at least, is it not?'

It was possible. It was beyond Tracy's experience, but they wouldn't be the first women in history who were drawn toward the bizarre. And this certainly solved the jealousy question. But no, *he's just trying to shock me now. There's nothing kinky about Firouzeh and Yvette. If anyone's kinky here, it's you.*

He sat back in his chair, pleased with himself, picking at the edge of his polystyrene cup, white cells settling on the table like dandruff. 'Now I don't want to go any further with this. The specifics in my family's case are very private, very personal, but you might take this last thought with you. People are strange fish, Tracy, stranger under our skins than others can ever guess. So what if some people make compromises with life? Who has the right to judge when they don't know the whys, hows or wherefores? What I've learnt in my time is that after the first couple of shipwrecks people will cling to the strangest flotsam to survive.'

Compromises, flotsam, strange fish, shipwrecks? She was more curious now to learn their secrets than before they started talking. Still, she was ready to concede something. The sophistication of the Sahar situation was beyond her ability to fathom.

Sam rounded on her now. 'But how about you? You must have your own romantic complications and complexities.'

'Me? Ha! Forget about that.'

'You must be overrun with young men, I'm sure. Teams of boyfriends making your life difficult, forcing you into unusual strategies?'

Tracy shook her head. 'No, I'm not into any of that. I'm boring. You might not know this but I'm the only twenty-year-old woman currently living in Britain who has never had a one-night stand.'

'Really? Congratulations.' He seemed impressed.

'So casual sex isn't my style.'

'Good for you.'

'No, I'm more into years of humiliation from that special someone.'

He smiled, but thought it polite not to reply this time, even though, in her own way, she had just proved the point he had been trying so hard to make.

Strange fish. Under the skin. Each and every one.

The Mercedes drew up to the unlit kerb and the driver looked about for a residential building. The car was surrounded by the empty semi-industrial lots often used in cinema to depict a nightmarish near-future. Sam insisted on seeing her to her door in 'a neighbourhood like this'.

'Seriously. No, I can walk from here, and it's easier for you.' Her arguments accumulated: she would be fine, a Mercedes should not be left unattended here, it would be stripped to a skeleton within seconds. But he ignored her, got out and they walked two streets before she nervously said, 'Okay, this is it, thanks.' He looked up. By then he'd deduced that she wanted to keep her living conditions a secret. 'Up there,' she said, pointing to the top.

He tugged open the door to a filthy, carpeted lobby. Carpet was a bad idea: it stank of human traffic. 'They're gonna clean this up,' she offered, as they went to the lift, which bore the ominous notice: 'Repairs in Progress'. 'Well, here we are,' she said. 'Thanks very much.' *Please don't come any further, please don't.*

'No, no, no. I promised Yvette. To your door. Who knows what those friends of yours have on their mind. They could be lying in wait for you.'

'It's not the first time I've taken this lift on my own, you know.'

'Still,' he shrugged, 'might as well see you up. And might be fun. Like going to the top of the Empire State.' The doors clanked and opened. 'You're going to take the lift? What about the sign?'

'Oh, that's been up there for months. It's okay.' She stepped inside first and faced him. 'It's okay. Promise.'

After a hesitation he cautiously followed. Inside, she pushed the top button.

'Ah, the penthouse,' he said. 'Very exciting.'

After the first lurch, which elicited from him a small 'whooa', they rode the first few floors in silence until he commented that the honest smell of human urine would have been preferable to having his nostrils burnt out by the disinfectant that had been applied. He pinched his nostrils, looked down and knocked with his shoe an empty needleless syringe into the corner.

She hadn't let anyone except Ricky get this close to home. Why was she allowing it now? She should have kept her employer in the dark. What a dump: it was doing damage to her standing in the restaurant.

Midway, they came to a halt. The compartment vibrated, stopped, then swung, somewhere — the numbers told them — between floors. Before she could explain that this was quite normal and that there was nothing at all to be afraid of, the doors opened. They gave way to darkness.

'Oh my God!' he said.

'This happens quite often.'

Sam stretched his arm protectively in front of Tracy, an instinctive act, and whispered: 'Stand back, no sudden movements, move back to the wall.' She was surprised at the strength he used as he drew her to the back, retreating from the dark precipice. 'Don't move. Stay as still as you can.'

She looked at him: he was hyperventilating. She tried to reassure him. 'It's okay, it'll start again in a minute.'

'Just don't move!'

'Okay. Okay.'

They stood there in silence and listened to the sounds of creaking metal cables, ghostly clanks and dripping water emanating from far below. 'It's like hell,' he said. 'Just look out there.'

He stared out at the only objects visible in the void: the vertical cables of the opposing lift, thick as a wrist, the flashing appearance of water droplets. 'Tracy . . . this telephone. On the wall here. Does it work?'

She shrugged. 'I think so. Used to.'

He went to work on it, his fingers clawed at the metal facing. 'How do you get it . . . how do you open the little door? It's stuck, look at this.' He pulled at the metal door until he got it open with his fingernails. Inside, a white receiver dangled on a hook and he snatched it up. 'Does it . . . connect directly, or what? What happens? How do I — ?'

'I think so, but . . . '

'Nothing's happening.' He waggled the hook. 'Nothing — nothing's happening. What's the matter with it? It's dead.'

'I don't think anyone's on the other end anyway. We just have to wait.'

'There's nobody there?'

'No.'

'This *is* hell.'

'We don't know who it's connected to actually.'

He stared at her, the phone in his hand. 'What?'

She shrugged at him. 'There used to be some instructions in there but someone stole them.'

Sam was stupefied. 'So who the hell is going to rescue us?'

'Rescue? No, no. It usually starts again by itself.'

'It clearly hasn't though, has it? We could be stuck here for Allah knows how long.'

She winced, more in embarrassment than from any fear of her own. 'It's probably going to be okay.'

'Not probably. We're absolutely stuck here . . . ' Sam had turned white, gripping the useless phone as though it was a lifeline, staring out into the inky blackness. 'Look out there. It's terrifying. We could plummet at any time.' She tried to smile. 'And I left my phone in the car. Do you have one?'

'No,' she said.

'You don't have a mobile phone? And you live in a place like this?'

'No . . . and yes.'

'I'm going to start shouting.' His chest was rising and falling. 'Let's both do it together.'

'What?'

'I think it would be better if we both did it. We can make more noise that way. I'll count to three.'

In the many times she had been left dangling here, she had never once thought of shouting. Perhaps because it was unlikely that anyone would either hear or, if they did, would even care. 'If you want,' she agreed.

'All right. When I say go.'

'Okay.'

'And don't move about too much. If we get pitched forward we'll probably fall for miles. Take my hand.'

She coyly threaded her hand into the one he offered. His palm was hot, a chubby hand cushioned with fat, moist with fear. She looked to him. 'Sam? I'm really sorry about this. This is *terrible*.'

'It's not your fault.' He wiped beads of sweat off his forehead with his free hand as a click sounded and the hum of power started up. The overhead lights flickered.

'Oh! I think this is it,' she said.

'What? The *end*?'

'No. I think this is it.' A loud clank of gears re-engaging rocked the lift. 'Shit!' Sam shouted. He gripped the far wall, steadying himself.

'There you go. See?' The doors closed again on the great void. 'I told you. Here we go. Going up again now.' The lift wobbled and rocked into its interrupted ascent. Gracefully, they rose again into the real world.

Sam's hand rode his chest as the indicator buttons for each floor flicked on and off again in smooth, reassuring succession.

'I'm just praying it doesn't stop again,' he muttered.

'No, hardly ever does that. It shouldn't stop again now. I probably should have told you actually,' she said. 'It happens all the time, and usually, just like that, between floors six and seven. Weird. But hardly ever between eleven and twelve. We should be okay.'

'Eleven and twelve?!' he shouted with some alarm. 'Why? Why . . .

doesn't . . . doesn't someone just fix the damn thing?'

Tracy observed that Sam's eyes were glued to the sequencing numbers as they approached the eleventh floor. 'This it eleven now. Oh don't tell me . . . '

Tracy looked up. The light came on, stayed on, went off and then became twelve. 'That's it,' she said. 'That's fine now.'

'How can you live like this?' He had been holding his breath. 'It's worse than Russian roulette.'

'It is getting pretty bad actually.' Tracy was glad she hadn't told him the full story of the building, given him the big picture, provided any more embarrassing examples of the adventures that went hand in hand with living in one of the worst council blocks in London: the vandalism, the caretaker strikes which had dropped work into her father's lap, the ankle-deep floods, the burglaries, the cracks in the plaster suggesting subsidence, the muggings of last year, even a balcony suicide, the yellow police tape cordoning off a section of the quadrangle for days afterwards. Besides, over twenty-three floors the lift was still infinitely faster, easier and, depending on your nerves, safer than the stairs. When the lift had once been closed, due to tenant protests about just this kind of disruption, and when the Schindler people had looked at their purposeful best, promising a breakthrough within hours, a pensioner had died from heart failure after reaching the seventh floor, one short of her destination. None of this Sam needed to know. These were facts of life best ignored.

When the doors opened on the top floor Sam leapt out onto solid ground and let out bellows of air, his chest deflating. 'We have been spared,' he said. 'Against the odds we have survived. This has been quite a night. Quite a night.'

'Well thanks,' she said, 'for seeing me up.' She held the lift doors open for him.

'You must be joking. I'm not going back down in that.'

'It's twenty-three floors.'

'I don't care if it's three hundred. Let it go, let it go.'

She let the doors go. She saw how badly the ride had shaken him. 'You'd better . . . come in, if you want, for a cup of tea, before you go.' What choice did she have?

'I should go.'

'No. Come in. You'd better come in.' What choice did he have?

'Please come in! Come in, of course, have a coffee. So nice of you to drop her off.'

Mrs Pringle invited Tracy's employer inside, as Eric, hearing a commotion, approached.

'Sam, this is Eric. Tracy's boss.'

Caught. Eric knew at once from the other man's astonished expression that he had been recognised.

Sam was busy joining the dots. 'Oh . . . of course, of course . . . now I see.' He laughed. 'Yes I see. Nice to meet you, Eric.' Sam winked at the man and fluttered his hand in a manner evocative of either the sea or a belly dancer.

'Nice to . . . um . . . see ya,' Eric replied.

'What?' Tracy asked, spotting the interplay. 'What's going on?'

'Nothing,' Eric quickly assured her.

By then Sam had crossed to the couch where, under the close eye of both parents, not to mention Tracy, he dropped down onto the cushions and settled in. 'This is very nice, utterly charming. That must be the whole of South London,' he said, motioning at the view beyond the balcony's sliding doors.

Tracy did her best to hide her torture, taking a long time to hang her coat on the hook.

'A million-pound view!'

'Fifty quid a week actually,' Eric reported.

'No! Cannot be.'

'Fifty-*eight*,' corrected Monica, as if it made a difference, which to her it did, as it was she who paid it.

Eric agreed. 'Close enough.'

'Incredible,' said Sam.

Tracy smiled wanly, enduring this.

'I used to love it. But I hate it now,' Monica said.

'She does not. Just wants a garden.'

'I hate it.'

'Like the Grand Canyon, quite spectacular,' Sam said, still taking in the view. 'You know, I have often found that with all of life's problems and burdens and so forth and so on . . . that a view, like this, that a *vista*, if that's the best word, is the greatest physician. You know?'

Monica and Eric forgot to nod, trying to see something in their own view hitherto overlooked.

'It's really the basis for our love of nature, I think, the fact that it heals us. And here you have it, right here. You're living in a place which is not only comfortable and *extremely* affordable but which is also curative. You know? And that is the meaning of home — the place where we come to lick our wounds, to recover and then to be healed.'

Three heads scoured their view for healing properties. Beyond the sliders, however, all they could see were a thousand points of light punching holes in a persistent, pernicious smog.

'This certainly is all most agreeable, I must say. You're very lucky. So . . . '

'So . . . ' answered Monica.

'So,' Eric mindlessly repeated.

'What is it you both do?' Sam asked.

Monica was in first. 'Me?'

'If you don't mind me asking?'

'Oh no. MI5 don't mind me telling people. Ha, Ha! They gave me clearance, didn't they Eric? Ha, Ha!'

'Ha, Ha!' said Eric.

'Teacher me. Plain old teacher. Pre-schoolers.'

'Really?' Sam appeared to be fascinated.

Monica laughed. 'Yeah. Well, play-group. One-to four-year-olds. Just the little'uns. Lovely at that age.'

Sam nodded eagerly. 'Because I think every one of you should be on the Queen's Birthday honours lists every year. Thank God for teachers is all I can say.'

Monica said she wouldn't go that far, and laughed again. She only led the kiddies in games and telling stories. But if he wanted to tell Her Majesty, she wouldn't say no to a life peerage. Everyone laughed at that. 'Whatcha reckon, Eric? Lord and Lady Pringle?'

But Sam *would* go that far, and further. 'Believe me. You have your right hand on the tiller of society. Various winds may blow but teachers steer the course. I'm not exaggerating.'

'Oh stop. Blimey.'

Tracy tried to smile but she was too busy working out what had come over her employer. She had never seen such a rapid attempt to charm the pants off her parents.

'A tremendous responsibility, though, far greater than politicians: you'll agree with that? What a wonderful thing to do, to influence a human being at their most impressionable, before the shell thickens. Wonderful. A parent with a thousand children. Congratulations. And I mean that sincerely.'

Monica smiled and shrugged, flattered as only a person who has largely given up on ever receiving another compliment can be. She turned to her daughter. 'Where did you find him? *He* can come again.' Sam laughed. Monica laughed. Eric's porcelain grin cracked as he looked at all parties like a referee.

Tracy smiled at Sam's act of magic.

'Makes running a restaurant sound so mediocre. And you, Eric, what marvellous feats of philanthropy do you perform?'

It was Eric's turn. 'Me? Nothing. Oh, you know, repairs. Odd jobs. Nothing at all. Whatever I can get me hands on. Bits and bobs.'

'Excellent.'

Tracy turned to Sam. In what way could he now transform a repairman into a Churchill? How could nuts and bolts save the world? 'Because I've been trying to find somebody actually, to do some work at the restaurant. Do you get the time to take on extra work?'

'Sometimes, yeah. Bit of this n'that. When the demand is there, you know. Well I *have* done. Go further afield n'that. Yeah. Sometimes.' He turned to his already amused wife. 'Haven't I, Mon?'

'Would you consider this as a serious offer? I'll leave my card here, please say you'll think about it. I might have as much as a month's work.'

Eric took the card for the restaurant he had previously described to his wife as a dive, a seedy bolt-hole. It now rebounded on him. 'Yeah, brilliant,' he said.

In the way that superb meals are followed by endless sweet delicacies, Sam was not finished with his extravagances. 'And what a very nice atmosphere there is in this flat. Real human warmth. Comfortable — cosy, I think you might have to kick me out.'

'Have a proper drink,' Eric offered, crossing the room. 'I've got some gin there.'

'Should really go.' Sam smiled at Tracy. She was stunned by his diplomatic turns.

At the modified gramophone cabinet Eric called: 'Sorry, bad luck, out of gin. What else? Go on. Have one. Might as well. Go on. Won't hurt ya. Yeah?'

'No, really, it's very late and I'm keeping you up.' He rose to his feet to shake Monica's hand.

'Are you from . . . ?' she asked.

'Persia,' interjected Tracy. 'He's from Persia.'

'Oh, Persia!' Monica's imagination filled with its own fair share of images, dusty and magical.

'Well then, goodbye and lovely to meet you both.'

Eric put his hand in the small of his wife's back as they followed him to the door. 'Oh and thanksalot for hiring Tracy.'

'My pleasure to have such a charming, beautiful waitress working for me.'

Tracy blushed. A quick round of handshakes ensued before the door was shut and locked three times.

'I think that's the first Persian I've ever met,' Monica concluded brightly, obviously uplifted, eyes shining.

'He's not Persian,' Eric responded with considerably less glee. 'He's more bloody English than we are.'

'Well then,' said Tracy, moving towards her bedroom, not wanting to face any further questions. 'Night.'

A fourth lock sounded as the snib on her door clicked home.

Eric and Monica remained where they were, Eric examining the fancy business card with its gilt, hieroglyphic writing and Monica staring out at her vista — South London, its light, its people — now seen in a new, more transcendent light.

Sam was not alone in the darkened street: Ricky Innes had been waiting some time for his 'Arab'.

The monumentalist had seen Tracy go in with her fat man from the restaurant. What boss took a waitress home, right up to her door? Only one kind, that was for sure. The kind who hand-picked his girls the way he chose fruit for his menu, picking the plumpest, freshest ones and pre-testing each with his horny thumb. Violence entered Ricky's blood. Waiting for the man to re-emerge and listening to Bob Seger on his tapedeck he became maudlin. He could visualise Tracy in the Arab's heavy embrace, locked in by his thick arms, her small face cupped — one he stupidly hadn't looked at enough when he'd had the chance — in this other man's palm like a rock melon, his other hand searching in the darkness for ripeness and firmness, pressing all the way round, his mouth

84

ready to close on it . . . no, it wasn't going to go this way.

Ricky would exact some revenge. He'd broken with Suzy Ballantine. She had wept over the phone, but he hadn't suffered a moment of remorse. When she accused him of being incapable of making love in an actual bed, he'd coolly hung up on her.

If he had been cruel to Suzy it was for Tracy's sake. Someone needed to suffer for this mess-up and it made no sense to wound himself. He needed to be fit and ready for the permanent investment he foresaw on the horizon, and also the type of lifelong unity neatly symbolised in a double headstone when the time came.

Recently, he had conceived their names, side by side, on a nicely rendered, twin-arching, double stone. It wasn't a bouquet of roses but it wasn't devoid of romance either. It was the common person's monument, their only immortality, and it was no accident that in English graveyards the cross of suffering had been steadily replaced by the 'head-board' of love: the grave was the eternal bed, after all.

He didn't start his car until Sam had walked some way off. He would follow the fat man home, learn his address, then devise a plan.

With slow menace he wound up his window. He squeezed off the hand-brake and prepared to roll in darkness after his victim, quite unaware that his invisibility was compromised by the word 'BASTARD' engraved onto the door of his car.

A week later, Tracy waved Sam and his wives goodbye and closed the Sahar front door, sealing herself inside a personal fantasy.

Sam had the unusual idea of seeing an opera. Firouzeh phoned Tracy, who agreed to babysit.

At first, Tracy didn't dare to move about the house. Had she been locked into Buckingham Palace and been free to roam about she couldn't have felt more excited.

She first went into the lounge: whitewashed walls, a white couch, pale, tasselled cushions. In defiance of London's weather it was the bright decor of a room in a hot country. She was determined to respect her host's privacy and would impose strict limits on any investigation she made of the house, but at the same time she was sure they wouldn't mind if she had a small look around.

She lifted the lid of the piano and depressed a weighted key to feel the pressure it gave back. She picked up a beautiful vase just to risk holding something so valuable. She trailed a lazy forefinger along chair-backs and over the coffee tables French-polished to reflective perfection. On a daisy-yellow slipper-chair, when she lay back, her right hand found a glass bowl of shelled brazil nuts. This was living, she thought.

She relished for a few seconds the knowledge that there was no one and nothing to prevent her from satisfying her every curiosity about this house and about the Sahars. She therefore built up in her head a check-list of things to do: there was an animal-skin rug to run her fingers through, the CDs to check out, the photos on the shelf to inspect, the paintings of Persian landscapes and the little items that lined the mantel-piece to study. She also wanted to pop her nose into the bedrooms upstairs to see how they were allotted. Her employers would not be home again for four hours.

At a mirror, she pushed a senorita comb into her hair. For now she was the lady of the house. Freeing herself of restrictions, she began her tour of touching, inspecting, tasting, sipping and reclining, as the first hour elapsed.

She pulled the *Kama Sutra* from the bookshelf. One glance inside gave her, interlinked and in sexual congress, three women and one man, the very scene she had never allowed herself to imagine about her employers! But instead of shutting the book she flipped the page, wondering if the action was continuous, like frames in a comic, but the next picture concerned three men masturbating into an artesian well. She went quickly back to the first plate. The man lay on his back, a passive taker of delights while the three plump women, their hair iden-tically coiled, grazed upon him like cattle. Tracy could see two quite simple ways in which the man could have returned the compliment of pleasure but the artist and the times had no interest in balancing the books. As dated as the picture was, it remained a blueprint for the likes of Ricky Innes, she thought.

Upstairs she twice checked the sleeping children, all four lying regi-mentally on their left sides, then returned to the lounge, each time overcoming the strong desire to open the doors of the adult bedrooms.

On the third trip up the temptation was too great. She turned the door-knob.

The master bedroom, the nerve centre of the Barnes love-nest, looked normal. She had imagined a four-poster bed at least, with swooping sashes fastened by ropes surmounted by a sultanesque canopy, a gold colour scheme throughout, matching white telephones, a place to which spies could come to practise being Arabian. Instead there was a wide English bed in a room that replicated the cool, tasteful minimalism of downstairs.

So this was it, at last, the sacrificial bed, the altar of delights? At least it was a super-king, she thought, big enough to sleep both Sam and his two wives. Otherwise, the room was a washout. It revealed nothing of how it all worked: *in detail*, who lay where, and who took what role, who instigated what, and how and with how many? Were the women bisexual? Was there a chair from where Sam just watched? There wasn't. Nothing. The room was a flat setback. There were two other adult bedrooms on the upper floor, their dressing-tables piled high with make-up and brushes and combs, but it was hard to know what these were for. Perhaps each wife used them for dressing. Or perhaps Sam visited *them* there; perhaps the women never came to him and it was Sam who did his rounds, secret knocks, keeping them in suspense, a kind of rota system, alternating between them.

It dawned on Tracy as she stood in the doorway that she wasn't worldly enough to imagine what was really going on. The women would need to come out with something. That was the only way she was going to learn anything. In the meantime, she wouldn't abuse the trust placed in her any longer. She started to close the door.

But then, the bedside telephone rang. In a crisis, she watched the phone vibrate, before she crossed the floor, sat on the bed and nervously picked it up.

In the crowded opera house bar at the interval, Sam ended his call and then switched off his mobile. 'She's fine,' he told his wives over the hubbub. 'Not a peep from the children at all.'
'Of course not' said Firouzeh. 'Now how about two vodka and tonics before the bell goes.'

Despite the storyline, a sentimental comic farce in which a young Romeo, whose love is seconded to a harem, sets about to free her, Sam was bored by the second half's interminable arias, and quickly buried himself in the programme notes.

On 12 March 1781, Mozart is summoned by the archbishop to Vienna, where the accession of Joseph II is still being celebrated. In the house of the Weber family, he embarks on *Die Entführung aus dem Serail,* The Abduction from the Seraglio.

In the summer of 1781, as the work progresses, rumours begin to circulate that Mozart is contemplating marriage with the third of the Weber daughters, Constanze; but he hotly denies this in a letter to his father: 'I have never thought less of getting married . . . besides, I am not in love with her'.

His writing is infused, however, by his slow-burning passions. While under his pen his protagonist chooses a path of self-destruction, the composer asks for his father's blessing on a marriage with Constanze, with whom he now admits to being in love.

In July 1782, the opera opens on the Burgtheater stage.

At the final curtain the composer is summoned to the royal box. His patron's response: 'Too many notes, my dear Mozart'.

Transparently, the heroine's name is Constanze.

As soon as the house lights came up Sam grabbed his coat.

When a key scraped in the lock Tracy threw herself onto the couch, a model of innocence. Only the raised lid of piano showed that she had moved a muscle.

Yvette and Firouzeh would have liked to stay up and talk but they were exhausted by the opera. They told Tracy she was welcome to borrow a CD of the performance which they'd purchased in the foyer. Tracy was very keen to listen to it. Only Sam joined Tracy for a quick nightcap while awaiting her taxi.

He complained he never had anyone to talk to at this hour. His wives were early birds. He put a match to contents of the fireplace as Tracy opened out the CD's cover notes to find the meaning of seraglio. Another visit to her dictionary might be in order.

'I see you've been reading,' he said. 'That's good.'

Tracy looked up. She blushed — the *Kama Sutra*! — before seeing that he had spotted a botanical atlas upon a near table which lay open on a coloured plate of orchids. The tinder burst into flame.

'Oh, that. Yeah, I flipped through it.'

'Wonderful pictures, aren't they?'

'Pretty interesting.' She wanted to go home. The longer she stayed the greater the risk of discovery.

'You had a good look then?'

'No. Not really.'

'Some other time. The shasta daisies are terrific. And thank you.' He took out his wallet.

'No. That was a favour. Please. Serious.'

'Don't be silly.' He offered twenty pounds.

'Thank you. Really. Anytime you need someone. I never do anything much.'

He smiled back, then took his eyes away. 'Really? Well, we may take you up on that.'

'It's such a beautiful house, it's no problem at all.'

He looked around him, as if considering his own surroundings for the first time. 'All their doing, not mine. Personally, I'm against luxury.'

She asked him what he meant. In her mind's eye she struggled not to see him as the protagonist in the reshelved *Kama Sutra*.

'When I was a child we had nothing much at all,' he began. 'My father only saw good fortune later on. Luckily, this colours you for life.' She shook her head, trying to rid it of debauched thoughts. 'It grooms you to appreciate the simple things so you keep your priorities. That's why I like my little table in the kitchen at the restaurant, and I have a simple office upstairs, one desk, one chair.'

All men are bastards, Tracy thought. They want a doting woman around, but they would want five even more.

'I think, for me, the problem with luxury is that almost nobody is worthy of it. Do you know what I mean? Nasty grim-faced people dressed up to the nines have always appalled me. It's a misuse of wealth. Magnificent artworks and rooms just dissolve the second one of those arseholes opens their mouths. The very second.' He snapped his fingers. 'Today, even, whenever I see a lovely house, I think "Fine, but are they happy?" and if I see a mansion I say "Well, they had better be" because rich people who are unhappy are especially disgusting.'

Happiness, Tracy thought, *is that what he's talking about*? She had been away. She had only just mentally freed him from an orgiastic free-for-all and still felt an irrational surge of repugnance towards her boss for his lacklustre and sexist performance. 'Yeah. I know what you mean.'

'Better, to my mind, a laughter-filled slum than an argument-filled penthouse. You know?' And here he inclined his head, 'Of course, I'm not altogether naive.' She smiled, nodded, giving him her full attention

89

now. 'The biggest problem is the argument-filled slum, but the point remains: how do we furnish *the soul* with luxuries?'

He's onto the soul now? This guy was amazing. 'Exactly,' she said. He isn't actually too bad looking either, nice eyes, nice smile.

His eyebrows were arched. 'That's what I want to know.'

'Mmm. Definitely. Yeah.'

With that, he picked up an antique and valuable-looking wooden ashtray and hurled it into the fire, where it splintered.

Her jaw dropped. She turned back to him, guessing what he meant by this bizarre explosion.

'Possessions!' he said. 'To hell with them. Do you know what I mean?' he asked earnestly.

Her eyes narrowed in bewilderment, but she nodded. 'Yeah,' she said. 'Of course. For sure.' She had nothing to hurl.

'I knew you would. You see, I knew you would! That's why I like talking to you.'

7

Community Action

All morning Monica Pringle had gone door to door until her knuckles were crimson.

Canvassing the top six floors of Melksham Towers, she hoped to drum up numbers for her petition which demanded of the council that the entire building be reduced to rubble and the above-signed tenants rehoused in modern council accommodation somewhere nearby. The men were uninterested, bleary and treated her like a Jehovah's Witness, and when she fell back on the mutual-aid female network, asking to speak to 'the woman of the house', she fared no better: women, she discovered, were even heavier door-slammers.

Although most people had been at home that Saturday morning — she could hear the commotion behind the doors, sense the eyes checking her out behind the peepholes — only a fraction went as far as to unhook their chains to talk to her. But even they declined to sign the petition, citing a fear of 'possible repercussions'. People wanted their rights upheld, but they wanted somebody else to uphold their rights for them.

'What's it about?' the latest fellow resident hissed through the crack in his door, angling a tousled head to read her 'Statement of Objection'. Monica had xeroxed it off at school the night before, optimistically allowing for a thousand signatures. So far, four had signed. 'You'd be the fifth,' she told the man, as though extending a high privilege.

He shook his head, but said, 'I'll tell you what, I'll take a copy for my wife. She reads these sorts of things.'

Monica took the elevator back up to her top floor. Before going any further she needed the pick-me-up of a cup of tea.

'So how did it go?' Tracy asked her mother, coming out of her bedroom when she heard the slam of the front door, the towel on her head twisted into a cupola.

'Still four.'

'Just four?'

'They don't care. They're happy to live in a pigsty as long as the rent's low. They'll moan and complain till the cows come home but you just try and get them to sign anything. They think it's an eviction notice.'

Eric had refused to use his small but untested leverage as a fixer to move the petition along. He didn't want it to hamper his work offers. The warm reactions he always had were important to him.

The phone rang for Tracy. As Monica cradled her cup against the cold glass of the high-rise window, steam fogging a halo around the cup, she eavesdropped on Tracy's replies.

By the end of the call Monica had worked out that Tracy had turned down an invitation to go out drinking with her girlfriends, preferring a quiet night in instead. It was the first time Monica had ever heard her daughter actually say 'No' to a friend on the telephone, let alone 'quite fancy staying in', on a Saturday night.

'Staying in?' Monica asked.

'Yeah. Might do.'

'Really? That's the ticket. Might do something nice then, eh? I'll ask your Dad.'

'Could do, yeah.'

'Get in some Indian or something? Chinese. Those sweet and sour pork balls thingummies you and y'father like. That'd be nice.'

'Be all right, yeah.'

'Not going out then?'

'Fed up with sitting in the pub. Boring.'

'Not much fun, is it. Never one for it myself. Even at your age.'

'That's bollocks. You were a total raver.' Tracy turned from the view they shared to look at her mother. In the slant of sunlight she looked unusually old: the unadorned cheeks blushed with blood vessels, small pouches slung under her eyes.

'What?' Monica asked.

'You should take care of yourself a bit more.'

'Y'what?'

'Well, you're getting on a bit, aintcha. Spoil yourself. Go to a beauty clinic.'

In dumbstruck defiance, Monica concertinaed her chin, producing three new ones. 'Well, listen to her ladyship, will ya.'

Tracy had turned back to the sprawling grey view.

Monica wasn't finished. 'And anyway, when do I get the chance to look after myself? When do I get the chance, eh?'

'Doesn't take long. If you want to do it. I could give you a hand with your hair.'

'Talk about the pot calling the kettle black. Anyway, my hair's fine. What's wrong with my hair anyway?'

'You haven't changed it in twenty years, have ya.'

'Yeah well, suits me like this, that's why. With a face like mine you don't have infinite choices. You'll get old one day too.'

'Other things would suit you as well.'

'No they wouldn't.' Monica was now furious. 'Like what?'

'I dunno. Loads of other things.'

'Exactly. Such as?' Monica had other questions she couldn't withhold. 'Embarrassing, am I? An embarrassment to ya?'

'What?'

'You embarrassed by me now? The way I look?'

'I can't say anything, can I. I'm going back to my room.'

'Well, before you do, Greta Garbo, here's some news for you, okay? You're gonna look like this one day. So I wouldn't get too . . . too *opposed* to the look if I was you.'

'I was just saying. God. Forget it.'

'We were all young once, y'know.'

'Forget it.'

'Well, thanks very much. That's lovely. Made my day. Any other suggestions?'

Tracy didn't reply. She wished she hadn't said anything. She rubbed the back of her neck, and considered going back into her bedroom but she didn't do it right away. 'Sorry, okay.'

'And yours is thicker than mine, remember.'

'No it's not.'

''Tis a bit.'

'Clips and bands. There's things you could do.'

'Clips and bands? And do what?' Monica stared at her as if her daughter were withholding a mystical key. 'Like what?'

Out on the balcony half an hour later, a band and two tortoiseshell clips in her hair, her ears exposed for the first time in years, Monica hoped the last of the sun would dry the last of the washing.

Tracy followed her out, wrapping herself in an already dried sheet, turning it into a veil. This sari effect was clearly intentional and Tracy tried various experiments with it, wrapping it this way and that, sometimes making of it a skirt, other times a full-length garment with enough left over to cover her head.

Sebastian Partridge opened the iron gate, came up the path flanked by miniature roses not yet in bloom, and tapped on the heavy inlaid front door.

His weeks had recently been made up of awkward visits such as this and they never failed to produce in him a light-headedness otherwise explained only by his great height and poor circulation.

'Hi,' he said when the door was opened by a striking, olive-skinned woman: his heart kicked him. 'My name is Mr Partridge. I'm from the Social Services. Could I come in and have a word?'

Allowed in by Firouzeh, he ambitiously chose a low camel-trader's leather stool, no more than a bicycle seat on trowel-handle legs. He was drawn by the peculiar force of the woman's wide eyes, her sea-coal irises flecked with amber, the elongation of her nose, her proud demeanour. His desire to impress her was compromised by the low stool, which forced his knees to come very nearly to his chin. He had wanted his choice of seat to appear culturally sensitive. Now he found it almost impossible to state his dark intention, his backside already numb, all sensation ebbing from his legs. He let his preamble run on about the price of good Turkish rugs in Notting Hill.

In her extreme elegance she nodded demurely and asked; 'Can I ask you now what it is you want?'

He confessed that this was just a routine check. The Sahars, he hoped she understood, were unconventional and on occasion his department had a responsibility to play the devil's advocate. His briefcase rested under the triangulated gable of his legs and he tapped it once: it sounded hollow. 'An article in the *Streatham, Clapham and Dulwich Guardian* . . . '

'Oh, that piece of muck!' Firouzeh exploded. 'So that is what this is about! That woman writer was a toad. Rude. Stupid — '

'I talked to her,' Partridge smiled. 'It's okay. But I still have to go through the motions.'

Firouzeh nodded, shrugged, relaxed. On these terms she could talk to the man.

He understood that there were four children. She nodded. And she was the mother? She nodded. And there was a second wife, also living in the house? Firouzeh nodded more slowly. This was quite unusual in a British context, he observed.

Without the slightest flicker in her black eyes, Firouzeh answered that it depended on what he meant by unusual. 'I'm a married woman. And I live with my husband. I have four children. We were married in Skegness, about, yes, about five years ago. What else would you like to know?'

Partridge was about to reply when the front door opened. A second impossibly impressive woman entered, followed by four highly groomed children, overwhelming Firouzeh and her visitor.

The clamour of shoes and jettisoned schoolbags was enough to end Partridge's dwarfish tenure on the stool. He rose to tower over the children.

'Everybody,' said Firouzeh, 'this is Mr Partridge from . . . ' She consulted the card she had been given, saw 'Child Protection Unit', said ' . . . the Social Services.'

Partridge's attempt to smile at everybody in the room individually, even at the smallest children, made it seem as if his head were mounted on a spring. It also marked him out as a superficial character. Breaking up families was bad enough without asking to be well liked at the same time. 'Hi,' he said. 'Hi. Hi. Hello. Hi down there,' and 'Oh my goodness, hello.'

Firouzeh sent the children upstairs. Yvette sat on the couch. The women then regarded the civil servant who had moved to the Persian armchair.

Where his job had been difficult before, it was now doubly so as the pair sat in sisterly perfection, and in matching emerald-green dresses. He gazed between one elliptical face and the other: desire was not a fitting bedfellow of enquiry.

He lapsed again into pleasantries and found himself, stupidly, mindlessly, smiling. He had always been mawkish in the presence of beautiful women.

'Would you care for a cup of Persian tea, monsieur?' asked the new mistress in a seductively French — *les femmes Françaises!* — accent. He nodded his acceptance.

'Then we should get back to your questions,' added Firouzeh, bending to a low table to stir the pot-pourri with her taloned index finger, setting free the fragrance.

'Yes. I can't stay long at all. I'm on a meter.'

The tea was brought in and the conversation continued with glances over the rims of glass teacups. It owed more to lies, diversion and conceal-ment than a governmental gathering of truths, facts or raw data. It was civil, polite but officially valueless. He commented on a striking painting in the Fauve style, and was told that it was by Sam. 'Really?' A palm-sized cloth-bound book was quickly placed in his hand, and he was told that the opening lines by Jalal al Din Rumi, the great mystic poet of Persia, had been its inspiration. Partridge was encouraged to open it and read:

> Listen to the reed, how it tells a tale
> complaining of separations —
> Saying, 'Ever since I was parted from the reed-bed,
> my lament hath caused men and women to moan;
> I want a bosom torn by severance, that I may unfold
> to such a one the pain of love-desire.
> Everyone who is left far from his source wishes back
> the time when he was united with it.

Partridge closed the book, moved, feeling converted but unsure whether a coded plea had just been made to him via a thirteenth century ruba'iyat. So thoroughly was he attended by these two women that the fragile clarity of his mission was lost in the assault of continental charm. 'I really must get on,' he kept saying, but at the same time his resistance weakened, his wits escaped, his official veneer cracked into a delightful mosaic of minor sensations. 'I only have a few more things to say.'

But he was stymied. Quickly he found himself appreciating every-thing from their dresses to the vased pansies on the coffee table until, in a crescendo of pleasantries, he stumbled almost by accident upon the actual purpose of his visit.

Specifically, he asked them, was the arrangement quite suitable?

The question elicited blank stares.

From a purely technical point of view, he said, the situation to an outsider was foggy.

More stares greeted this.

'How do you mean?' asked Firouzeh.

For example, and here he cleared his throat, there was no doubt the house was run to the highest standards — he glanced from the regimented books to decanters, vases, portraits, cinched-back drapes — and the children's material needs were evidently well provided for, but he had increasing difficulty in understanding the 'quite unusual nature of the central relationship'.

He is obsessed, thought Yvette.

My children, reacted Firouzeh instinctively.

Yvette, shrugged. 'What does he mean?'

'I mean the formula,' he blurted in his own defence, badly outnumbered. 'I suppose I mean the *sexual* formula.'

Obsession.

My sweet children.

'I mean, I couldn't pretend to understand how it works. Please tell me what *you* call it.'

The two women didn't reply, forcing him to first cross and then recross his legs in an exhibition of acute discomfort.

'How can you ask this?' Firouzeh's face reddened. 'It should be clear, if you just look around you, that the children have all they need. Were there ever children so well cared for?' It was true. Partridge felt no impulse to deny it. 'Plus, they have the obvious advantage of two mothers. Think about that.'

'Fine,' he conceded.

'Is that not all the answer you need?'

Sebastian Partridge smiled. 'Okay, well let's . . . perhaps we can . . . leave that there for now then.' The house did look to be in order, though it was dangerous in his job to take this as final proof. Luxury, he'd learnt, was no guarantee of propriety, and injustice often kept a fancy address.

Yvette refilled his teacup.

He sipped at the offering, smiling at his hostesses over the glass rim, and returned to wondering which of the two was the more beautiful. Perhaps the French one had his heart, he thought as he drank. But she was very thin. No, on reconsideration, perhaps the Arab one after all, more fulsome and exotic, holding more bedroom promise.

When he was eventually shown out ten minutes later, having announced he would come back again when perhaps Mr Sahar might also be in, something he said would be very pleasant given 'everything I've just heard about the man', he was under the quite false impression that his official house-call had been something of a success. When some time later he snapped out of this delusion and realised the extent of his ineffectiveness, he came to the sobering conclusion that he might be in the wrong line of work altogether.

Sam was briefed when he came home. The full report worried him. He had married two women under common law, and although it was all legally above board, he knew they would all come off second best in any official run-in. He would phone Ridley, his lawyer, his sole link now to the establishment, a varsity man, big on contacts. 'Ridley will take care of it. And I know what he'll say. Keep our heads down. Simple as that. Lie low. So what did you do with him? What happened?'

'I made him tea,' Yvette happily reported, her shoulders leaping as she shrugged.

'Tea? Is that all?'

'I don't think we have anything to fear,' Firouzeh nodded with a wink. 'We had a good talk to him.'

Sam brightened, guessing the treatment the man had received, a veritable bath in ass's milk. 'I see. I can imagine.' But Sam's face remained clouded. He knitted his fingers. The key to their long-term success had always been a low community profile.

'He even left his card. Like a brush salesman.' Firouzeh handed it over and Sam put on his half-moon glasses to examine it. 'It's routine. That is all he said.'

'Partridge? Is that a real name?'

'He said it was.'

'I trust you charmed him then. Thank goodness for you both.'

Yvette laughed. Firouzeh said encouragingly, 'Tell him.'

'Well,' grinning, 'as he was going, I found an excuse to tighten his tie.'

'Oh my God. Did he blush?' Sam finally grinned.

'Like a *pêche*.'

Together they all laughed. He draped his arms over their shoulders, a fat temple dog bolstered by two gleaming jade cats. 'Then we might be all right,' he concluded. 'Lust has saved us again.'

In the Sahar garden, Ricky Innes dropped over the wall onto the grass and rolled to his feet, staining his knees with mud. Greco-Roman statues in a moonlit garden greeted him as he heard the skittering hiss of a chain unspooling very quickly across the flagstones.

Still wiping dirt off his hands he turned to see two large dogs come straight at him from round the corner of the house. The animals' mouths were open for a savage attack as he reeled back against the wall, awaiting the inevitable, raising his arms to protect his face.

And then, just as the dogs were about to leap, the chains miraculously cinched tight, arresting the hounds in mid-air, choking off their barks with a yelp, less than two feet from him. But now he was pinned to the wall, inches from their snarling mouths, the dogs pulling so hard that their collars dug into their muscled necks.

'Whoaa,' he cautioned. 'Easy. Easy.' But nothing could calm dogs in this state. Their upper lips were drawn up to reveal wet gums, their eyes bloodshot, they had a perfect instinct to kill.

Inside the house, initially unaware of this drama, Sam re-read Partridge's card as though it contained encryptions. When he heard his Dobermanns beyond the french doors, he turned.

'Now it starts!' he said, oddly connecting the disturbance to the card.

At the doors he turned back to his wives, lifting his empty hands: 'I need something! Give me something. Quick!'

'Don't go out!'

'Sam, no!'

'Give me something.'

Ricky saw the french doors open and the figure advance across the lawn towards him. There was nothing he could do. The dogs were barking up a storm. In the half-light Ricky saw that the man was carrying a huge curved blade, some kind of sword. The scimitar flashed reflected streetlight at him. 'Oh shit,' he said. He had drained six pints of lager before coming here. The beer-fuelled lust for havoc was fast becoming a dim memory.

With the sword in both hands, Sam appeared at the foot of the garden steps. 'Don't move.'

'You gotta be joking.'

'What do you want?'

'I'm an animal lover. Can you let them come a bit closer?'

'What do you want?'

Ricky Innes looked down at the animals. 'Look, just call 'em off will ya? I meant to come in the front way. I'm a friend. Call 'em off. Please.'

'A friend? What are you talking about?'

'Of Tracy's. Tracy Pringle.'

'Tracy?'

'I thought she might be here that's all.'

'Ad, Asad!' Sam whistled, dug the point of his sword into the lawn and then jerked on the two chains: the dogs yelped, drew back on their haunches but panted loudly. 'You climb into someone's garden, looking for someone who doesn't live here? You didn't see all the guard-dog signs. Are you mad?'

'I love her, that's all.'

'You love her?'

'Yeah. Tracy. I love her. I wanna marry her.'

Sam stepped forward, in line with the dogs and their arsenal of teeth, to get a better view at the intruder. 'So, it's you again.'

'Yeah. How's it going?'

'I don't believe it. The troublemaker! You have the nerve to climb into my garden after that? I should let these dogs go right now.'

'Relax, okay, if she's here, I wouldn't mind a word, that's all.' He pointed up the path. 'She's in there, isn't she? See, I know what's going on. I'm not daft. And I'll tell you something. You should be ashamed of yourself, old bugger like you.'

'You're an idiot.'

'I know what's going on.'

'The first thing you should do is keep your mouth shut.'

Ricky nodded. 'Fucking hate dogs.'

The dogs snarled again and Sam jolted their chains. 'Tracy is my waitress, not my housekeeper. And from what I've seen the last time we met, I think you'd better stay well away from her.'

'Protecting her now, are we? Well I know what you're up to. Fucking disgusting. You're shagging her, ain't ya?'

'*Shagging?*'

'I've got your number, mate. Don't think I haven't. I've got your number.'

'Are you quite finished talking?'

'Yeah. I have.'

'Then we should get a move on. I haven't got all night.' Sam picked up his sword again.

'A move on? Where?'

'Under Islamic law I have a few options. I am obliged to take action now. You should have thought harder before climbing over my wall. This is just the beginning of it.'

'Beginning of what?'

Sam suddenly took on an aspect of the dogs. 'Now you pay.'

'Pay.'

'Yes. Pay.'

'Pay how.'

'You have invaded a traditional home and I fully intend to exact the traditional punishment, which befits a thief.'

'A thief? No way.'

'A thief. You are a thief. And you're not the first I have had over the wall either but you can be the first to carry the message back to your racist friends. Someone has to pay and it looks like it's you. Now get up that path.'

'Why?'

'That way, up the steps, we're going inside.'

'No. Inside? Why? No. Why?'

'Because I need something sharper than this sword.'

Terror lit up Ricky's face for the first time. 'Okay, I'm sorry, okay? I'm sorry. Let me go you won't see me again. How's that.'

'Too late. Someone must pay.'

Ricky gawked at the sword-wielding maniac before him. He credited the mad Arab with the will to do anything, to cut off a hand, or something worse. They were always on telly killing people, throwing stones. They had the killer instinct bred into them, took bloodshed to a whole other level. It was almost religious, their belief in violence. 'Please,' he now pleaded. 'Come on. Just let me go.'

'Up the steps or I let my dogs go.'

'Please.'

'Up, thief. Up!'

Ricky had no choice but to start up the steps, shimmying round the dogs. 'Okay. Okay.' The dogs were close behind him, held back only by the Iranian's loose grip on the chain. Several times the hot burst of moist breath penetrated the back of the young man's jeans.

He climbed the steps and prayed only that he wouldn't excite the dogs further by stumbling in the dark.

'Now I teach you a lesson,' he heard the voice behind him say.

The carving knife descended, slicing a triangle of thick, Black Forest cake. Passing cleanly through its subject, it reached the cutting board with a heavy thump. Yvette then proceeded to pass out portions on hand-painted china plates.

Already supplied with Turkish coffee in a silver cup so hot to the touch that he had to wrap both its handles with his napkin, Ricky Innes was full of gratitude. 'Nice one. Grazie, grazie. Thanksverymuch, yeah.'

With his feet up on a low stool, being served like a king, he looked at Sam. 'I really thought you was serious back there. Thought you was gonna have me Germans off. Had me going.'

'That was the whole idea.'

Ricky looked around the room until his eyes stopped on a wall scroll. The eastern writing looked like the disorientated squiggles left by a borer beetle. He followed the letters with the sharp chisel of his eye, curious about the professional challenge posed by its calligraphy: he had never done a gravestone for an Arab. He would almost certainly need a specialist tool.

Ricky and his host were left alone to talk.

'Now then, you say you love her.'

'Love who?'

'Tracy.'

'Oh, Tracy. That's right, yeah. Had a few problems, but yeah. And she loved me till you comes along. Got her a ring and everything.'

'I see.'

'And so when I heard that you and her were mucking about I got a little . . . a little bit upset, shall we say.'

'Nobody is mucking about with her, I assure you.'

'Anyway, I came here to talk it over basically. To have it out.'

'Which is what we are doing.'

'Exactly.'

Sam nodded. 'Right. Then I have a suggestion. I don't know who gave you the impression that she was anything other than my employee, but — '

'You drove her home. I seen ya.'

'I drive a lot of people home. I may even drive you home. It doesn't mean that we're mucking about with each other.'

Ricky nodded. 'Good point.'

'Does it?'

'No.'

Sam sighed and regarded his uninvited guest: a bleak advertisement for the next generation, studiedly unkempt, vainly so, cocky, street-smart, a ring on his *thumb*, a stud in his nostril, hair gel serving to keep his hair disorderly. The soles of his high-tech sports shoes confronted Sam, snarls of multi-coloured rubber wrapped around two ovoids of imprisoned air. All these pseudo-scientific advances, Sam thought, just to carry this caveman to the pub. Was this the modern British prototype? *And Tracy had said yes to this?*

The boy wanted to talk again. 'See, the problem is she won't even listen to me, so I know something must be going on. If you're not messing with her then somebody is. I thought it was you. Won't even talk to me on the phone. But all I wanna know is where I stand, see?'

'Nothing you say makes logical sense but I can see a solution.'

'What?'

Sam had the kid's attention now. 'I could talk to her. On your behalf. If you promise never to come here or to my restaurant again. Then I could relay what she says back to you. Would you like me to do that for you?'

His looked stunned. 'You'd do that?'

'I might.'

'Why?'

'Because it's the only way I can see to stop you from bothering people.'

Ricky could live with this. 'Fair enough.'

'Is it a deal?'

'If you could do that, if she'll talk to ya, yeah. You reckon you could do that?'

'What do you want me to ask her?'

'Just . . . I dunno.'

'Think of something.'

'Just . . . y'know, what's going on. That's it. Just what's going on, that sorta thing. Why won't she talk to me. I can explain everything. Stuff like that.'

'You just want to know what's going on.'

'I just wanna know what's . . . yeah.'

'I'll ask her then just . . . what is going on.'

'You'll do that for me, then?' He suddenly looked twelve. Could his ball be thrown back over the garden fence?

'Leave me your number. I'll call you. Don't call me. And then I never want to hear from you again.'

'Brilliant. Thanksalot.' Back comes the ball.

'Are we agreed then?'

'Not a problem.'

'Now be gone.'

'What?'

'Hop it.'

The kid paused. 'So you weren't serious about that lift then?'

At the front door, Sam Sahar watched the young man walk down the path and felt the sentimentality of a zoologist releasing an unequipped species into the wild. Ricky scampered away and slipped back into his tough, natural habitat.

8

Setting in Motion the Wheel of the Law

Oarsmen were measuring their strokes on the grey Thames as Tracy and Sam strolled down its bankside path under the cover of the London planes of Battersea Park. The evening light caught finches rising to a standstill over the fast-flowing river. She interrupted his narrative to point out the golden roof of the Peace Pagoda.

When the path forked they veered towards it.

The walk was all Sam's idea. There were a few things he wanted to tell her. Comfortable in his presence, she still had to be nervous about any meeting set up on the pretext of passing on important information. *What have I done now?*

The four seated Buddha, aureoled in gold leaf under a double-layer pagoda roof, hands in the principal positions of meditation, lent irony to Sam's discourse on the value of aerobic exercise.

Sam reeled of the main devotional positions as they circled: Dispelling Fear Buddha, Calling the Earth to Witness Buddha, Setting in Motion the Wheel of the Law Buddha, and lastly, the Preaching Buddha. 'That symbolises the prophet's first sermon.'

Tracy mimicked the hand gestures of the idols as they circled, performing a dyslexic sign language, before committing the precise combinations of finger and palm to memory, all under her aisle system. For quick reference she labelled the aisle 'Devotion'.

At the first pause in his instruction of the Buddhist *mudras*, she said: 'This is great. All this. Everything.'

'This?'

'Yeah. Just . . . everything.'

With a purifying intake of breath she turned and looked down the river to where the struts of Albert Bridge were delineated by light-bulbs. A cool breeze refreshed her face. 'I like being with you. I hope you don't mind me saying that.'

'Really? Why is that?'

'I dunno. You're funny.'

'I see,' he said, pondering this, nodding heavily, and wondering how he could bring her round to the topic of the intruder. 'So . . . you like humour. That's good. And what else makes you happy?'

'Easy. Hotel rooms. Staying in them.'

'Hotel rooms. So how many times have you been happy?'

'Eight.'

With this quick answer he rolled up his shirtsleeves, tight on his thick forearms. He would have to take another tack.

'Yvette says you're magnetic,' she said, interrupting his thoughts.

He coughed. 'She said that? Yvette? Well, you need to know that she drinks. I can accept that I may look okay through the bottom of a glass.'

Tracy wasn't sure if he was joking. Did Yvette have a problem? 'So how did you meet them both? And why did you decide to have two wives anyway? I mean, did your father have two? How does all that work? If you don't mind me asking you all this.' She couldn't hold back all her questions any longer and was very relieved to get them off her chest.

Sam faced the river. He shook his head. He didn't hurry his reply. 'My father? He only married once. You have to understand, that having more than one wife is very unusual in this day and age. Even in Iran it's hardly ever done any more. It's not thought desirable, really. The historical necessity for it has gone. Plus, it's bloody expensive, if you want to know the truth.'

'Then why?'

He sighed, fortifying himself for a complex reply. 'Well, it's a long story. A very long story.'

'So you keep saying.'

He consulted her expression; it pleaded with him to continue.

'They haven't told you themselves? All the hours you've spent together? Whatever happened to feminine gossip?'

He sighed again. Her interest was as intense as that of a biographer.

'What if I tell you it's all based on honesty. That this is the start and end of it. Obviously, when you're sharing a partner you need honesty like you need oxygen. Without honesty you're lost. So how's that?'

'And . . . ?'

He was increasingly uncomfortable. He rubbed the bristles on his neck. 'You should really ask them. Why don't you ask them? My decisions were relatively simple compared to the decisions they had to make. Honestly. They gave up the chance of having men their own age, for . . . this.' He threw his arms cruciform: self-mocking Buddha.

'And . . . ?'

'And what? I've told you. Honesty is all I have to offer them. That's it. And this just happened to be more important to them at the time than having a man each to themselves. Believe me, I was as surprised as you are now. But they had their needs, their sorrows, their own troubles. Much of romance is matter of timing. Mine turned out to be immaculate.' Looking unhappy, he held up his palms. 'And that's it. One thing led to another and here I am, living in the suburbs of south London with an old-fashioned *Mal-E-dzeh* on my hands. But who am I to argue with such an attractive fate?'

'But how did it start?'

He realised, finally, that she was not going to go away. 'Let me put it this way for you then. And you should work for the police department by the way. They have nothing on you.'

'The police were involved?'

'The police — ?' He had slipped up. 'No, well . . . in a way. Look, no. Look, we are just three people who for one reason or another solved some of each other's problems.'

'You always make it sound like an accident,' she said. 'Accidents like that don't happen.'

'An accident?' He faced her, sensing his wives and their wagging tongues in her question. 'Why do you choose that word? Yes, that's truer than you know. Much truer.'

'So how can it be an accident?'

'None of this is what I wanted to talk about. I wanted to talk about you.'

'Me?'

'Yes. I'm here on a mission of sorts.'

'Okay, but first tell me about you, then I'll tell you anything.'

It was a stand-off.

A park bench near the river would be the scene of the great confession. Tracy walked over to it, plonked herself down, challenging him to join her. He shook his head, let out an aggrieved sigh — hell had many guises, many of them beautiful — and finally dragged his feet across the stones towards the unavoidable rendezvous.

The story, when he had finished it some thirty or forty minutes later, exploded with something of the force of a hand grenade. Tracy's eyes were glazed with emotion. And he was similarly moved: it was hard information to impart.

Involving each of the wives and himself in equal measure, it was a tale of collective hardship but also collective triumph. 'I'm so sorry. Nobody said anything! If I'd known . . . well, I wouldn't have . . .'

'Wouldn't have? What? Been so curious? Yes you *would*.'

She put her hand to her mouth in a gesture of guilt. 'I think that's one of the saddest things I've ever heard.'

'I am not trying to win a prize.' Moved again by his own story he opened out his handkerchief and wiped his whole head, eyes, cheeks and the shining dome of his crown.

Tracy shook her head, going over again the real-life drama in her head. 'I mean, what happened to Firouzeh was bad enough, terrible, but poor . . . poor Yvette, she never said *anything* about this.'

'But no one is to know. You have to promise me this. This is just between us.' He adopted a fierce look.

'Just us?'

'A pact. Yes. Just the four of us.'

She agreed. It went without saying. She was more than happy to be included in this inner circle.

'And now you see? I am not the great womaniser you thought.'

'I didn't think that.'

'Everyone does. This great sex-fiend. It's understandable, I suppose. And yet here I am, with two wives, with two wives who never come near my bed. That's some kind of harem. It is almost funny.'

She didn't think it was funny. From where she sat, and knowing his full story now, a completely new light had fallen on him. His big head, the large counter-sunk spirals of his ears, the broad nose and hairy throat, all suddenly added to the nobility she now attributed to him. As she had listened this past half-hour, the litany of selfless acts had remoulded him in her eyes into a figure worthy of her highest esteem. His size, his age, his seriousness, even his verbal diarrhoea, his balding head, his podgy childlike hands and his watery eyes, were all matters of indifference now; in fact they were essential aspects of a new attraction, for who wants to tamper with a heroic character? Any alteration is vandalism.

'So you see,' he continued, 'everything in my life has been an accident. As you say. Fate worked like a kitchen cook to bring us all together. Even you.'

'Me?'

'Even you. Yes. What kind of accident is it that I am here telling all this to someone like you?'

The last light had faded. Other strollers came into view only as they passed under promenade lamps. A lone oarsman on the water, a surreal invention in the dark, steered between the bridge's black buttresses. She sniffed.

'I've upset you,' he said.

She brought her hands to chest height, thumb and forefinger joined, right palm outward, left palm inward.

He watched this act of prestidigitation. 'What are you doing?'

'Remember?' She held up her hand. 'Setting in Motion the Wheel of the Law.'

'Of course.' He stared at her, impressed again by her, and putting out of his mind yet again the recollection that he had business to transact on behalf of a lout. 'Brilliant,' he said. 'You have a brilliant mind, you know.'

With this, they looked at each other. It was inconceivable that he should suddenly lean forward and kiss her, but he did. He was a family man, a man of responsibility. If his own bed was barren, a twilight zone of zero activity, then that was no excuse. And yes, of course she was young and attractive, but she had a life with people her own age to live. At the same time, it was impossible to say whether he instigated the movement of faces together, or whether it was her doing. Suffice it to say it caught both of them off-guard and each looked as surprised as the other. 'Oops,' Tracy said as she withdrew.

'Oh dear.' He instantly felt the weight of repercussions. His hand went to his mouth to verify the accident.

'What was that all about?' she asked, smiling, pulling back. She was young. Youth was for gambling.

'I have no idea.'

'Was that me or you?'

'I have no idea. I assure you.'

'I think it might have been . . . '

'This is ridiculous.'

'I mean, you're married. I mean, bloody hell. Twice.'

'Technically, yes. I'm aware of that. But as you now know, it's not exactly as it looks from the outside.'

'So?'

Again their eyes invited the other forward, both guilty. 'So,' he said.

This second kiss was less tentative, much less a politeness. It made both of them close their eyes. Then, pulling back just far enough to speak, Sam gasped; 'We have to stop. I'm sure.'

'I know.'

'Disastrous.'

She smiled, thrilled at their mutual failure. She knew they were both anticipating their third kiss and that such protests were no more than caresses, stimulants to even greater feeling. He took her hand quickly, placed another behind her head and pulled her forward.

Unlike all the kisses in her life up to this point she didn't need to drift off to anywhere else or to escape into some fantasy and replace with imagination what was lacking in reality. It was all here, the sweet oblivion of the pop songs, where everything drew to a standstill. The leaves stopped their stirring, the oarsmen forgot how to row, even the pull of the Thames was nullified by their Rodinesque kiss, and it all remained in suspension, in the service of the moment, until one paradisal bird, finally drew air and climbed into the sky, releasing the world from its heavenly stasis.

'That was lovely,' Tracy said as they drew apart. Like guilty children, they smiled at each other, the surly older employer and the dreamstruck ex-shopgirl employee.

'Wow,' he replied, using a word he'd never used before.

'Lovely, yeah,' she said.

What the hell am I doing with this girl? he asked himself half an hour later. It was not too soon for a post-mortem.

Sitting under an oak in the darkness, while her head rested on his chest, he was free to ruminate. He put his nose in her hair — a small but unthinkable action only half an hour before! — and smelt green-apple shampoo. Life was certainly miraculous.

'Incredible to think,' he said.

'Mmm,' she murmured, almost asleep.

'Here we are. And a few minutes ago we would have blushed to hold hands.'

'It's nice.'

In our fortresses we rarely lowered the drawbridge, he considered. What a waste. Look what we missed. Standing aloof from each other was just a bluff waiting to be called. The great romancers, among whom he didn't include himself, knew this and acted on it. The walls were immaterial. Every averted glance was actually an invitation, every unreturned phone call a petition, every aggression a request to be stroked . . .

No, he upbraided himself. He was getting into dangerous territory. He had no right to extrapolate so much from a kiss. He smelt her hair again, an alien smell, and put himself on a different mental track. He didn't know her at all, even now. This was the truth. Nothing further was going to happen between them. Just because he had finally admitted to someone else a deep, intramarital loneliness didn't mean that Saaman Sahar had been offered a worldly invitation to end the platonic incarceration of his marriages.

He shook his head at how his thoughts had returned him to the starting point. He looked down at the lovely stranger curled in his arms. He must resist her. His family came first. And he was far too old for her. They were worlds apart. Kisses revealed nothing, he told himself. When they said goodbye tonight it would be as two unknowns who had bumped into each other. The real drawbridge came down only a few times in every lifetime. No, it was even worse than that. It came down hardly at all.

It was time to take her home, and to settle this.

The next morning, however, nothing had been agreed. Everything was a loose end. Sam had said nothing when he had dropped her off, pecking her on the cheek and speeding away.

Tracy took a bus to Mortlake Street, crossed diagonally in front of the old newsagents whose tabloids were held down with black, painted stones, and walked into the Clapham Library. From the librarian she requested a book on Islam. Directed towards 'Religion' she was told to try her luck.

On a low shelf she eventually found three versions of the Koran but couldn't decide which to take. They ranged from a small 1908 hip-pocket version, with tiny print, through an Oxford Press copy hammered out in the 1950s, to a modern Penguin paperback with an upbeat cover. After agonising between alternatives she gave up and decided on all three. As she couldn't tell which was the most authentic or decide whether the most modern translation would be the closest to the truth or the furthest away from it, she had no choice.

By the time she reached the checkout desk she had a stack of books under her arm including an account of the role of Islam in the modern world, which the *Times Literary Supplement* on the cover called 'a clear and readable account of a large and complex landscape'. She thought she might need a roadmap in such a large and complex landscape, and smiled at the joke in her own head.

While waiting her turn she glimpsed into the browned pages of the most ancient Koran. It read like one huge poem, full of terms like 'smite', 'admonition', 'mercy', 'exhort', 'felicity', 'Heaven'. The word 'Moses' surprised her, 'Jesus' even more, 'Hell' and 'Creation' with a capital C.

At the desk the librarian flipped the books face up. Tracy felt a blast of pride at being seen to borrow such works — *Attention everyone: Tracy Pringle of Flat 2312, Melksham Towers, is borrowing three copies of the Koran, and yes, she will be available for autographs on the library steps afterwards.*

Unasked, and temporarily a scholar, she told the librarian: 'Research.' Blip-blip-blip-blip.

She smiled at him and took her tracts and the next bus home.

'I'm tired. I'm off to bed.'

Eric checked his watch. It was 9 p.m.

He looked at his wife and then returned his eyes to the television.

Behind a locked door, she began her secret studies.

She had problems immediately. Drawing up her knees to become a lectern and opening the most readable version at random, she found the first lines virtually incomprehensible. Her spirits deflated.

Sam would later explain, beside the restaurant's steaming coffee machine (where he wouldn't laugh at her) that the *saj* style of the writing presupposed a familiarity with Bedouin society which she couldn't be expected to have. Processes, not things, are described in it. Each sentence is like a road washed out at intervals which can only be travelled if you are prepared to leap over the gaps, as it were, from association to association. You need to make jumps, and project yourself into the ancient desert environment of the Bedou. He closed the Holy Book and handed it back to her. 'You really have to *imagine*,' he said, 'all the stuff that for them was too obvious to spell out.'

But without this insight, on her first night of study she was lost in her own blind travels.

She decided to concentrate on one small but typical section and work on that.

> *By those that pluck out vehemently*
> *And those that draw out violently*
> *By those that swim serenely*
> *And those that outstrip suddenly*
> *By those that direct an affair.*

She read it three more times. Still nothing. What 'affair'? And who were 'those'? And why were they so busy, plucking and drawing and swimming and outstripping? She wondered if it would be easier to understand in another translation. Locating the exact verse by its numbers, she found what seemed an entirely different passage altogether:

> *Consider those that rise only to set*
> *and move with steady motion*
> *and float with floating serene*
> *and yet overtake with swift overtaking*
> *and thus they fulfil the behest!*

'Fulfil the behest'? What? It was too difficult. It was hopeless. She was getting nowhere. It was clearly a riddle of some kind. All she could do was to earmark the page, an old school habit for dealing with anything she couldn't understand, and not so much to note it for later study, but rather to record the intellectual defeat: at the end of the year her fifth form maths book was an uncloseable wedge!

Similarly, she didn't think she'd ever return to this passage. But she was wrong. Two days later Sam was to iron flat the bent corner with his big thumb, glancing at her as he did so as though it were a mistake to mark a holy page in this way. At the back of the restaurant he put on his half-moons and prefaced his response with the disclaimer that he was a poor interpreter of the sacred text himself, and not the best person to ask. 'Well, okay, for a start, I'm not quite sure,' he said, squinting more in an attempt to comprehend meaning than simply to read the words. 'All the translations are so . . . so different, you see. But if I had to hazard a guess, the verse makes me envisage . . . the night sky . . . surely the night skies in the desert. "Floating serene" implies that. I think that is what is suggested there.'

'The night sky? But where does it say that?'

'It doesn't. But that's the point. As you know, the stars are unusually brilliant in the desert. So I would say it is referring to celestial bodies, stars, things like that. You have to imagine sitting around a campfire, imagine the crackling olive branches, the camels in a circle about it, the Bedous silent, following the smoke upwards with their chins towards a dazzling sky, towards Allah.'

She nodded. She was more than willing to call up this scene before her, an obsidian sky pinpricked a thousand times with light. 'I'll have another go then.'

'And this last line, I read as "and thus they fill the *Creator's* behest". Insert the Creator there, Allah, you know? Praise be upon him. Try putting in the missing links.'

She took the book outside after her shift, the sky an impenetrable grey. She sat on the smoker's box and reread the passage, inserting the concepts of rising stars, bodies moving in orbit, floating through space, overtaking one another, all under the direction, the sway, of the one creator.

'You see,' Sam said, joining her later for a smoke, 'the holy book isn't an easy read, simple as that. It's what is called a cryptogram, a book of symbols. It's saying that reality can't fully be grasped head-on. If you try, it recedes like an horizon. You have to use your own intellect and imagination. That's what marks the Koran out as being so different from the Bible. By editing out the obvious it requires that you do some work. Like the best art. And in this effort, the idea is that you reach another level of consciousness, one which spoon-feeding would never *ever* awaken.'

In her bedroom, ambition returning, she flicked to a new section and would not turn off the light until she had read at least one line she could understand. When she found it, she read it several times, waiting to reach

114

a state of higher consciousness but happy in the end to settle for simple comprehension.

The life of this world is after all nothing
but an enjoyment of self-delusion.

She carried the consolation to sleep, along with her reflections on Sam's park-bench revelation, harbouring in passing a sad thought for Yvette and Firouzeh, before revisiting the kiss which for a few seconds had stopped most of the clocks in Creation.

Tracy found the Cecil Street bookstore while shopping. She looked in at the window display: gold-painted palm-leaves wreathed an Islamic candelabra.

She pushed open the door, wandered around the lightly scented room, her eyes struck by the unfathomable Arabic titles, gold and silver calligraphy on Bible-thick books, all under the occasional gaze of a young bearded male attendant who otherwise entered figures into a calculator. Tap-tap-tap-tap-tap.

'Need help?' he asked when she passed by the counter. He was bookish, in a collarless shirt, moist-eyed, with a feminine tilt to his head, studying to be a cleric, she guessed, but racking up his hours in a bookshop first, getting his feet wet in the community before then.

'Umm, yeah. Definitely.' She had already prepared her question. 'Do you have anything in English?'

'English?' The young man smiled. The soft brown eyes glinted through the large-rimmed glasses. He had a brash London accent. 'No. Not much actually. Depends whacha looking for?' His voice was a surprise, barrow-boy cockney. 'I fink we got the Koran in English, but not a lot else.'

'Not the Koran,' she shook her head. 'I've got three versions of that already. Actually, I need something to help me understand it.'

He seemed impressed. 'Yeah? Three? You read 'em then? I fought you might be new, that's all.'

'I wondered if I could find something like an introduction.' She looked about her.

He nodded and came round the counter. 'Right. I'm with ya. But we're mostly Arabic texts here.' She followed him down the length of the shop. Could this East Ender read Arabic? 'You might be better off in the

Islamic Education Centre then,' he said. 'In Battersea or somefing. Otherwise, we've got a few videos in the corner you could take a look at.' The young man had to be a second- or third-generation Briton, and with him she felt a lot less intimidated, marginally less a tourist without a map. 'But as I say, depends on what you're looking for, really.'

'Just . . . just . . . I'm not sure . . . what Islam is about really?'

'Oh. What it's about? Right. An introduction.'

'Just something.' *Why do I have to sound so idiotic?*

'Right, just something to answer your questions, then. About what its all about?' Again the feminine tilt to his head. He was a first-class enlister.

'Yeah.'

'You definitely need an introduction to the Koran then, cos it's all in there. It's all in the holy book.'

'Is it?'

'All the fundamental questions, yeah, get answered in there.'

'Just that sort of thing then.'

'Working out the times we live in. What we all want. That sort of thing, innit.'

She nodded. 'Yeah.' She chuckled. 'I'm definitely looking for that.' Tracy's grandmother used to talk this way about the Bible.

'Everything's changing, but where's it going? That sort of fing.'

'Exactly.'

'Everything being questioned, everyone's experimenting, but it's not joyful. There's no joy.' As he spoke his eyes searched the shelves. 'No inner peace. People in big numbers, searching. That's what brings people in here. But the Prophet, peace be upon him, well, he points us towards the timeless answers. Infallible truths.' He had barely blinked. His forefinger roamed, ready to jab at the first book that came close to an English introduction.

'If you have that then,' Tracy said, 'something like that. That's great. In English, though.'

'Right, we'll . . . nothing here, y'see. We'll try over here.' She followed him to another corner of the shop. Here the shelves contained videos and magazines. 'Got some audio-visual.'

She could read these titles herself and her eye immediately fell on the words 'Cat Stevens'.

'Oh, Cat Stevens!' A favourite of her parents, she had adopted him for herself years ago. Except that he wasn't Cat Stevens any longer. He had renamed himself Yusuf Islam, and, as she learnt from the young man, now lived quietly somewhere near Ladbroke Grove in a triumph of reinvention.

She had loved his music ever since she had been curious enough to go through her parents' record collection. Neil Diamond had not interested her, the Beatles were too happy, Pink Floyd too paranoid for a thirteen-year-old, but Cat Stevens had filled the maudlin, sentimental, day-dreamy gap. Despite the all-consuming beard — ever the badge of artistry, a rejection of the outward — he had struck a romantic chord in her and so she had taken the copy of *Tea for the Tillerman* and the old record player with her into the sanctuary of her room to indoctrinate herself with the man's singular downbeat view of the world.

As with most self-educations of this sort, the nostalgic lessons she learnt never left her.

An old record player, jammed with a 20-pence coin onto repeat mode, had ensured that both sides of the LP were played so many times that each note, each nuance, each vocal inflection took root in her peculiar imagination. Once, when Ricky had driven her to a party, she got the chance to demonstrate her devotion to his repertoire. As they neared the Blackwall Tunnel 'Father and Son' came onto Virgin Radio. She began to sing along until radio contact was cut as they slipped under the Thames. In Cat's absence, diving underwater, she kept on singing and when the car surfaced again into daylight, nearly a minute later, her words dovetailed perfectly with the returning maestro.

'Oh yeah,' the young man said, handing Tracy the video. 'That's good. That's well worth watching.'

She turned it over in her hands, saw she had enough money on her to buy *The Making of the Last Prophet*, which, as the cover stated, featured 'an exclusive interview with Yusuf Islam'.

Perhaps she could hear Cat's side of things. From the horse's mouth. 'Yeah, I'll take this. Is it in English?'

'Should fink so. He's English, in 'ee.'

She couldn't wait to get the video home. On the bus she read the back cover, learning how he had gone back into the studio. She hadn't heard about this. She felt again the old excitement of the fan anticipating a new album.

Fortunately, no one was home, so she went straight to the TV, broke the wrapper and inserted the tape into the machine.

And there he was. In eastern robes, he was seated at a desk flanked by heavy books, reconceived as an eastern liturgical scholar. His voice had the same unmistakable tone of the records, mellow, rich; the beard was as long as the young man's in the bookshop. He hadn't been in a music studio since 1978, he stated cheerfully, looking anything but regretful. Her hero talked comfortably about his childhood as a West End theatre-rat when show business entered his blood like septicaemia. Fame came too easily. He had always been on a search for higher meaning. Then, hospitalised by tuberculosis, he had begun a revaluation — Tracy mentally listed the great albums of this period — which had primed him for Malibu Beach when, caught in a rip-tide, he had had an epiphany. Locked in the Californian surf, he promised himself to God and a huge wave lifted him back to shore. From there, and with his brother's intuitive gift of a Koran, it was easy to walk away from the silliness of rock and roll.

Tracy replayed the account twice and then let it run on. The life of the last prophet was the great untold story in the west, he told her. Descended from the same line as Moses and Jesus, Mohammed was an historical figure above kings and conquerors. The west suffered a mental block — its own great misfortune — and terrible misconceptions existed. Yusuf himself had not been truly content until his conversion. His own life was now blessed. Asked further about the music business, he looked away and laughed.

Tracy had to go to work. She would be late. She took the lift down and boarded another bus, knowing now that Yusuf Islam had gone back into a music studio after all these years to record only three Islamic songs. His real purpose had been to narrate his own miniature biography of the Prophet for CD and cassette.

Perhaps she could write to him?' she thought at the back of the bus, slowly tearing up her ticket. He was a Londoner too. She wasn't a heavy-weight thinker, but she was interested in things, she was no dummy, and she had a good memory. Couldn't she, too, glimpse the grand design, the big picture?

Firouzeh's favourite film in the whole world was *Gone with the Wind*. She'd first seen it as a young adult in pre-revolution Iran, where even a bad translation could not dull its romantic appeal. Under the aegis of the hyper-westernising Shah, it had played to packed houses.

In fact, Rhett's famous doorway rejoinder, prudishly mutated into, 'Well, my love, the future is up to me,' was somehow even more poignant, more bewitching, and struck her squarely in the pit of her stomach, releasing tears under her *hijab*.

Unlike her friends, she had always thought Ashley the better bet and was delighted to see the back of Rhett, the big moustachioed baboon.

Years later, in a hotel in Bucharest, when she spoke better English and tried to watch the unedited original, she switched it off after half an hour, missing the romantic power of understatement inherent in the poorly dubbed voice-over.

Yvette, on the other hand, the real movie buff, was a lover of Federico Fellini, the master of *over*statement. She had developed a recent obsession for *City of Women* which promoted the fantasy that under our beds lay a trapdoor which allowed us to ride down a vast spiralling slide, sweeping us past the scenes of our lives, with our loved ones and dearly departed waving back to us, depicted in tableaux to the left and right. She adored the idea of being able to consort with people on the other side so easily. It was, an overeager shrink had told her, simply her way of expressing the fact that she was only living to see her dead husband again.

With such high cinematic standards, neither wife expected very much from this evening's movie, which revolved around a shell-shocked lawyer getting his act together just in time to reprieve an innocent man. Firouzeh muttered, 'Bullshit America.'

Tracy sat between them. Yvette gripped Tracy's forearm on one side, while, on the other, Firouzeh turned inward to share a Diet Pepsi from the same straw. The movie had not yet started.

Nervously, Tracy made her pronouncement: 'I really like Sam.'

The reply came in synchronised unison: 'Of course you do.'

Having ventured to the edge, Tracy threw herself into the unknown. 'No. I mean, I think I'm falling in love with him.'

Despite the bombshell neither of the two legitimate wives took their eyes from the screen where the trailers had drawn to a close, the feature about to roll. Yvette lobbed popcorn into her mouth continuously while Firouzeh, straw in mouth, gripped her Pepsi like an oboe, and drew a vein-flow of liquid upward. 'Good,' she replied.

'You both don't mind . . . then?'

'About time. We were beginning to worry about you.' Firouzeh held out the drink for Tracy. 'We have been planning it, anyway. In case you didn't notice.'

The house lights dimmed on Yvette's grin as the curtains closed, only to part again a few seconds later. The screen swelled to its full width and the movie began with an orchestral flourish.

'Then you know that we kissed?'

'Oh yes,' said Firouzeh lackadaisically. 'He was very happy about that.'

'Shhhh!' Yvette was reverential about films. 'Can we watch please?'

The movie finally began: a realistic character became hopelessly embroiled in an unrealistic turn of events, ending after many close shaves in a superficial but uplifting redemption.

9

The Temporary Wife

A large map of Iran was now pinned to Tracey's bedroom wall. She had also bought, at a stall in Camden market, a miniature ceramic elephant whose perforated hide could support six incense sticks at a time.

She took her books into the bathroom. Submerged to the chin in long, deep, energy-sapping baths, she regulated the taps with her toes and tried to summon the Bedouin landscapes Sam had evoked. On the twenty-third floor of her council flat, with her teacup kept warm on the bath's edge, and with her texts just above the waterline, she summoned, as she read, the vast salt deserts of the central interior, the Iraqi citadel of Aqaba and the 'lynx-ridden marshes' of the Caspian coast.

As their park walks became more frequent she was now always certain of having something to discuss, touting a knowledge of Sam's homeland that outweighed his own. 'Really? I didn't know that,' was his most common reply. Where possible he tried to play the sage but often her questions went over his head. To live inside a country and culture didn't make you an expert, he confessed. 'Actually, it usually makes you blind as a bat.'

During these 'meetings of minds', as Sam christened them, he was increasingly at pains to point out that they were also 'stolen moments' and that they would have to end.

'In fact, this should probably be our last meeting.' Despite the active encouragement of Yvette and Firouzeh, who seemed happy for them to spend as much time as they liked together — 'it's good for his heart, keep him walking' — he couldn't continue like this indefinitely.

But each afternoon when they met before work and held hands on an unpopulated section of path, adamant that this was their last walk, they realised again and again that any talk of calling it off was an irresistible aphrodisiac.

They only ever met to say goodbye, to call a halt to it all, but their emotions were so hugely magnified by their attempts to reduce them, that they rushed the stages of romance and leap-frogged straight into passion. Sensible and morose talk about the impossibility of a future made them so depressed that they had no choice but to set a date for a new meeting, invariably another walk, in the vain hope of restoring some kind of order to their feelings and to bring them back down to earth.

But neither the final, the final final, nor the *absolutely-last-time* walk ever came off as intended, and in a maze of penultimate walks, they consistently failed to see that they were moving so far away from their intention that they had become quite incapable of ever fulfilling it.

Sam spoke of his exhaustion first. 'If we're ever going to get things back to normal,' he finally said, 'then I think we have to stop saying we're meeting for the last time. It's obviously fatal.'

In an effort to lift them out of this vicious cycle, Tracy accepted an invitation by three girlfriends to go out to a local nightclub: she hadn't been returning their calls for some time.

She left work that Friday night without saying a word to Sam, tried to dance in the middle of the spinning lights, laughed for an hour at nothing at all, drank three rainbow-coloured cocktails and then, bemused, depressed, flat, sat watching her friends spin like dervishes in the centre of the jumping crowd.

The touch on her shoulder made her spill her drink.

'Did he talk to you then?' His hair shone with excessive amounts of gel.

'Did who?'

'Your boss. Did he talk to you?'

'My boss?'

'The Arab geezer.'

'Get lost, Ricky.' Fumbling in her purse for a coin, she escaped him, ran to the pay-phone beside the cloakroom and dialled a memorised number.

Twenty minutes later, she hurried across the road towards a slowing

Mercedes, hopped into the passenger seat and was swept away from the club.

In her wake, his stiff hair resisting the rain, Ricky Innes was left to observe the nature of her departure and to deal with the sudden facts of this double betrayal.

When Sam pulled up in front of his own darkened restaurant three days later Tracy thought he was joking. She had spent good money on her hair, and bought a new dress. 'This is it,' he announced. 'It's all ours! And tonight, I cook for you.'

On a high stool in the kitchen, glum with dismay, she watched him stir a dozen saucepans and narrate the origin of each dish. He had shopped that morning for specialities, he shouted, kumquats from Peru, organic bell-peppers from Oxfordshire, herbs cut hours before, tiny mushrooms picked by a friend from the base of a tree split by lightning. He had conceived a sylvan banquet she would never forget. He took particular delight in ending each dubious anecdote with a cymbal clang of pot-lids.

She was slow to be convinced. No combination of vegetables could salve her disappointment. She was angry. In one stroke, her love was upturned and everything was draining away. What was she doing with this kind of man anyway? With all his problems? *I'm making a terrible mistake.* A hundred reservations stepped from the shade into the light.

The final banquet partially appeased her. She had to admit that he had made a huge effort. And the table, an oasis of light, was not without seductive power. 'Taste!' he said over the unveiled starter, a basted eggplant supporting a mandarin-sesame sauce. 'Taste!'

She did. And was transported. It was more than excellent.

'Food is one of the last magic carpet rides that we have left,' he said with a full mouth. 'Executed perfectly, you should soar!'

By the main course, she was well on the road to rediscovering her enthusiasm for Sam, and by the exquisite dessert — a marinated plantain under a burial mound of rose petals — she was seized with a sudden desire to advance this relationship to the next stage.

'There!' he said, setting down a golden spoon with a satisfied clang on the china plate, looking at her over the remnants of his culinary triumph. 'And so what now?' It came out as a challenge. Now it was her turn.

She amazed herself with her next utterance. 'Bed,' she said.

He gaped at her. Nothing in his reaction indicated that he was ready for this.

'Unless you think we're rushing things.'

'No.' He was determined not to stammer. 'Of course not. No. I'm just wondering . . . no I was just wondering myself . . . that age-old question.'

'What question? What question is that?' She was ready.

'That most ancient of questions. Of course. Your place or mine.'

Sam and Tracy checked into the Marilyn Suite at the Hilton Metropole on Praed Street just after 11 p.m.

Hanging up their coats they sat on the tautly made bed and looked about at their empty room, a chromed love pad, but quite appropriate for a descent into madness. Warhol's photo-portraits of Marilyn Monroe glared down from every wall onto a bed much wider than it was long: the effect was that of an auditorium.

'Awful,' Sam muttered. 'Not how they described it at all. They said it had a balcony. We should go somewhere else.'

'I don't think we need a balcony.'

'All the same.'

But Tracy wanted to try and make this work. As he nervously loosened his tie and removed his jacket she set about taking a few of the pictures down and stripping back the silver-foil-like bedspread.

Less offended by decor, he sat again on the bed, hard as a trampoline, and contemplated the next step.

'There is something I've just thought about. And I think it might be nice to do it,' Sam said. 'A bit old-fashioned, but I think you might like it.'

'It's not kinky, is it?'

'Kinky? No, it's something from old Muslim tradition. But unfortunately I didn't plan ahead. I don't have the equipment.'

'Equipment?' She began to look worried.

He then explained that there was an old, old Muslim tradition that governed encounters like this. 'I read a short passage from the Koran, that's it. But I doubt if the Hilton Metropole stocks a copy of the Koran.'

She nodded vigorously. 'You might be surprised.'

'I know. I'll make a quick call.'

She watched as he went over to the phone, dialled and waited. This was not how she imagined the evening proceeding. It was doing nothing for her nerves.

A voice came on the line. 'Firouzeh? It's Sam.'

He had phoned Firouzeh! Tracy blushed.

'Listen, my dear. I'm phoning from a hotel. Yes, a hotel. Of course with Tracy, now listen — what? All right. All right.' He covered the receiver and faced Tracy. 'Firouzeh says hello.'

Tracy tried to smile. 'Hi.'

'She says "hi" back. So are we finished? Okay, now listen, I want you to find the Koran on the shelf, yes, it's somewhere, and read me the *seegheh* passage. You know the one . . . Yes, of course I want it for that reason. Calm down. Just go and get it. I'll wait. I want to copy it down. Are you looking now? Can you see it. Okay. Thank you, my dear.' He looked back at Tracy. 'She's got it now. She's just looking it up. It's really a very charming protocol. In the old days men would have to recite it before seeing a whore.'

'A whore!'

'But it's really rather beautiful. I'll get it down and see what you think. We don't have to do it at all, but you're so interested in anything Persian I thought we would do it for you.'

She nodded nervously. 'Great.'

He spoke into the phone. 'Have you got it? Yes. Read me the first line. Yes. Yes. Okay, that's it. Okay, let me write this down.'

While Tracy waited patiently he sat on the bed and transcribed the Arabic text on nicotine-coloured hotel paper.

'Okay I've got it,' he finally said, then thanked his wife, put down the phone and faced his mistress.

'She doesn't mind?'

'No. I think they were both expecting it. Even hoping something like this would happen.' Tracy's look of astonishment made him continue. 'I know. It's all very odd. All of it. I know. Nobody on the outside looking in would believe it. But we're not on the outside, are we?'

That was true enough, Tracy thought. 'No we're not.' You had to know at least as much as she did herself to even begin to understand how such taboos could be so casually transgressed, and even then . . . 'It's pretty odd on the inside as well,' she said.

He returned to Tracy on the bed with the text.

'So what now?' She hoped it promised something romantic.

He pumped his shoulders to release tension. 'Well, first I must read this, this passage, and then you must verbally give me your permission. That's the last thing. And then we can begin.'

'Begin?'

'To make love to each other.'

'Okay. I permit you. How's that?'

'No. More officially than that. And it comes later.'

'Okay. I'll try and be more official when the time comes.'

'Good. And then I must take some heart pills.' He cleared his throat. 'Okay. Now we can start. Okay. First the reading.'

'And this will make me . . . a what?'

'This? Okay, well this will make you a *seegheh*.'

'A *seeg-heh*.'

'Yes, *seegheh*.'

Tracy filed it under Beautiful Terms.

'A temporary wife. Let me read it to you.'

Reverently he read the transcribed passage in his hand. She listened carefully to the soft Arabic music of the words. She calmed as she listened, relieved at least that he did not know the passage off by heart. She wanted the illusion that this was the first time he had had cause to recite it. When he was finished he looked up from the piece of paper, his mood more settled.

'There's, it's done.'

Tracy Pringle was now his temporary wife. And by extension, he was her temporary husband. The mood of frivolity had vanished.

'Was that all right?' he asked.

'It sounded lovely.'

'And now then. Do I have your permission? Tracy?'

'Now?'

'Now. Yes. Do I have it?'

'Yes,' she said earnestly. 'You do have.' Then added 'To go ahead'. She smiled sweetly, but then decided her tone lacked gravity, and tried again: 'You have my undivided permission.'

'Please take this seriously.'

'I am. I am. I think it's beautiful.'

'All right then,' he was sweating heavily now. Beads on his brow. 'Do I have your permission?'

'Yes.'

Instantly they slid into each other's embrace. Over his shoulder Tracy saw she had forgotten to take down two portraits in the bathroom, and that they were under the double gaze of these remaining pink and yellow Marilyns. It was not a great leap to transmute these into Firouzeh and Yvette.

The life of this world
is after all nothing
but an enjoyment
of self-delusion.

They began to make love. It was sweet, silent, tender, protracted, and performed with the lights off, the physical pleasure diluted by an impossible reservoir of affection. He took his time, something she welcomed as a refreshing change, and placed so many kisses on every part of her body that she had to gain his attention and ask him to proceed to the next stage. At last they coupled, and when it was over, twenty minutes or so later, Tracy cried but could not tell him why. She had intended at some point to say 'I love you', but had completely forgotten to do so.

Sam drove her home.

'That was amazing,' she said.

'Don't exaggerate. I'm not a stud.'

She was forced to recollect her imprisonments under the pneumatic, fluorescently lit Ricky. 'Thank goodness,' she said.

Later, in the foyer of Melksham Towers, they kissed outside the lift and then she went up alone. He remained to ensure the lift did not victimise her again on the seventh floor. He was right to do so. He counted the numbers aloud through seven but when eight did not appear he took the stairs two at a time, arriving exhausted and panting on the seventh landing several minutes later only to find the illuminated floor numbers blinking on and off again in smooth succession. He made his way back to the ground, an invalid with his hand over his galloping heart. This girl was going to be the end of him!

As Sam closed his own front door lightly, so as to not disturb the house, he wasn't altogether surprised to find both his wives on the couch in their dressing gowns sipping tea.

'Good,' he said, and moved towards them.

10

Stress

Monica's migraine had begun as she sat in traffic that morning on her way to the pre-school. All day it had accompanied her, making itself felt on the right side then, around noon, moving over to the left where it sharpened and sent occasional stabs to the back of her left eye.

By the time the book-reading hour started at 2 p.m. she was trying to be careful with herself, speaking just loud enough to be heard at the back of the class, but not so loud as to worsen things. In between instructions, with just an hour to go, she pinched the bridge of her nose and rested her eyes for a few seconds at a time, hoping to make it over the four o'clock finishing line. Unless she was good to herself, she knew, she would be in for a hell of a time.

She was just preparing the class for a story about monarch butterflies. What colour are they? Who has seen one? Where can you see them?

Several small eager hands went up, waving for her attention.

'Samantha? Orange, good. Brown? Not really. I have a picture here, so you can see . . . that it's . . . well, it's more of a reddish brown, isn't it, a red brown. And how long are its wings? Anyone? No, they're not this big, this is just a big picture. No, they're *four inches*.' Her emphasis caused a widening of most children's eyes. 'Rachel! What am I talking about? Are you listening to me? What am I talking about?'

'No.' The automatic answer would be useful for the girl's whole life, but not right now, not here.

'What am I talking about?'

'Butterflies.' She knew after all. She would go a long way.

'That's right. Butterflies.'

A knock sounded on the door. The play-group leader wanted a word. At his side stood two highly timid Asian children.

'This is them,' he said. 'The Cambodian children.'

'Great. Come in. Hello.' Monica crouched to speak to them, her head hurting badly now. 'I am Mrs Pringle.' She enunciated each word. She knew their English was virtually non-existent. 'You are going to be part of our play-group for a little bit. How do you feel about that? Play some games? Games? Listen to stories?'

The children didn't nod. Their eyes radiated fear. To them she must be highly suspicious, a new western type to deal with — the smiling female stranger — and for all her friendliness was just as dangerous, for all they knew, as the Khmer Rouge.

Monica had been informed that their parents were asylum seekers who, because they were not yet deemed refugees, had only been provisionally afforded free pre-school care: in other words, they could be sent home at any time.

'Would you like to come in and sit on the mat with the other children?'

The brother and sister held hands in a strategy of mutual protection. Monica had been versed on the family background in the staffroom at lunchtime. They had travelled many thousands of miles on foot and by makeshift boat, then aircraft and train just to make it to this point, passing through several worlds and several lives. She guessed that these two had seen enough in their short lives to make them justifiably wary of anyone for a very long time.

She took their hands. 'They'll be fine,' she told her colleague and closed the door. With a hand behind each head she steered the children into the room, a makeshift paradise papered with crayon drawings, giant mushrooms and rabbits and puffy white clouds, in reds, yellows and dill-pickle greens. From the big mat the other toddlers glanced at the foreign twins with no particular interest, as if they were just another aspect of the continuous entertainment.

'Everybody? This is Lon.' No nod from Lon. 'Lon. And Tang. Lon and Tang.' A few giggles from the girls at the back. 'They are from *Cambodia*. Now, does anyone know where that is? Where Cambodia is?'

'By the seaside.'

'Yes, well by *someone*'s seaside.'

Very soon the visitors had taken places on the mat and, like the others, were staring wide-eyed at the picturebook, listening beyond comprehension to Monica, at least superficially assimilated into the rainbow-coloured world of the child.

When Monica got home she dropped her bags and keys on the table and went straight to the bathroom. She took a bottle of Nurofen capsules from the cabinet and held four of them in her mouth until she got back to the kitchen where she leant over and drank straight from the tap. 'Ow,' she gasped. She cooled her forehead with her wet hand.

She definitely didn't want anything to eat tonight. Eric could have the leftover Persian that Tracy, at his request, brought home every night and that now occupied most of the fridge. Monica was not sold on the taste anyway. Still, she had forced herself to eat enough that she had learnt some of names — *haleem bo-demjune,* and *masto khiar,* or something like that.

Eric, on the other hand, had not got past calling the dishes 'that aubergine, walnut thing' or, when putting a call through to Tracy mid-shift, suddenly hungry, 'those y'know's in yoghurt'. He had taken to the food with a vengeance and several weeks had passed since he had cooked himself a fry-up.

She peered in vain into the freezer compartment to see if she had any ice-cubes she could hold to her temples but found only more containers of frozen Persian. In desperation, she decided to take a nap with the curtains drawn.

In the darkened bedroom, the painkillers helped her to go off. She awoke, feeling only marginally better, around 9.30.

In the lounge, Eric was happily watching TV with his fingers inter-laced behind his head. 'Migraine?' It was said without sympathy. She knew he relished times like this, when he had the place to himself in the evenings.

'Tracy wants to talk to us tonight,' Eric announced.

'What about?'

'God knows. Called me while you were asleep.'

'Well what time?'

'When she gets in.'

'Some kind of trouble or what?'

'No idea. Couldn't talk. Cuppa tea?' he finally offered.

'Mmm. Be nice.'

She took his vacated seat and stared at the programme. They paid an extra £35 a month for this satellite service and she never watched it. The whole building was dotted with little dishes, a thousand ugly hearing aids eavesdropping on the world. A reporter was telling her that this year, for the first time 'in ages', the McLarens were expected to win the Constructor's Championship. A victorious pit-crew jumped up and down excitedly.

Eric shouted from the kitchen, 'Why does it worry me when I hear she wants to talk to us?'

Monica was feeling too fragile to shout back, and waited until he came in with two cups of tea.

'Because . . . ' she took a sip, and kept her eyes on the Formula One car revving on the grid, 'because it's never happened before.'

'Fixed a window. Rewired a bit of number 2307's lighting,' he said, his eyes on the set.

She nodded. It was ludicrous really. Like any successful couple, they liked to believe they were a team pulling in the same direction, and yet, whenever she thought about it, which she tried not to, there she was, trying her hardest to force the council to pull this building down, to destroy the place, declare it a death-trap and put a wrecking ball to it, while he, at the same time, and with no sense of irony, pottered around with his hammer and nails and quietly made a living out of patching it up.

The observation didn't surprise her. He had always been happy to leave things as they were, plastering over the cracks as they appeared but otherwise content to live his days alongside imperfections while she, on the other hand, had aspirations towards perfection and had always needed to test the reality of everything. If she thought about it, they were fundamentally at odds on a level so profound as to render the whole arrangement ostensibly meaningless, but neither of them wished to talk about it for fear of the consequences.

And yet, here they were, side by side, a technically happy couple by normal standards, the cheerful carpenter and the restless demolition expert wife, their warring energies buried like nuclear waste, throbbing underground, while they above ground went about their normal life, plainly hoping the canisters of mutual denial would hold out for a lifetime.

She looked at the TV. It was very hard to tell who was winning the race now underway. The vehicles overlapped each other continuously.

When Tracy came in the door it had gone 11.30. She wasn't alone.

'Mum, Dad, Sam gave me a lift home again.'

Sam was breathless, his nostrils flared, porcine after the climb.

'Tracy, you should've said!'

Eric apologised for the lift's failure as if it were his fault, and acted as if they were old friends. Monica watched the two men shake hands vigorously and affectionately and noted the hugely changed atmosphere. Eric apologised for not getting back in touch 'about that little work offer of yours' then added that he and Monica were extremely grateful for the amazing changes they had seen in their daughter.

'Not me,' he puffed. 'All her.' Sam turned warmly to Monica. 'Lovely to . . . excuse me . . . to see you.'

She took his unnecessary umbrella and tried to smile. It hurt her head and she decided to convey her hospitality from then on with small nods and slow gestures.

'Let's all take a seat, shall we?' she said.

Once on the couch Tracy broke the ice of their collective anxiety. 'Mum, Dad, you're probably wondering what we want to have this talk about. Well, Sam's asked me to marry him. And I said yeah.' She hoped this would cover it. Now they could drink a toast with the champagne they had brought.

Shock sometimes has instant after-effects but for Eric the first symptom was retardation. 'Who did?' he asked. 'Marry who?' He looked from his daughter to his wife. 'What's going on?'

Monica had no desire to say anything.

'Sam and me. Me and Sam. We wanted to tell you first. It's really sudden. But we're gonna go for it, we decided.'

Tracy had anticipated the ensuing silence and so filled it at once with a report on how hard and how long and from how many sides they had looked at everything, taking everyone's concerns into account along the way. 'Obviously, I'll be moving out but I'd like to involve you all in our plans, which are still . . . y'know . . . ,' she turned to her fiancé, her rehearsed smile becoming a beam, ' . . . it's still early days. But we want both of you to be part of it all. So, what do you think? Surprised, or not? Or did you see it coming? Sam didn't think you would.'

A monarch's butterfly's wings are four inches wide, thought Monica.

'I think we can say they didn't see it coming,' followed up Sam, trying to laugh, taking over and adopting the same slightly idiotic look of delight as his latest wife-to-be. 'They're shocked. Of course.' He shifted uncomfortably in his seat and played with his tie-knot. 'And I completely understand why you would be.'

Monica and Eric had glazed over.

The Constructor's Championship would come down to a race between the McLarens and Ferrari this year.

'But there's something else,' Tracy said. 'I haven't told you this yet, and it sounds worse than it is, but Sam has two wives already. I'll be his third.'

So who knows where Cambodia is?

'Two wives?' Eric managed. 'This is a joke, right?'

'Dad — '

Sam interjected, cutting off his betrothed, judging that a bald rendering of the facts could do irreparable damage. 'What Tracy is trying to say, I think, is that as a Muslim by birth I am allowed up to four . . . but Tracy will definitely be my last. I won't take another after this. If that . . . if that is a concern.'

By the seaside, by the seaside, by the seaside.

Before Monica ran to the toilet to be sick her vision began to blur and distort, transforming the lounge into a fish-bowl where even the voice of her only daughter, talking to her, asking for understanding, became distant, far removed, abstracted. She tried to focus her mind but it was filled with the bizarre and solitary image of a butterfly.

Like Lon and Tang, she was too afraid to take her eyes off the creature, fearful that if she did, even for an instant, every certainty might vanish and the future go out like a light.

Eric got her back from the toilet and calmed her down. Often after the nausea phase, the pain of a stress migraine would fade, especially if he massaged her scalp. He stood behind her chair as Sam and Tracy looked on and tried to move the pain around. Pain, it seemed, didn't like to be unseated.

'Mum? Are you all right?' With her eyes shut, Monica was breathing regularly and deeply. Tracy had staked everything on the fact that Sam had so utterly charmed them on his first visit that they would eventually warm to her decision.

'Don't you think you could have said something?' Monica asked weakly.

'Mum, there wasn't even anything to say until a few days ago. It took us both by surprise.'

'*You* by surprise?' Eric replied.

'Thanks, Dad.'

'Don't thank me, all right?'

Tracy sighed. She could tell that this was going to get worse. 'Dad!'

Eric shook his head. 'I should have flippin' known.'

'Stop it.' Tracy could sense the build-up.

'Shoulda known. I woulda fixed it too. Believe you me. Woulda fixed it for good.'

'I'm not a stove, or a hinge, Dad. I don't need fixing. I'm just getting married.'

'Yeah! Into a fucking harem!' he said. Monica winced with pain. 'Unbelievable! Into a fucking harem.'

Sam sat forward. 'I just have to say, it's not a harem. I want you to know. It's not anything like a harem. My great grandfather had a harem, and this is nothing like a harem.'

'Well thanks a bunch for that,' Eric replied. 'Thanks for the words of bleedin' comfort.'

'Monica, Eric,' Sam continued, 'I know this is difficult, and I completely understand how you must feel, but perhaps if we properly discuss this.'

Eric snorted. '*Difficult?*'

Tracy: 'Dad!'

Sam pressed on. 'And my own parents won't be happy about it either, if that is any consolation. They'll think I'm mad. And yes, there's a lot on the surface that won't make sense to you right now, but perhaps you should know that I don't actually sleep with my other wives.'

'Oh, so you need some fresh stock then? Gone off the other two, ship in my daughter then.' Eric almost had to laugh. 'And then you say that you think this might be *difficult* for us? Got a lot of mustard, I can say that.'

'Eric — '

'Listen here, right? You haven't got any idea what this is like for us, so don't start telling me how it must seem.'

'Eric,' cautioned Monica.

'And a harem is *exactly* what it fucking is. So don't patronise me. And there's only one thing you need to know buddy boy: it's not flippin' happening. Right. So now hop it. Scoot.'

'Eric.' Monica's soft remonstration was only partly due to his loss of control. His outburst had caused him to double the pressure on her temple: she was suffering in the jaws of a vice.

'Okay, okay,' he said, alleviating the pressure, going to work on his wife's shoulders. 'And I'll tell you something else for nothing. You get this for free as well. I know she might be twenty and all that, but I'd call the cops before I'd let something like this go ahead. I wouldn't hesitate either.'

'No one's gonna call the cops,' Monica contradicted.

'Dad!'

'Try me.'

'Dad! That wouldn't make any difference. It's fully legal anyway.'

The term 'fully legal' aggravated Eric more than anything else.

'Maybe in Baghdad it's fully legal, but just try — !'

'Tehran.'

' — you just try — '

'Tehran,' Tracy repeated.

' — Tehran what?'

'He's from Tehran.'

Sam sided with Eric on this. 'Let him go on, darling. It is important he speak his mind.'

'Thank you very much. I really need you to tell me that in my own home. And don't call my daughter darling.'

'Eric,' Monica whispered.

Sam demurred. 'No, go on Eric. You're obviously angry.'

'Great, well I'm glad you're finally getting it. I should have put my foot down the minute I realised she was working in a fucking kebab joint. That was my own mistake.'

At this Tracy leant forward in exasperation, hands reaching out to him as though she were a toddler again on the playground swing wanting her father to lift her away, to rescue her. 'It's completely legal. You've gotta calm down.'

Monica had started to cry. 'How can it be legal?'

Sam explained. 'It's legal because we're not getting married properly. Okay, that did not come out right either. I mean, it will only be a *symbolic* marriage.' At least this stalled the crisis; two bizarre new concepts now had to be contemplated at the same time: a four-way marriage of

135

only symbolic value. 'I am, legally speaking, still an unmarried man. Please listen if you can. My two *existing* wives, I haven't actually married them properly either.'

Neither Eric nor Monica even bothered to look at him after that. Their concern shifted a hundred percent to their daughter: she was a three-year-old blithely crossing the road in heavy traffic. She was in peril again. The Pringles were rigid with fear. *Grab her, just grab her!*

Tracy suddenly guessed the nub of her parents' worries. 'I think they're worried that you're a *polygamist*.'

'Oh no, no, no,' Sam quickly assured them, happy if this was the only problem. 'Not at all. If that's all you're worried about.'

'Tracy!' shouted Monica, with no thought for her headache any longer.

'Is that what you're worried about?' Tracy asked her parents.

It was too late. A juggernaut was bearing down on all their lives. Tracy was playing on the road again and looking the wrong way. But a parent had no hesitation in flinging themselves into the smallest gap.

'Tracy!' Monica shouted again. 'Just stop and think. You're sounding like an idiot.'

'I know.'

'We need to talk about this alone. We need to be alone.'

Sam prepared to rise. 'I'll go.'

'*No!*' Tracy shouted, forcing him back into his seat.

'I'll go — '

Monica turned on Sam. 'Then go. Then go. Get out. Please. Eric, get him out. Get him out.' Eric stood proudly at his wife's shoulder as she pointed the man towards the door and watched as he obeyed her. 'Please get out of our home. Please. Just go.'

With his face draining of blood, Sam complied, crossing to the door, picking up his coat en route. 'You only have to ask me for something once. Over time, you will find that.'

Tracy couldn't bear it. 'I'm coming with you.' She jumped to her feet, scooped her things from the table and almost reached the door before him. 'I'm coming too. Let's go.'

'*Tracy!*' Eric shouted.

'Let's go.' Tracy left with Sam.

The front door slammed. Eric and Monica were left alone. They couldn't move immediately. They stood there, bereft and paralysed.

Something had just gone terribly wrong, something vast, but, like the window of their flat, the view was too big to take in all at once.

The first person to move was Monica. She went to the fridge to look for something cold to press to her pounding temples.

'Monica? What are you doing?' Eric called, in no state to be left alone.

He followed her in and was appalled to find the freezer door open and Monica holding a tray of frozen Persian food against her forehead. Her eyes were shut and she was sighing in relief. 'Oh God,' she moaned. 'I think I'm gonna collapse. This helps though.'

'Mon! Can't you see what that is? That's his fucking food!' He grabbed the foil container from her as if it endangered her.

'I don't care what it is. It's cold.'

'We're not having that stuff in our house. We're not having it in this house.' From the freezer he stacked the foil containers into a tower on his left hand until it reached up to his chin. 'Not in this house. Persian muck. Not a single fucking one. Not. In. This. House.' With veins fluting his neck he crossed the room and hauled open the kitchen window.

'Eric! No! You can't — '

'Out!' Eric had tears in his eyes as, one by one, he hurled the heavy packets of frozen food into the night. The trays spun into black space. 'Gone!' he shouted as he flung each one in a silvery flash. 'Out . . . out . . . out . . . out . . . '.

From the twenty-third floor, the icy meteors hurtled down towards the unyielding planet.

'Stop!' screamed Monica, her hands clamped over her temples. 'You'll kill someone!'

'Gone!'

'I think that went okay,' said Tracy blackly.

'Mmmm. Terrific.'

They stood in silence as they waited for the lift.

'Did you feel that?' Sam finally asked.

'Feel what?'

'Can you feel it now?'

'What?'

'Sudden . . . like a very small earthquake.'

Tracy tilted her head, concentrated, seismically alert. 'Oh that,' she said. 'There's movement all the time.'

'Movement?'

'Settlement. Causes stress.'

'Stress?'

'Whatever they call it. Stress, I think. The building is under stress. That's the building relaxing.'

'Don't you mean collapsing?'

'The whole thing moves a lot.'

'Oh.'

'Mum's . . . ' she sighed, trying not to cry, catching herself. 'Mum's trying to get something done about it, written dozens of letters.'

'And you still *stay* here?'

She looked at him. 'Oh,' she said.

'What?' His eyes widened with worry.

'The champagne.' She had never found the right moment to pull out the bottle of champagne. She drew it now from her shoulder bag.

'Never mind.'

They both looked at the bottle. 'There,' she said, setting it down beside the elevator doors. 'Let someone else have some fun with it.'

They both stared at the expensive bottle.

'Sorry about all that, Sam.'

'Come on,' he said, 'Let's get out of here before it's too late.' He tugged her hand and drew her into the stairwell where the hard echoes of their footfalls — bang-bang-bang-bang — accompanied them down to the ground.

11

A Wedding Dress

'I feel like Shahrazad.'

'Oh you mean —?'

'From *The Thousand and One Nights*.'

'Remind me again?' Sam had a dim memory of the most famous product of Persian literature, buried as he had been in the literature of his adopted country. Tracy, on the other hand, steeped in it since birth, thanks to Burton's translation and her mother's love of fairytales, knew it almost inside out. Her early dreams had been textured by it, and her daydreams were still coloured by its palette.

She filled him in. On the islands or peninsulas of India and China, King Shahryar discovered that during his absences his wife had been regularly unfaithful — 'What's regular, in those days?', 'Shush!' — and so killed her along with all of her lovers. Then, loathing all womankind and blind with rage, he began to marry and then kill a new wife every day until no more candidates could be found.

His vizier — 'A vizier is like a minister', 'Thank you, I know that' — has two little known daughters. One of these is Shahrazad. 'Now it comes.' The other was Dunyazad. The elder, Shahrazad, having worked out a scheme to save herself and the others, insisted that her father give her in marriage to the king — 'Can I speak?' 'No' — and although her father is afraid, terribly afraid for her welfare and for what will happen if she marries the king, he has no choice and so offers his daughter, and that evening it starts — 'What?' 'Wait' — and before the king can sleep with Shahrazad she distracts him with a story, but leaves it tantalisingly incomplete — 'A tease' — promising to finish it the following night — 'But?' — But the following night — 'Of course, always a but' — she adds another story — 'And another and another' — and they are so entertaining, and so tantalising and the king is so eager to hear the ending — 'surely —', '*Shhhh!*' — that he puts off her execution from day to day to day to day — 'Until the end of recorded time?' — until he finally abandons his cruel plan.

'Brilliant,' he said. 'And I, presumably, am the king?'

'Yes,' she said. 'You actually don't like women at all.'

'I don't?'

'No. You think you do. But you're really just a bachelor at heart. You don't believe in love at all. But by accident you've got yourself stuck in a . . . in a kind of . . . marriage-go-round, charging about, marrying anything that moves.'

'And you? You fit in where?'

'I'm tricking you into doing something, just like Shahrazad.'

'And why do you say that?'

He was driving. He slowed, pressed the indicator lever and prepared to turn out of the heavy traffic.

'Because I notice things.'

'Oh. I see. Like what do you notice?'

She looked out of the passenger window. Tourists in the sunshine, shopping bags bulging, Saturday morning couples joining hands to run the gauntlet between traffic lights, before slowing, releasing their grip, walking on again as individuals. 'How nervous you get when we talk about the arrangements.'

'Old habits, that's all.'

'How you leave the room and leave it all up to me and Firouzeh and Yvette. They said they've never seen you take such a sudden interest in the garden.'

He sighed and loosened his collar. 'I can't get a word in edgeways, that's why, so I just go into the garden.' He saw a gap in the traffic and surged the Mercedes forward, making the tyres squeal, inches away from a disaster on the car-choked roads of London. 'Particularly Firouzeh. She's overseen all my weddings,' he laughed lightly. 'She's a veteran of the damn things. You're in good hands with her. No one better. You don't need me. But go back, you didn't finish the great story.'

'What do you mean?'

'*Alf Laylah Wa Laylah*. The end of it. You should learn that. You forgot to mention the twist in the tail.'

'There isn't a twist in the tail.'

'Of course. The king falls in love with Shahrazad. Seduced by her tales, probably stupefied by them is more likely, his faith in women is restored. She saves him. And from then on he is completely rehabilitated, all thanks to her. Completely a new man. The end.'

The car rejoined the traffic. He switched on the radio, trying to find a channel. He glanced at her. She looked maudlin, frustrated, was still looking away from him through the window.

'Chopin,' he said, finding something. 'Good. Maybe this will make us happy again.'

Firouzeh and Yvette were waiting for them when they pulled up. Ten minutes later Sam dropped all three women off in the casbahs of Knightsbridge.

Sam excused himself. 'I'll give you ninety minutes, is that enough time to bankrupt me? Or would you like longer?'

They let him go, he would hamper them anyway. 'Go back to your adding machine then,' Yvette told him. 'It's your loss.'

'You can say that again,' he told them, winding up his window.

With malicious intent the women turned to face Harrods. They would start the buying spree in the shoe section.

'Let's work from the ground up,' Firouzeh said with a grin, towing Tracy by one hand towards a hungrily revolving door, while Yvette pulled on the other.

'Definitely the ground up,' agreed Yvette.

To which Tracy, leaning back like a water-skier, replied, 'Do you mean me or the building?'

'I've started a notebook,' Monica called from the balcony where she reared cacti in yoghurt containers.

Eric nodded and lifted by its plastic drawstring the last can of his six-pack from the floor and popped the tab. 'What for?' He tasted his beer, a new brand. Its quality resided in the after-taste. He looked past his own slothful reflection in the sliding door to his hyperactive wife, a silhouette against the grey sky beyond.

'Tracy phoned. I've talked to her.'

'What did she say?'

'I wrote it down for you in a notebook.' Monica came back inside, shut the door with a gloved hand.

'You wrote it down?'

'Yeah. So I could remember. Get comfortable.' She took off her gloves and picked up the notebook by the phone.

'I am,' he said.

'Crazy things. You should have heard her. Utter rubbish.'

'Well, go on.'

'Religious things.'

'Getting all of it from him, in't she. It's gonna happen. I told y'that. He's full of it.'

'Oh, and she wants us to come to the wedding.'

'Ha!'

'Gonna drop off an invite.'

'Ha! Tear it up. What else did she say?'

'Well, sounds like she's turning into a Muslim.'

He looked instantly worried. 'What makes you say that?'

'The things she says.'

'Like what?'

'Apparently . . . the first known reference to the Immaculate Conception of Mary is . . . is apparently in the Koran.'

'Exactly. This is all from him.'

Monica flipped two more pages. 'Hang on, that wasn't the bit.' Monica searched. 'Okay, here it is. The older we get the less joy we experience.'

Eric looked away, then nodded. 'How the hell would she know?'

'Exactly.'

'Oh, and she says you're a Muslim.'

This stopped him. 'I'm a Muslim?'

'And so am I. We're both Muslims. We just don't know it yet.' She stared at him, happy to have found something conclusive.

'Well, she's right about that.' He turned sideways in his chair. He gripped the armrests, almost lifting his own weight. 'She didn't say that?'

Monica searched for the entry. 'Yep. Anyone,' she reported, 'who . . . hang on . . . somewhere? . . . anyone who *submits*, here, submits and *surrenders* to the Almighty God, is basically a Muslim. Because that's all that Muslim means. Someone who submits and surrenders, submits and surrenders to, like I said, the will of Almighty God. And we do that. Or claim to, she said.'

'That's him bloody talking. That's bloody what'shisname. I could wring his neck.'

Monica read on. 'That's what it means in Arabic apparently. Submits and surrenders. And if we say the same thing in church, she said, and if it's the same God, then we're all Muslim too.'

He nodded automatically. 'Unbelievable.'

'Like a fish is already Muslim.'

'She said that? Fish?' He needed a cigarette. Lit up.

'And the sun is Muslim. And Jesus was a Muslim.'

'Right, oh Jesus was now. Course he was.'

'She asked me what he was if he wasn't Muslim.'

'How about Christian? Or a Jew? How about Jew or Christian?' Eric had lost his temper. He sucked heavily on the cigarette. The next time she phoned he would answer it himself.

'I said that. That's what I said. How about a Christian?'

'What'd she say?'

'Wrong.'

'Wrong? What do you mean wrong?'

Monica consulted the notebook, read: 'No. Doesn't . . . doesn't ever call himself one in the Bible.'

'So what'd you say?'

'I said that wasn't the point. He doesn't have to call himself one because he *is* one. His name's Jesus *Christ*. That's a pretty strong clue. Then she said the Bible says we're meant to worship God. Not Christ. The one God.'

'Let me get the phone when she rings. From now on I'm talking.'

'And if we do that, talk straight to God, then we're Muslims.'

They looked into each other's faces to see if the other had accepted this as a remote possibility. 'Anyway, she's invited us to the wedding as well.' Silence dominated the room. 'What shall we say? We should say something.'

With Tracy describing herself as 'barely religious', and Yvette a third-generation agnostic, it was left to Sam and Firouzeh to draw upon their traditions to inject some mystique into the planned wedding ceremony. The exercise found them unusually determined to revive the sentimental protocols of their homeland.

Tracy asked for Kahlil Gibran's 'On Marriage', the gentle lyric of two trees growing together without suffocating each other, but she accepted Sam's point that this was an inappropriate number of trees in their case and so traded it for a poem by Walter de la Mere.

Tracy had not given up all hope that her parents would show up at the last minute: she had slipped an invitation under their door, but told everyone she wasn't holding her breath. Apart from a couple of telephone calls to let them know that she was safe and well, she had not been home since the disastrous night of her wedding announcement. She had slept, meantime, in the small guest room downstairs, curling up like a lost cat on a single bed, left alone at night with the buzz of the refrigerator, while above her family-to-be slept in presidential luxury. But it was her choice. She liked the fairytale scenario of this scullery-maid-soon-to-be-mistress. And she also respected Sam's desire not to overuse the *seegheh* protocol She was determined to let the household function normally until the wedding. The makeshift bed seemed the perfect place to sleep until that day arrived.

> *Assembling everybody in the great hall of the palace,*
> > *the King announced his decision to spare the life of his bride.*
> *Next he summoned his Vizier, Shahrazad's father, and presented him*
> > *with a magnificent robe of honour, saying:*
> *'Allah has raised up your daughter to be the salvation of my people. I*
> > *have found her chaste, wise, eloquent, and repentance has come*
> > *to me through her.'*
> *The city was then decorated and lit with lamps; and in the streets and*
> > *market squares drums played, trumpets sounded and clarions*
> > *cried out.*

The wedding was memorable for its ostentation, its cultural flavour, and for the odour of chrysanthemums which, in several dozen bouquets, lined the tented rooms erected at the back of the house to take the hundred or so invited guests.

It was further enhanced by the glowing rapture of the bride and the near-adolescent joy of the groom who, courtier-like, supported her hand throughout the ceremony, his palm a rostrum for her fingertips.

Otherwise, the fact that Tracy was from Clapham Junction, that she had irreparably broken with her parents in doing this and that the two silk-resplendent bridesmaids were nothing less than the current wives of this ageing Lothario, was neither noted in the service nor reflected in the faces of any of the guests who packed themselves into the lounge for the official service.

The wedding had all the ingredients of one of Tracy's daydreams when she used to sit on her supermarket stool. If the girls in Sainsbury's could see her now! It was her decision not to invite them. They would never understand the subtleties of her new life.

In opening the service, the celebrant, a veteran of several hundred weddings on both sides of the Atlantic and a scholar of ancient Persian culture, invoked the pre-Vedic God of light, Mithra, with a quick glance at his watch.

Seated on a stone bench in front of a three-tiered display containing the symbols of life, love and good fortune — honey, a bowl carved from crystallised sugar, a mirror, as well as a Koran, all manner of flowers and painted eggs — Tracy and Sam held hands and smiled into each other's faces. Sam quieted the slight tremor in his bride's hand.

Sam wore a traditional costume of Northern Persia, agreeing to this only after Tracy's passionate pleas had worn him down and whittled away at his stubborn western leanings. For the first time in years he dug into a chest and found a full-length *abbah*, roses embroidered into the hem and a disastrous Ottoman-style fez, relics not used since his undergraduate fancy-dress parties when he had played the eastern mystic, the desert prince, for the amusement of the waspish girls of Oxford. For Tracy he agreed to wear it again.

As tradition dictated, a cloth was held over them by four happily married women. Yvette and Firouzeh took a corner each, Abdulla's wife and Sam's lawyer's secretary another. Firouzeh and Yvette both took leave, however, to stand on a stool and grind blocks of rock-sugar over the canopy, the drizzle of crystals symbolising a blessing that their life together would be sweet.

After that Firouzeh took a needle and sewed a single stitch into the fabric.

Looking up, Tracy asked of her groom: 'What is that for?'

'That? That just symbolises the sewing shut of the lips of the mothers-in-law.'

The wedding guests clapped their hands vigorously.

Seated on the bar-stool, Monica smoked a cigarette. Eric read the paper. Both were aware that at this moment their only daughter was now entering into marriage with a much older polygamist.

'What's the time?'

He looked at is watch. 'Two thirty.'

Monica took another heavy puff.

'What are you smoking for?'

'What do you think.'

They had both adamantly refused to attend the wedding. Still, the invitation had not been disposed of, and now sat propped up against the telephone, as though at the perfect damaging moment Monica might pick up the receiver and fire their official objection into the bosom of the ceremony.

'Be happening right now then I s'pose,' he said.

Monica didn't reply but instead looked out of the window at the hapless view, trying to decide whether she had loved her daughter too much or too little.

Central to the wedding ceremony was the bride's verbal acceptance of Sam's offer of marriage: Sam's agreement was taken as read.

'I will ask you three times.' The celebrant gave a wry smile. 'Now it is up to you if and when you answer.'

Tracy had been schooled by Firouzeh in every detail of the very Persian art of playing hard to get. At the first invitation she closed her eyes and looked away, causing widespread delight. Centuries of chauvinism was being addressed and the women's high, warbling ululations rose and filled the room.

'Ah! She must have gone into the garden to pick some flowers,' the official intoned, hushing the women, segueing into a 4000-year-old Farsi poem on that subject before returning for the second invitation, pointing his finger at Tracy this time with great seriousness, as though her acceptance was now in doubt and asking, in a catarrhal voice: 'And now, will you take him, this fine fellow, who says that he loves you to distraction, even to the detriment of his career?'

A second time Tracy looked away at the question.

And again came the deafening approval of the women. 'Now she has gone to collect rosewater! Will she return in time? Such a beautiful wedding, but is it to be? Doesn't she want to get married to this fine man?'

A second poem on the subject of rosewater ensued, and it brought Tracy to her third and ultimate invitation. She was warned in Shakespearean tones that her husband's fate was in her hands. 'This time we ask you to stay and not wander off. No more gardens. Speak now if you wish to accept this man. We have locked the doors. Answer all those who love you. Will you take him?'

Consoled, the assembled women nodded: Tracy could now agree.

But Tracy's silence was even more extravagant than before. Sam turned and looked at her, the smile frozen on his face. Even the old celebrant, experienced in a thousand protracted acceptances, was in new territory.

Tracy looked about her. She mistakenly viewed this moment as a practical opportunity to review the wisdom of this marriage. Forgetting the lesson spelt out by Firouzeh, that the bride should accept the third invitation as rapidly as possible, thereby putting her groom out of his misery, she understood that this last call should be the most lengthy of all. Therefore she looked with pleasure around the room, misinterpreting the looks returned to her. Finally, from above she encountered Firouzeh and Yvette's gaze through the mesh of transparent cloth. Neither woman offered urgent looks: if Tracy had real doubts then perhaps a recess should be called. The snowstorm of sugar stopped.

The official could do nothing but notch his outstretched hands higher and higher in a picture of desperation, until Tracy finally returned her eyes to him. Seeing his discomfort she spoke at once. 'All right,' she said softly.

To Persian ears this was another tongue. Tracy clarified herself, 'Yes, I will', allowing two dozen strangulated chests to release sighs of heavy relief.

Tracy had to squeeze her new husband's hand to revive him. Had his heart stopped? Slowly, though, as applause circulated, he revived enough to lift her veil and kiss her intimately on the lips. They were married.

Then came the exchange of rings and the licking of honey off each other's pinkies. But she was not prepared for the instant outpouring of gifts that followed. Bracelets, pearl necklaces, gold watches and the treasures reserved for a married woman flowed into her lap, and in such an avalanche that Sam was having a job getting them into the ceremonial chest before they were crushed underfoot by more guests eager to get close to bestow more presents.

'Oh my God,' Tracy kept saying, with each new unbelievable gift. Thousands of pounds worth of presents passed through her fingers in a few minutes.

With that the ceremony was complete, and the banquet could begin.

A troupe of Persian players led the procession to the back of the house, where, beyond the french windows, the tents held the majority of the guests. Second in line came a group of belly dancers, spinning and bearing flaming torches. Behind them were the smiling bride and groom. A good proportion of London's wealthiest Persians rose to their feet in applause, wetting Tracy's face with their kisses as she passed. The train of her dress washing over a fallen blizzard of rose petals. Sam led her to the centre of the parquet dance-floor and to the strains of a marriage anthem, they waltzed to the collective delight of their audience. Sam's eyes didn't leave her.

After a feast prepared by Abdullah, several glasses of champagne and numerous performances by the artisans, the dancing guests pushed back to form a festive circle around Yvette, Firouzeh and Tracy, clapping in time as the women united in a display of wifely affection, sliding in and out of each other's arms like a single serpent unwinding itself from sleep. They vastly outdid the professional dancers who had preceded them. It was at once hypnotic, celebrational and not a little erotic. Many of the men raised surreptitious eyebrows at Sam. Imagine being the man, their looks said, who had the pleasure of imposing himself in the middle of this lovely serpent!

The clapping grew louder and as Sam watched his wives he was forced to worry about his seemingly redundant role in the scheme of things.

'Congratulations,' Sam's lawyer said, clapping him hard on the back. 'Lucky man. Oh my God, unbelievable.'

'Thanks,' Sam replied after a moment's hesitation. 'Yes. Yes. I am. As you can see. Very . . . very lucky indeed.'

12

Meridian

The children were left in the good care of a young Bavarian alpinist who carried Nabokov in her rucksack. In addition to her normal duties, Firouzeh asked this golden Gretchen to keep her aquamarine eyes on her shoes whenever Sam was around; another marriage would kill him.

Tracy had often fantasised about her honeymoon: the trousseau assembled weeks in advance, the ambitious itinerary, arriving exhausted by the Orient Express with five enormous trunks, the platform full of triple agents . . . but in reality she chose Blackpool, via Greenwich. Tracy rode in the front of the car beside her husband; the other wives sat in the back.

With the brief stop at Greenwich Tracy wished to baptise her wedding present from her co-wives, a carmine-studded wristwatch. She had decided that it should be wound and set in perpetual motion at the chronographic centre of the world.

Climbing the Old Royal Observatory hill, they waited in the cobbled courtyard for a party of Japanese sightseers to expose a mandatory quota of film. Tracy then lined up her toenails along the international Meridian Line, a long red stripe bordered in brass. Sam read aloud from a brochure: the prime meridian was the actual borderline between east and west, and therefore, he added, the perfect point to launch their marriage. To the amusement of the Japanese on one side and a band of English schoolgirls on the other, Tracy stretched out her arms like a weather-vane along the borderline, and tried for a second to actually sense the definition of the hour from which every other time is derived. She seemed to be making a birthday wish and when she opened her eyes she said she was ready to set her watch.

She had two choices. For £1 a machine nearby issued a ticket stamped with the time, accurate to within one-hundredth of a second. She chose, however, to enter Meridian House itself, and consult the foremost authority on global horology, ticking away in its dark steel casing.

The atomic clock stood in the centre of the room, a shining tablet of steel whose only decoration was a simple, digital display near the top, on which fifteen red digits were readable for the first twelve places, thereafter tumbling too fast to be of use. Accurate to within a millionth of a second, Tracy set her watch to it and on that purest of times, the fourth of March, five past one, GMT, she celebrated her new life, her real one, which had just begun.

In the hotel lobby in Blackpool, pleased to be out of the car, the party suffered the condescension of the clerks when they took adjoining rooms, signing under the name 'Sahar, party of four'.

At 7 p.m., Sam ordered a honeymoon *diner à quatre* in their room. If the bell-hop was suspicious he gave no sign. The meal was a whole baked salmon à la lyonnaise in lemon vinaigrette washed down with a white burgundy of rare vintage.

At 9 p.m., too full to sit any longer at the small card table, the women slipped inside the tight envelope of the bed's top sheet, hoisting it up over their heads. Sam, affected by the wine, turned and viewed this humpy Himalaya of brides and imagined consecutively climbing all three peaks. 'I can see that the hour for mountaineering has finally arrived.'

Within minutes, however, he had managed only to reduce each of the women to giggles.

The noise of three laughing women can carry a long way, and outside in the hall, being slowly tortured by curiosity, the bell-hop held his ear to the door. Hearing the smutty giggling within, he chewed his thumbnail. He waited for the scandalous noises to mature into something else but other guests returning to their rooms forced him to leave his station.

Inside, crouched at the foot of the large bed, the master of all he surveyed, Sam tickled each anonymous foot without mercy. He was trying to identify, from the laughter he generated, which feet belonged to his newest bride.

150

With the sheet over them, the women complicated the game by interlacing their legs, and their erratically sized feet, three mongrel sets of two, made his task genuinely difficult. He knew the first laugh well enough: nine years had schooled him sufficiently. 'Stop it, I give in, stop it!' shrieked Firouzeh, swiftly withdrawing her foot at the faintest flutter of Sam's forefinger. And also this second one, yes, he knew this as well, her painted toenails giving her away, a detail he had never so much appreciated: also, no one giggled like this girl, such a feather-light spirit, even after so much sadness! But the third, what courage, what stubbornness, what fortitude she had and no matter how dextrously he tickled, how lightly, how elaborate the patterns he traced or how varied and delicate his scratchings, he still could not produce a titter. This one was too nervous to laugh, made serious by pledges, weighed down with oaths: without question he had located his bride.

'Now, like the prophet Moses, let me part a heavenly sea.'

Having deduced their placement, he collapsed between them and floated on top of the sheet on his back, a playful walrus bobbing on a pitching ocean. He could feel their currents, each surge through the cotton: he closed his eyes, concentrating on their five-fathom undulations, the passing caresses of the marine life, wicked crabs and lobsters nipping deliciously his underside, which, if unable to make him laugh, made him at least croon in ecstasy. He basked amid these beauties with a happiness he had never known before.

'Now then,' he said, 'which fish shall I devour tonight? It is becoming increasingly difficult for me to decide. Perhaps a three-course meal.' But it was an idle joke. He was no satyr and who knew it better than they did?

With a tug, he unmasked them. With melodramatic gasps they redrew the sheet to their chins, pretending a coyness that none of them had possessed since they were fifteen. Three *demi-mondes* averted their eyes, clapped their cheeks, and mimed a virginal burlesque. Brute, devil, wolf: would his cruel demands never be satisfied?

'I've got about five minutes, before I fall asleep,' he added.

Firouzeh and Yvette took this as a sign to go. They slipped out of the room and allowed the newly-weds their consumative hour.

The door was bolted, the telephone taken off the hook. Sam kissed the palms of Tracy's hands. She had incredible hands, a violinist's. Her eyes grew tender and she looked at him with love. Then they helped each other out of their clothes.

151

'Oh, my pills.' Sam reached across to the bedside table, locating them among his assorted nose-drops, antacid mints, analgesics, his eucalyptus pastilles, Epsom salts, cough lozenges and ear-plugs: the allies of his middle age. He washed down the medication with a quaff of champagne before passion was given the floor.

Up before the other guests, the newly-weds descended to the dining room to take an early breakfast at a window table. That morning the room had all the sepulchral stillness of a church. Birds glided above the pier outside and a calm ocean lapped against the pebbles with the apathy of an ageing lover.

'Take off your ring, I want you to see something.'

'See what?' She slid it off her finger.

On the inside face — 'they inscribe it before they mould it' — were five letters, which, to read, required one complete rotation of the ring: 'symbolising a day,' Sam instructed.

'Z-A-H-I-R?'

'Zahir, yes. Arabic in origin.'

Tracy was delighted to find that her ring had inner dimensions, mystery, surprise: For a second, and before she had even learnt the meaning of the letters, she conjured a daughter to whom she could impart their mystical meanings: 'Look inside,' she would tell her child, 'read what it says.'

'Well, do you want to know what it means or not?' he asked.

'Course,' she said, returning. 'Yeah, keep going.'

'It's my new name for you. And it has many meanings. Many.'

'Such as?'

'Okay. For instance, one is "notorious". Or "visible". And it is also one of the ninety-nine names of God. But history also tells us that *Zahir* was a name given to a famous, a very famous actually . . . sort of . . . well, it was a copper pot.'

'Copper pot?'

'Mmm. It resided actually at a school in Shiraz in Persia many centuries ago, and this is why, my sweet, my luck, I give you the name.'

Tracy nodded, weighed being renamed after a copper pot, then instead of taking this as an insult, realised that a restaurateur probably valued a good pot more highly than anything else.

Sam ducked his silver teaspoon into a halved grapefruit and lifted the teardrop of pulp to his mouth.

'Why?' she asked. 'Why a copper pot?'

He fixed her with a look of almost depraved intensity. 'Why? Well because . . . because it was fashioned, in such a particular way, such a *remarkable* way, Tracy, through techniques of metallurgy now utterly lost in antiquity, that . . . '

Things were certainly improving, she thought.

' . . . that whosoever looked upon it, even once, could thereafter think of nothing else, nothing on heaven or earth but this little copper pot sitting inauspiciously in a little corner of the world. As a result,' he said, waving his spoon at her, 'a jealous king, and there is always a jealous king, intervened and his dictate is legendary. He instructed that the pot, and I quote from ancient Sanskrit sources, "should be sunk in the deepest part of the sea . . . lest men forget the universe".'

Tracy could not blink. It was better than she'd thought.

'And so, *Zahir*, for you, who could make men forget the universe.' He took up her hand. Remarkable, she thought. He kissed it. Ancient, she thought. He set it back down. The universe.

After a second's thought she looked down at her inscribed ring and then slid it back onto her finger.

'That's beautiful.'

'I had you worried there? With the copper pot thing?'

'No,' said Tracy. 'Not really.' But when her eyes looked back up they were rimmed with tears. She had the sudden feeling that she had come a long way.

'Are you okay?' He quickly reached into his jacket for a handkerchief.

'Yeah. I'm. I'm just not . . . ' she looked out of the window to where the boats were moored to the pier, 'used to getting married, I s'pose.'

13

Charity Ends at Home

At about one o'clock Monica got a phone call in the staffroom. It was Eric to say that after seven years of inaction and pretence he had finally taken matters into his own hands.

She interpreted this to mean that he had found a real job.

Her heart jumped at the thought. *Has hell frozen over?* But she was not entirely surprised either. He had been making noises for several days, a rolling thunder building towards something momentous, making comments about changes being in the air, insinuating an urge to get his life moving again, and physical signs too: ordering his tools, laying them out on the floor like a street vendor, counting up his ring spanners and chisels and nail-punches and scribbling an inventory on a musty shred of paper.

But this was not the case. She was wrong. With a voice quivering with emotion, Eric told his wife that after a seven year ban he had simply busted into Tracy's bedroom, splintered the latch and taken stock of the interior.

'I'm telling you, you have to come home and see this right now.'

Over the phone Monica could hear that he was excited. She was stunned to hear what he had done without consulting her. They had respected their daughter's demands for so many years that even though Tracy had moved out forever, a sacred pact had been broken, a promise betrayed. Monica had become used to the arrangement. Living in a house that hid a forbidden room afforded her life a certain mystery: how many run-down council flats had that? And now Eric had destroyed the conditions by which it might be possible for Tracy to ever return. Not even the terrible marriage announcement had done that, and Monica had not given up hope that somehow it would fall through.

Eric's voice was breathy and tense. As he urged her to drop everything at once and get home, a secondary curiosity grew in her. Many times she had wondered what her daughter had been up to in her room. It had been locked against them for six years after all, and she would be lying if she said that she hadn't ached to kick the door down herself, find clues that would solve the mystery of her daughter.

'It's the worst thing you've done, Eric.'

'I used a jemmy.'

'I can't believe you did it.'

'Popped right off its hinges. Could never get in to oil them, y'see.'

'Put the door back on right now.'

'You've gotta be joking. Anyway, can't. Come home now and see. You've gotta see this.'

'It'll have to wait. I can't just walk out.'

'Then come as quick as you can.'

She sighed, looked through the window at the children who were starting to run riot. 'Okay. Okay, I will. I've got to go.'

She put down the phone and went back to her room to read to the children.

The children stared at her. 'And so what do you think the handsome prince did then? Anyone?'

The children were quiet, bored, until one boy, tipped towards anarchy, piped up: 'Ate her?'

The group erupted into giggles. Even the youngest of them, the two- and three-year-olds, fell into each other. Here it is again, Monica thought. *Every day it's harder to hold them.* Even at their age the fairy stories didn't cut it any more. The baddies were too easily conquered, the goodness outdated, the dénouement of marriage repetitive and dull. Someone had unhitched the gate to their tranquil garden. Now everyone's kids wanted to play in the traffic.

Still, Monica had a way of dealing with these post-modernisms. 'That's right, Axel. He ate her, good boy. So what do we think of that? What do we think?'

The assembly screwed up their faces in unison, revolted, jointly jumping the imaginative ship. 'Yuuuucccckk!'

'And how did he eat her? Anyone tell me? On toast? How?'

'*Yyuuuuuuuucccckkkkk!*'

It was a risky business, this: just one child reporting stories with cannibalistic endings would land her in trouble. But Monica the professional had to try something.

'No!' shouted the first boy, his lesson learnt, his grisly idea already sour in his mouth. 'No, no, no.' He was on the point of tears.

'No. That's right. So don't be silly, Axel. And sit down now. They love each other. They love each other, okay. And people, who love each other, what do they do?'

Maxine: 'Get married.'

'Good girl. That's right. They do.'

'And then they eat each other,' Serena Armitage interrupted, no joke intended, just trying to say the right thing.

'Don't be silly and sit down, all of you. That's enough!'

At the back of the class, as quiet as mendicant monks, the Cambodian children smiled but never once actually laughed. As if they believed they had done something wrong, something inexpressibly bad, they barely moved a muscle all day. Their dismay was buried far too deep for Monica to shift. Dozens of times each day she intervened in their play, giving them a turn when they missed out, compensating for their lack of tenacity. It had no effect. When their father, a youngish man of no more than thirty and with no English beyond a tourist's phrasebook arrived at five o'clock each day, he was invariably the last parent to collect his children. They grabbed his hands with relief, not at all taking his arrival for granted, and walked towards the bus-stop at his side, heads lowered, looking exhausted as if recovering from an ordeal. Monica read this as evidence that their days with her were doing them no good whatsoever.

After a few songs and one round of musical chairs the first parents arrived in dribs and drabs. Today, Monica, bursting to be on her way, cut short her parent-teacher chats. Tracy's room was on her mind.

After half an hour only Lon and Tang remained on the mat. And as usual they stared at the window towards some country or thing they couldn't see. Monica watched them in silence until the phone rang.

'Where are you?'

'Still here.'

'What the hell's going on?'

'I don't know. One of the parents hasn't shown up again. There's nothing I can do.'

'This is ridiculous.'

'Tell me about the room anyway.'

There was a pause. 'No.' He sounded bullish. 'You have to see this for yourself.'

'What's going on, Eric? Stop being so ominous. It's only a flippin' room. What did she do?'

'No!' Eric was now as wound up as he had been earlier. 'Just come home.'

'I've got kids here. There's nothing I can do.'

'Get Rita to look after them.'

'Everyone else has gone. I'm here alone.' He tutted on the other end of the line. 'So just wait. It's not an emergency.'

'That's what you think.' Adding a further intrigue, he said: 'Just wait till you see the walls.'

She put down the phone. The children had not moved. They looked like little statues, rendered serene and tranquil by their unbroken melancholy.

The phone rang again.

'You're still there?'

'Mmm.'

'What kind of parents are these? It's nearly an hour. They're three-quarters of an hour late!'

Monica's nod turned into a shrug. 'It's a tricky situation. They're refugees. They hardly know English.'

'What do you mean refugees?'

'Asylum seekers actually. Their parents are. They don't even know yet whether they're gonna be accepted as refugees. They're beneath refugees on the ladder, can you imagine that?' There was silence on the other end of the line. 'The worst case thing is that they could be sent home again, just turned around and dumped back where they came from.'

Eric's reply took a second. 'Yeah, okay. But who leaves their littl'uns waiting around for three-quarters of an hour?'

'It happens. Quite often.'

'Nup. Some of these other cultures are weird.'

'I've got to go now.'

'Some of these other cultures. They just don't work.'

'Stop it.'

'Hardly work in their own country and then they bring 'em over here. It's just a joke. Look at you, sitting there, waiting for these people. It's all breaking down, innit. It's a joke. It's all breaking down.'

'*All* cultures are weird, if you're gonna look at it that way. We're just as messed up. I see it every day.'

'Don't make me laugh,' he said. Then he sighed. Across the wires of London she fired him back a sarcastic sigh in return.

'Wait till you see it,' he told her. 'The room.'

'I don't even want to know.'

'Yes you do.' He hung up. The *clack* chimed in her ear.

Monica would give the children's father another quarter of hour. She dug and found some cordial in a cabinet for the kids to drink to take their minds off waiting. Then she rang up the only number she had been given. Every parent had to provide a phone number on the first day. There was no reply.

The official procedure, which she had never had to employ, was to phone two numbers. Both were listed in the back of her roll-book. The first was for the Social Services who would send over a social worker and then escort the children to an overnight shelter. This meant reports and assessments, but it was better and far less ominous than the second number on the list, which was to the police.

'What is it?'

'I wanna bring the kids home.'

Eric shouted into the phone. 'Home?'

'If I ring everybody as I'm supposed to do then it's gonna ruin their chances.'

'What *chances*?'

'Becoming legal citizens. If it goes on their record, which it would.'

'No.'

'Eric — '

'It's not our responsibility!' Eric was aggressive. She knew he had adopted his usual line: that there were enough people in the country already, in the world, whom he had to be nice to. Also, why should one family, a struggling one at that, cover for the failings of other parents, a specific problem here but also a root problem in society at large. The best countries had the best parents. Weak parents — and therefore weak countries — sent trouble down the line for everyone else: someone

158

somewhere else had to cop it, clear it up, accommodate it, defuse it. Even the defence of your country in war could be viewed as a mass undertaking to make up for the mass failings of a mass of parents elsewhere. Paying more in taxes, feeling insecure on the streets, forking out huge sums to insure your possessions against theft and wilful destruction, fighting all the evil works of yesterday's children, it all amounted to the same thing: picking up the tab for other parents. And looking after Cambodian refugees, while their footloose father was off playing mahjong or indulging in some other delinquency, was definitely an act of thankless surrogacy. 'Just don't go getting us into anything, for God's sake!'

'But you have to see these poor kids.' She softened her voice, speaking to an imaginary baby.

'For God's sake, Monica. Can't you see it?'

'See what?'

'What's going on here! What stinks? What stinks about the whole arrangement?'

'What arrangement?' With a turn of her head, Monica was able to monitor the children through a gap in the door while her husband built his hostile case against them. Cross-legged on the carpet, they stared vacantly into space.

'Things like this refugee thing. The pressure this puts on ordinary people. And you know why? Cos once they get here they don't flippin' know how to live here, so what happens? Someone's gotta carry the load.'

'Eric, what are you banging on about?'

'Refugees. Refugees. Who don't know how to be parents, decent parents, proper parents. They don't deserve to live here.'

Monica thought twice about saying it, but did so anyway. 'And you know how to be a parent, do you?'

'No. Not a fucking clue. But I wouldn't leave them waiting for an hour at their age. That's criminal.'

'I want to bring them home.'

'Don't even think about it.'

'So we don't ruin their chances. Of living here.'

'Over my dead body.'

'I'll see you in a minute. I'm bringing them.'

'Like fucking hell.' There was a sudden silence at the end of the line.

She expected him to hang up. She waited. She could guess that he was staring out the window, over the city, perhaps winding the cord around his forefinger.

'Eric?'

'No,' he said. And then he hung up.

Monica waited another quarter of an hour and then began to prepare the children for the drive home. They had begun to whisper to each other, guessing that their father had let them down, and that something unusual was about to unfold. Still, neither of them showed fear or grief.

In the carpark Monica made them stand aside as she unlocked the doors of her Mini Metro. They would both ride in the back — it was safer.

The solitary figure crossed the street and ran towards them calling ''Ello' and 'Sowwy' repeatedly. From his silhouette as he ran, the slightly bowed legs, the unseasonable short-sleeved shirt, she knew who he was.

'Oh good,' she said, smiling diplomatically, for the sake of the children. There would be time later to rail against the father.

The man slowed to a walk and waved.

'Oh good,' Monica repeated. The children ran to their father's side. He bent and kissed the crowns of both heads and then continued with them towards Monica.

'Sowwy-sowwy-sowwy. Thank you. Sowwy-sowwy-sowwy. Thank you.'

'That's all right, Monica replied. 'Very late. Very late. You are very late, Mr Sung.'

'Yes. Yes.'

She tapped the face of her watch, emphasised a frown. 'Very very very late.'

The man offered his thin feminine hand, his face corrugated with contrition, his forehead drenched with perspiration, his chest was pumping. How far had he run? Monica shook the hand. 'Just good you're here. Lucky. No one is hurt.'

'Yes. Yes.'

'They're beautiful children. Look after them.'

'Yes, yes, yes.'

'Look after them.'

The man would not stop shaking Monica's hand. 'Yes, yes, sowwwy,' he said, again and again.

Sitting in his armchair, Eric brooded with a can of beer and a cigarette for company.

Any second Monica and her refugees would pour through his door. He visualised barefoot boat-people in san-pan hats so thickly dispersed about his lounge he'd be crushed where he sat. Monica wasn't simply bringing two kids home with her: she was importing a global dilemma into their living room. In one single face he saw the millions. No wonder he always lowered his head and hurried past the city's destitute.

And as if he didn't have enough to cope with, Tracy's marriage was burning holes in his mind, even bigger than the ones his index finger was exploring in the armrest of his chair. He had prepared a plan of sulky behaviour which Monica would only appreciate in its fullest form as the hours passed. He had drunk most of the six-pack.

At the front doorway she stopped and looked at him. It had all been a storm in a teacup, she told him. He didn't respond. The children's father had shown up after all. When she didn't move he saw that she too had a point to make.

'Eric? So what the hell was all that? I want to bring two little children home and you make out it's the end of the world. Well, I think it's disgusting. I'm just glad I waited. Just think, if I hadn't. Their whole lives might have been . . . might have been different from now on.'

He nodded, chastened — he knew his philosophy came out as mean-spiritedness — and looked back out at the view, sealing with a lick the paper of a hand-rolled cigarette.

Monica turned to see that Tracy's door was ajar. The room was dark inside. She looked back at him. She counted five empty beer cans at his feet. 'So, what's all this about? You're drunk. What a great performance. Now you've invaded our daughter's privacy.'

'I bloody-well wasn't gonna be sober for Operation Save the Children.'

'So have you been right in? Into Tracy's room?' No answer came. 'I asked you if you'd been in, grumpy!'

'Aren't I allowed to go into my own daughter's bedroom, even after she's moved out?'

'And have you been through her things?'

He didn't answer.

'Well, I think that's terrible.'

'Do ya,' he muttered. 'I haven't touched her things. Just go and have a look for yourself.'

Monica couldn't move. 'No. I'm not going in there.' Although extremely curious to see inside the room herself, she was now afraid. Eric's behaviour had told her that she was in for a shock. She had butterflies in her stomach already, the large wingspan variety. It was only Tuesday and a Tuesday shouldn't be the day of the week that everything in your life changes forever. And she wanted to get back at Eric. 'I'm not going to come down to your level.'

'You know you want to. So go on. Just go in. Get it over with.'

From where she stood she couldn't see into the room. 'I need a cup of coffee.'

'Coward.'

'Drop dead.'

'Coward.'

He rose and went to run a bath. Twisting both taps to full pelt he undressed in the steam. He had no use for his drunkenness now. Complex issues required his wits and he wanted to clear his head. His daughter's room had to be deciphered and also the mystery of how Monica could keep herself from immediately taking a look in there.

He stepped into the water, lowered his haunches down and then sank all the way to his chin in the piping tub, the water gliding up his body in a grateful caress until it settled in a crew-neck. The shower hand-piece in its bracket dribbled water on his toes and a wafer of soap by his head filled his nostrils with the scent of apple.

The first thing he did was pee. A nimbus bloom of yellow clouded his crotch as he let go. It blotted the surface in the shape of an unknown country: Australia? He had no idea whether his wife had witnessed this indignity, because by the time she spoke from the doorway he had just paddled the water clear. He might just have got away with it.

'What's going on?' he asked her innocently: it was more like Africa by then.

'I don't know.' She clutched her coffee tightly. She had been crying. 'I can't get those children out of my mind.'

'Are you going to take a look or not?'

'I don't know.' She wiped her eyes with the back of her hand.

He pursed his lips. 'You come home, go in the kitchen and just start crying?'

'I know.'

'What do you want me to do?'

She had already decided. She looked at him clear-eyed and he realised she had come into the bathroom only to tell him one thing. 'I want you to lock up her door again.'

He splashed a handful of hot water over his face and closed his eyes.

'I'm not joking. Lock it again. Please.'

'You're not even gonna take a look?'

'I know. I know it sounds stupid, I can't explain it, and I won't even try, but I don't want to know. It's still her room. And it's only Tuesday. It's all just a bit much for a Tuesday I suppose.'

Eric shook his head. His ears were at the waterline. Monica's voice was almost marine. What's happening? he thought. Tracy had always been a subject on which they could agree. They relied on it. It was a staple of their marriage. Their joint hysteria over her upbringing, the shared alarm and worry and happiness had always produced a harmonious foundation upon which almost everything else was balanced. Now the old table suddenly had three uneven legs.

'I'm not joking, Eric. Eric, I'm not. Lock it up.'

'The lock is totally broken. It's done. It's open for good. So . . . I dunno . . . if you want to walk past it every day, for the rest of your life, if you can do that, if that feels like normal behaviour, then fine, and not even show the slightest interest in what your daughter's been up to and not even face the fact that she's gone for good, which is probably what this is all about, right? Then, fine and dandy. Treat this arrangement like it's normal. But me, I've moved on.'

'Big man.'

'That's right.' He splashed the water. 'Big man.'

'Fine,' Monica said, reaching a dead end. She couldn't ignore the room forever.

'Great,' replied Eric. He felt assured of eventual victory. He gave her a day. Two at the very most.

Over the next few days, the temperature between the couple fell to subarctic.

Barely exchanging a civil word, Monica and Eric went about their daily routines in moods of bitter rivalry. Increasingly repelled by known habits, repulsed by the most familiar of acts, scents, rituals, annoyed by even the sight of each other crossing the room, they began to wonder how they had ever been attracted in the first place.

The war soon extended to the subconscious channels. A ditty hummed by Monica at breakfast would, under normal circumstances, have haunted Eric the whole day as he pottered about the flat. When she came home in the afternoon, with her head a chamber of little voices, he would usually reinfect her with it, so that she, in a late reprise, would hum it softly as she took off her make-up and wonder to herself where she had heard it and why she was humming it. But even this subliminal conversation, one of many that had given their marriage meaning, now failed to take place. All the lines were down: the wires sparked in the void. And all the while, Tracy's bedroom door haunted them: slightly ajar, flapping with every breeze, clumping loudly with every rapidly opened window. It slowly whittled away at Monica's resolve. She tried folding a small piece of cardboard and jamming the door shut lest she be driven mad by the reminders, but Eric spotted it and pulled it out, sabotaging her plan and plunging their marriage back into crisis.

Significantly, neither mentioned the piece of cardboard, nor its removal — a clear sign of how merciless the war had become.

By Day Three Eric took a new approach. After a noisy dinner-time dish-clearing display, he rinsed his hands in the sink, dried them on his trousers and announced: 'Right then.'

She watched him aghast as he crossed the room into the hall and entered the sacred bedroom, shutting the door behind him.

Monica went straight to the lounge, took his chair and pretended to watch a TV boxing match between two anaemic Britons.

Eventually, he came out.

He sat on the couch, keen to display his calm, sated mien. She refused to react. Even when he went into the kitchen, noisily made himself a cup of tea, and then re-joined her in front of the set. She couldn't bear to look at him. Every minute that he had been in Tracy's room would cost him, she promised herself. She would slowly take her revenge. She would make him pay somehow. She was dumbstruck with rage. Eric had never before seemed this black a character, this menacing, twisted, petty. Like the moon, he had a dark side where no light shone at all. Their marriage was in deep, deep trouble.

For Eric, though, it was precisely their marriage that he was trying to save. If Tracy had gone, and of course she had done so, then he wasn't going to stand by and let his house be turned into a mausoleum. He'd give it another week, he promised himself, and then if he saw no improvement or way forward he'd pack his things, force Monica to admit that Tracy was gone. From the outset, even during their motorbike-riding hair-billowing engagement, they had only ever wanted one child because they had both wanted to preserve a degree of freedom, to stay *young*. And now that kid had grown up and handed them their freedom back, they were miserable! If they were no longer enough for each other — if that was the hard truth of it — then he'd rather find out sooner than later.

In bed, the only place where they were forced to be close to each other, they had stopped relating completely, lying spine to spine, a beast with two bellies. The rift had been made even more complete by Monica's decision to retire earlier and be firmly asleep by the time Eric switched off the sports channel.

And then the breakthrough came. It took Eric by surprise. Nothing about that evening had alerted him to Monica's capitulation, and when he awoke at some hour of the early morning to find her side of the bed empty, he actually thought she'd done it: run out on him, gone forever.

He vaulted from bed and found her running a torch over the walls of Tracy's bedroom, staring at the creation he now knew well, but too secretive to use the light switch.

'This is what you were on about?' she asked him, when she heard him at her shoulder.

'I told you, didn't I.'

'Bloody hell,' she conceded.

Monica would later say that to save her marriage she had caved in against her own better judgement. She would also maintain, to his annoyance, that she found nothing at all irregular in the contents of that bedroom. This lie was her charge for having singlehandedly saved the marriage, and he let her claim it.

'I'd . . . expected . . . ' she muttered, 'I s'pose I expected . . . '

'What?'

'All sorts of things . . . '

'I know.'

'But this is . . . well, this isn't . . . so bad.'

'Bullshit. This is weird.'

'It's . . . no, no it's not. It's nothing. It's just a young girl's thing. It could be a lot worse than this.'

Their heads swivelled as they tried to absorb the amazing welter of images plastered everywhere on their daughter's walls, a seamless collage of a thousand cut-out pictures. 'I can't believe you got so excited about *this,*' she said, trying to keep her voice level.

'She's obsessed. I didn't have any idea.'

'You just don't know about young girls, that's . . . that's . . . '

'Obviously.'

' . . . your trouble.' Monica's mouth hung open.

'You don't think this is even a bit odd?'

She hesitated. 'No.' Her lie was born.

'Come on. Look at this. No wonder she lives in a fantasy world. Is it any wonder? Living in a room like this'd space anyone out.'

'It's not the room that caused it. She made the room.'

Eric turned on the lights and the work as a whole sprang to life, but Monica still didn't lower the torch. Like pyjama-clad tourists in a gallery they stared at the walls and ceiling: not a square inch remained of the original wallpaper — faggots of bamboo on a tapioca background. It had been obliterated. Tracy had turned her room, had *transformed* it, transfigured it, into a mural of the fantastic. Each character, cut out from comics, magazines, books, postcards and posters, vied for space and crowded or partly obscured the next so that any observer felt that a lifetime would be required to take in all the images as they came to life, peeping around the edges, forcing their way to the bustling surface. The longer Eric and Monica stared at Tracy's creation the more three-dimensional it became, drawing them further in.

'Did you know she was into all this stuff?' Eric asked.

Monica shook her head. Not once had Tracy intimated this obsession with tragic heroines, castles, deserts, mountains, movie stars. In one crowded corner alone, Monica spotted Guinevere, The Lady of Shallot, Marilyn Monroe, Joan of Arc, Ophelia, Rapunzel.

'Scary, don't you think?' Eric asked. At last he could share this with his wife.

'Not really. Quite beautiful actually.'

'I'm worried that it's happening again.'

166

Monica shook her head. 'This is fine.'

'You don't know that. It could be starting again.'

'You don't know young women.'

Eric relaxed slightly. He was prepared to admit this. 'How she could've stayed in here for five minutes beats me. Makes me feel sick in seconds.'

'She made it, I s'pose it's how she wanted it.'

'Disturbed, I thought. Got me worried again.'

'This took years. You can see. It's actually amazing.'

'No wonder she wants to hook up with some exotic geezer, living with this all around her.'

They stood there in silence.

He sighed. 'Reminds me of the time we done LSD, remember?'

'Yeah.'

'I'll start peeling it back tomorrow. Let's go to bed.'

'Mmmm.'

'Come on.'

But neither turned off the light or moved an inch. They remained where they stood: it was impossible to stare at the walls for any length of time without becoming ensnared by some narrative or other.

'It's your fault,' Eric stated. 'I blame all this stuff on you.'

'Why?' Monica's tone was dreamy, her eyes roving.

'Force-feeding her with all this rubbish when she was little.' His own eyes darting across the walls, 'Arabian Nights, fairytales, all that fantasy rubbish and what-not from the day she was born.'

'You've got to read to them. But *she's* done this. This is her. I stopped that years ago.'

He shook his head in disbelief. 'Only child, y'see.'

'Yeah.'

They both waited for something to take them from the doorway. But they were too absorbed. They recognised the room for what it was: an astonishing insight into their child's mental life, a map of her mind. They had to concede that they barely knew their daughter at all.

When they made it back to bed, sleep now impossible, the image-filled walls shifted into their own heads.

'Got me worried about her again,' he said.

'You were worried over nothing.'

Eric tossed and turned over, picturing a bull with a javelin in its ribs, a burning castle, an embattled army, the teeth of a lion. The harder he tried to sleep, the less likely it became. 'This is bloody ridiculous,' he muttered.

Monica was wrestling with her own images: a downy bed, a petalled reservoir, the bulls-eye on a peacock's tail. After a short while they wound up in each other's embrace.

14

The Arrangement

Picnickers with children and retired couples from Manchester filled the beach resort in early March. A portly Persian man promenaded affectionately with three young women making an unusual late-afternoon addition to the Blackpool crowds.

During the week-long honeymoon Tracy tried not only to get used to her new place in the four-way unit but also to adapt to the looks and attention of the general public.

Sam stemmed a rivulet of melted ice cream before it reached his heavy, gold wristwatch. 'I've had these for twenty years, these looks. But I have to say that in all that time, it never got out of hand. I have never had sufficient cause to strike someone. And that is something that cannot be underestimated.'

The idea of Sam hitting anybody was ridiculous to his wives. His hands were as small and fat as a child's; his arms almost too short to reach over his head to touch his opposite ear. He was clearly a man who needed a docile country. England had been his first choice.

'If there had been violence here as well I could not have taken it. Not with the scorn I received, but on balance, I cannot complain.'

Tracy objected on his behalf. 'How can you say there isn't violence here? You can't say that. You almost had some the other week.'

Firouzeh waved her hand. 'Don't get him started, please.'

Sam put his hand on his first wife's shoulder. 'Firouzeh and I argue about this all the time. Well, I argue, she listens. Well, I think she listens.' He was having a good time here: three beauties, a political discussion, sunshine.

169

'You will never get him to say a bad word about England,' Firouzeh responded. 'You would think he was old school tie the way he talks. He's stone deaf to any criticism of this country.'

'Not deaf,' Sam countered. 'Not deaf. Just balanced. I'm impartial. Perfectly placed to see it how it is.'

'Deaf *and* blind.'

'I take a world view.'

Firouzeh had suffered her own fair share of racial slights. She could quote the same race statistics, but did not. Every country was good and bad. It was not a competition. 'You're wasting your breath,' she told Tracy. 'When I first came over he was bloody wearing Union Jack underwear.'

'That was a joke!'

'Some joke.' Firouzeh shook her head.

'Why is everyone so blind to how well off we all are?' Sam threw up his hands, a ritual question.

'What about that time in the restaurant? That was almost a brawl.' Tracy said.

'That? That was nothing. I'm not talking about some kid a drink or two over the line mouthing off utter rubbish. I'm talking about the real world, the real one. Where people feel terrified in their beds, where armies move against you, waking to the thunderous approach of tanks, producing mortal terror, actual terror, not just some hiccup in your day. I'm forever grateful to England for that, for protecting me from all that. Forget America, totally gun crazy — this Right to Bear Arms and Bury Your Own Loved Ones malarkey. England is the last haven. Perhaps Switzerland, Australia. As the refugees all say, it is a kind country. It is a fact. I tell you, the worst that has happened to me here has been a picnic in comparison to what I might have encountered. A picnic.'

Firouzeh had drifted into thoughts about her children. Yvette's mind preferred to rekindle memories of her own honeymoon in Portugal one high summer. Only Tracy listened, as usual.

'And that is why, of course, this country has such a good and great reputation among the world's dispossessed. And why, when they are all sitting in their refugee camps with their pencils chewed to a stub with trepidation and after a list of unknown countries on a bit of paper is put in front of them, possible destinations, they tick the box marked Great Britain.' He drew a tick in the air. 'Maybe a few tick Sweden but mostly it's here.'

Tracy grabbed the break in the monologue to have a thought of her own. How many people, she wondered, walked around perplexed about the actual state of *the world*? This, in her eyes, made him a great man. A weird one, but also a great one.

'So. If you are the citizen of a bypassed country and are looking for a top-shelf nation to live in, where you might get a few insults and jibes and intimidation from time to time, the odd threat or isolated bit of rough stuff, but where you shouldn't actually have to live in fear of your life, then the rule is get yourself to Dover, get a ticket, a plane, a boat, the back of a lorry if you have to, but get yourself to London, to Birmingham, to Aberdeen. And as quick as you bloody can because the world is burning, I'm sorry to say.' In his grandiloquence he lifted his arm, raised his voice to address the surf. 'Come all you bloody millions, to Blackpool!'

Several dozen heads turned to look at him. A passer-by even sounded a derisory hiss.

'Ah,' Sam said as he spun to see the man walking away. 'Hear that? There it is. The great English tut.' He laughed. He was in high spirits. 'I love that. That sums it up. Somewhere else it might be the report of a rifle or the clump of a machete. But here? A tut. Now you see what I'm saying? Thank God for countries like this, countries where people can tut in peace and uphold the past and focus on leaving furniture and china to their heirs.'

'Stop talking now,' Tracy interrupted, unhooking her arm, turning her own head away and for the first time giving in to embarrassment. Yvette and Firouzeh retained distant, wistful looks on their faces.

'Yes, chatterbox, shut up,' Firouzeh agreed. 'First-generation intellectuals. On and on and on.'

'Over there,' Tracy pointed, changing the agenda, reimposing the honeymoon. 'Come on. We'll all have a go on that. Come on. Everyone has to give it a go.' She raced ahead, searching for change in her pocket to pay the man, waving the others over.

'On that? She has to be joking.' Sam scratched his bald patch.

Where they had been merely noteworthy before, strolling arm-in-arm, they became a full-blown seaside attraction once they mounted a bicycle-for-four, veering giddily along the waterfront.

With Sam aft, half off his seat, laughing hysterically but from necessity pedalling for dear life, and Tracy fore, also pedalling but steering so

171

badly that the bike appeared magnetically drawn to the gutter, Yvette and Firouzeh were sandwiched in the middle. Sensing their redundancy, both women took the first chance to call a halt.

They dismounted, cited headaches, and returned to the hotel. The real honeymooners perservered for a few more minutes but soon returned to the hotel as well to get on with the real business of the honeymoon: the transformation of high spirits into horizontal, seaside bliss.

It began while Monica was at work. Eric popped his head into Tracy's room, shook his head in dismay then closed the door again. But within ten minutes he was back again, this time with a cup of tea. He sat on the end of her bed and took in the creation.

Instead of removing the montage as he'd threatened to do, instead of just getting out the steel-edged scraper and stripping the walls back to their bare plaster, Eric began to while away a considerable amount of time in his absent daughter's room.

Sitting on the bed or in the bedside chair after Monica had gone off to work, he scanned the walls, immersing himself in the intense gallery of events, growing increasingly familiar with its vast cast of characters. With the situations vacant pages of the *Evening Standard* open on his lap but with no jobs circled, time would pass so quickly that, apart from the odd fix-it job around the building, he was soon getting less and less done with his days. Staring at Tracy's room left little time for anything else.

When Monica rang to ask how he was getting on, he lied. 'Found an interesting job in the paper.'

'Did you phone up?'

'Bit far out. Be three hours' travel every day.'

'Is that too far?'

'A bit, yeah. Hour and a half each way.'

When she was gone again, he would go back into the bedroom.

The problem was that there was so much to take in. In one five-minute period his eye might roam from a blind-folded matador, a team of Mongolian horsemen, an Elfin King and his wives, Madam Butterfly, a Viking ship, Maid Marian, a Cyclops, a French court, pages, giants or a reclining Buddha, to Sinbad the sailor, a chateau, young couples entwined in embraces, celebrities of the English stage, an African tribeswoman identified in subtitle as a Masai, Errol Flynn, a Renaissance madonna, Elizabeth Taylor as Cleopatra, Bluebeard, a mermaid, four musketeers and an Amazon Queen venerated by a thousand slaves. Before he knew it he was reeling, the mug of tea cold in his hands. It was time for lunch already.

Drawn by the seductive tug of his daughter's empty room he went back in again in the afternoon, spending hour-long chunks in there, only managing to escape minutes before Monica came in from work.

'So did you take the pictures down?' Monica asked.

'Tomorrow. Few things came up. Do it tomorrow.'

'So what did you do today?'

He had to think about it. 'Bit of a funny day,' he concluded.

Monica nodded. There was little she could infer from that: his funny days were numerous and impenetrable.

The next evening, however, when she came home, she found the bedroom door open and the light on. She caught him at it. His voice called her in.

He looked up at her, his eyes filled with the light of discovery. 'She's getting it all from this stuff,' he declared.

'Getting what?'

Tracy's books were all open on the bed. Compact discs had been taken out of their cases and their lyric sheets spread out on the floor. 'All her ideas. Her funny ideas. Harems and Arabs, all the rest of it. It's all here. Tell you something. Her meeting him was no accident.'

'I hope you're not prying into her things.'

'Just started looking at some of the things on her bookshelf, that's all. And you should see this stuff.' He was in an excited state. Tracy's room could have been turned over by a team of detectives. 'Every bit of it is here. Every bit. Siddown. Siddown. Look at this.' He raised books. 'Omar bloody Khayyam, right? Kahlil Gibran, the Arabian Nights, it's full of harems. Siddown!' Monica reluctantly sat on the edge of the bed. 'I told ya, didn't I. She's living in cloud-cuckoo-land. Look at this, opera, she doesn't even like opera.' He held up a CD. 'But look at the title of this! *Seraglio* something. Mozart, Read the translation on the back. Read it. Turn it over.'

Monica did this. 'So?'

'*Abduction from the Harem*. From the fucking harem. So she's sneaking off to the opera now? I don't think so. No, she's got her eye out for anything like this. Anything in this area. All the pieces of the puzzle come together. Can't you see? She's obsessed. This is a long-term obsession, building up for years.'

Monica couldn't contradict him. The evidence was persuasive.

'She's been searching out this stuff, Mon, hunting it out, wherever she can find it. Look at this, look here. Loves Cat Stevens, right? Always done, right? Well look at him here. Look at him on there. Yusuf bloody Islam!' He rapped his finger on the cover. 'Cat bloody Stevens that was!' Eric then passed her the video: *The Making of the Last Prophet*. He tapped this one's cover as well, conclusive proof. 'This is what started it. Look at him on the cover. Right there. I've been reading the bit on the back. Converted to Islam, the whole bit. So what does she do?'

'So what's your point?'

His look told her he thought this should be obvious. 'Whaddaya mean what's my point? My point is . . . my point *is,* okay, that Tracy, always in her own head, right, wearing out these records in her room here behind a locked door, okay, until one day, what happens? He converts — '

'Who does?'

'Cat. Bloody Yusuf, okay. He converts. Her hero converts, so what does she do?'

'She marries into a harem.'

'And that's part of it.'

'Is it?'

'It follows on, dunnit. It follows on. Natural progression. She starts boning up on this Islamic stuff, and it's a natural progression.'

'So Cat Stevens is behind all this then?'

'So it's no wonder she goes off looking for someone like this Sahar geezer. All this stuff spinning round in her head. She goes out looking for a job. What's it gonna be? No Chinese restaurant is gonna do it. She's got it all worked out in her head. She probably goes into every fucking Far East joint and kebab house in South London. I bet she even chucked in the supermarket job on purpose. She had it all planned.'

'You make it sound like *The Colditz Story.*'

He didn't appreciate the inference, that he too was in thrall to some fantasy. 'Mon, she went out *looking* for him. Like she looked for pictures to put on her wall. Built it all up in her mind. I even doubt that he chased her at all. I reckon she went out after *him*. Then, when she found he had two wives already she must've thought all her dreams'd come true.' He pointed at the walls. 'He didn't stand a chance. And now we know why. Because this is what the inside of her head looks like.'

Monica turned to look at the walls, redefined now and forever as the inside of her daughter's mind. 'Don't be silly.'

'And that's not all,' Eric continued, 'It's my guess that she's halfway to being a Muslim already.'

Monica looked up. 'Why? Why is she?'

He rose and took the copies of the Holy Koran down off her book-shelf. 'One, two, three, Mon. I mean, not one, okay, not two, a bit odd, but three? That's a flipping fanatic!'

The three Korans, overdue from the library, made Eric's case irre-sistible. 'She's not a fanatic,' Monica limply replied.

'Even your churchy grandmother only had one Bible.'

Monica got to her feet. Eric looked at her. 'We shouldn't be in here,' she said.

'So what do you want to do?' He was spent.

'I don't know. But let's get out of here for a start. Let's just get out of here.'

On another front Eric tried to contact Tracy. He got as far as talking to the Sahar au pair, but got little sense out of her. The party was some-where in Brighton, she thought, but she was not allowed to give the number out. The girl was not impressed by Eric's explanation that he was the bride's father and that it was extremely urgent. She merely took his number and said she would forward the message right away.

But no return call came.

Eric next proposed he ring his uncle, a retired private detective of sorts — actually an investigator of insurance claims for Norwich Union — now living in Camberwell on a pension. For a small sum Uncle Wally could go to Brighton and dig up Tracy. He might even be persuaded to put her into a car and bring her back. Eric was serious.

'Don't be ridiculous, she's a grown woman.'

'Well, she's not acting like one. And we've got to do something.'

In the end, Uncle Wally, a testy depressive with a colostomy bag, was not called. Monica merely spent more and more time in the bedroom, closing the door behind her, running out the clock until her estranged daughter returned from her week-long honeymoon.

Over a supper of Indian takeaways, and with some pride, Eric said 'She's even got me up there. Just saw it today.' He appeared in a line-up of manly legends, right between Charlton Heston and Marco Polo.

'I know. I'm there as well.'

'That shot of me when I was water-skiing, remember?'

'I know. I saw it. Can you pass the rotis?'

'So you saw your one then?'

'Course.' She took a warm bread from the oily paper bag.

'Beautiful shot, actually.'

'Thank you, sweetheart.'

'No, I just mean the photography.'

She threw a roti at him. She was a good shot.

'Hey!' he said.

Perhaps it was only a further coincidence but Monica's behaviour seemed to be increasingly affected by the marathon visits to the room. She dressed with more flamboyance than usual, wearing odd and varied combinations of clothes and jewellery, as if the room had begun to influence her as it had her daughter. 'What are you dressed up like that for?'

'Just experimenting.'

He knew what was going on. 'I think you're spending far too much time in that room.'

'Speak for yourself.' She lifted the napkin so that only her eyes could see above it, then spun round and left the room.

Her dialogue even started to feature the odd playful non sequitur. When one morning he asked Monica to remember to drop off the rented video, she shouted, 'Whatever you say, Signor Augusto.'

'Oh Jesus!' he replied. 'What the hell does that mean?'

'Nothing.' Monica went out to the lift.

'Don't you flip out on me as well,' he called after her.

On another occasion, Emily Powell called by to borrow napkins for her dinner party, Monica responded to the knock by calling out: 'Get that will you, it's probably the maharaja.'

Eric let this go by. He didn't want to knock himself out with things that would cure themselves. Marriage was about gliding over the bumps. But still, the strain of worry was getting to them both.

'The au pair says they get back tomorrow,' he finally announced. 'So we can get back to normal.'

176

'I'm sure she'll phone tomorrow then.'

'Let's invite her over to dinner.'

'Won't come. Not unless we invite the two of them.'

'No way. We've gotta talk to her alone.'

'Why don't we . . . I know, I s'pose we could go and see *her.*'

'I'm not setting foot in that house.'

'You're not leaving many choices.'

'I could always follow her again. Grab her.'

'What about going to the restaurant?'

'What restaurant?'

'*Their* restaurant. Book ourselves in. Surprise her.'

'Are you joking?'

'We've gotta do something.'

'Mon, we need to get her on her own, talk some sense into her. What good is going to the restaurant?'

Monica sighed. 'It's a first step. We haven't spoken in weeks. It's a first step.'

'The best week of my life,' the sunburnt ex-Sainsbury señora decided, new jewellery on her wrists, clasps in her hair, unpacking overfull bags the day the newly-weds returned to the family home.

She set the latest trinkets — a tortoiseshell hairbrush, gold earrings, Raybans, a beautiful camera no bigger than a matchbox and a credit card — on the blackamoor bedside table.

Yvette helped her unpack. 'Where do you want to keep things like jeans?'

Tracy had bought the pair Yvette was holding up more than five years before, on the precise day she had decided that she had stopped growing. She would throw them out now. They represented her old life.

'No, keep sem.'

'Just dresses now.'

'Only dresses?'

'For a while. It's nicer if we all wear the same thing, isn't it?'

Yvette looked horrified. 'The same sing?'

'Mmm.'

The Frenchwoman stared at her sister-wife. 'You are joking, yes?'

Tracy had got the wrong impression. 'But you and Firouzeh —?'

'Not the same, non, non!'

'You dress . . . yes you do . . . kind of . . . the same. So I thought that I'd just —'

'How could you sink ziss!'

'But you do dress alike!'

'Tracy, just because we share z'same husband, ziss does not mean we are some Siamese twins. Oh my God. We dress nussing alike.'

Firouzeh came out of the walk-in wardrobe where she was revolutionising the layout, taking down hangers and making room for Tracy. 'Who dresses alike?'

'Tracy says we do.'

The two women stood side by side. They looked identical, at least to Tracy: dresses of similar length, hair drawn back in similar styles. They even shared the same look of consternation.

'We don't want you to be like us,' Firouzeh said.

'No,' agreed Yvette.

'Your job is to make Sam happy.'

'Oui. Just make him 'appy. Ziss is all you 'ave to do.'

Tracy inclined her head at this, taken aback. 'My job?'

Firouzeh nodded.

So this was to be the arrangement.

Firouzeh and Yvette looked at each other, as though something fundamental had been left out of the explanation of how the ship would run. 'Of course, Yvette and I and have everything else under control so you don't need to worry about any of that. There's nothing else for you to do. You can simply concentrate on Sam!' Firouzeh grinned. It was all very simple.

Tracy remained silent but her eyes revealed that she was upset.

'It's perfect,' Yvette said, encouragingly.

'Yes, perfect,' Firouzeh agreed. 'You see, we had it all worked out.'

A vast empty space had been allocated for Tracy in the wardrobe. The question was how to fill it.

She stared at it later, when she thought she was alone.

'Don't worry, *ma petite*,' Yvette whispered over her shoulder, accurately reading her mind. 'It will soon fill up.'

'But I don't have anything.'

'But you soon will.'

It had not dawned on Tracy that by marrying a wealthy man she would inherit a wealthy woman's problems. With her survival issues settled, the rent paid, no job needed to get by and with a very well-oiled system already in place in this pristine house, she had been lured into a position where, alarmingly, she had all the free time in the world. The idea was terrifying.

Her life as a checkout girl, and before that as a troubled teenager in a council flat, had not prepared her for this. Were she a spoilt brat she would know exactly what to do, just how to occupy herself now, how to luxuriate in it. Tracy, however, was left with her first feelings that a life free of problems was no life at all. Without a crisis to manage, minor or great, without the daily fight for survival, *what the hell are you supposed to do?*

Moving about the house during the day, while Sam was at the restaurant going over accounts, she brooded. She fought anger at being tricked. No wonder Firouzeh and Yvette had been so accommodating, she thought. No wonder they had been so utterly devoid of female territorial instincts! They had never planned to give anything up! Sam did not interest them sexually. Tracy was welcome to him. But only him. No more than him.

She went to find her co-wives; perhaps she was misinterpreting them. She found Firouzeh going through her children's school clothes and listing new items she needed to buy.

'Anything I can do?'

Firouzeh thanked her but left in her no doubt that her function was exclusively that of being a good wife. 'Just look after Sam.'

Tracy went back down the stairs, biting her tongue.

Yvette was just then in a discussion with the old family cleaner. Tracy stood and listened. When the old women had walked away Tracy said she didn't mind helping out in domestic areas. She'd noticed that the rubbish needed putting out. When was collection day? Yvette laughed. On no account would Tracy be allowed to do any such thing. She should, rather, think about the world that had now opened to her. What, for instance, did she want to buy? Sam was a rich man. 'You haven't even been shopping once yet.' She could join a health club, take a morning massage or a beauty treatment, plan a holiday or a party. The world was her oyster.

'You've got to be joking,' Tracy said.

Yvette explained that this was nothing: a lot of Persian wives spent most of their time organising their own cosmetic surgery. 'They get

179

z'works done, z'noses, z'cheek bones, z'breasts, z'liposuction.' Her hands shaped exaggerated body parts in the air. 'It is crazy but they do whatever they want. You can do the same, anysing you want.'

That night, Sam confirmed all this over a late-night supper cooked by Firouzeh, wiping his neat moustache with a napkin rolled by Yvette. 'The house and children, all the practical things are taken care of. It's a standing deal. But this leaves you free to do anything you like.'

'I wish everyone would stop saying that! The next time anyone says it,' she warned, 'I'll pack my sodding bags and go back home. I will.'

'You want a divorce already?'

'No one told me about this.'

'Why is that so bad, to decide what you want?'

Tracy had hoped that by getting married such questions would have been resolved, but here it was again, and twice as large as life. 'Firouzeh said it was my job to make you happy.'

He smiled. 'Isn't it?'

'You'll be lucky.'

'What is the problem?'

'She said it's *my job.*'

'And it's my job to make you happy.'

She shook her head. 'It makes it sound like it was . . . like you needed someone to fill a vacancy and I got it. Like this was all a giant conspiracy of theirs.'

'It was. We are the poor victims.' He laughed. 'But you must have realised how busy they were in the background. They had wanted for a long time to find someone for me. They have been playing Cupid for years. Saying I should date this divorcee, I should phone up that one. Actually, by the time you came along, I had completely forgotten how to romance a woman, if I ever knew how. They felt it was their job to find someone for me. To repay me for what they think I've done for them, I suppose. And so they paved the way for us together. But you understand all the reasons behind this.'

She recalled his revelations on the park bench. She nodded. But she felt no better about the realisation that she had been bagged like wild game in a pre-planned operation. 'I still want to work in the restaurant,' she announced.

'You don't have to.'

'Yvette does.'

'If you wish. Anything you like.'

'And I'm thinking of doing a course. I'm not sure. Studying something.'

Again he nodded. 'Courses are good. Improve yourself. Good idea. What are you interested in?'

'I'm not sure. I'm quite interested in learning a bit more about Persia.'

'Persia! Really?'

'And maybe about world religions.' She felt she needed to explain this urge. 'Trying to read the Koran made me feel stupid but I got quite interested.'

'It's a good idea. I like this idea, great.' Study was, he continued, the only way to ensure that the soul, the eternal — but she cut him off. She didn't want a homily right now. 'And something else,' she said. 'For the record.'

'Anything, my love. Don't you know that?' He reached for her hand.

'The day that making you happy feels like a job is the day I'm out of here. Do you understand that?'

'Of course.'

She rose then and without a kiss gave him a foretaste of what such a departure would feel like.

What had he said? he wondered, his fork suspended halfway between his plate and his mouth. It couldn't have been his fault. She hadn't let him get a word in. This in itself was a bad sign. Had she lost her taste for his speeches and philosophising already? Unbelievable. How quickly one wife could become just like another, the polygamist thought, as he returned his fork to his plate and resumed his solitary midnight meal.

But Tracy wasn't the only one who would struggle to acclimatise to the new arrangement. No sooner were they all settled under the one roof than the earlier wives experienced their own teething troubles.

Having encouraged Sam, in a hundred ways, to openly display his feelings for his new bride, they were not quite prepared when his first grand bouquet was delivered while they were all at the breakfast table. The first wives, happily satisfied that their advice had been heeded, soon became moist-eyed and had to leave the rose-scented table in a rush when they were too vividly reminded of what they had been missing for years.

'Oh dear,' said Sam.

'What can we do?' Tracy asked. This wasn't going as smoothly as she'd imagined.

'Nothing. We can't win. It's impossible.'

And so the perfect arrangement, so easily maintained during the high delirium of the honeymoon, was suddenly found to be imperfect: for the forseeable future, though, it remained the best idea anyone had.

The calendar of courses felt impossibly heavy in Tracy's hands. The contents page alone listed hundreds of papers. She had half a mind to turn around and walk away.

But Yvette and Firouzeh had taken her there themselves, put her up to this — as with everything else it now appeared! — giving her the thumbs-up sign before they drove off. If she caved in now she would only have to explain later why her life suddenly wasn't worth improving, and why she'd given up on herself, why she'd thrown herself onto the human scrap heap at twenty, and why the logic of making Sam happy was suddenly a sufficient solution for all the questions of her life.

In comparison with such a scene, listening to a lecture series entitled 'Anthropomorphic Polytheism', seemed comparatively easy.

Tracy had queued at the reception desk of the adult education centre for twenty-five minutes to get hold of this copy of the calendar. The first lesson she had was that further education lay at the other end of a great deal of waiting.

She also noted, as she turned the pages, how earlier travellers had highlighted their preferences with red ticks, exclamation points, asterisks and bold parallel lines in the margin. These trail-markers revealed the mysterious paths down which a hundred others had already disappeared. Could she really follow them? By now the brains of these pathfinders were filled with science and novels, with arguments about archaeology, architecture, the make-up of cities, the law, the problems of the Third World. She looked up. Such students crossed the void between buildings in the wind, clutching thick books to their breasts. To her they all looked brilliant, sharp, privileged and confident. She felt like an impostor. Only Firouzeh and Yvette's encouragement kept her a second longer in their company. 'You're smarter than any of them,' they had said.

She quietly requested an enrolment form from the matronly secretary. She received it with the level of respect Moses might have displayed for the Ten Commandments, then retreated to a corner where a dozen similar hopefuls bent over their calendars.

Tracy scanned the list of topics on offer. She had her eyes peeled for any mention of Islam or Persia — she could always drop the papers she didn't like — but she could only find three courses that came close. These would have to do. She read the details. Six lectures a week was plenty. With essays to write, extra books to read, it would more than fill up her empty days.

She wrote down the course names on her form in careful big-lettered capitals then returned to the desk and handed it in. The woman nodded as she checked it through. 'That's fine,' the woman said, then went to a cash register to total the cost. Tracy handed over her new platinum Amex card, thanked the woman when it came back and then took a campus map and followed its directions to the bookshop. She bought all the recommended texts, some fifteen books. It was quite a load. Lugging two carrier bags she then sought out the Comparative Religions Department. Everywhere there was a queue. From a department secretary she took a programme of lecture times and a second map, showing her the layout and the location of specific lecture halls. Additional course notes were passed to her at an alarming rate. She was told to go down the hall now and get several more booklets. By the time she made it back out onto the street she was swamped with documents. She splashed out and caught a taxi back to Barnes to begin reading. In the taxi she nervously opened the first textbook: she wanted to read all the opening sentences. She filled her lungs and lowered her head. By the tenth sentence she raised her head again. All of it had been comprehensible. 'Thank God,' she said to herself.

Tracy Pringle was now a student. Proclaim it from the rooftops, write it large in the sky.

'Student?' asked the taxi driver.

'Yeah,' Tracy replied and gave the directions for home.

Ricky Innes came out of nowhere, intercepting Tracy as she walked up to the front door, her arms laden.

'I can't believe you married that slimebag,' he said, catching his breath. 'Oh man. That dirty old man.'

'Who told you?'

'Your mum. Tell me you didn't marry that scumbag.'

She turned to him. He looked just the same: pained, anguished, on a quick break from work, blasted rock dust nested in his hair. He had crossed the road from his slab-heavy van, whose morbid load pulled it very low on its axles. The back door was ajar: she could see inside the stones readied for the dead.

What a grim job you've got, Richard Innes. No wonder you want the gory details.

'You wouldn't understand, Ricky.'

'What wouldn't I understand? Because he's what? Banging all three of you at the same time? That it? All three?' His eyebrows were raised. He drilled these words at her, intending that they stand the test of time. 'You all sleep in the same bed then, do ya? Just tell me that? So who shags who, Trace?'

What had he meant to her? A respite from loneliness, an attempt to join the human party. Beginning to think she had a real block about men, she had plucked one from the crowd: one as good as another. But even then, what had she been thinking? Handiwork on a gravestone couldn't have wooed her completely. The heart ring, which had cured her eye problems, must have also blinded her.

'I'll go if you just tell me,' he promised. 'You all sleep in the same bed? Tell me that and abracadabra, I'm gone.'

She considered telling him the truth but then decided against it: far better to make him pay. If this was what was bothering him, had him stewing in his septic juices, then let him marinate in it! He couldn't hurt her now.

Ricky reported all that he learnt some hours later, back in his flat. 'She told me she was!'

Bruce rolled a joint laced with MDMA, which he would share, and shook his head. 'No way.'

'She's banging all three of them. Some fucked-up four-way lesbo harem thing.' Ricky sank his face into his hands.

'I bet the Arab watches.'

Ricky groaned. This was quite likely.

'Dirty cunt,' Bruce said. 'What are you gonna do?'

Ricky lifted his head. 'Do?'

'What you gonna do about him?'

'Whadaya mean?' Ricky studied his pal.

'You're obviously gonna get your own back in some way?'

'Am I?' Ricky had mooted a few courses of action but had not let them crystallise: He could drive a nail into Sam's car tyre, terrorise him, or release maggots through the letter box of his front door, a teeming sea of larva for the foreigner to find. Piecing together threatening notes from newspaper headlines was another possibility.

But these ideas were amateurish. 'No, no, no,' Bruce said. 'You wanna shake someone up?' He licked shut the joint. 'Then something's gotta die.' It was a statement of mere fact, not to be argued with or diluted.

'Something?'

'Yeah. Not necessarily him. But something.'

By putting a light to the cigarette and partaking of it in turns the two of them could really explore the realms of revenge. Bruce, the teacher, arrived first at the *coup de grâce*.

While the iron was hot he dispatched Ricky to a late-night grocery store while he went out to his truck and dug around for a length of thick copper wire he knew he had in the boot. By the time he came inside Ricky was waiting with a packet of Lincolnshire sausages. 'So what's this about? What do we do now?'

Bruce relit the joint, pondered the unlikely ingredients lying upon the table and then went to work, explaining the process as he went. In this way Ricky learnt that an old sausage, if left to rot for three days in the presence of copper, would form a powerful and barely traceable poison: one highly palatable to large dogs. Sam's two guard dogs should die. Those damn wolves, who had craved a piece of Ricky not so many nights ago, should be eliminated. It was no more than that 'fat shagging Arab' deserved and it would send an anonymous message to Tracy: that someone loved her enough to go ahead and kill two dogs.

Once the kebabing was complete, both men stared at their work, studying in silence the poisonous valentine before them, mustering in their drugged stupor the rapt concentration of chess champions deliberating their next move.

Tracy would never have guessed that her parents would actually show up at the restaurant. The booking had been made under a false name so as not to alert her, and had she known she would have been in knots of anxiety. There had been no communication between them since the night she had stormed out. She had even picked up her clothes in a clandestine fashion, phoning her parents repeatedly and hanging up when they answered until, finally, she found no one at home. She whizzed across town in a taxi, making further checks with Sam's mobile phone, and instructed the driver to keep his engine running as she rose in the lift, cleared out her room and, ten minutes later, re-entered the taxi with two bulging cases.

As she approached their table with menus in her hand, however, she felt only inclined to smile. It was, in fact, incredibly good to see them. But what would their feelings be towards her?

Monica nodded apprehensively at her costumed daughter. Eric merely grimaced. He would make no pretence at being happy. Tracy blushed in response. This visit was the last thing she'd expected. 'What's going on?' she asked.

'What's it look like? Hungry, aren't we?' Monica answered, with a wink at Emily Powell, who smiled at Tracy.

Eric coughed into his fist and pulled out a medicinal cigarette. Tracy leaned forward with a lighter before he could find his matches, a flame springing up at the end of her thumb. He stared at her, the unlit cigarette in his lips. But she did not return the look, her eye poised professionally on the flame, until he finally bent forwards and staunched it with the tip of his cigarette. Quickly then he lowered his head into a menu he already knew by heart, as Tracy used the same flame to light the candle on their table.

'Hi,' Emily Powell waved, buoyant at the far side of the table, all this a tremendous wheeze to her, her mourning period preserved only in a brooched scarf, a black cardigan.

Eric's eyes darted from the menu to his ethnically transformed daughter and back again. He had told Monica that too many people were unprepared for this for it to be a good idea. He had finally agreed to come but only to limit the damage.

'Y'look beautiful,' Emily enthused.

'Lovely, yeah,' echoed Monica. 'Amazing.'

The full-length dress flattered Tracy. She gave a little curtsey. 'Thanks. Not too bad, is it. So . . . what can I get you?'

'Beer,' Eric blurted. 'Drown my sorrows.'

'Oh shut up you,' Monica laughed, hitting his arm.

'Right,' Tracy said. 'What one do you want, Dad?'

Monica jumped the queue. She wanted a gin and tonic. Emily took

Tracy's advice and settled on a house white. 'It's quite nice.'

Eric chose a Heineken but wanted to proceed at once to ordering the food.

'No, slow down, slow down,' Monica remonstrated. 'Plenty of time.'

Tracy fled to the kitchen. Her emotions overcame her. She put her face in her hands as soon as the kitchen door swung shut, screaming under her breath, partly in anxiety and partly in excitement.

'What?' asked Yvette. 'What is it?'

'My parents! They're here! I can't believe it.'

Yvette had yet to meet them, and she and Abdullah squeezed up to the crack in the door. In the background Tracy described them, who was who. Yvette said they looked very nice and begged to be introduced. Tracy replied that this might have to wait until after her heart attack.

She organised the drinks and ferried them back out.

Monica spotted the engagement ring at once. 'Look at that!'

It was a diamond ring of impressive vulgarity. Tracy slid it off and handed it to her mother, who had never seen anything like it.

'Me neither,' Emily said. 'Just look at that.' The diamond sat in a cluster of emeralds.

Eric stole only sideways peeks at it. He could not afford to be beguiled. It was huge, he had to admit, but he saw its value only in terms of a brand-new motorbike, a deposit on a house, a better car, two months on a deckchair in Torremolinos. The ring came a distant second to all of these. 'Nice,' he agreed, then went back to his menu. 'With these prices, no wonder he's got money. Can we order now?'

'No,' Monica said. 'I haven't even looked yet.'

Monica rose and announced that she would pop into the ladies. Tracy said she would go with her. Emily's eyebrows rose approvingly. Eric shot a new look of displeasure at his wife.

As they stood at adjoining basins Monica wanted to know how Tracy was doing.

'I've never been happier actually, Mum.'

'Really?'

'I mean it.'

Monica nodded into the mirror. 'We'll never agree. But you know that. Or you should. We'll never think it's right, or good, or even gonna work out, but we want to keep up contact. We're here, so don't cut us off. All right?'

Tracy softened. 'Mum, course I won't. Course I won't. I wanted you to come to the wedding.'

'Pigs'd fly, sweetheart. Your dad's shoes turned to anvils just coming here.'

Tracy decided to take the next step. 'Come over some time, see for yourself. It's totally normal. Come over for dinner. Ask Dad.'

Monica shook her head at her daughter's reflection. 'He'd never come.'

'Ask him.'

She turned to look at her directly and didn't immediately rule it out. She was desperately curious to see how the set-up worked on the inside, view the big white house of her imagination up close, find out how it was really furnished.

'I mean it, come over.'

'Eric wouldn't.'

But from the pauses Tracy deduced that eventually, somehow, things might find a way of working out. She left it there.

Monica tried to find herself in her child's profile, but Tracy's new look masked any resemblance. She imagined her own hair combed back in a tight chignon.

Tracy refastened her hair clips. 'Then come on your own.'

'I couldn't do that. Be a divorce.'

'No, there wouldn't. Sam's parents are flying in from Tehran next week. To check me out, I think.'

'You've got nothing to prove. If you wanna know, I don't really wanna know what you get up to, to be totally honest. I'm scared to find out. I'm only managing it this far so long as I keep myself in the dark about all that other stuff.'

'I don't believe you.'

'What do you mean?'

'You must wanna know. Otherwise, you wouldn't be here, would ya.' Tracy confidently reapplied her lipstick, subtly overpainting each lip in the French style.

Monica watched this evolution, the sophisticated woman blooming on the face of the young girl.

15

The Marriage Guide

Sam was there to meet his parents at the arrivals hall. Parking on a double yellow line, he left his hazard lights blinking. He had been alerted to his father's frailty in the last year and guessed the long walk to the Terminal 3 carpark would be too much for him. So what, he thought, if he got a ticket. His parents had come to celebrate him!

But the real reason behind the visit was clear. He had written to his youngest brother, Sassan, encamped with his division in the desert, making his feelings about Tracy clear: 'She's much more than I could have hoped. And much more than a bloated hippo like me deserves. I certainly can say that this time it is the real thing.' Running out of room, he wrote vertically up the margins. 'Never happier. Must come and visit soon. You not me, I mean. Love and wishes. S.'

The letter took no time to wing its way into the hands of his parents. Enraged by the irresponsible news, they vowed to address the arrival of a new non-Muslim wife by flying out to take him on. Their first son's moral universe was clearly collapsing. They did not exaggerate when they said they were prepared to risk their lives to do it, and so booked their flights. This 'marriage jamboree' had to be curbed.

Across the cold terminal floor, bow-backed in one of his loosely tailored pin-striped suits, his fine, snow-white hair floating on his head, padded his father, pulling a wheelie-case like a pet, his usual sheaf of meaningless family documents under his arm, his small feet pit-patting on the tiled floor. He looked to Sam much like a retired magistrate these days, hurrying to secure the acquittal of a condemned man. Sam raised his arm and waved.

189

A few metres behind, eternally ten years younger in appearance, but by some miracle of age now several inches taller, laboured his mother, unassisted as she fought to control a trolley towering with cases, looking this way and that way for her wayward son, still vigorous, dressed with the prim formality of a 1950s American housewife: black shoes, dark stockinged legs, the hem of a dun-coloured dress below the knees, a trademark pashmina tied over her shoulders and a scarf drawn down so low on her head that it visored her eyes. Peeking over the rim of the Raybans on her proud nose, she scoured the gaping gallery for the prodigal.

Sam caught their attention. Relieved to have made the connection, they almost smiled back as they came towards him. How foreign his parents now seemed to him, these desert nomads. After small formalities, hugs and kisses, a swift gift of pistachio nuts was made. Fatima had crazily smuggled lamb sausage through customs, at great risk of embarrassment; also the best candy from Shiraz, several loaves of flat bread. It occurred to Sam, however, that his parents' primary contraband was themselves.

He flagged them towards his just-ticketed car. He glanced at the bill. Eighty pounds. He couldn't wait to get away from the airport.

Slipping into top gear behind a black cab on the M4 he asked in his bourgeois Farsi if they had enjoyed a happy flight.

'The journey was as off-putting as senile nudity,' Mostafa replied curtly. The airline staff had run out of both halal food and mineral water. They were both exhausted.

After some prompting, the old man went on to report on the political climate in Iran. With his watery eyes aimed out of the window, trying to detect signs of hope in an alien landscape of back gardens and allotments, he stated that his own sympathies were divided between the clerics and the students: one represented his values, the other rights he also believed in. He was at a crossroads not dissimilar to that of his country. Sam nodded. How often had he heard his father link his fortunes to that of his nation.

At a set of traffic lights, Sam was made to justify anew his forsaking of his homeland in favour of a meatless restaurant business.

He reiterated that he had not forsaken it. On the contrary, the murmur of it was always in his blood and he felt the loss of it more intensely and purely than ever. In fact, he assured them in a raised voice, the impact of the diaspora upon him had been devastating. Since his

190

flight from the Revolution his life had lost its natural pulse and tempo and he doubted that he would ever regain it. 'So you see, my dreams will not let me forsake it.' He was a different man now, part of a lost generation, a dislocated class: not even on the ladder of British society, he was somewhere off to one side.

His parents' response was hardly comforting. If his life was upside down he should not be surprised. They were happy to see him but he must see that he was no better than a drug addict, too charmed by his demons to see any way out. Apart from doing his duty in marrying Firouzeh, a brother's obligation, he was a good-for-nothing, a washout. And now, with a new wife to boot.

They rode the rest of the way in silence.

Once inside the house, his parents, pleading exhaustion, brushed past their son's assembled wives and disappeared to their upstairs room to which they summoned their grandchildren. It was clear that normal civilities had been suspended.

The following day began with an emergency.

Shortly before dawn, Fatima knocked loudly on the door of the master bedroom. Sam was called into the hall and Fatima spoke quickly in her native tongue. It was the hour to pray, she told her son, the sun was about to rise, and they had lost all sense of direction.

Sam clapped his hand on his head. He had completely forgotten to provide for this. He knew that the *sunna* dictated fifteen minutes of Mecca-directed prayer before sunrise, with four further and longer sessions to follow throughout the day. The clock was ticking, sunrise was almost upon them. His parents were badly disorientated and it was his fault.

'I have no idea, Mother. Stop, let me think.'

Sam was embarrassed that his parents should learn in this way that he had long ago stopped observing the daily practice of devotion. He calmed his mother's fears and sent her downstairs to wait. He would come up with a solution.

Back in his bedroom he pulled on a dressing gown.

'What is it?' Tracy groggily enquired.

'They need to know the direction of Mecca.'

'And you don't know?

'No idea.'

Tracy jumped out of bed and hurried with him downstairs to find that the entire household had been awoken by the predicament.

The emerging day, a miserable cloudy London morning, was too heavily overcast for anyone to even hazard a guess as to the true direction of due east. Untypically, Fatima had forgotten to bring her compass. She had realised her oversight on the plane but had remained calm. Always a good son, Sam was sure to know the bearing for the holy city.

They gathered in the kitchen. Tracy the sun-worshipper remembered that the morning sun came in over the oak tree. Sam's parents gave her their full attention as she pointed: 'East . . . east . . . east . . . over there.'

Sam translated this for his parents. But it was rejected. It was not sufficient just to face east. They knew from the in-flight magazine that Mecca lay many degrees to the south of due east. Facing the oak tree, Fatima extended her arms, pointing to both the fridge and the oven. So which way was south?

Opinion was divided, leaving his parents no choice but to insist on being taken to a mosque regardless.

'That is, if you know which direction there is one.'

Firouzeh volunteered to drive them after breakfast to the grand mosque beside Regents Park. The children could come along on this mysterious ride. Sam, meanwhile, once the shops opened, would take the other car and go in search of a store that would sell him a compass before noon.

The parents retired upstairs to pray, making their protest felt.

Several hours later, and after two slams of the front door, Tracy found herself alone in the house.

She had barely enough time to plug in the kettle to make a coffee, when a knock came at the door.

Sunlight streamed over the official's shoulders, blinding her. 'I hope this isn't an inconvenient time,' Partridge said.

Her heart sank.

Mr S. Partridge, Sebastian on his card, Seb at the door, apologised for calling at what appeared to be a somewhat inconvenient time, before being led to the couch. He wanted only to have a look around. He had with him an official court order permitting an investigation into the family's living arrangements. He had hoped the entire family would be in, but this was no matter. He wouldn't take long.

She told him she needed to make a call and left him on the couch.

In the kitchen, she picked up the phone. 'Come on, come on,' she said to herself.

Sam had had a terrible time finding a shop that even looked as if it might sell a compass. In the end he pulled into an electric appliance superstore. At the counter he tried to attract the attention of the harried shop assistant, but the man was attending to an earlier customer, placing a second cellular phone down on the counter beside a first.

The customer, a nervous suburbanite, had entered into a slow internal debate, one which Sam had to endure as he waited his turn. The choice was between a £45 model or going all out on a more expensive brand. This ruddy character with rolled sleeves winced many times, pursed his lips and shifted his weight continually in a ballet of indecision. Sam's patience was at breaking point. The choice seemed a simple one and Sam had long since made up his own mind: the first would be broken in a month; buy the second one.

But the customer, after five full minutes of agony, seemed no closer to making a decision. Sam could no longer contain himself. 'The second one. Please. Just buy the second one. I'll even buy it for you, how's that?'

The customer faced him, flushed, shocked.

'I'm sorry,' Sam apologised. 'It's none of my business, but it's an emergency. The difference is clear. Spend the extra.'

The man looked as if he were on the point of hitting Sam, or of running out, such was the physical change that came over him. He turned back to the assistant. 'Just give me the cheaper model. Anything to shut this prick up.'

'Great,' said Sam.

'Watch it!' The man shot him a *don't push me* look.

'I just have been, for ten full minutes. What choice did I have?'

When the phone was packaged and paid for, and after the man retreated with an ugly glance, it was Sam's turn.

'Can't do that sorta thing, mate. Everyone's busy.'

'I know. I should know better.' And he did. 'I'm sorry. But I just need a compass?'

'A compass? What sort of compass?'

'A simple compass that's all.'

But they did not sell compasses. Such technology was too old for this hyper-store. Too old? thought Sam, hearing this. What did that mean? The attendant was sorry. They used to stock them. They'd stopped years ago. No demand since the market went digital. *Digital!* The *Telegraph* reader in Sam was outraged. But if Sam was interested, the man said, and for a bit more money, he could sell him something similar: he enthusiastically unlocked the glass display cabinet and pulled something off a plastic stand. He set it in front of Sam.

'What is it?' Sam asked.

'State-of-the-art'.

'Obviously. But what is it?' In its leather sleeve the box-like instrument could have been anything.

'It's a global positioning system.'

'Global — ? What's that? I just need a compass.'

This device could fit into the palm of his hand, Sam was told. Take a look. Pick it up. Feel it. Weigh it. You had to love it. 'Electronic directional finder as well, satellite guided. Signals bounce off the ionosphere.' This store worker loved saying ionosphere. Such jargon gave even the smallest people the illusion of boundlessness. 'They bung exactly this technology onto military warheads nowadays. Remember the scuds? Same as this going into Iraq. Pop.' He made a suction-breaking sound and then drove his fist into the palm of his other hand. 'Just the business.'

Sam nodded, trying to visualise his aged, old-world, technophobic mother operating this object of mass destruction. It was ridiculous but he could not rule it out. 'Well how much is it?'

'Four hundred and forty-five quid. Out the door. It's yours. Wrapped. And that's with the recharger'n all.' The man looked confident, as if the item sold itself, as if the future needed no help from him. 'And then you wouldn't only be able to find a needle in a haystack, mate, but a needle in a haystack *on the other side of the world.*'

Sam nodded. 'That's all very well. All very impressive. But I just want to tell where north and south are.'

The man looked at Sam with diminished respect. 'North and south, mate? Yeah. No worries. That's what I'm saying. North and south, east and west, what I had for breakfast, and the current value of the Japanese yen. That's what I'm saying!'

'I want to know . . . I just want to . . . be able to tell . . . ' But he stopped himself. He was not going to tell this PlayStation groupie about his parents' specific religious needs. 'I just want to be able to find the direction of a certain city, that's all.'

'Right. Like Mecca, yeah?' The man winked. Sam blushed. 'Right, so all you do is load that in. Okay look, quick demo, but it's all in the booklet, y'turn it on here, flip through the menu like this, key in the name of the place you want, 6000 cities worldwide on the database and hey presto . . . ' He keyed in M.E.C.C.A. ' . . . Robert is definitely your mother's brother. That's the little arrow there, see it?' Sam nodded, leaning forward. He could see the small arrow. That was simple enough at least: an arrow was a technology his mother might trust. 'It's just trying to establish a satellite link.'

'Oh,' said Sam.

'And when it does, you just point your boat or your car or your magic carpet right at that and you're guaranteed to be accurate to within five metres anywhere in the world, but that's on a bad day. It should get you to within two.'

Sam smiled and nodded. They waited for the device to contact a satellite. Oh, the infinite bamboozling abstractions of modern life! They terrified him at the same time as they excited him. But with what supreme betrayal of human destiny would it end? Invention was leaving the soul far behind.

'No, damn. Have to be outside really. But it'll definitely work if you take it outside. So, what do ya say? Wrap it or not?'

By then another customer was already waiting for service, shifting uneasily beside Sam, becoming impatient. The attendant noticed this, and to avoid a recurrence of the previous scene told the man, 'Be with you in a minute mate, all right?' Sam also smiled an awkward apology. He would not be like the previous customer, but he was still uncertain. He wanted a simple compass, not a device to steer a killer rocket. He felt the pressure of the purchase. Soon it would be noon. But £450? Just then his cellphone rang. 'Bugger,' he grumbled, pulling it out of his pocket. 'Sorry,' he told the other bargain hunter.

'So watcha wanna do?'

'Ah . . . ' said Sam. 'I suppose . . . it's just . . . can I take this call?'

'You wanna take that call?'

The man at his shoulder sighed heavily. Sam turned on his phone. 'Okay! Bugger it. Wrap it,' he said. 'Just wrap the blasted thing.' He took out his wallet and tendered his credit card as he spoke into the phone.

'Just don't let him go upstairs,' he told Tracy via the microwaves of London. 'Whatever you do.'

'Why?'

'Just try and hold him in the lounge until I get there.'

Tracy put down the phone. When she returned to the lounge Mr Partridge was no longer on the couch.

She raced up the stairs, took them two at a time, to find him already craning into the master bathroom 'Very,' he said with a long pause, 'impressive.'

He faced her. 'Haven't got long, you see. Sorry. Thought I'd make a start. Left the authority form down on the coffee table for you to read.'

She nervously stared at him. 'Who said you could . . . could do this?'

'All in the document. On the table. Sorry for the intrusion.'

Tracy knew very well that Firouzeh wouldn't have accepted this, not with her ferocity, or Yvette with her guile: they would find a way of stopping this man and getting him back onto the street. Tracy, however, couldn't think of anything to say that would stop him.

'Anyone up here?' He pointed up the hall.

She shook her head. Her heart was racing. 'No. No one. Nothing.'

'Great. I'll just get on then. Don't mind me. Few minutes. Just go on with whatever you're doing.' He turned and went into the next bedroom. She didn't follow him in and waited to receive his comments as he re-emerged. 'Mm hmm,' and 'Good' and 'Okay, great' and 'Lot of adult rooms.' Slipping from one room after another, he asked whose each was, scribbling a brisk note on his clipboard, before entering the next room and shouting back: 'Right, right' or 'I see' or 'lovely'.

'So this is the main children's bedroom, then, right next to the . . . ,' glancing at his notes, 'right next to the master bedroom?'

She felt sick. She couldn't move. Her distress was unbearable. She was now certain she was permitting disaster and certain tragedy to occur but she was no better than a deaf mute in mounting a defence. Whatever the outcome of this, she would be responsible. She had to act, she knew it. She was about to say something, when he came back up the hall with a satisfied smile, lowered his clipboard and announced that he was done. 'Right then, shall we go back down then?'

Back in the lounge she fidgeted and looked out of the window. Sam must arrive any second. He was stuck in traffic. She had phoned him three times already, reached him in his car, trapped at some set of lights. She told him she had failed to stop the official going upstairs. In his absence she had ruined everything.

'So is it an open relationship?' Partridge asked her cordially.

'Open?' She knew what he was getting at, but refused to add to her list of mistakes by giving him new ammunition.

'Do other men or women ever participate in the sexual side of your group marriage?'

'What are you talking about?'

'I simply need to know how these things work. Are you allowed to take other partners? Under this arrangement?'

Tracy ruffled her eyebrows. 'Other partners?' By playing dumb she might just get through this ordeal.

'I'm just trying to compile a picture here.'

'Are you allowed to . . . to ask these kinds of questions?'

'Oh yes. That's why I was sent. To ask them.'

Tracy nodded. This at least was believable.

'Oh, a car,' Partridge noted, turning his head. 'Somebody else?'

They had both heard the car arrive, and Tracy stared at the door, waiting to be relieved of her terrible duties.

Sam finally burst in the door, his tie loosened, his sleeves rolled up ready for action, with a box under his arm. As soon as he saw the scene, the official rising from his chair to be introduced, he slowed his pace and he transformed himself, his expression of deep anxiety metamorphosing into a civil smile. 'Oh hello,' he lightly greeted his guest, steering himself first towards Tracy in her chair, where he bent and genteelly kissed the top of her head with great tenderness, effecting an intimacy that negated the official's presence. 'My sweet one. You look wonderful. Lovely dress. Is it new? Oh and good news. I have a compass, but not as you have ever seen one. It can guide a bomb.' He gave her the package as if it were a gift. Partridge had simultaneously been gifted a brief insight into a loving fully functional marriage. He turned to face the public servant. 'And now then . . . who do we have here?' He smiled, stepped towards the visitor. 'How do you do. So pleased to meet you. Welcome. Saaman Sahar.'

'This is Mr Partridge,' Tracy supplied, just now aware that she was trembling. She folded her hands.

'Oh good, the famous Mr Partridge.' The two men shook hands

warmly, the official towering over Sam as he continued: 'Now what seems to be the trouble?'

Partridge assured Sam as they both sat that this wouldn't take long. He had already taken a brief look around and only a couple of points remained to be clarified.

'Good,' Sam said, nodding his approval to his wife. 'It's important you get the full and proper picture. But let's just take a second.' And before anything further could be said Sam began to establish that his guest was comfortable, offering refreshments and modifying the formal atmosphere with Persian witticisms. 'What do you think of our home? It provides a wonderful view of the real world, do you not think?'

And: 'By the standards of most foreigners we keep it very clean, don't you think?'

And: 'And let me apologise if that chair is uncomfortable, it was designed for fat people.'

'I've talked to the children's teachers,' Partridge interposed, 'and the play-group workers, and for the most part they are aware of your situation and are quite unconcerned, which is good. A good sign. The children seem to be doing well, which is always a clear sign.'

'Very well. Yes. But first, would you mind if I ask you to take off your shoes?'

'My . . . ?'

'If you would. I am serious. My parents are with us now. It's one of our traditional observances, when a house is used for prayer. I'll join you. I forget myself.'

Sam led the way and bent to untie his own laces. 'Please. If you would be so kind.'

Partridge watched him, waiting to see if this was yet another joke, even looking to Tracy for assurance, before realising that his host was quite serious. His tall, thin frame became a veritable paper-clip as he bent over.

Socks revealed, Sam gathered up both pairs of shoes and set them by the door with the others of the house. 'Thank you. And anyway, that's much more comfortable, don't you think?' Sam returned to his chair, wiggling his toes. 'Good. Now we can talk.'

Tracy's relief was enormous. Everything would now be all right. Sam would see to it. Even her recent failures would be repaired.

Partridge tried to turn the conversation back to official business. 'It's about your children. That's why I'm here.'

198

'What would you like to know about them?' Sam asked, taking the lead.

'You have three?'

'Four actually.'

'Oh yes, four. Yes, I've got four names here. Mostafa, then —'

'The older ones are top of their classes, but this could presumably be from cheating. Living as they do in an immoral household it comes naturally to them.'

Partridge smiled and significantly lowered his clipboard. Tracy took this as the first good sign. 'But no one is actually saying — '

'No, *I'm* saying it. Terribly immoral, by most people's standards.'

'Well . . . '

'Otherwise, well, you wouldn't be here, would you?'

'Well that's not entirely — '

'You would otherwise be unconcerned for the children, who exhibit no signs of damage, as you can see, if this were not ultimately a question of . . . yes, morality.'

'Well, my job is not exactly to judge — '

'Isn't it? Isn't it about your view as opposed to ours?'

'It's not my *place* to judge people's morality, Mr Sahar. That's your own affair.'

'No, I can't accept that remark. It would make your job impossible.'

Partridge nodded uncomfortably: he was being sidetracked. 'The children are all that I'm concerned about.'

'I thought we had established they're fine.'

'No. I'm not at all sure we have.'

'No?'

'Well, I need to decide, well not me personally, but my office does, that . . . that they're not being exposed . . . '

'Oh, exposed!'

' . . . to harmful, possibly *very* harmful experiences, which may be inappropriate . . . inappropriate for children of their age.'

'For example,' Sam said 'let me help you out here. Group sex.'

Tracy's knuckles turned white in her lap.

Partridge stared balefully at Sam and Tracy. 'Well, are they?'

'Or . . . or they are even being invited to *participate*?' Sam added heatedly. 'We can keep going, perhaps they are not even being asked: perhaps they are being forced . . . Is that what you think?'

Had these last questions not been the exact ones that Partridge had been sent to ask then he would now have shrunk from them and blushed. He held his official pose, returned his host's stare and, suddenly grateful that this most distasteful aspect of his mission had just been performed for him, he felt a surge of relief. 'Well, not in so many words.'

'Mr Partridge, are we degenerates?'

'No one said you were.'

'You're here to find physical evidence to that effect, though. As it is impossible that you could ever find proof that we were moral, as you cannot take a photograph of a man's soul, morality isn't reliant upon an action but more often inaction, unlike immorality which always requires an action, then you are therefore here for the first reason. But you and your office require evidence where *none exists*. And though you look for it, but can't yet find it, in the faces of my wives or my sweet children or in my own face where you are most likely to find it, and though you'll try to insinuate it in the layout of the house, which I presume is the reason you are so keen to look around, you will still fail to get the photograph you need.'

'I'm not here to take photographs, Mr Sahar.'

'So let me speed up the process so that we can conclude it. Yes, the bed is big enough to accommodate three. Does it? Either believe me when I say no or else you'll have to break in in the middle of the night. Also, I do not have a jacuzzi, even though one originally came with the house. Make of this what you will. The room was turned into a nursery. What else? Oh yes. I have three wives. Under Muslim tradition and British law I am high and dry. I recommend you speak to my lawyer for clarification. The laws of polygamy do not concern themselves with common-law marriages like these. Which returns us to the issue of morality, the only area in which we are truly at odds, but the one area in which you say your office is not interested. Really then, Mr Partridge, it's my turn to be blunt. I think you should really ask yourself what on earth you are doing here?'

Partridge couldn't reply. In his entire life he had never been so elaborately told to bugger off.

Sam smiled and marched on. 'Do you have children yourself, Mr Partridge?'

The official was limp with exhaustion. 'Two.'

'Two? No wonder you look tired. Doesn't he?' Sam turned to Tracy, who nodded. 'Are they at home now?'

'Well, no . . . they're . . . they're not exactly with me.'

'Not with you.?'

'Divorce.'

'Oh I see.'

'They're with . . . with their mother,' Partridge added, his voice trailing away to a whisper, 'they're both . . . with their . . . with their . . . ummm . . . mother. In Wales.'

Tracy stared at Partridge. He seemed to be changing by the minute. Robbed of shoes, bombarded by a fusillade of enquiry, he had lost much of his earlier authority. His official cloak of antagonism was being transformed into a strategy of ingratiation. 'I'm sorry,' he said. 'My . . . my boss looked up my notes, those I made after my first visit, she's the co-ordinator of my branch, and she . . . well, in the light of a very serious complaint — '

'Complaint?

' — an anonymous complaint, yes, she requested more information, shall we say.'

'What complaint?'

'Well, I don't need to tell you that in an English context, your arrangement is unusual. Not unheard of, but unusual. But that wouldn't be enough to concern us if we didn't have information that — '

'Information?'

' — yes, that the children might be at risk.'

'This is from?'

'I actually can't say. It was from an undisclosed source.'

'Undisclosed? You listen to anonymous complaints?'

'Actually, we have to. Genuine callers often need to remain anonymous for their own protection. Many times we have relied upon — '

'Mrs Acherson. It's her, isn't it. Aisha's teacher. I knew it.' Sam did not bother to conceal his contempt.

'I won't be drawn on names.'

'Well, with Mrs Acherson, you must bear in mind that she has only been in charge of her school for forty-eight years, so to some extent she is still finding her feet.' Sam could contain his anger no longer. 'Mr Partridge, I hope you are not threatening my family because of the rantings of a pea-brain?'

201

The man held up his hand. 'I shouldn't do this but . . . no, it wasn't Mrs Acherson. We had an anonymous report, from a very concerned party, that the children are . . . perhaps being incorporated into . . . your . . . shall we say . . . adult activities.'

Sam's face flushed red. 'How dare you. Really, how dare you.'

'The matter has also been passed on to the police. You may receive a call from them as well. So you see, it's very important that you help me establish a few things about how you run your private life.'

'Who would make such a call?'

'I suppose a concerned member of the public. Someone who knows you.' Partridge turned to Tracy and found her trying to calm herself. She was visibly shaking.

'No. No, no. Stop. I don't know who you've been talking to, but that is not *information* you've received. Information implies truth. What you have heard is hearsay, shocking rumour, based on jealousy, envy, bias, probably racism.'

'Still, we had a report. And it worsens matters if you refuse to discuss your private life.'

Sam had had enough. 'Did you ever think that it might be because it's *private*? He shook his head. 'You people are extraordinary. Do you know how angry I am right now? I don't even know how anyone could make such a depraved call! The suggestion is evil. Evil!'

'I'm just doing my job,' Partridge offered lamely.

Tracy looked worried. Loss of temper didn't seem a good strategy right now. 'Sam — '

Sam stared at the man. A decisive point had been reached. 'I think you should go now. Be gone.' He batted his hand. 'Hop it.'

'Just tell him,' Tracy urged her husband. 'Just tell him.' *Tell him, and then he won't exist. He'll disappear.* She turned to the man. 'It couldn't be more innocent, believe me. It's not what it seems.'

'Tracy!' Sam was quick to stem any leakage of critical facts. 'He has no right.'

'If you . . . if you knew the whole story — '

'Tracy, no!'

She faced her red-faced husband. 'What?'

He stared back at her, willing her to silence. 'Not this way.'

From this point, Partridge knew that he was wasting his time. 'I see. So the children are fine because you say so?' The rhetorical question left no doubt in anyone's mind that the situation had degenerated to the point of hostility. Sam had placed the official in an impossible position, and for this there might be repercussions.

Sam calmed himself. 'Sir.' He softened his tone, held out his hand. When you grew up in a buzzing Persian market you retained the instinct for diplomacy. 'You are speaking to an immigrant. Please. We have an exaggerated respect for certain rights. Many of us have lived without some of them, and now we're quite addicted to them. Therefore, I am not asking you for anything. Not a thing. Except privacy, and the rule of law you expect in a civilised country.'

'I think I had better go now.' Yes, the man needed to go back to his office now, as quickly as he could, reinstate himself as a reasonable man again, a likeable sort, wash himself clean of this episode. Only a government job paid you — and badly — to go up to a total stranger and accuse him of incest.

Sam sighed. 'Is it simply too much to ask to be left alone?'

Partridge sighed. 'You have really missed the point. We just need to satisfy ourselves that your children are safe and well. What is wrong with that?'

'But you've already spoken to the teachers, you said. Right? So you already know that they are.'

'Well, actually, there were one or two troubling discoveries. They *slightly* concerned me.'

'What discoveries?'

'Did you know that Aisha, for instance, has had to be disciplined several times this year for truancy.'

'That? And you're worried about that?'

'Aren't you?'

'She sneaks away to a friends place to play CDs, for God's sake! I know all about it.'

'Is she an unhappy girl?'

'It is time for you to go.'

'She's also been borrowing money off other girls. Did you know that?'

This detail took Sam by surprise. 'The world functions on credit, Mr Partridge.'

'Does she not get pocket money though?'

'None of the women in this house can keep to a budget.' But Sam was on the back foot for the first time.

'And then Ali's teacher says he has wet his pants on a couple of occasions recently.'

'This is ridiculous. This is like the work of secret police. Is urination now a cause for a fascist invasion of my house?'

Tracy had to intervene again, lay her hand on Sam's forearm.

Partridge took a deep, steadying breath. He was almost done. 'Not on it's own, no, but then Haman's teacher says that he won't settle, noticed slight behaviour problems, and has been violent to one of his classmates, actually stealing a — '

'Yes, a 10-pence mathematics protractor from him! In revenge for the earlier theft of a set of valuable collectors cards from his desk. It's a dog-eat-dog world, Mr Partridge.'

'So on their own they are nothing, but they have a cumulative impact and when I reported these to my superiors, well, let's just say they have begun to grow slightly concerned. And that is why I have to request your permission to allow us to take a further precautionary step. Don't be alarmed by this — ' he glanced at Tracy, a cooler head, petitioning her already for support — 'but we would like to quickly interview your children on some occasion that would be suitable, just ask them a few questions, just to satisfy my department's concerns. And if that goes well then we can leave you completely in peace ever after.' He smiled. 'So could we have your permission to do that, do you think?'

'To question my children?' Sam was shaking, on the point of eruption.

Partridge had been obliged to voice this request. To bring this news to this family had been his task. But he did not need to listen to the response.

'And ask them what exactly? If they have been interfered with recently? So you want me to allow you to get each of my children in a room, like fascist police, and traumatise them with sexual questions? You want to ask if I've been paying visits to their bedrooms? Is that it? Yes?' Sam was shouting.

'At this stage I just need to know your answer, Mr Sahar.'

'*You need to know my answer to that*? Are you stupid? Are you an idiot? You should get out of this house. This is what you should do!'

'Fine.' Partridge shot a frustrated look at Tracy. But she had turned away from him now. 'I'll take that as your answer.'

'You do that.'

'Well, thank you for the tea.'

'You have no respect! If you don't leave this house this instant I cannot be responsible for my actions.'

'Oh, I'm leaving.' Partridge reached for his case, snapped shut the twin locks. 'I'm definitely leaving. So thanks very much.' He had one further thing to add. 'You know, these are not easy things to ask.'

'Just get out.'

'Thanks very much.'

'Be gone!'

Tracy saw him to the door. Outside on the step, Partridge took deep breaths and turned to her with a parting request. The man was truly churned up by the meeting. He was not as hard as his tasks. 'Try to talk to him.'

Tracy did not appreciate this insider's tone, which implied they were co-conspirators. 'No. I won't. He's right.'

'It won't look very good if he won't let anybody talk to the children. Tell me you'll at least discuss it with him. For the children's sake.'

She eventually shrugged, mostly to just get rid of him. But then, before she could avoid it, he surprised her. He reached out and took her hand. 'Good. That's great,' he said. He squeezed it. She hardly believed this was happening. 'Thanks.' He gave an overfamiliar smile. 'I'd really like to help you. But with his attitude I can't.'

Her hand was then released. He retreated quickly down the path. Perhaps it was only a way to emphasise a request, but Tracy understood that in the midst of chaos the official had just made a pass at her.

Shutting the door, Sam called from the lounge. 'Is he gone? Good. I was going to kill him. Now come here and help me find Mecca.'

To distract himself Sam opened the device's instruction manual. He quickly observed that he had to stand in the back garden a dozen paces away from the house for satellite contact to be established. The LCD display quickly told him: 'WAITING FOR SIGNAL'. As he aimed the hand-piece at the sky it seemed barely possible that Saaman Sahar would receive his curious information from far above the clouds.

With his thumb he keyed in the five-lettered city. The tiny screen went blank. Was the crazy thing working? He wondered if it had packed up, but the power light was still on so perhaps it was redirecting its energies to other tasks as the human body did: and then a small arrow appeared, shimmering, fish-like, a compass holding its direction whichever way he turned. It pointed steadily over the roof tops. By a small mental extension, over land and sea, he imagined Mecca.

What an amazing world, he thought. Information streamed across space, inhabiting the air we breathe, and not only in wave form, but as X-rays, laser beams, binary signals, electrostatic pulses, all of it bombarding us. He remembered visits to the dentist as a child, the man popping on a lead apron and stepping into a side room before he would even think about taking a single X-ray. But today these rays were ungoverned. Carrying libraries of mostly banal data, they saturated the air, passing invisibly through buildings, people, even the unborn foetus, then entered the earth, reached the dead, infiltrating their silent bones with some fool's email! Even in his own garden, holding this instrument in hand, he stood in a blizzard of 1s and 0s. But without a battery, what? It all ceased to work, the whole kaleidoscope came crashing down. And what were we left with? A few rusty principles. Half a dozen truly animating truths. When you dropped a stone it fell; when you put metal into the flame it expanded; when you slid into a bath you displaced your volume; and now, unless this device was sorely mistaken, he was being told that Mecca lay roughly to the south-south-east, between the garden shed and the new plum tree he'd planted the year before. But could he trust it?

He didn't trust it. The soul required that the earth remain comprehensible and Sam wanted simpler truths. There was one thing he knew for sure: nobody would harm his children. False information could flood the galaxy, but his children were certain of protection.

He had worked himself up. His mind was racing. Who was investigating these issues? Who were the watchdogs? No money in it, therefore we are on our own. He should toss out his mobile phone, he barely used it anyway. A world that worshipped convenience was heading for a fall. He switched off the GPS and went back inside with his news.

'It works, but only outside. I hate these things. Still I think I've got it.' He held up the device. Inside, it struggled to commune with its satellite, the arrow flickering, a dying force. His point had been proved.

Tracy was pulling on her coat. 'Good. That's great.'

'Where are you going?'

'Aren't you worried?' Tracy's face showed her anger at his ability to sideline the recent exchange.

'Of course I am. But what can I do? What can I do? I'll call Ridley, let him look into it. And now, enough.'

'Be back soon.' Tracy headed for the door.

'Don't worry. We're going to be fine.'

She stopped at the door. 'I shouldn't have let him go upstairs.'

'Where are you going?'

'Back in an hour,' she called, and closed the door.

Tracy burst upon the play-group. She demanded to speak to her mother, rapping on the wired glass of the classroom.

In the corridor, Monica faced Tracy. Her daughter was clearly upset, the lids of her eyes already swollen and red. 'Tracy? Has something happened?'

'Tell me it wasn't you. Tell me it wasn't you who phoned.'

'Phoned?'

'The Social Services. Just tell me. Was it you?'

'Who phoned the Social Services? Tracy? What's this all about?'

'It *was* you, wasn't it. You and Dad, like you said you would.'

'Settle down. Did what? What are you — ?'

'It's *so* like you and him. To go round the back way. Just like you used to do to me at school. Phone the teacher and tell them things about me. Most kids had to worry about the bloody teacher telling their parents something about *them*, but fuck . . . I had to worry about my parents grassing to the teacher!'

Monica became annoyed. 'Now calm down. And lower your voice!'

'A Social Services guy came round this morning. And it looks like there's gonna be some kind of trouble. They're concerned about the children. They're gonna investigate. And you call yourself a teacher? Ha! You make me sick actually. Oh, and don't bother contacting me again, all right?'

'Tracy! nobody phoned anyone, so calm down.'

'Well who else would have done it?'

'Trace —'

But Monica couldn't stop Tracy from walking away.

Behind her a row of four-year-old faces had crept up to the glass. Monica spun to see them. 'Get down from there!' she shouted, re-entering the room.

Tracy took a cab home. From the empty garage she deduced that

207

Sam's parents had stayed on at the mosque for the noon prayer. She found Sam in his upstairs office, pointing his new gadget this way and that. She arrived at his shoulder. 'Did you work it out?'

'Yeah,' he said. 'Works fine up here.'

'So which way is it?'

He pointed. 'That way. Right over there.'

She followed the line of his arm and shifted until she faced that direction. 'So I'm doing it now? I'm facing the right way?'

He adjusted her shoulders a couple of degrees. 'Pretty good. If we can trust technology then that is about exactly right.' She seemed instantly transfixed, focused on the direction. 'Are you all right?'

'Mmm,' she said.

'Then let me go and get the Hoover. This place needs a clean.'

When he returned a few minutes later she was still facing towards Mecca. 'So where did you go?'

She turned to look at her husband, a Hoover-hose snaked around his neck. 'What?'

'We can't tell my parents. They'll only worry.' He searched the vacuum cleaner for an orifice for the hose.

'The other end,' she told him. He found the hole. 'I've just been to see my mother. I've got something terrible to tell you. I think . . . I've got a feeling it was my parents. Who phoned the Social Services.'

He stared at her. He refused to believe it.

'Remember how they said they'd phone the cops?' she said. 'When we told them we were going to get married?'

'Yes, but they were just angry. That means nothing. Tracy! That's a terrible thing to accuse them of.'

Not expecting this reaction, Tracy found herself suddenly on the back foot. 'They . . . threatened to do it. And also, I thought, why now? Why are the authorities worried suddenly now? It must be to do with me.'

'Stop it. Tracy, I don't believe you accused your parents. How could you suspect such a thing of your own parents?'

She became silent.

'I will phone your mother and apologise. Hopefully they'll forgive you. My God, how did she take it?'

Tracy shrugged. 'Not well.'

'I am not surprised.'

Tracy looked at him then as if realising a huge mistake. 'You don't think it was them?'

'Of course not.' He hugged her. She buried her face in his shoulder. He cradled her head with his hand. 'We shouldn't've got married,' she said.

'Definitely a mistake,' he softly replied.

The car containing their extended family pulled into the drive. He switched on the Hoover, and began to vacuum for the first time in his life.

By the end of the day, the makeshift mosque in Sam's office had worked out perfectly. Fatima and Mostafa were able to retire into the room whose walls Sam had stripped of year-planners, charts and calendars.

Largely undisturbed, they were able to conduct their devotions in peace, hands held up like books in front of their faces, bowing twice then kneeling to rest their foreheads on the desert stones they'd carried all the way in their leather cases, reciting aloud the Arabic principles, palms flattening on the carpet in praise.

Only once or twice were they bothered, and then only by their grandchildren, who, quizzical and innocent, crept into the room like tiny *jinin* to watch the ancient ritual in progress, eyes wide in fascination, ears taking in a new spiritual language but diluting it at once to a game, once or twice venturing close enough to faintly tickle the soles of their praying grandparents' bare feet, for which they received stinging looks of rebuke.

Tracy pulled them out of the room. In a strong whisper she scolded them, sent them downstairs, shooed them away like sheep. She stopped for a second to make sure the door was firmly shut, testing the knob, twisting it but pushing it open. The slightly opened door permitted her a view of the antique ritual.

Inside, in soft unison, the elderly couple were bent forward on their knees, heads almost touching the ground, showing a suppleness that greatly belied their age, their fluted prayers combining to produce a low hum. She pictured her own grandmother, struggling to kneel at church in her last years: the old dear, buried now in East Wickham with an empty plastic vase above her, would never have been able to get up from such a position. And yet, by their daily practice, Sam's parents had remained as nimble as teenagers.

As Arabic phrases rose from the floor, Tracy felt as she always did in front of people at prayer: mystified. Unable to sense an iota of what presumably enthralled them — the ecstasy, the communion, the peace — she was left admiring their discipline, and was drawn only by the lush ambience of the ritual, the differentness of the activity. If religion was finally the point of life, if devotion was the key, if surrender to a gentle God was the reason for existence, then her life was a huge waste of time.

She had spoken about this to Sam, who liked the topic enormously. He had tried to cheer her up, quoting the great nineteenth-century Jew, the Baar Shem Tov. 'He was very interesting on this point: a real religious experience can only really come after the age of thirty-seven, the baptising age of the spirit. Before that, forget it. Trying to connect with the soul is a waste of time, you don't have the spiritual equipment. Just wait a few years,' he'd told her. She had nodded, memorising the name, Baar Shem Tov. Yes, maybe she just needed to be older. She wondered how old Cat Stevens had been at Malibu, while he was tossed in the surf, contemplating death. She must watch his video again. She didn't want to disturb Sam's parents or push her luck any further and so she shut the door respectfully and excluded herself from the world of religious activity.

On her way downstairs she pledged to win over her in-laws somehow but right now the children needed controlling and she sent them into the TV room with a Disney video.

The house became still. But even with the mystic incantations far out of earshot, a house containing people at prayer was not a normal house. The mere knowledge that it was taking place made the adults creep about speaking as though in a church or a mosque.

Sam called Tracy over to the phone.

'Who is it?' she asked.

'Your mother. We've just been talking. We both agree that you're mad but what can we do? Talk to her. Make up.'

'No, no, I'm not talking to her.'

'Yes you are. Respect your mother.'

Tracy took the receiver as Sam watched. For a long time she contemplated hanging up. She heard her mother calling 'Tracy?' on the other end. She screwed up her face as if she'd eaten something bitter, then put her ear to the receiver.

Sam smiled as he listened to Tracy's piecemeal apology. When she put down the phone she left him standing there.

He called after her, hoping to kiss the back of her freckled hand, to cup and to covet and to kiss her delicious face, but his only consolation was the sight of her butterfly hand flitting up the balustrade in six bursts of flight as she ascended the stairs.

It became clear that Sam's parents favoured, in descending order, the children, Firouzeh, Sam, Yvette — whom suffering had elevated — and lastly, at a binocular distance, Tracy. They had not so much as risked a glance in her direction.

Determined to force upon them a word, a look, a measly exchange, Tracy posted herself in tight doorways, even at the foot of the stairs or outside the bathroom door, hoping that by some fleeting contact they would have no choice but to acknowledge her. Still they pushed past her at every turn as if she didn't exist. In a cool swish of robes, heads lowered, spines bent, mother preceding father in a demonstration of the art of the rebuff, they glided up the stairs or slipped out of a room. Their only comment to her came in the form of the resounding slam of their bedroom door.

Taking on the duty of serving at the breakfast table earned Tracy no more attention than her increasingly modest attire. Her demonstrations of love for the children were as ignored as her exaggerated displays of respect for Sam. 'What have I done wrong?' she asked him.

'Be patient. Be respectful. Be generous. Give it time.' He suggested she challenge his father to a game of backgammon. The old man had no greater passion and if she could beat him he would respect her forever. Though victory was unlikely — he was a veteran of many thousand campaigns — the act of putting up a good fight would force him to re-evaluate her. 'He is the key to winning over my parents, the Trojan horse by which you might sneak into the walled city.'

Tracy shook her head. 'I've hardly ever played. I'm terrible.'

This didn't matter, Sam said. His father would realise this at once, her efforts would be transparent to him. As long as she tried hard he would approve of her. 'The game is some kind of barometer for him. A distillation of life. Don't ask me, but until you play him you are invisible.'

That afternoon she set up her trap on a low table in the lounge and waited. After an hour Fatima and then Mostafa, as usual travelling in his wife's slipstream, drifted through the room. He stopped as expected, unable to resist an inspection of the solitary game, but his face instantly

211

compressed in agony. Not only had Tracy set up the board incorrectly, an offence to his soul, but she was adding to her own ignominy by advancing the pieces after every shake in a zigzag fashion up the board, lifting them off at the end like runners in a hundred-yard dash. Seeing this he barely noted that she was rolling all four dice plus both gambling cubes at every throw. He withdrew in disgust at what he could only take as another western brutalisation of a sacred tradition.

'How did it go?' Sam asked, when they were alone in the big bed, her head on his naked chest.

'Terrible. He just looked, but then walked on.'

'He didn't join you?'

Tracy shook her head.

Sam was baffled. 'I don't understand that at all. We'll have to find another way. But now, let's forget about them. They don't rule this house quite yet.'

He enfolded her in his arms and they began to kiss until she let slip with a happy but loud moan.

'Ssshh,' he said, lifting his finger to his lips then pointing at the wall which separated them from his insomniac parents. 'Very quiet. Very quiet indeed.'

On another front, Firouzeh began to feel pressure from Fatima. 'Assert yourself,' the older woman secretly instructed in Farsi.

'You don't understand. This is not a competition, Mother.'

'Are you crazy? A harem is nothing but a competition.'

In line with this, Firouzeh found seductive night garments laid out on the end of her bed which, when returned to Fatima, with the apology that they were not her sort of thing, caused the elder woman to release a torrent of complaints about the comparative harlotry of the other two wives. Something had to be done to limit their competing allure, Fatima complained.

A campaign of feminine sabotage began.

Over ensuing days Tracy and Yvette noticed that items of their make-up disappeared. 'I left it right here, under the mirror! I know it! What is she up to?'

Next, Tracy found that all her new silk underwear had vanished from her drawers. Only the tattered ones had been spared in the *putsch*. But before Tracy could raise the matter, Yvette revealed that all her French perfumes had been ruined. Diluted with water, the lids left off, the remaining scent had been left to waft away. When personal items of clothing belonging to both women had to be lifted out of the mud under the washing line, Tracy decided to talk to Sam.

In emergency session, Sam told his wives to be patient. His parents could not stay forever. And it was not possible to change them: time had hardened their attitudes to the density of lead. The best strategy was to ignore these divisive manoeuvres. Out of sheer frustration they might abandon them.

But at dinner, he showed that his own nerves were not exactly intact. He banged his glass on the table. 'English, please! Tonight we will speak in English!'

He knew that the imposition of this foreign language would restrict his mother to a half dozen pleasantries, and his father to even fewer. 'It is unfair to talk in Farsi and it stops now,' he said in Farsi. 'If anyone wants to talk to me in future you know what language to use.'

He grumpily picked up his knife and fork and began to eat his first meal as a defiant monoglot.

'English?' his mother retorted, in her native tongue. 'The language of thieves, homosexuals, bomb-makers and whores.'

Sam's mother had sent Firouzeh a Muslim marriage manual shortly after her emigration but it had never been opened. Tracy might read it now, Firouzeh suggested. It might contain a few tips that might impress Mostafa and Fatima.

Tracy had foreseen difficulties ever since Sam had translated and read aloud to her several of the most recent letters from his parents. His first marriage — ran their sharp correspondence — was noble, dutiful, commendable, even pious; the second could be narrowly tolerated owing to the tragic circumstances; but nothing could excuse the third, which was an absurdity.

Not only was she British — they wrote in a scrawl rendered illegible with passion — and with no knowledge whatsoever of their ways, but she was a child. Even Sam's much younger brother, Sassan, courted women older than she. Also, and as the Blessed Prophet taught — warning enough! — where it was impossible to deal justly between co-wives, then marriage should be limited to only one wife. This was unequivocal. How had Sam misread this? If, as Sam openly admitted, he felt 'quite different about this one', then wasn't that proof of favouritism? Therefore, how could he deal justly with each woman, when he openly favoured one?

213

He was in deep water, out of his skin, they wrote, as only a parent could observe, and they would travel all the way from Tehran to his door with one intention: to bring him back to his senses and to quash this last mistake.

But as avidly as they pursued their first son around his huge house, attempting to engage him in this vast and overripe conversation and force his surrender, he always managed to escape, slipping the noose and leading them into the *cul de sac* of an empty room, then leaving them to ponder how he could have exited it, looking to the bookcase which perhaps concealed a secret door, then turning to discover, standing right where they should have found their son, this upstart girl! The impudence of it! The impropriety! On each occasion they swiftly lowered their heads and fled the room, seeking another part of the house where this interloper in their son's affairs would surely not have the audacity to follow.

Time after time, the durability of their bedroom door was tested.

Retiring to her own room, foiled for the hundredth time, Tracy opened her hand-me-down *Easy-to-Follow Muslim Marriage Guide*.

She fell into a synopsis of the marriages of Mohammed.

The Blessed Prophet is born c. 570 in Mecca. At the age of twenty-five he marries his employer, the caravan owner Khadija bint Khuwaylid, a wealthy and intelligent widow some fifteen years his senior. Despite this age difference they are a happy match.

When he turns forty, he receives a vision and begins to preach, exhorting people to repentance, prayer and belief in the one God, Allah.

In 619, after 24 years of marriage, Khadija dies. After her death, and for practical and political reasons, he takes two new wives. The first is a fifty-five-year-old widow who assumes responsibility for his four motherless daughters. The second is the six-year-old virgin, A'isha, a daughter of his best friend. By this union, he forges important links between three tribes. This second marriage, not consummated until the girl is of age, becomes ever more loving as the years pass. As she herself records: 'After I ate one part of the meat on a bone, I used to hand it to the Prophet, who would bite the morsel from the place where I had bitten. Similarly, when I offered him something to drink after drinking a part, he would drink from the place I had put my lips.'

To A'isha he grants religious duties, permitting her to speak for him in his absence. To both wives he also permits relaxed freedoms radical by the customs of the day.

Mohammed next marries an argumentative widow, whose fiery nature has scared away many suitors. Trust builds between them. To her the Prophet will eventually leave his text of the Holy Quran for safekeeping.

His fifth wife is a pious widow whose husband was martyred. Poverty-stricken and alone, he is obliged by her plight to marry her, naming her Umm al-Masakin, the Mother of the Poor, for her generosity to the destitute. She dies only a few months later.

Umm Salama is the pregnant widow of his cousin. Reluctant to marry Mohammed because of the profound love she retains for her lost husband, she is persuaded by what she learns of the Prophet's life. At his deathbed, she prays that she and her entire family may be taken by Allah instead, so long as The Prophet is spared.

His adopted son, Zayd, then divorces a girl brought up under the Prophet's own supervision. The Prophet marries her to resolve a delicate situation.

The Muslims are attacked by the Mustaliq tribe but are defeated. The Prophet's seventh wife is among the booty.

The Prophet is contacted by the Negus of Abyssinia, who is distressed by the plight of a thirty-six-year-old widow, the niece of his son-in-law. A wedding is performed by proxy.

It is unclear if he marries the Jewess Raihana or merely maintains her as a maidservant. It is certain that she accepts Allah and becomes a Muslim.

When a Jewish soldier is killed in reprisal for burying alive a Muslim man, his beautiful widow is taken into Mohammed's household as a maid. The woman, however, requests 'a more honourable fate'.

The Prophet marries a last time: to an elderly widow, the sister of his uncle's wife. The marriage is to mitigate her sufferings and see her well-placed.

In 622 Mohammed is forced to flee to Medina with his many wives to escape assassination.

In 630, he conquers Mecca and, by then sixty, receives a revelation from Allah limiting the maximum number of wives to four. As his ten surviving wives have all been declared 'Mothers of Believers', however, he does not set them aside.

He dies in Medina in 632 at the age of 62.

16

Common Law

In the corner of the office behind his chair a dismantled fly-fishing rod and triangular net rested. Three stuffed fish on mahogany discs dotted the walls. The barrister's family had manorial rights over the Preseli Hills, which were a source of trout streams and also of the stones used at Stonehenge. Sam had known him since Oxford, and Ridley was his restaurant's first and most loyal customer.

'Mushroom them,' he said. 'That's what we've got to do. Mushroom the buggers.'

Nobody in Ridley's office, and there were five, needed this horticultural term explained. To appease the social agency they need only to be kept in the dark and then fed on shit. 'I have received a letter. The Social Services wish to speak to you, Sam, and the children's mother, Firouzeh, in person. Both are requested to visit their Fulham offices next Monday to discuss the nature of their domestic arrangement.' Ridley fired the piece of paper onto his desk with dismissive contempt. 'This is no big deal. I think we can go along with this. Of course, I'll be there as well.' He made no pretence at disguising his excitement, relishing his role as rescuer, magician, miracle worker, legal leviathan. His walls were bedecked with certificates, his desk with telephones, briefs folded lengthways were tied with red ribbons; a great number of case-books were opened face down upon each other forming tall pagodas. Between these legal pillars he alternately stretched back with a squeak of springs in his big executive chair and, upon the dispatch of a cogent point, lunged forward to plant his elbows on the leather inlaid desk in an A-frame of hairy forearms. He was a class act.

He was also a lawyer's lawyer, a bright star in whose eyes scintillated the love of the chase and the general *tally-ho* of jurisprudence. It was said that with an incisive flash of wit he could reduce to nothing the laboriously compiled case of the prosecution, and several times in his career, while representing clients thought undefendable, he had forced judges to do a *volte face* and upbraid the prosecution for their temerity in considering that there had ever been a case to be heard against Ridley's client. Law was as susceptible to charm as any other area of life, and for Mr A. Ridley QC, winning had its own values, its own moral imperatives. He had no problem, therefore, in securing, with an ornate valediction on the sanctity of justice, the freedom of numerous villains or in fact throwing many an innocent person into the muscled embrace of criminals. Like the real world, the courts marched to a strong Darwinian drum. Better sharp teeth than a good heart.

His reputation had long since been assured. In recent years he had mellowed alarmingly, keeping to old clients the way an old trout hugs the gentler river banks, humouring high rollers, artists with deep pockets, glamour pusses, and liberating them of their cash with the finesse of a pickpocket. 'Just to be on the safe side,' he added.

'There is nothing to discuss,' Sam replied, sitting between his wives. In his mind, the entire inquiry was a moral outrage. 'We shouldn't dignify this by agreeing to it.'

Tracy wanted to hear Ridley's thoughts. 'Please. Go on.'

'Well, we know a couple of things. They had an anonymous report, then followed it up with a house inspection and visits to the children's teachers. As an unfortunate result, I think we can now conclude that they are thinking orgy, orgy and rubber sheets and God knows what else, even that the children are involved somehow as well. These images are rampant.'

'Ha!' said Sam, tersely. 'Here's what I want you to do. Throw that letter away in the rubbish and say we're taking the matter to our MP. This is a clear case of harassment. We'll take it to the Race Relations Board.'

Ridley was already shaking his head sagely. Suggesting to him a defence on the grounds of racism and institutional bias was akin to asking a Anglican minister the whereabouts of a decent prostitute: they'd know exactly where to find one but they were professionally obliged to advise against it. 'That will only incense them. No, I recommend you do as they

217

say. Meet with them. I think you'll have to trust me on this, Sam.'

Sam sighed. Ridley was an authoritative presence, hard to contravene.

'And remember how I got you off the last thing.' Ridley's evocation of the last time he had represented them had the Sahars turning and looking at each other. 'Remember that.'

The sudden mention of this history clearly alarmed the family. Ridley really knew how to press the emotional buttons. The women fixed on their frozen husband, reaching out to touch the hands folded tightly in his lap. Tracy put an equally concerned hand on Yvette's shoulder, drawing a weary shake of the French woman's head.

'And that was *close*, if you remember. But I got you through it.' Sam had to nod at the memory: It couldn't have been closer. 'So you might just have to go with me on this as well. Now listen, and you need to know this going in. You'll be up against a group of desperately well-intentioned civil servants, so be very afraid. There'll be a psychologist there, I expect. This person will press you to allow them to interview your kids. These people will all be desperate to be the good guys. And if the whole liberal humanist mind-trap doesn't scare you shitless, then realise that half of the women and *all* of the men are going to be very very deeply conflicted about this. And not because they're revolted by their preconceived ideas of your life together, no, but probably because they'll be *jealous*. They'll be envious! And therein lies the problem. Because your average politically correct liberal humanist can't afford to admit to himself, or to herself, that they're jealous. So they'll have to do what they do with all their most interesting instincts, repress them. And this is where they become dangerous. You know what movies the film censor bans?' The Sahars stared at him, in no mood for rhetoric. He was onto the movies now? 'You know which ones? The ones that give him an erection. That's his sexual barometer. Excuse me ladies, but it's true. They ones that stir his true nature. They take out their own moral discomfort on the object of greatest interest. They'll talk about the children, the children, the poor children, but they'll secretly be thinking that four adults must not be permitted to have this much fun.'

'But we're not having that much fun!' Sam protested. 'Are we?' The women shook their heads. 'Especially not now. Come to the house. My parents are there. It's like a morgue.'

'Nonsense, I'm jealous myself. Simple as that.' Ridley seemed not to have heard him. 'Three gorgeous women, and so forth. No one will

218

believe for a second that you're having a bad time. Forget it. No, the panel will deal with you in the same way they'll have to deal with their own fantasies. They'll repress them. And consequently they'll try to repress you. They'll have no choice. That's the trouble with liberals.'

The following Monday, in the foyer of the government building, the lawyer's lips pressed as close as a lover's to Sam's ear to whisper his final entreaty. 'You know what to say. And keep it brief. Short answers, for God's sake, short answers, Sam.' Sam nodded. His calcified heart dropped with a clunk. 'I know, I know', he repeated as he and Firouzeh followed his counsel into the lift, murmuring to himself, 'I know,' exhausted by a night of panicked self-tutelage. Expecting to face an imposing panel, he was relieved to find in the room a single, large mahogany table around which they would sit, facing each other. The woman he presumed to be in charge waited at the head. Sam and Firouzeh were led to chairs. As they sat, Firouzeh, at his right, squeezed his arm. He nodded at her and then faced his panel. Seven people eventually took up seats opposite, and apart from 'Partridge in a Queer Tree', as he had been dubbed by the Sahar household, all were unknowns. Only then did Sam gain a full impression of the forces arrayed against them: except for one black face, surely a token, he and his wife were the only foreigners.

The official faces were shrewd, focused, adversarial. How odd it was that the matter to weigh so heavily upon them today should be his own bumbling romantic history. Sam sighed. The walls of our houses were increasingly made of glass. Still, in the face of great provocation, he would show these meddlers true English manners. In the face of their cavalry charge he would give them a lesson in British dignity, pride and the benefit of holding one's fire.

The springy, red-headed woman at the head of the table called the meeting to order. Half a dozen manila folders were opened in near-unison. What have they got on me? Sam worried. It looked like an entire dossier! He longed to know what he was filed under. 'polygamist' or perhaps 'sex fiend'. How far they were from the truth.

With a courteous welcome, the redhead outlined the reason for today's meeting. It was a serious and delicate case, the woman began in a cool, mannish voice. Due consideration would be given to all parties, the children's welfare to be placed before all others, and she requested everyone's full co-operation. *They mean me,* Sam thought. *Well, I'm here, am I not?* After a swift round of introductions, in which Sam learnt that three of the panellists were psychologists, the Social Services spokeswoman was invited to make the first representation.

The only black woman in the room identified herself. She would make the department's case. This heftily forearmed Trinidadian wore a black dress enlivened only by a huge silver brooch which strongly resembled the George Cross. A wolf in sheep's clothing, was Sam's assessment. Her tone, in its deceptive warmth, set off warning bells. *Minorities to pull the trigger as usual. Ridley was right.* This might be a liberal minefield after all. Firouzeh, beside him, gripped and regripped white-knuckled hands in her lap. The safety of her children was at stake.

Outside in the lobby she had said, 'When I came to this country, who would have imagined we would get into this kind of trouble?'

'It's me,' Sam said. 'My fault. Too many marriages.'

Sam received the first question. He sat forward in his seat, straightening his spine, his moment of truth upon him. His cuffs rested evenly on the table's edge. Short answers, short answers, he told himself; this, and fire above their heads.

But with her initial question, an awful loquacity took hold of him. Justifications and evasive explanations flowed out of him in a torrent. He was overprepared. Worry had made him too eager. A certain anxiety was to be expected, his family life was on the line, but as Ridley's hand rose to his face to tweak the bridge of his nose, indicating that he was worried already, Sam might have seen that he was talking too much.

The question had simply been whether Sam was the children's legal father.

His last statement before he finally ground to a halt, expressions of surprise playing on the faces of the panel, was 'So you see, I am and I am not'. He looked to his lawyer and his wife for a reaction. Both faces showed concern.

'Thank you,' the lead official replied. 'Now then, we have quite a few questions but not so much time. So if we can keep our answers short.'

'These are complex questions.'

The Trinidadian smiled. 'Well, let's try at least.'

He was being told off. He shook his head in dismay. If they wanted the truth then this wasn't going to be quick and easy, he wanted to say. His life was Byzantine in its complexity.

Further questions followed. The request for brevity was ignored. Sam could find no way of compressing his replies to anything under a dozen sentences. If this was the mark of a con man then so be it. What was his immigration status? If they wanted to know he would tell them. What did he do for a living? What religion was he? None of these were easy questions for a man like Saaman Sahar. And when did he first come to Britain? Under what circumstances did he meet Firouzeh, the children's mother? A huge subject! There was no perversity on his part in any of this. He wished only to animate a greater truth which, by its nature, was complex. If his explanations produced a haze that the public commonly associates with a liar, then it was hardly his fault.

Ridley had by now turned his head away. Firouzeh's fine-fingered hands were chalky fists.

Only the falling angle of her head informed Sam that he was going too far, and prompted him to change his line. To the next few questions he became almost curt. To him it felt unco-operative, but if this made people happier then so be it.

The Trinidadian wished to discover something of the children's home environment. 'And so how many wives *do* you have, Mr Sahar?

'How many?' Sam obfuscated.

'How many, yes. At last count.' His interrogator smiled at him.

'Just three.'

'Would you like to clarify that? How many are you married to under common law?'

'All three, I believe. This is not a breach of the law. As you should know.' He wouldn't say more. He was beginning to bridle against these questions.

'All three?'

'I am a Muslim by birth, which entitles me to four. I am exercising restraint.' Had Sam looked to his left just then he would have seen a dark Ridley shaking his head. He would have seen a deeply unamused Ridley.

'Then let me ask you. Have you ever slept with all three women at the same time?'

'I take it you mean have I had sex with all three at the same time?'

'Is that the usual arrangement?'

Gripping the arms of his chair, Sam looked to be resisting a tornado. 'No. I have never slept with all three.'

'No?'

221

'If you mean making love to. No. I would not. None of us are very interested in that and I'm not even sure I would be capable. I am a very ordinary individual.'

'Just . . . individually then? The sex?'

The sex? Yes, this is what excites them, Sam thought, the sex. With no proof that the children were harmed, it was all they had. But why should he humour these people? He should not even be here. The last time he checked it was still a free country. 'No. It's not like that at all.'

'Then how is it?'

'None of your business. None of your bloody business. As I said, we are not breaking the law. I would prefer not to talk about our marriages. You said yourself. You are concerned for the welfare of the children.' He was pushing back and forth in his chair now, his earlier poise lost. His hands, instruments for Persian emphasis, were coming into strong use, his right hand a chopper thumping on the table. 'Can we move on now, please?'

The panel was taken aback. They shared collegial glances. The Trinidadian turned a page in her notes. Sam hoped this marked a change of approach. She wished now to turn to another subject, to the question of Sam's character, which had a heavy significance on the children's welfare. All would benefit from knowing what kind of man he was.

'Four years ago you were tried, is this true, for manslaughter?'

Sam shook his head in disgust, even chortled. Here it comes at last, he thought. *I could have bet they would drag this up!*

'Please answer.'

Ridley intervened. 'My client, quite rightly, is within his rights to ask what this has got to do with the children?'

The facilitator who had been quiet for some time spoke up again. This was not a court case, she emphasised. There was no need for such caution. Nothing would go on record. It was merely a fact-finding exercise. In this context the panel required Sam's full co-operation. Not as a matter of courtesy, either, but as one of necessity.

Ridley turned back to Sam. 'Do you mind?'

'This is an outrage.'

'Let's just get this out of the way, shall we? It's easily dealt with.'

'I don't care. It's none of their business!'

'What do you want to know?' asked Ridley, red-faced, a hand going out to hold Sam's forearm.

The Trinidadian resumed. 'You were found not guilty — '

'*Can someone tell me why this is relevant?*' Sam charged, his right hand banging on the table a second time. There was a limit to how far he could be pushed.

'We are just interested to know how you came to be, within a relatively short space of time, married . . . ' *Say it*, Sam thought, 'under common law at least,' *Spit it out then* ' . . . to the wife, to the widow, of the man whom your car struck and killed?'

Sam rose to his feet. The panel watched him. Perhaps they expected Sam to continue his Rabelaisian oratory. 'Thank you,' he said widely, addressing everyone. 'Firouzeh. Shall we? I refuse to co-operate with this panel one minute longer. You have no honour and you have no power to ask me about this.'

Ridley was also on his feet. 'Sam, Sam,' he chanted. 'Perhaps . . . perhaps if you wait outside for a minute, while I speak with the panel alone.' He soothed the bureaucrats. 'I'm certain we can find a way through this. Mr Sahar, as you can see, is very agitated right now.'

'I took her under my wing. And let's leave it at that!' Sam added.

'Sam. Get some air. Firouzeh? Let's take a break.'

The facilitator nodded her consent.

'Thank you,' Ridley replied.

Sam took a step away from the table and faltered. One leg was dead. It had gone to sleep and he fell back against the table.

Thinking that he had perhaps collapsed from the emotional strain, several officials gasped. He held up his hand. *Pick it up, Sam,* he told himself, rattling his thigh, trying to get some circulation going. *Pick it up.* So much for a big exit.

And so with Firouzeh's help he set off for the door, an old goat supported by his strapping young wife. This was a hell of a time for a display of premature senility. He reached the doors and broke out of the room.

Sam's refusal to answer questions on this topic was not only rooted in contempt for the process. He was not lying when he said he was not sure he had it in him. The best he managed, before Ridley stepped back inside to map out a new way forward, was to say, 'It was a matter of the heart.' But this sounded pompous, even to Sam's ears.

Firouzeh volunteered to find coffee. Both their nerves needed steadying. As he sat in the public reception area, with scenic pictures of Australia taped to the walls — did they wish to politely suggest perhaps that people like him might be happier elsewhere? — he recalled the tragic events, the pulverising emotions that had marked that period.

Within himself, he tried to recall his best retelling of events, which had been to Tracy on the park bench. He had captured the essence of the tale that one time, earning a kiss. But he had been inspired then.

Sam waited, as Ridley and a panel of strangers fossicked through his life — *his* life — a cut-price biography, skating contemptuously over events which had tossed him into a hole so deep that it had seemed for a time that even the highest of the high-class shrinks he employed could not help him. He'd taken medication back then which would have sedated a wild boar. Yes, all the top quacks had my number back then, he reflected as he waited for coffee. *I was lucky to come out alive.* After all, he was a Class A client, a walking jackpot for a therapist. His troubles were not just some petty phobia, some flaky emotional problem. No, Saaman Sahar had decided he had murdered somebody: accidentally perhaps, but no relief came from thinking that. If there was a remedy, a way out for him, he believed it would take him years to find it. In actual fact he was to be free of the guilt and terrors within a year, thanks to Yvette.

What a story! The future severed, unable to see a way ahead, under spiritual house arrest, until a kind spirit in the form of the dead man's widow — his widow! it still seemed bizarre — answered his calls. An angel of mercy with the amnesty of forgiveness under her arm.

But how could he tell a panel of mercenaries this?

23 October, 7.38 p.m. Guillaume Berger, an accountant, crosses the road with his wife Yvette en route to a taxi rank; they are due to dine with family friends in Queensway at 8 p.m. The offending car, driven by a Mr Saaman Sahar, travels southwards, allegedly within the speed limit. Mr Berger steps into the road. Mr Sahar's car knocks Mr Berger down.
8.22 p.m. Victim is rushed to St Mary's Hospital, Paddington. Two initial roadside breathalyser tests find excessive levels of alcohol on the driver's breath, despite the driver's claim to have drunk only a single glass of wine.
8.28 p.m. In police custody the driver gives an inconsistent negative blood-alcohol result.

224

10.35 p.m. Victim pronounced dead from internal injuries. Deceased's wife needs to be sedated: declines autopsy; asks for cremation.

Midnight. Charges of manslaughter levelled against Mr Sahar, despite the inconsistencies.

26 October, 3 p.m. Funeral conducted. Driver and his wife attend. Widow's mother unable to attend funeral services due to ill health. Widow collapses. Has to be placed under the care of doctor.

16 February, 3.30 p.m. Judge Harold L. Cummings finds in favour of the defence, citing discrepancies in police evidence over actual level of blood alcohol in driver's bloodstream on night in question. Case dismissed. The driver is permitted to go free.

Dismissed? Free? Just like that? That was hardly right, Sam reminded himself as he looked around for Firouzeh. What about the nausea, he recalled, the insomnia, the weight loss, the ghost that waltzed through his rooms, not to mention the shrinks he had shelled out a fortune on, so many of their business cards in his wallet that it was impossible to close: were all these dismissed with the rap of the judge's gavel? Hardly. It was not that easy. No legal finding, no technical sleight of hand could assuage the guilt that came from knowing you had killed another human being, snuffed out a human soul. This was Sam's lot. And even before he thought about what he had done to that person's loved ones, especially his widow, it was overwhelming.

He remembered the therapy group he made himself join, the Guilt Group, as they dubbed themselves. Eight others sat about on hard chairs under fluorescent lights in an anonymous prefab in a Battersea school-room with large crayon pictures pinned to its walls: dinosaurs, lizards, words like 'caterpillar' on the board.

For four months these sessions had been his only respite. They had stirred his feelings around but hadn't actually cured him. If anything, they made the problem worse. Even his boredom with his emotions didn't translate into a cure. Still, this didn't stop him going and sitting beside Stevie in the checked shirt, a railway switchman whose thoughts had strayed one morning so that he forgot to throw a switch. He lived with the consequences: two passenger cars off the rails, pitched five metres down a siding, forty-four people wounded, twelve dead. Twelve! Sitting by Stevie, Sam felt at least a little better. In an instant Stevie had been marked, as Sam had been, but no one in the group could match him for numbers. He was the king and his speeches always drew the most respect. He sat there tweaking his baseball cap, trying to patch himself together, smiling at Mary-Anne, the attractive young mother of two whose youngest son died on his way to a birthday party when his skateboard went under a school bus. Sam felt like a lightweight next to Stevie.

Death was the sole unifier, and Sam fitted in with these human cot cases, all hit by a thunderbolt and desperate to recover their balance, but only half-believing they deserved to.

Like them, Sam shared his stories, hoping for the weight to lift, for lightness and good humour to return while doubting it ever could. In his life he had never felt such sadness. As Trudy put it, Trudy who had told her younger sister who'd been drinking to drive home alone without her after a party, tossing her the car keys then returning to a conversation with a handsome young man, which ended up in an amputation below the knee for the younger sister, it felt like being cursed.

But neither the group, nor the medications, nor all the self-help books, made the slightest difference. The only weight to budge an inch was from around his midriff. And as the pounds of contentment fell away from his body and his misery deepened, only the intervention of Firouzeh arrested his decline.

How idiotic he'd been! An expert on grief, a connoisseur, was living under his nose. Why hadn't he turned to her earlier? He knew the answer. How could he trouble this former widow with his own troubles? He wouldn't make her revisit her own past tragedies.

What changed things was Firouzeh's offer to become involved. The loss of Sam's brother had altered her profoundly but she didn't want to push the lessons she'd learnt. She had planned to wait for Sam to ask her for advice, but when the weeks passed, and as she watched his state worsen, she finally had no choice.

She began her master-class one morning as they took coffee in the garden. She really had only one point to impart but its explanation would take some time, and many hours of discussion. The point was this: happiness was not simply the remission of pain but an aspect of the pain itself.

He nodded, said he understood, but gave her such a good impression of being mystified that she felt encouraged to proceed.

Her own loss, she told him, speaking in their native Farsi, good for straight talk, had changed her forever. If he had been affected like her

226

then he could not go back to being who he had been before the accident. In a small but fundamental way he was a different person.

Sam had gulped. She continued.

If he pretended otherwise his thoughts would turn inward and become parasitic. Her fingers formed the shape of a claw and his eyes were drawn to them. His mistake, she said, would be to try to say that nothing serious had happened. He was a different man now.

'But I don't want to be any different.'

'Too late.' His waters had clouded but deepened forever. On a moment-to-moment basis he would find himself a heavier person, more earthbound, slower to laugh, less likely to act out of character. He would be more averse to risk, but the state was not without its advantages.

'Oh really? What's left?'

'You will be a better listener. You will listen with more understanding.'

Sam nodded. It was a bitter potion. He almost regretted the insights that had already penetrated him deeply.

'A better listener, more understanding of other people's pains, and therefore a better person all round.'

Small compensation, he thought. The fun from life removed and in its place sincerity. *Fuck sincerity*, was his first thought. 'I hear what you're saying,' he replied in English, the world's best tongue for clichés.

Sam listened as she went on, taking it all in, accepting the poisoned chalice of her ideas. He tried to look on the bright side. Truths, even hard truths, brought their own relief. Firouzeh encouraged him to embrace his melancholy. And he realised, at last, that he had no choice. He was already there.

Sam could remember vividly the fragility of the doorbell under his index finger on that first visit to see the dead man's widow. The wiring was bad. He had to wobble the button from side to side to make a contact.

He straightened his tie. His heart was pounding. Firouzeh had put him up to it.

Her face at the door was pale and the veins fanning out in a delta across one temple seemed to throb visibly. Her deep French accent and her croaky voice made him at first mistake her invitation to enter as a rebuff.

'Yes. I should go,' he agreed. 'But first, I just came to give you these.'

The hot-house peonies had also been selected by Firouzeh. Useless on his own, he was happy to be directed. And he would continue to be.

'*Non, non,* please, *non.* Come. Come in, please.'

Astonished, he went in. They sat at the window. He learnt that she had stayed on in London in a suspended act of mourning. He told her that he couldn't move on until he had at least talked to her. Via Ridley and police records he tracked her down.

They sat in the bay window of the crumbling flat in Southall, in the heart of little Bombay, *garam masala* literally on the breeze, and spoke with miraculous ease. She bore him no obvious grudge. This astounded and humbled him.

Her circumstances were desperate. She only had a temporary room courtesy of a public charity, but her money had run out. Her mother in Arles was bed-ridden, an intestinal disorder. Yvette Berger had only been married a year, he heard. No provisions had been made for her welfare.

'It was our second honeymoon,' she told Sam calmly.

His heart broke. Twisting with unrelieved anguish he listened as she told him that she didn't blame him. She knew the truth. Her husband had always been irrepressible, excitable, a puppy prone to explosions of energy. One such explosion had propelled him out into the road without looking, slipping her grasp: his own fault. She did not hold Sam responsible, though it was bad to drink and drive.

'I only had a single glass of wine,' Sam confessed, his own tears forming.

'I believe you. And I told your lawyer this.'

He didn't want to hear this. Resisting her absolution — he didn't deserve it yet — and touched by her pained beauty, a face that should have guaranteed her earthly happiness, he told her his wife's story in a single passionate outburst. The comparisons struck the French woman at once. Sam passed on the advice which had helped him: 'Never expect yourself to love in the same way again'.

Yvette nodded. She knew this to be the case already. Was it women's wisdom? 'Tell me some more about your wife. I would like to meet her.'

He continued, sure now that he was speaking truths. He had taken care of Firouzeh under a Persian custom. He had taken her in, married her in a common-law ceremony on the death of his brother, also by car accident, and he had been grateful to be in a position to do so. At least he could lift from her shoulders the financial burdens. He wouldn't bore

Yvette with his own troubles, which were insignificant next to hers, but the fact that he had missed the chance of marrying for love was something he had never regretted. It was an honour to be of help. And now he had an offer for her.

'Offer?' she said, inclining her head.

What Yvette needed now was simple, he told her: the money to rebuild her life. He could be of help. He was not a truly rich man but she could have what she needed. Take it. No limit. 'You know, I did not even have the chance to say a word to you after the accident.' No, he had been dragged into those breathalyser tests!

'I could not have talked. So it does not matter.'

'So please think about what I have said. I am in a position to assist you financially. And it would help me to help you. It is actually a selfish offer.'

She couldn't believe her ears. She refused at once, no doubt wondering who this man was, this stranger, this man of tragedy, springing from nowhere waving his wallet. She shook her head. It was nice to talk to him, she said, but now she had things to do. She had an errand to run. And a small job interview. A French travel agency needed a part-time receptionist. He rose, and apologised for staying too long. She showed him out.

'Thank you,' she said, as she shut the door.

He stood on the street, contemplating the conversation, smiling for the first time in months. Pleased by her light rebuff, she had proved by her refusal of money that she was exactly the angel he thought she was. A second factor had also pleased him. Before she had closed the door he asked if he could call again.

'Yes,' she had told him.

The answer had surprised them both.

My goodness, did I ever call again, Sam remembered. Within a couple of weeks Yvette had replaced the Guilt Group in his personal recovery process. He sent his apologies to its leader: 'Been going round in circles. Hopeless. My fault. Best to the others. Read Kierkegaard. S.S.'

His value to Yvette? That was harder to answer. To this day he questioned it. If he went back over the events, where one emotion bled into the next so that within a year Yvette had miraculously moved into his life, into his house, he was none the wiser. It certainly had nothing to do with money: well, almost nothing. She accepted nothing from him for months. And it was hardly emotional support he had offered, as she was entirely self-sufficient in this regard, and it was Sam who needed those talks more than she. No, he ought to be ashamed of himself, going to his victim for succour, for absolution even! Why did she stand for it? *She pitied me, say it. Simple as that.* But no, that wasn't true either, he didn't ever recall pity in her eyes. It was a friendship, an odd one, and leave it at that. He nicknamed her *fereshteh*, angel, within days.

The reasons for marrying her had another cause.

Its principal name, its chief architect? Firouzeh.

Only after Yvette had begun to come to the house, he recalled, did the grieving French widow at last start to open up and allow any insight into her own hardship. Robbed of the love of her life, living in a shoe-box, and on a bank overdraft, her life was an endless crisis. Under Firouzeh's guidance Yvette discussed her own struggles for the first time, and started to gain something in return. Relegated to the background, Sam had little to do with this second phase. In fact, his work had largely been done by then. He had coaxed Yvette to their house, introduced her to Firouzeh, and then retired.

As he would continue to do, he stood patiently on the perimeter, gazing in at the feminine chemistry at work with a mixture of pleasure, curiosity and envy. It was abundantly clear that the involvement of Firouzeh, who had suffered bereavement in not dissimilar circum-stances, made all the difference to Yvette's life at that time, and it was no surprise when they began to behave as best friends, arranging outings, invitations to dinner, exhausting each other on the phone every day or in conversations deep into the night. In actual fact, Firouzeh's ideas — he had to admit — probably benefited from his absence as interlocutor. Twice as powerful, her words reached Yvette undiluted by his trademark orations. Yvette perked up immediately. She brightened visit by visit. As Sam had gone to Yvette, so Yvette now came to Firouzeh, her knock at the door becoming as familiar as that of the children.

With a vanity like his it was hard to accept that he hadn't helped at all. He had set up the conditions for healing to occur, established a climate of honesty, but the real work was done by Firouzeh. In a million years he could not have made Yvette admit her loneliness, or confess her plight: a woman in a foreign country fighting heavy demons, and heavier debts. It had not even occurred to him to offer her a job: the one thing he could do.

'Ask her. Just ask her.'

'She'll never do it,' he had argued. The offer was insulting. 'A man who takes your husband's life is hardly someone from whom you wish to take orders.' But he was wrong.

She was desperate to work again. She had thought he would never ask.

And so Yvette began as the Taste of Persia's newest waitress. She found her feet at once. Even the moodiest customers were charmed by her and he attributed a sudden rise in business and compliments about the food to her alone, the scenery being just as important as the taste to the average gastronome. Also, he was finally able to show his appreciation, his deep gratitude for her forgiveness, in monetary terms.

Able at last to cover her modest outgoings, if not make inroads on her substantial debts, and with deepening friendships with Sam and Firouzeh, Yvette no longer talked of returning to Paris, a city that contained too many memories. She needed the freedom of a new place now, she told the Sahars.

'Good,' said Sam, at last beginning to feel his conscience lighten and the weight of guilt to lift.

But Firouzeh was not finished yet. Interrupting him as he did his books late one night, she asked him to come downstairs. She had something to discuss.

When he arrived in the lounge he found a flute of champagne waiting for him. 'What is the occasion?'

Firouzeh had just spent the day with Yvette. Had he seen her flat recently? It was not fit for rodents, although the place had no shortage of them. Firouzeh had felt like crying when she left Yvette there, trying to coax heat out of a leaking radiator, and doing battle with a hot-water boiler whose pilot light would go out if anyone in Southall exhaled.

'What do you suggest?'

They had three empty rooms. It was a sin. What a waste under such circumstances. If Sam asked her — and Sam should be the one — then Firouzeh was convinced that Yvette, with winter approaching, might just agree to move in. And what an asset she would be! The children already loved her, having shortened Sam's *fereshteh* to Fresh. There was no end to what they owed her.

Sam did not need to be convinced. He was only slightly annoyed that again he had failed to lead the way in the promotion of ideas which would pay off his moral debt. But this was not entirely the full story. Yvette was a gorgeous woman. He was not blind to her beauty. Could he trust himself not to make a fool of himself, were she to live with him under the same roof? He had placed her on such a high pedestal he was fearful that his physical appreciation of her might in some way make itself felt. And he didn't want this. What an insult it would be to a woman who had already suffered so much by his hand. Hoping he would not feel continually uncomfortable with the arrangement, he agreed.

With one proviso. Firouzeh must ask her. He did not want the invitation — he searched for the word — misinterpreted.

Firouzeh looked at him, surprised. The amplitude of her eyebrows was immense. She was speechless for several moment before responding, 'Yes, well if you feel that way, then I should definitely be the one to invite her.'

Sam blushed and turned away, hurrying back up the stairs to the safety of his numbers, where, over his books, he could at least be in control.

As winter's ravages set in, darkening the gassy skies of London, and even bringing on a snap snowfall which reduced the lush, painterly parks of high summer to a stark pencil-sketch, Yvette Berger packed her bags and exchanged Southall for Barnes. She was welcomed with tremendous jubilation. She had never been so touched in all her life, she said. The children ferried her bags up the stairs, tiny barefoot sherpas, the whites of the soles of their feet flashing as they rose.

'Welcome,' said Sam.

Yvette kissed him on both cheeks and hugged him tightly.

He broke loose and hurried up the stairs, heaving the biggest case in pursuit of the children.

'What did I do?' asked Yvette.

'Nothing,' Firouzeh replied. 'He's just shy. He's just very shy.'

They were now only a step away from committing themselves to a state of affairs the outside world would forever look upon as bewildering, but by then, each of the key players was so mutually indebted to the other two that it was hard to keep up with the rocketing level of generosity and respect being paid, repaid and paid again in the Sahar house.

In such a climate, a surreptitious kiss on the mouth could not be regarded as delinquent. Rather, it might be seen as inevitable. And that his first kiss should then be followed by a second, in the steam-filled kitchen of the restaurant one wintry night, is hardly surprising. Sam had not expected it, dreamed it, wished it, fought it or regretted it, ever, but as Yvette drew her hot, fruit-flavoured mouth away from his — her lipstick, he later discovered, was impregnated with the aroma of peaches — he was no longer the master of his own destiny. His internal gyroscope went haywire. Having no idea that she now felt much of the pressing gratitude towards him that he'd so long felt towards her, he wondered if she was teasing him. He backed away. Surely it was wrong, he said. This was madness. He apologised. Whatever he had done to motivate her action he regretted.

'Done? How can you apologise for saving my life?'

With these few words, his resistance vaporised. In a tempest of emotions and with nowhere else to go, first she, and then he activated the idea inside themselves that they were destined to be lovers. As impossible as it might be to explain this, they kissed a third time, falling into each others embrace, gratitude, friendship, loneliness and devilment fusing into a facsimile of desire so close to the real thing that it was indistinguishable.

Anxious that Sam find the romantic love she could not provide, Firouzeh encouraged both parties to explore their fragile new feelings as quickly as possible. In a breathtakingly short space of time, Sam found himself sitting up in his bed, his heart pounding, awaiting the turn of his doorknob. And when it came — and oh, what a lovely, loaded, explosive turning it was! — he was ready for her. Forewarned by fits of giggling from both women at the dinner table, he had a candle burning, incense fuming on the dresser. As he could never forget his lifelong debt to her, he saw his role in a servile light. And she seemed sad, heavy, nostalgic as well. Crossing a boundary she had not navigated since the death of her husband, she had lost all mirth. Yes, she was undoubtedly lovely, he thought, as her chemise fell to the floor. He reached out an arm and she came into his bed. He would please her. He would give this angel a new gift. It would be sweet, tender, with a dead man alarmingly present, but first he needed to recite a piece from the Koran.

Yvette understood from the first that the status of temporary wife was not binding. Since it could equally accommodate a one-night stand or a relationship stretching forty years, it could be easily revoked. Off she could go. The Muslim procedure of simply saying 'I divorce thee' in triplicate would serve. She was happy to agree. He read slowly and carefully and when he put the book down she pulled him down on top of her.

Bingo, two wives. *And me the great bachelor,* Sam thought as the panel inside weighed the wisdom of his emotionally driven decisions. What had happened? With this second marriage he had let his private life go public, floated like a company on the stock exchange.

But his romantic relationship with Yvette had been short-lived. Only one week. There had been no real basis to it, beyond need. Yvette was the first to speak. She apologised for involving him in her recovery. A certain number of wrong turns had to be expected. He fully understood, he said. He awoke after that first night together to realise that, as desirable as she was, he had no hope of viewing her as anything other than an angel. Each time they made love his heaviness and guilt returned. It had to end.

In honour of their sentimental settlement, and as a sign of their lasting respect for each other, Yvette refused to revoke the mantle of temporary wife. If the day came when she met another man and wished to do this, then she would approach him again, but she would not do it lightly. She rated Sam so highly, she said, that she was honoured to be called his wife. Also, the children had become accustomed to having her around. It was a shame to disappoint them.

As for Sam, he had no choice left but to dust off the old belief that he was at heart a one-man band. With two wives down the hall, Saaman Sahar ludicrously steeled himself to sleeping alone again in a bachelor's bed.

Sam recalled these loverless years as he thought of Tracy again, his true love, his magical zahir. What a leap of faith this girl had made — phenomenal, when he thought about it. That she was not driven away by the absurd situation as soon as he had explained it under the plane trees that day in the park was a miracle. She had taken his hand and looked at him in a way no woman had before. He supposed it to be a look of admiration. Little did she know what a paper boat on a windy pond he had been.

Still, how an English girl of twenty could comprehend and finally accept a peculiarly Persian brew of marriage, sadness, tragedy, guilt, high-minded courage, turgid emotional baggage and gloves-off honesty, he would never know. Perhaps she would snap to her senses one day and head for the door. Until then he just had to conclude that the ointment of life caught many strange flies.

Ridley emerged from the corridor, looking for him. Sam waved and the lawyer sat down. 'Where's Firouzeh?'

'Went for coffee. But I don't blame her if she went home. This is absurd. We have to stop this.'

Ridley had news. 'They want to put something to you. Will you come back in?'

Silent, Sam looked out into the street at the passing traffic, at the first sign of dusk.

Ridley waited for an answer. 'I'm on your side.'

'With the money I pay you, you'd better be. What do they want to ask?'

'They want to put it to you themselves. It's about the children. They're adamant about the need to talk with the children. We can place restrictions on them, however. Name the place, set the times. Insist that you and Firouzeh are present.'

'And this is all they want to say?'

'I think we're going to have to give them this, if we want this over with. Which, after all, is the goal.'

Sam shook his head, gravely. 'I can't agree to that. No. I cannot agree to that. My children will not answer questions of a sexual nature. What greater insult?'

'Sam, be careful. These departments have powers.'

'I did not come to this country for this.'

'Calm down. It's just checks and balances. It's awful, I agree. But it's the lesser of two evils. Talk to Firouzeh.'

But Sam shook his head again. 'I have talked to her.'

'And what did she say?'

'She said we'd do anything, but we would never agree to expose them to questions like that.'

'Think of the children.'

'Exactly.'

The roadblock stalled Ridley. His collar dug into his bull neck as he twisted it. 'What do you want me to tell them then?'

'Tell them just that. I will answer any of their other questions, about

235

Yvette, my mistakes, anything. But the children must be left alone. Tell them.'

Pausing in the middle of the road to wait for a gap in the traffic, Sam saw Firouzeh holding coffee in two paper cups. The men watched her come through the automatic doors. She looked tired but ever hopeful as she came near. 'What is happening,' she asked. 'Am I late? I had to walk miles.'

Neither Sam nor Ridley replied.

17

The Party

'We'll take the matter higher, that's all,' Sam told his wives in confidence. 'But we won't be pushed around and allow them to talk to the children.'

The meeting with Social Services had ended badly. No settlement was reached. While the panel maintained its demand that the Sahars submit their children to questioning by a child psychologist, Ridley raised the Human Rights Act of 1998 as a basis for a legal objection. Sam had loudly voiced his intention to contact his local MP. He was ready to go over their heads. The European Court of Human Rights was not out of the question!

'We have challenged the secular establishment, you see. So we are in for a fight. Polygamy sticks in their throat. That is why they have put so much stock by an anonymous report and a couple of pairs of wet school shorts. So it looks like we will just have to test the boundaries of multiculturalism.'

Sam was excited. Principles were at stake. As long as British society continued to ignore the separate laws of its minorities, he told his wives, it could not claim to be multicultural. Within Britain, a parallel set of laws had operated for years, but one completely unrecognised by the state. The customs of religious and ethnic minorities had no legal status here, but change was in the air. Fortunately the focus was shifting to Brussels. The new Europeanism meant people like the Sahars could go round the stick-in-the-mud Brits, circumvent the stuffy law lords. If German transport laws could affect British truck drivers, Danish meat standards change the cut of an English steak, then perhaps certain Muslim customs could be enshrined in the great British charter. 'Ridley even thinks we will be a test case. We could get the newspapers behind us. This is racial harassment.'

'The papers? Oh no.' Firouzeh had seen what the papers had done to them once already, turning a local community against them. 'I hate all this. I dread it.'

'We have a right to fight all the same. Thank God we have got money behind us,' he told them.

'So what can we all do?' Tracy asked, her fingers knitted in anxiety.

'Right now?' Perhaps barricades had to be erected, doors nailed shut. 'I think we should have a dinner party,' Sam announced. 'Let's keep up our good spirits. Believe it or not, we have a right to those as well.'

His parents were soon told that Tracy's parents had also been invited. Both sets of in-laws, Sam hoped, might find comfort in each other's displeasure. He received no reply to this jibe.

Despite the heavy undercurrents, the dinner party began very well. Both sets of parents made a point of mentioning early that they were extremely disappointed with the arrangement. Both were keen to see it revised as soon as possible, and, they hoped, reversed. With Sam acting as translator — and hence his own executioner — Mostafa and Fatima expressed to the crowded table their profound disappointment in their son, a despoiler of the family name, and sympathised with Eric and Monica who must feel the same about their daughter, a girl young enough to be their son's daughter. It was shameful, shameful. Something had to be done.

Tempering his parents' words as much as he could, Sam could not quite derail the depiction of himself as a son who had betrayed his parent's deepest dreams. Heaven knew what would come of such a hopeless boy, he told the Pringles, allowing the humiliation of the word 'boy' to stand. 'We have given up looking for any sign of hope.'

'Really?' Eric replied, becoming quite chirpy.

'I see,' said Monica, asking for her glass of water to be refilled since no wine at all was on the horizon.

'Oh yes,' said Sam. 'He is a dead loss.'

Eric looked at his daughter, resplendent at the other end of the dinner table. He barely recognised her. She was dressed becomingly in a jade-green velvet dress. Jewellery too. Were they real pearls?

'Also,' Sam added, after Fatima had dictated several new humiliations, 'we thought vegetables were supposed to make people thin . . . so what is happening? . . . just look at him . . . he is a waterhog . . . worse than ever . . . he looks like a . . . like a . . . ' Sam struggled to translate the word, before remembering with dull resignation, 'oh, yes . . . a pumpkin . . . a big, overlarge pumpkin. Now can we finish with this?' Sam suddenly petitioned the table, throwing down his napkin. 'Or not?'

Monica and Eric laughed, delighted by this self-assassination. When Mostafa and Fatima did likewise the success of the evening was assured.

Afterwards, the group split along gender lines.

'We're at war, you and me, basically,' Eric said from a very comfortable armchair, a saucered teacup on his knee, some kind of green liquid inside. 'I know I'm in your house and everything, under your roof and all that, eating your foodn'all, and it's been very nice, lovely, but you need to know that I'm not finished with you, not by a long chalk. Basically, you're not having her. Simple as that. So it's war. Cheers.' Eric was pleased with this speech. It was hard to fault. Hard talk from a calm mind. He had wanted to get this out all night, face to face, and it had come out perfectly. It was a father's duty to put himself on the line. He felt almost victorious.

'I can understand that, Sam nodded, conceding nothing. 'And I respect that.'

'Good then. Just so as you know.'

Eric glanced over at the women. The first wife was translating for Monica something Fatima had said. The old girl bent round her interpreter to search Monica's face for a reaction. It was a hell of a dynamic. A Barnes-style Camp David. He returned to his conversation. 'Just so you know.' He sniffed at the rim of his cup and swirled the contents.

'I know this must be hard for you to take,' Sam ventured further, under the silent uncomprehending scrutiny of his father sitting several feet away, 'but when we get enough time I think I can explain why I have ended up in this tangle with three wives. Man to man I think you could understand.'

'You wouldn't change a thing though, would you?' Eric asked, lacing his words with scorn. 'That's the point. You wouldn't bloody change it. You're happy as dog in a lamp-post factory, and you know it.'

Sam was grateful for the show of paternal temper. It provided evidence that Eric was tackling the issues at last. It was the first step to acceptance. 'No Eric. Now that I'm in this happy situation, I wouldn't change it at all. It offers me a lot. I can't lie to you about that.'

'Then leave it out. Do me a favour.'

'I'm a very fortunate man, no question. What man could be unhappy? Look at them.' He indicated the women. 'It seems to me I've offered very, very little to the world and yet in return I've been given the keys to a secret garden. As a man you must be able to sympathise. Imagine, three wives who love you, and who also love each other.'

'Hey, keep on talking like that and I'm walking out of here, right? I'm here as a father, pal, okay? So watch it. I'm not here as . . . as "a man." '

'I understand. Of course. You're right. You're talking as a father, I know, but you asked me if I'd change things. And my answer is simply no. And I will wager, Eric, nor would you.'

Eric stared at him, even contemplated hitting the man. *This guy is really pushing it now.* 'The next thing you're gonna tell me is you're knackered. The huge demands of having three women? Well don't start, all right? I don't wanna hit ya but I will.'

'Well, actually, I *am* quite tired. But it's not what you think.'

'You've got a flipping nerve.'

'You do understand that I sleep only with Tracy, don't you?' Eric did not reply, holding the Iranian in his fixed gaze. 'Because it is the absolute truth.'

'I know that's what you'd like us to believe.'

'Eric, you have to believe this.'

Eric changed the subject. 'I need a refill.'

Across the room, Monica learnt about the Islamic dress code for women. What she did not know was that underneath the modest outer robes which women wore into the street, a free-for-all was taking place.

'A shame to cover everything up then,' Monica said.

Firouzeh translated this to Fatima who shook her head and gave a passionate reply.

'On the contrary,' Firouzeh reported back. 'The imagination is the best clothes designer.'

Monica nodded. She had never looked at it that way.

Finally, jet lag, moral fatigue and naive questions forced Fatima to sit back in her armchair and fall almost instantly into a deep sleep. A light snore surfaced now and again.

Monica mulled over what she'd learnt while Firouzeh and Yvette went off to make more tea, choosing the private moment to ask Tracy if she was a lesbian.

'Mum!'

'It's not a stupid question.'

'What are you like? We just share the same man, that's all, not each other. Blimmin' hell. Is that what you and Dad thought?'

'So . . . so you don't all sleep in the same bed then?'

'Been fantasising again, have ya? You betta watch that.' She laughed. 'So *that's* what you've been worrying about.'

'Hey, don't worry what I've been worrying about, just tell me yes or no.'

Tracy sighed. 'I'm the only one who sleeps with Sam, all right? We told you that. Satisfied?'

'Y'sure about that?'

Tracy was about to say yes, when she paused. 'Well, sometimes we all . . . '

'I knew it!'

'Every now and again we all have a bit of a cuddle. But that's all.'

'A cuddle? So what's a bit of a cuddle then? The mind boggles.'

'Just that.'

'I wanna know the truth. I'm your mother.'

'Oh, are ya?'

'Just tell me.'

'I just did. You've got a filthy mind, that's your trouble. Now give it a rest.'

But Monica's imagination still could not paint a satisfying picture of the bedroom situation. 'So . . . what's that like then, this cuddle?'

'Whaddaya mean? It's nice. That's all. It's nice.'

'Nice, is it?'

'Yeah. Look, just cos you can't imagine it doesn't mean it's filthy.'

Monica stared at her daughter. 'Well, thank God for that at least. Me and your Dad thought maybe you'd turned into a lesbian.'

'Well, you can take a holiday now, can't you.'

With a swift jerk of her wrist. Monica knocked back the last of her tea. 'All right. But I'm not finished yet. I want to know why the others don't sleep with him.' She leant forward. 'What's he done to them?'

'Look, he's lovely. He's really great. It's everyone else whose being disgusting.'

'Who's everyone?'

'You.'

'Oh thanks very much. And I tell you one thing. I know you don't really love him.'

'Oh yeah? So how do you know that then?'

'Because you wouldn't be able to share him if you did. Human nature. I couldn't share your father.'

'No one else would want him.'

Monica and Tracy turned to look at Eric, just then picking something out of his ear. Feeling their gaze he turned and gave them a small wave.

'And I'd rather share a first-rate bloke,' Tracy observed, 'than have a completely useless one all to myself.'

Monica swung back to Tracy. Her face was red. 'That's a terrible thing to say about your father!'

'Who said I was talking about Dad?'

Tracy left Monica with this question and went into the kitchen. Monica tried not to look at her own husband from then on.

When all his guests had departed and his wives had gone up to bed, Sam took his cigar out onto the patio as usual and blew smoke at the moon. The party had drained him, but unlike the rest of the house he couldn't sleep. In his slippers and robe he contemplated the tragi-comedy that was his life just as two sausages fell from the sky.

They landed at his feet: *plop . . . plop.*

It was an astonishing miracle. He looked up into the sky at once for the large birds who had perhaps dropped this carrion but the sky was full of stars and stars only. Could it be that he had just witnessed a miracle? Were miracles out of the question nowadays? But what divine meaning could be ascribed two rancid, heaven-sent tubes of meat? For a vegetarian it could only be a dark harbinger of the end of the world. Or perhaps, when the sky rained meat it was Allah telling him that his twenty-year-old diet of green vegetables should end.

He looked back down at the two items on the paving stones, odd-smelling, turning them over with his foot, and realised the likely truth: neighbourhood brats, up to mischief, wanted rid of uneaten meals and had selected his two dogs as beneficiaries. Not a bad plan, except that both were kennelled on the other side of the house, well out of range of

Sam's parents who, in their ageing insomnia, liked to roam the property at all hours, and who, like most Persians, considered dogs low, filthy and utterly untouchable. Sam's ownership of two hounds was just one more nail in his coffin.

Sam set his cigar on a vacant Roman plinth. Popping indoors he came back out with a dustpan and brush. The best place for such jetsam was the compost. They were not worthy of his prize animals. The worms would appreciate them more.

He made his way through the tree-dark shadows, feeling from memory for the large plastic compost bin at the bottom of the garden. The dogs barked in the distance and he shushed them over his shoulder. His hand closed on the plastic handle on the lid and he lifted. A pent-up gust of moist, warm rot rushed upward and he drew back. Millions of worms were certainly doing their job in there, breaking everything down into their fundamental minerals — a timeless process, a microcosm of society, he thought — sticks, vegetable peel, grass, leaves, all organic matter, reduced to the stew and effluvium whence even he, Sam Sahar, was merely on loan. Perhaps both sets of parents, speaking so critically, were right about something: In the midst of decaying orders certain codes had to be defended, even at the cost of the emotions. This was the earthly battle as they saw it. An act of resistance to natural forces: timeless values upheld against the rot of today's throwaway world. Was he himself just an agent of decay, a lower-order worm working away in the dark, eroding everything? To them he certainly was. To his own parents he was a traitor to tradition, and to his in-laws, a terrorist, crossing borders to lay charges in the centre of their lives. At least this was how they all made him feel. He would stage no more dinner parties. Why should he host his own persecution? Depressed, he tossed the rank sausages into that great, frenzied process and resealed the bin.

He sighed. Getting back up the garden would be a lot easier. The house was softly lit by streetlights. He was in dire need of a pee and then, after that, the slumbering warmth of his youngest wife. The red beacon of his waiting cigar, with its glowing tip, guided him back towards the patio and his home, of which he now ached to become a tranquil inhabitant.

Monica and Eric lay in bed high above the same dormant city. 'How would you feel about it though?'

He refused to answer the question. To do so would invite trouble.

243

'Tell me,' she urged.

'Sleep,' he murmured. In protest he thumped his head a third time into his feather pillow.

'But how would you feel about it?'

'Ridiculous question.' Still, he knew that the topic could no longer be dismissed purely on the grounds of improbability. Normality had been left far behind of late.

'Tell me.'

'I don't want to sleep with two women, okay? I've never thought about it. End of story. Satisfied?'

She pondered his reply. 'Big liar.'

In frustration he pulled the covers almost entirely over his head.

'As a man. It must appeal though,' she said. 'Three women in your bed. Do anything you like. Like a kid in a sweetie shop.'

Eric took his time replying. 'Look, it probably means I'm impotent or gay or something, fine, but it wouldn't interest me.'

'It's all right to say you've thought about it.'

'I'm not greedy, all right? So leave it. I don't want three cars either.'

'Now I know you're lying.'

'Three television sets. What's the point? How many fridges can I use? I only want one. One decent one. That's what you are. Solid, reliable — '

'A fridge?'

'I don't need more than one woman. If that's all right with you. So sleep. Ridiculous question. Christ. Anyway — '

'Anyway what?'

'How would you feel, if I ask you the same question, about having two more men in here? See what I mean?'

Her silence eventually became disturbing. 'How would I feel?'

'Stupid question. Just go to sleep.'

'How would I feel?'

'Good night.' He pretended to breathe heavily, as if already on the edge of sleep.

She sat up in the darkness for some time.

'Night,' he said, turning to see that she was still awake.

'Night,' she said. But she didn't lie down.

The police had no sooner arrived than they had left again, taking with them all four children.

Firouzeh had to be held back by a large officer with whom she wrestled in vain. Woken in their beds and asked to put on bathrobes, jumpers and slippers, the children were dazed and only half aware of their predicament. The older ones, however, knew enough to be unconsoled by Sam's repeated promises that they would be all right. 'Go with them,' Sam told them, when it was clear he could not stop this from happening. 'We'll follow right behind you in our car.' He tried to keep his voice calm for their sakes, concealing his desperate emotions. 'Firouzeh, stop it, let them go.'

'Mama?' Aisha pleaded, dressed only in a full-length flannelette nightgown and a bathrobe, her oval face full of confusion and fear as a policeman's big hand ushered her towards the front door and the night. 'What is happening?'

Firouzeh, unable to oppose the officer's large arms, could only scream her protest. When Sam tried to follow the children down the path he was held back at the door. 'It's okay,' he called after them. 'Go on. They'll look after you. We'll follow right behind you.'

The children were led away — holding hands as they had been taught to do when crossing the road, avoiding danger — to a waiting van in which they sat, stunned, and in the case of the youngest one, hysterical, trying to break out of Ali's stronger grip but restrained by a brother who saw safety in their togetherness.

With the children inside the van, Sam erupted. The anger held at bay for their sake was unleashed. 'Get out! Get out of this house! Get out now!' The biggest cop released Firouzeh. The one barring the door to the dining room, which held back Yvette and Tracy, stepped away. The third and fourth were also happy to retreat as quickly as they could. 'Get out!' But when Sam tried to speed them up, putting his own hand on an officer's chest, he was swiftly repelled. Thrust backward, his head hit the door-frame. It was a wincing reminder that private property held no meaning at all in times of public inquiry.

Yvette and Tracy, who had been duped into stepping into the dining room to permit 'a private word with the parents', spilled at last into the hallway, ready to do battle. The black police van outside, however, was already running. Within seconds the remaining cops, all but one, were aboard.

This last officer, a tall, young, black man, not devoid of sympathy, adjusted a disturbed tie and told Firouzeh that the children's clothes and personal belongings would be sent for in the morning. He was keen to show them his own emotional discomfort and apologise for the disturbance, the upheaval. Unlike his colleagues, he wanted to show he had not just swallowed the official line.

'Unpleasant business,' he said, biting his lips. 'Always is. But we gotta keep the kids' interests in mind.' He told them to try not to worry: the children would be taken to a temporary safe house for the night, while an assessment took place. As soon as it could be proved, over the coming days, that they were in no danger then they would be returned home at once. He was sorry about the whole thing. 'Cos you seem like decent people to me.' Firouzeh saw this lowering of his official defences as an opportunity to attack. She was a mother: she needed an object for her ferocious sense of injustice, and he was all she had. With her hands she tried to strike his face. Sam leapt forward, tried to pull her out of the man's grip, out of his big hands, but Firouzeh was strong. It took a few seconds of both men's combined efforts to subdue her.

This officer then withdrew down the path, jumping up front with the driver. No sound came from the children as the van drove away, although Sam would say later that their screams were quite audible to him, and that their echo would follow him for the rest of his life.

When Fatima and Mostafa were belatedly drawn from their beds by the shouts Sam had to explain to them that while they had slept the family had been decimated. His mother added to the screams already threatening to shatter the house, while his father, who had anticipated trouble as a result of the court case, shook his head from side to side.

Tracy closed the front door in a daze, repeating to everyone and no one: 'I'm so sorry, I'm so sorry.'

Firouzeh had fallen to her knees as if hit from behind, and a bout of paralysis left her unable to get up, keeping her there, refusing all offers of help. Her statement was clear: she would not move until the children ran safely back through the front door. To budge an inch would be a clear betrayal of a mother's duty. And so as Sam made several desperate phone calls she stayed where she was, buckled in agony, finding in the cold polished flagstones a reasonable place against which to softly bang her head, sending dry-mouthed wails into every corner of the house.

Into the phone Sam shouted fevered instructions. He could think of nothing else to do, as one call drifted without result into the next. It had gone two o'clock and he counted on people being up. He made wild calls: to his lawyer (who was on his way); to the police, who refused to release the address of the safe house where the children had been taken, despite his furious protests; then a series of less cogent calls — he wasn't thinking straight by then — to someone on the council who was a big fan of his restaurant, perhaps something could be done at board level tomorrow; to the JP who had just married him; even to a retired cop whose only tenuous connection to Sam was that he used to sing baritone in the Anglican choir. Maybe he could turn wheels within wheels, even at this hour reverse these corrupt workings, grease some palm, ply money at some corruptible point. But Sam got nowhere as he repeated over his shoulder, to the remnants of his family, his promise that he would take care of this. Finally, he became bogged down in wrong numbers and engaged signals. As he used up his contacts he found himself lost in the wires of London. His notepad was already black with the corrected numbers of absolute nobodies given to him by complete strangers. He put down the phone.

In this furnace of enquiry, he knew the actual truth: he had led his whole family into this madness, placed them in danger by his own hand. This third marriage had been the big mistake: he had always wanted too much for himself. *Greed, greed, greed.* Once again, just as when he had been marooned between floors in Tracy's old, festering lift, a useless telephone hot against his ear, assistance was not forthcoming, the doors of his *life* were opening now, revealing oblivion. That same solid scream rose up inside his chest. Help! he wanted to shout, help! But, as Tracy had said in the lift, who would hear?

Tracy was at his shoulder, checking his progress, her sweet breath upon him. Even now she touched him. 'Anything?'

'I don't know anybody. I thought I *knew* people. I don't know anybody.'

She heard pure distress in his voice and put her arm around his waist. 'It's okay. We should drive after them.'

'Don't know where they've gone. Wouldn't tell me. Some foster home apparently. Would defeat the point of taking them if we could follow.'

'Ridley. What about Ridley?'

'He should be here by now.' Sam went back into the hall, saw Firouzeh still on the floor where he'd left her. The pang of responsibility shot through him again. 'Can you take care of Firouzeh? I'll try some more numbers.'

247

Tracy nodded. She returned to running between all the wounded parties: Yvette on the couch gazed into blank space with an anaesthetised face, unscrewing the cap on a tiny bottle of Bach's Rescue Remedy, as though the essence of a flower would do some good; Fatima, on the stairs, wrung her hands ritualistically and then bowed her head into them in earthly petition. To them Tracy brought tissues, to others an embrace, but like Florence Nightingale she was too outnumbered and lacking in the vital supplies to do much good on this kind of battlefield. She kept it up however, helping Mostafa to a chair, putting water on to boil, until Ridley arrived.

'Now, I'll try and get an order to have the children returned to you in the morning,' Ridley promised. 'All going well, and bearing in mind that their offices don't open till 10 a.m. — I feel just awful, I have to say — I'd hope to have them returned to you by noon tomorrow. But I can't promise anything.'

The plan met with no opposition. He turned to his chief client. 'Sam? Is that all right?'

But Sam's mind had broken off into a hundred minor thoughts. 'I take back what I said about this country.'

Ridley's brows crossed. 'This country? What did you say?'

'It's not fit.' Sam looked back at his solicitor. 'It's not even fit to be on the list.'

'What list?'

'The list.'

'I'm not with you, old boy.'

'When they offer countries to refugees. In those transit camps.'

'Sam, what are you talking about? I think we really need to focus right now.' But his words had little effect.

18

The Proposal

Sam passed Firouzeh in the doorway to the garden. He put a hand to one cheek and kissed her on the other, looking into her eyes. 'It will be okay, my *joonie*.'

She left without a word and went straight up to her room.

He sighed heavily. The onus of responsibility for this maelstrom was on him alone. He had been the one to so vehemently oppose the interviewing of the children, misjudging the tenacity of the government department. He had always idealised his adopted country, letting this blind himself to its bite, to its very real teeth. He should have known better. Having as a young man seen American support planes fill the sky with thunder as they backed Iraq in the long war, he knew what it was to deeply fear a democratic, purportedly peace-loving western country. How frightening, how villainous America had seemed with its God-like technology and payloads of TNT, with your home next on its target list. He'd placed Britain in a different box, however. Like France it had joined the rank of ex-empires, specialising in food, holidays, memorabilia and anniversaries. He had attributed to it the benign good humour and generosity of a paternal grandfather: long in the tooth, with only ever something good in his pocket. He certainly never believed he would be woken by a knock at the door at 1.30 a.m. to be confronted by official thugs. Not ever! But he would never be fooled again. He was now at war with this country. And he had discovered within himself a first-rate ability to hate.

Tracy was in the garden patting the dogs. Here again Sam had slipped

249

up. He should have trained his brutes to bite policemen.

'Any news?' she asked.

'Ridley is at their head office right now. He will phone through when he knows anything.'

Tracy nodded. The dogs, oblivious, hunkered on the ground, waiting for a new command. Sam scratched the older one between the ears. The dog instantly relaxed its muscles, slumped and rolled over to expose its hairless, nippled belly and scrotum. The point of Sam's shoe eased the animal's flea-ridden agony.

It was near to the end of the first full day of the children's abduction. Ridley was yet to establish their actual whereabouts. It was standard practice, the Sahars had been told, to deny the deprived parents this essential information. They had to be satisfied with the official consolation that the children were safe and well in a recognised safe house.

'I've closed the restaurant for tonight. Told Abdullah not to come in. So you have a night off.'

Tracy held a flower between her thumb and forefinger but did not pick it. 'I keep trying to imagine where they are, but I can't.'

He put his hand gently on her head. 'Ridley says we'll definitely get them back tomorrow or the next day. He's sure we can come to some arrangement with them.'

'They haven't even got a change of clothes.'

'They provide them with new ones.'

'Like prisoners! Jesus!'

'They are plucky children. They are strong. Even Mostafa, can you see anyone pushing him around? Haman I am more worried about. And Aisha. The older ones have more to think about. I don't want them to think. That's all I'm hoping. I hope they are watching television. If they can lose themselves in stupid programmes, then they will hardly know they have been away.'

'It's my fault,' Tracy said.

'Stop it.' He aimed his forefinger at her.

At this point the phone rang. Yvette, inside, came running to the doors.

'It's Ridley,' she called.

'So far I have managed to get us a hearing for six weeks' time. I hope to get this moved to an even earlier date, however. I can work quicker than they can.' Ridley smiled from the rattan armchair.

'Six weeks!' Firouzeh shouted. 'It would take six weeks?'

The general uproar took several minutes to die down. The family could only guess what such a period of separation would do to them. Certainly the children, if not the parents, would be affected forever.

'Now just listen,' Ridley resumed. 'There's a couple of other things we could do. I've put in place a compromise by which we could have the children home by tomorrow.'

'Tomorrow?' Sam asked.

'And provided we then take the right approach at the hearing, and are properly positioned, then that could well be the end of it.'

The family waited to hear what this compromise might be.

'Okay, so here it is. Tracy and Yvette would move out. As soon as possible. Tonight. Remove any possibility of contact. Only under these conditions would the department be prepared to let the children return. They saw the refusal to let the children be interviewed as an effort to conceal something. They were in no mood to compromise but I brought them around.'

Ridley let this proposal hang in the air.

No one spoke.

'I know that what I'm asking won't be easy for you, but the choice is yours. You can have the children home tomorrow but Tracy and Yvette would have to move into, say, a hotel. Of course, there couldn't be much contact, except on a formal basis, until the hearing. We couldn't take risks.'

Ridley could see that he was not going to get much in the way of feedback and so chose to advance to his second point. 'Which leads me the next matter. Now there isn't so much urgency for this, but if you agree then I suggest why wait. It's this. The polygamy thing has got them rattled: two wives, one of them English — sorry, Tracy. The English connection probably bought it close to home. And as its unlikely to impress the judge when we get to the hearing stage we might as well defuse this now. Plus, if you then consider that Firouzeh is still not a resident of this country, lacking a legal status, then this visa question has to be faced as well. Sam? Head on, I think. We need to get ahead of the play here. And you can't go on wangling these visa extensions forever. If the other side gets wind of this it won't make our job any easier.'

Sam, Tracy, Firouzeh and Yvette stared at him, players from a dumbshow.

'So what I suggest is this. Immigration problems and even a nasty extradition is a real danger for Firouzeh if things get any worse, as well as the resulting loss of the kids and break-up of the family. So what I suggest is this. And you'd better brace yourselves. Are you ready? You'll bloody hate this. Sam, it would really help me if you'd marry Firouzeh.'

This might as well have been said in a foreign tongue, such were the looks of incomprehension returned to Ridley. The lawyer scrutinised the frozen faces. 'Did anyone hear me? Let me know what you think. I'm feeling lonely here.'

Sam was the first to find his tongue. 'What are you talking about?'

'Sam, don't be like that. I've put two proposals to you. I need you to get serious.'

'Sorry for being so light-hearted.'

'I'm trying to get the children out of state care. And it would help if you married one of these women!'

'*Marry* one? I've married them all.'

Ridley gave an exasperated sigh. 'I mean registry. Just for appearances. If the mother of the children is your legally wedded wife, a legal resident . . . you get my drift? Then I can see a way through this. We know a couple of things. We know what the SS are thinking, so let's play them along, let them run with the bait, then reel them in with a legitimate wedding licence.' He mimed fighting a heavy fish on his line. 'Gotcha!' His invisible rod snapped vertical and then faded in his hands. 'Let's surprise them with a model of marital stability. But before that, let's get the children returned. From now on I think we'll have to seriously play down wives two and three.'

Wives two and three looked pale. Sam was already shaking his head. 'Play down? How far play down?'

'I mean, not in their face play down. Not in their face. After the hearing, when we prove that there was never anything untoward going on, then you can go back to how you were.'

Sam scratched his chin. The women variously covered their faces with their hands as the reality of the situation dawned.

'We just have to find some other way,' Sam demanded. 'There can't be inequality. For us that would ruin everything. There has to be another way.'

'Tracy and Yvette will have to move out tonight. And if I can phone through with that assurance we can have the children returned in the morning.'

The change in the room's climate amounted to a drop in cabin pressure. Tracy jumped up and ran out. Yvette and Firouzeh followed.

Sam was left alone, slumped lifeless in his couch like a fish which has battled so hard for freedom that it is dead by the time it is plucked out of the water.

No one decided that Tracy and Yvette would go. They just packed their bags and went.

Ridley had already made the call, before the end of office hours, confirming a 'breakthrough in negotiations'. Wives two and three would be gone from the family home by ten o'clock that evening. The house would be available for inspection before the children's return; no obstruction would be put in the department's way.

Sam arranged the hotel booking. By mutual agreement they chose the Marilyn suite. Two single beds would be moved in to replace the big double. 'Why not let it end where it started?' Tracy told him. He said that this was not funny.

She apologised. 'No, it's not,' she said.

He kissed her on the lips and told her the pledge he'd made to himself: he would not sleep on their big bed until she returned. 'Don't be daft,' she said, but he was stubborn. He would think of her without pause until she came back home for good and in triumph after their victory at the hearing.

'Well, one thing at a time,' she said, as she bent and zipped up her suitcase. 'Now let me get dressed.'

Yvette and Tracy had decided to go out in style. They were not prepared to slink away like social embarrassments.

Each woman dressed in elegant new clothes, and spent on hour on their make-up. When they descended the stairs Firouzeh and Sam, as well as the speechless Fatima and Mostafa senior, witnessed their descent.

'Stunning,' murmured Firouzeh, not knowing whether to smile or to cry.

Sam could not find his voice at all. He pulled out his car keys and went out to the car.

In the front doorway the three wives hugged: they refused to let this crisis divide them. Both the separation and the proposed marriage of Firouzeh to Sam would be an opportunity to show just how durable and wide-ranging their philosophy was, in spite of the attacks.

Sam tooted his horn. Tracy and Yvette left Firouzeh crying at the threshold, waving to the car as long as she kept sight of it. As far as she was concerned, the night, into which her children had been taken, had once again claimed two more victims.

Très en beauté in a black and white dress, Yvette put down the phone. 'It's on the way up.'

Her first act as a hotel guest, and to properly christen the new arrangement, had been to order champagne at a ridiculous price, but the extravagance was failing to buoy them up. 'I feel like a criminal on z'run.'

'It's only temporary so let's try to enjoy it.' With a long face Tracy smoothed the silver bedspread up and down with her palm. They had to look on the bright side, she said. Hadn't Ridley got the children back, and after only two days? Then he would settle this too. They'd be back home within a few weeks. 'Anyway, I'm the one who should be flipping out.'

'Why?'

'Because it's all my fault. That's why. Like Ridley said. A third wife, and an English one. Brought it close to home. That's what started it. You never had any trouble before I came along.'

'Don't listen to him. I don't like him anyway. His eyes are unkind. Like this!' She tried to imitate his myopia. '*Inquiétant*!' She squinted heavily. She shook her head, her hair tumbling loose. 'A skinny man with a big stomach cannot be trusted. Worms. My *maman* used to say ziss. Such men have stomach worms.'

Tracy laughed, as the room service knocked.

She didn't feel the need to keep a clear head for her lectures the next day. They would take care of themselves. Just as justice would take care of itself. Not permitted to be there for the children's repatriation, they both intended to spend the morning sleeping off a huge hangover. When they awoke they would phone and confirm that the deal had gone through.

'I have never been in a courtroom,' Tracy said, uncorking the bottle with her thumbs, sending the cord thudding into the ceiling plaster, making a dent. 'What do you wear, do you think?'

254

Yvette shrugged. 'What does it matter? We will be invisible, remember?'

'*Touché,*' Tracy said. 'We have to be invisible from now on, don't we?'

'*Oui. Touché.*'

They raised their glasses and touched them without a sound.

The dogs were the first to awaken to the children's return. Able to receive news on clairvoyant wavelengths, they sprang from the hot paving stones trailing their chains and surged to the french doors, yapping wildly, rousing the house.

Thinking he had another intruder, Sam threw open the doors and came into the garden, ready this time to let the dogs obey their animal instincts and dine on whoever they found.

Firouzeh came to the door also, ribbon around her neck, tying up a party balloon. 'What is it?'

'They heard something.'

'We should leave them off their leash.' She suggested.

'They've been off for two days already.'

The dogs, which had calmed down, then burst into another round of excited barking, running to the garden wall and putting their front legs up on it, scratching at the brick.

'They're back,' Firouzeh said, taking extra-sensory readings of her own. 'They're back!'

A people carrier pulled up outside the house two minutes later. A social worker, not Partridge, opened the back doors and the children, in strange clothes, raced up the path, their faces breaking into smiles. They were an ocean wave of affection and it broke over Sam and Firouzeh simultaneously. Sam could feel anger underneath his relief. What should never have happened, in the first place, would never happen again.

As Sam predicted, both Mostafa and Ali, with the saving amnesia of children, looked freshly returned from a surprise holiday. Haman and Aisha, however, had longer faces, ones which told a story of broken nights, of a fear of the unknown and the burdens of responsibility. It was to them that Sam went, wrapping arms strongly around both their heads, holding them tight so as to leave no mistake in their minds that he understood exactly how they felt, could envisage what they had been through and would make amends. These wounds would heal, all their questions would be answered — he would see to it — and they would work together to erase these events entirely from their memories.

Monica re-entered the lounge. Eric looked up from a documentary to ask where she had been, but knowing the answer full well.

'In there,' she said. It was no longer necessary to name the room.

He shook his head. 'I'm gonna strip back those walls.'

'You keep saying that.'

'I know, but I am. What were you doing in there anyway?' She stood at his shoulder. 'I was . . . I was just writing. In the notebook.'

'Notebook? Did she phone? What did she say this time.'

When Monica didn't reply he turned to look at her. 'Well?'

She said that it was difficult to talk while he was watching T.V.

He rose, switched off the set and placed his hands on his hips. His look suggested that no greater act had been done by a man for a woman in the annals of matrimony.

'You better read this then.' She handed him the notebook at the relevant page. 'Read from there. This is what she said today.'

He read it closely then looked up at his nervous wife, worried himself. 'What does she mean? Mean by *exposed*?'

'He was some old guy in the park apparently. She was nine or ten. He came out of the bushes and opened his coat.' Eric stared at his wife as she raced to nip his rising emotions in the bud. 'He didn't touch her or anything. She just walked away, told her friends and they all had a big laugh about it. We don't need to get worried about it. But she's apparently only just realised that she never told us about it. And now she's wondering why.'

'She phoned you up to say this?'

Monica shrugged. 'No, other things actually. Much bigger things. But that came out.'

'Bigger things?'

Monica could see from her husband's chest that his defensive capacities were on alert and that his posture had noticeably changed. As a man of action he saw the protection of his family as a physical act, in a primitive sense. His task, his area of specialisation, to provide, defend and repel. In some sense he had a retarded role. There seldom being anything to repel, he was on a virtually constant holiday. But he relished this low level of responsibility. But now, the siren had gone off, and he was called to battle stations. The task for Monica, as he saw it, was to intuit, to finesse, to alert him to the family's subtler needs.

'They've had to move out. Her and the French one. They've moved into a hotel for a bit.'

'They're breaking up? Why didn't you say?'

'Don't get too excited. The kiddies were taken. By Social Services. It was dreadful. And so to get them back Tracy and Yvette had to move out.'

Eric's sudden burst of enthusiasm faltered. 'They took the kids? They can't do that, can they? You mean they actually took them?'

'Well, they did. They did. Sounded awful. Just terrible. The way Tracy described it. Must be something to do with that earlier thing. Somebody making complaints about them or something. But they came in the night.'

Monica had read poetry as a girl. She often came out with these high turns of phrase. *They came in the night* was pure Monica.

'What hotel? Where is she? I'm going down there. Is she all right? What's going on? Fucking hell, rapists in the park, kid being seized — what's next? This has gotta stop, Mon. We've gotta put our foot down.'

'You're welcome to talk to her. You don't always have to quiz me to find out what's going on. You're not a cripple. Pick up a phone yourself.'

'The phone's your thing. I wanna see her. I'm going down there. Where is she? What room.'

'You wanna go now?'

'Yeah. What hotel?'

'Well, I'll have to phone first.'

'I'm waiting.'

Eric was ready to go, on red alert. He went to the coat rack and pulled on his coat. Valuable minutes were wasted, he felt, while Monica made her call.

A chaffinch wheeled and stopped on the branch of an ailanthus, the tree of heaven. From where they walked, down the forking path, Tracy could see the golden dome of the Regents Park mosque which, now that Ramadan was under way, the month of fasting and purification, Sam's parents must have made their second home. She pointed it out to her father. He grumbled and looked away.

He returned to his chief subject. 'What the hell were you doing in a park anyway, at that hour?'

'I was playing. It was years ago. We always did that. Dad, it wasn't that late.'

'I don't remember letting you go out alone at that age.'

'Dad, there's something important I've got to tell you.'

'I don't remember that.'

Poor Dad, she suddenly thought, looking at her father as he refused to listen, his thickening nose, new wrinkles, jowls even. *He looks old all of a sudden, my fault, that's me. Guilty again.* It was a cause of further distress to her that she had thrown him into turmoil too. He had turned his big gentle face towards her, concern and anxiety engraved there: the face that had always broadcast the word 'don't', now projected the tamer word 'please'. Was this old age? 'There's gonna be a court hearing in a few weeks' time. I just want you and Mum to know.'

'What's it about then?'

'About our children.'

'*Your* children? Come on.'

'Yeah, we think of them as our own anyway.'

He shook his head. This was where they differed. 'Tracy, they're not yours. You'll know when you have your own what that feels like.'

'So what does it feel like?'

No, he didn't want to answer questions like this. 'A lot different anyway,' he managed. 'You can't just go out and pull a family together, like you're trying to do. You make your own. Then you look after it with everything you've got. Everything you've got!' He bunched his fists, as if he was talking to another man.

'Is that what you do then?'

He took this as a criticism. He had it coming. 'Take your mother. She's trying to help so many people. Take on every cause in the book. But her main concern is you. And me. The family. There's a reason why a family is built this way. Because it works. One person does one thing, the other something else, everything balances up. And I'm not much fucking help. Useless lump of dead weight.' He swung out his leading left leg, compensating for the delicate ankle on his right, tottering like an old man. 'But it still works out, because the basic structure is sound. Not like this thing you've got yourself involved in, I can't see any structure at all.'

'It's not that different actually. There's a structure. It's just that these people haven't turned their backs on others just because they have a different surname.'

'Oh come on, Tracy!'

'It's true. I know what you're like, Dad. I remember the time Mum asked you to join up with a Save the Children Fund. I've never seen you so hot under the collar.'

'It's a rip-off, that's why! All the money goes into administration. The fat cats drive big cars. And the kids that do get helped are ostracised by their villages.'

'Just because some guy at the pub told you that.'

'He knew what he was talking about.'

'Not everyone thinks like you, Dad. Fortunately. Thank goodness.'

'I think you'll find they do.' He paused for breath. 'Anyway, I think what happened to Sam's kids is awful. That shouldn't happen.'

'I know.' She decided not to tackle him on certain points, even though she saw big contradictions in his argument. 'We all freaked out. I panicked as well. It was bloody terrifying. Police came n'everything. The children screaming, it was awful. Awful. But Sam's lawyer got the order revoked eventually. But Yvette and I have to stay away.'

He shrugged, nodded, kept up with her, a lame duck beside his youthful, energetic, dreamy daughter.

'Anyway, I hate this country now,' she said. 'Countries who are led by regimes act no better that this.'

Regime was not her word, he thought. He could detect her pseudo-husband in her conversation, the bastard was slowly radicalising her. 'So do you think they can win the case? What does this lawyer think of their case?' He was at pains to exclude her from these distant battles.

'Ridley says that anything can happen in a London courtroom. Anyway, I'm at the Metropole. I wanted to tell you. Just in case you wanted to, I dunno, contact me.'

'Contact you? Course we wanna contact you, Trace. Come off it. I'm still doing your frigging bedroom up for you. Well, I'm about to.'

She sidestepped the subtle invitation to return home by pulling out a gilt card. 'Anyway, here's the address.' She handed him the hotel business card.

'Living in a hotel, eh? Like bloody Gloria Swanson.'

She smiled. They used to watch the old movies together, play Guess the Actress on Saturday afternoons. 'Well, it's not actually that fancy but Yvette and I have to lie low for a few weeks. And Sam is going to have to officially marry Firouzeh. Legally married now. It has to look like Sam is only married to one woman for a bit.'

Eric looked wan. He shook his head repeatedly. None of this was easy on a father who wanted for his only daughter a long, breezy, single life for some years to come, one in which he continued to loom large, until, when the time came, a son-in-law came along in the father's mould, a safe pair of hands who would hold the older man's interests dear, and who could eventually take his place at the Sunday dinner table and in a hundred kindred ways amplify Eric's version of the world, breathing new life into it. But such hopes were now ashes.

He looked at his daughter. Her eyes were on her shoes scuffing pebbles. 'What did I do? Tracy? I must have screwed you up. I lie awake at night now trying to work it out. What did I do to screw you up this much?'

'You didn't.'

'I've started wondering now if it was . . . maybe it was this flasher? This pervert?'

'Dad!'

'Those bastards have an effect. I've read about it.'

'Don't be stupid.'

'So maybe you're only attracted to perverts now. I'm trying to work it out.' She stopped walking, refused to go on, shaking her head in amazement. 'Well, it's possible, innit? That can be how it works. You get attracted to the things that mess you up. Don't ask me. I'm just trying to work this out, that's all. Or maybe it's me who messed you up somehow.'

Tracy shook her head. Her high hopes for this walk were gone. 'Dad, you didn't screw me up, okay. If I'm screwed up then I did it all by myself.'

'We should turn around now.' Without waiting for her he turned and started back.

She knew this mood of his. For a while he would be silent now, grumpy, withdrawn, working off his adrenalin while working out his next point. He hated talks that required quick answers. He was a slow thinker, a heavy deliberate head-scratcher, a weight-shifter, a room-leaver. Given time he could be as sharp as the next person, even sharper, but his success rate slipped away dramatically when rushed. Playing chess with him, she had only to rush him with an urgent 'C'mon, c'mon', for his queen to fall, by an absurd oversight, to one of her pawns. He'd resign, upending the board. 'Look, we're all screwed up,' he finally countered, 'some piece of us anyway. But you can't let that tiny bit rule you.'

'You're invited to the wedding as well. If you want to come.'

Surprised, he faced her. 'What for?'

'To support me. To support us. My new family.'

He was aghast. He took a full minute to reply, by which time they had almost returned to the park gate. 'Look,' he concluded, 'we'll always support you. You're our daughter. And if you wanna go down a big dead end with your life we can't even stop you then. But I'll be buggered if I'm gonna *help* you go down it, no way, sorry. Don't ask me and your mother, Tracy, to *help* you go down it.'

Saaman Sahar married Firouzeh Afzalur at a civil ceremony on a cold Friday morning at an hour which still permitted him to open the restaurant that evening.

After the meeting with Ridley it was clear that if the children were to be protected, the fine balance of their cohabitation had to be staked. The continuous sight of the children, arriving home from school and flushed with good health and ignorant of the depressing proceedings, was enough to decide the matter.

In contrast to the festive mood of the most recent marriage, this one was conducted in a state of near-catalepsy.

Not a single flower had been purchased. To underline the funereal air three men in dark coats, waiting to whisk the justice of the peace off to a burial, stood at the door with hands clasped behind their backs.

The only respite in a ceremony devoid of embroidery came when the official asked Sam for a ring. Sam had so downscaled his ambitions that he had completely forgotten to buy one. At this point, Firouzeh slipped off her current ring and passed it over to her fiancé for its immediate return.

Sam answered the JP's confusion with a smile.

The couple, thus ringed, muttered perfunctory vows and signed the register with a faulty ballpoint. Tracy and Yvette witnessed beneath.

Sam then took his leave, kissing all three foreheads, waving himself out of the door while the bride with her bridesmaids drove away in a taxi, the newly legitimate wife asking to be taken home at once so she could get out of her dress immediately.

A sour civil case was now ready for Ridley to make.

Sam's parents made no pretence at disguising their approval of this turn of events, praising with open enthusiasm a wedding ring they had seen many times before. 'Oh! *Ajab khoshgeleh!*' they gushed. '*Cheghadr Maheh! Vay, Che ghashangeh!*'

Sam yelled at them, 'Enough, please! You've seen it a hundred times.' But their retort was that Firouzeh had always been so busy — 'so much busier than anyone else' — that until then they had never been able to fully appreciate it. The ring was worthy of a true wife.

Insensitive to Sam's discomfort in the wake of the enforced wedding, they gave Firouzeh Persian delicacies from high-street stores, monopolised her at the dinner table in long discussions in Farsi on the rights and wrongs of western housekeeping, and attributed to her the lost mantle of *soccoli*, most favoured wife. The strategy was as transparent as it was outrageous. They found the house so much tidier now, so much more well run, they said. They sensed a strong Muslim hand at the helm. And now it was time for them to make preparations to return to Iran. Sam picked up the phone and found seats for them on a plane leaving in three days' time. The visit was over.

All that remained was to counsel Sam in the matter of his children. He must not play about with their safety a second longer. The other wives must be discarded at once. In the lounge, with the door shut, their raised voices reached the length and breadth of the house. It was time for him to take stock, they told him. Enough of this playboy lifestyle. Who was he kidding? One wife, one wife only was all he had the skill to manage. As a boy Fatima had not been able to trust Sam to go out and bring home a loaf of bread. What on earth did he think he was doing having three wives?

They begged Sam to erase the names of the other two from his memory.

19

Happiness Is

When Tracy awoke on the first day of her third week in exile, she looked across from her narrow bed to its twin. The sight of its sleeping inhabitant, auburn hair coursing off the pillow, the feathered eyelids shut, reminded Tracy that she was once again in a hotel room, not in her own bedroom at all, and that her vivid impression of family repatriation and courtroom victory had only been an aspect of sleep.

Because the chamber maid's knock was yet to sound on the door it must be before 10 a.m. She pulled herself from bed, and slid her feet into slippers. She was hungry but balked at eating either the hotel's individually wrapped butterscotch biscuits or its chocolate mints which sat on a white saucer in the mini-bar. Neither did she wish to dress and go down to the breakfast buffet. Like every other one of the fourteen other mornings that had followed the judgement, she simply went into the bathroom, wiped her face and brushed her teeth, put on the white bathrobe with the hotel moniker over the left breast, and sat on the end of her bed to stare out of the window until Yvette awoke.

When Yvette opened her eyes ten minutes later and said, as usual, 'What time is it?' as though they were two women in a hurry, two women with full itineraries, with meetings to attend, promises to keep, Tracy replied, as usual, 'Before ten.'

'Shit. Too early.'

Yvette knew as well as Tracy that to wake up at any time before ten left them both far too many hours to fill, too many hours in which to contemplate their predicament, and therefore far too many hours in which to become depressed and pessimistic about the future.

Yvette rose, stretched, then dipped and touched her toes, something she did easily. Going to the sideboard, she unwrapped a butterscotch biscuit and popped it into her mouth: 'Hungry.' They had tired of hotel food within days, and as with shopping or visiting art galleries and museums, nothing on the menu now interested them.

Since Sam had decided it was unsafe for them to continue working at the Taste of Persia they had very little to do. Yvette had taken to watching every French movie in town, while Tracy kept to the college's library, trying to keep her mind on what she was reading. This was hard enough. Nothing stuck now. She might read ten pages and close the book with only a vague impression of what she had spent the last hour studying. The dates, the names, the facts — her forte — slipped out of her memory.

Side by side they sat on one bed and stared out at the view until, as the first milestone of the day, the maid knocked on the door. They usually took turns calling 'No thank you!' but this time they called together. The maid's cart could then be heard wheeling away down the hall. Both women listened to this as long as they could.

Tracy finally went to a lecture. The man talked about the 'democratising power of the spirit'. It didn't sink in. As her fellow students scribbled down notes, snapping over to clean pages, she could only think about the danger that her marital situation posed for the children's welfare. In fighting the agency they were playing Russian roulette with their future. They had a right to fight, but the cost of losing was far too high. Sam was too angry to admit it, but if the judge found against them, the children would be taken away permanently.

She could see the situation as Ridley must have seen it all along. She should just bow out, do the noble thing, Yvette as well: let the Sahars return to being a normal family. That was it! British society could breathe again. Sam could serve his vegetables, Firouzeh answer the phone. Yvette would return to Paris, find work as a model, while she became . . . a what? What would become of her? A scholar, or a gold-digger, taking rich husbands until the jewels ran out? Or would she head back to the retail checkout business? It didn't matter. The children mattered. Only the children. Yes, she decided, it was time to undo the damage she had done.

Eric used a bevel-edged scraper to tear back the layers of collage in Tracy's bedroom.

It was astounding how many layers had been built up. Where it had hardened he had to resort to a chisel. It was a work of art he began to fully appreciate only as he destroyed it.

Monica came in with Emily to discover how far he'd got.

'Eric, I think you should stop. I feel awful.'

'No. Why? What's up now?' His chisel took triangular chunks out of the wall. 'You wanted it down this morning.'

'Cos . . . I dunno. It just looks terrible under there. It's like a vandal's been through it.'

'You said you wanted it off, so it's off.'

'No I didn't. It's just you were always banging on about it, I said you might as well get rid of it then, if you're gonna bang on about it.'

Eric shook his head. He looked to Emily for understanding. The edge of his chisel was partly embedded in a horseman, a Mongol warrior: his cap a fur rim, the horse's nostrils flared in mid-escape. 'Unbelievable.'

Emily scanned the room. 'Bit of a work of art, innit?'

'Was,' said Monica, glibly. 'Was a work of art.'

'For God's sake,' Eric said.

Emily's sympathies were naturally for the artist. 'Did you ask Tracy?'

'Oh yeah,' Monica replied, miffed. 'Just told us to do what we like with it. Doesn't mind. Was a teenage thing, she said.'

Eric took over. 'Course we did. So I start to take it down, okay, because madam here tells me to take it down, and now I'm suddenly ruining the fifth wonder of the bleedin' world!' He shook his head and let his chisel fall. 'So tell me, do you want me to leave it up or not? And Em, I want you to listen to this. Well?'

Monica looked around the room at the surviving dramas, most of them familiar now, but even these were damaged. 'What did you do to them?'

'I prepared it for stripping.'

With her imagination she had to fill in the blanks to repair it. 'Do what you like now then. You've wrecked it already.'

She turned and left the room. Emily shrugged but said nothing.

'Jesus Christ,' Eric shouted to both women.

Over coffee, Emily updated Monica on her daughter's academic successes at Cambridge while Monica reciprocated with depressing news of Tracy.

As usual, it was a balance sheet of contrasting achievement. Monica fell silent, became maudlin, drifted into her own thoughts, mouthing only a repetitive 'Really?' and 'Oh'.

'Some of them film themselves having sex.'

This refocused Monica's attention. 'Who? Christina does?'

'And God-knows-what-else. No, not Christina. Probably even take a camera into the toilet. And then send it out live on the internet. This friend of hers. Another student, not Christina,' Emily said.

'Oh, I thought you meant Christina.'

Emily laughed. 'No, this friend of hers. Her and her American boyfriend pay all their tuition fees by filming their sex life. Making a packet. They send it out live on the worldwide web thingy. On the internet. Charge people to watch. People pay.'

'Just make sure it's not Christina.'

Emily frowned. 'I know.' She hadn't thought about this, and now worried, remembered how children often test their parents' reaction to their activities by citing a friend. 'Oh, don't tell me that.'

'You think you know them, but then they bloody surprise you,' Monica said. 'I tell ya.'

'Who's having sex on the internet?' Eric asked from the doorway. He had a bemused look on his face.

'Em.' Poker face. 'Aren't you, Em?'

'Mmm,' said Emily with a good-spirited nod, still worried by a dizzying notion that Christina had been turned from an A student into a cyberspace porn star, but happy to play a trick on Eric.

'She's suggesting we do it as well. Film ourselves having sex. Whacha think? For the worldwide web?'

Eric snorted, waved his hand and left the doorway.

Monica laughed. 'Might have to find myself another stud, though.' She looked back at Emily who had drifted off. 'Em?'

'Now that you mention it, she never asks for money.'

'Who?'

'Never short. Christina. Gawd, you've got me really worried now. Always new clothes.'

'Em, oh stop it. Christina's not like that. Oh stop! She's top of the class. Too bright for that sort of carry-on.'

'Mmm. Still.'

'But if you're still worried there's an internet café in the new Tesco.' Monica laughed. 'Look her up. Log on.'

Emily couldn't smile. 'You're right. We're fine. And don't you worry about Tracy either. She'll be all right.'

'I know she will. I know she will. But we don't bring them up just to be *all right*, do we.'

'Well, I'm just all right,' Emily realised.

Monica paused. 'So am I.' They laughed. 'Bloody hell, I tell ya, I can't even cry any more. It's even beyond that.'

Emily nodded. 'So how is she?'

Monica poured more coffee. 'Bit better. The judge has broken up the harem thing at least. Thank goodness. Tracy and the French one have to stay away from the big house. And he has to stay away from them if he wants to keep the kiddies. Thank goodness for common sense.'

'And how's Tracy?'

'Not the best. Not the best.'

'So where are they staying now?'

'Still stopping in a hotel, but her and the French woman are looking for a flat together apparently. They want to stay together.'

'Must cost a packet to live that long in a flash hotel.'

Monica poured the cream. 'Mmm.'

'Wouldn't mind meself. No cleaning,' mused Emily. 'Room service.'

'Beauty parlours once a week.'

'Really?'

'Things like that. Oh, I'm sure. Hair's always nice anyway.'

'Nice for some. How much does a beauty parlour cost these days then?'

'Dunno. Thirty quid? Couldn't tell ya. Never been, have I.'

'Thirty?'

'Least.'

'We can afford that. Why should they have all the fun?' Emily was serious.

Monica looked at her neighbour then turned towards Tracy's bedroom from where she heard the renewed *chip-chip* of Eric's chisel. 'What are you doing on Tuesday then?' she said.

Emily laughed. 'Having a luxury facial with you, looks like.'

When Eric heard Emily go, he finished up and went through to talk to his wife. He found her in the armchair, reading from her notebook, the journal of controversial comments. She didn't look up. He lit a cigarette.

'I thought you were going to try and get a few more signatures this morning.'

'Mmm.'

'The petition has to go in on Friday, dun'it?'

'Mmm.'

'What's she been saying now then?'

It took her a few seconds to reply. 'Fastest growing religion in the world.'

'What is?'

'Four hundred and fifty million now. In 1907 there were only half that many. Interesting.'

'Interesting, why?'

She looked at him. 'Cos it must be offering something.'

'Repression. People look for repression. That's all it is. Explains why people get married.'

'Ha, ha. I thought you weren't going to smoke in here any more.'

He ignored this. 'Why must it be offering something?'

'Because . . . because it's getting millions of converts. Not like us, who are born into a religion and just stick with it come hell or high-water. These are *converts*.'

'Hell or high water?' He had to laugh at the irritation he felt at this remark.

'And we don't ask questions. But some people are searching.'

He drew on his cigarette. There was a limit to how much change he would tolerate. 'Bollocks,' he said. 'Course they're searching if they're on the wrong track. We don't have to search cos we're on the money. We've gone past go and collected two hundred, in't we.'

'I thought you'd say something like that.'

'You only search when you haven't found what you're looking for. Simple as that.'

Now it was her turn to chortle. 'You mean we have?'

'Well, I have. Obviously you haven't. I mean look at you. You think you need to keep a journal just to understand your own daughter.'

Her reply was whimsical, but he wondered if it was not becoming true. 'I do actually.'

She went back to her book.

He stewed for half an hour then went into another room. He returned only to reproach her. 'Fancy a pint?' he found himself asking instead.

'Y'what?' She was squinting now and massaging her temples, fighting off the beginnings of one of her headaches.

'I thought we could pop out for a pint.'

She looked up at him until it seemed like the oddest suggestion he had ever made.

On the landing in their coats, waiting for the lift, the oddity of this outing was still to recede. The single downward arrow in the silver plate was illuminated. They both stared at it.

'Living dangerously,' he smiled.

'We should take the stairs.'

'Bugger that.' He drew on his cigarette.

'Enough cigarettes.'

'Quitting tomorrow. Got no wind left.' With one fist he thumped his chest. 'Stairs'd kill me. But quitting tomorrow. Watch me.'

'Look at that,' she said. 'Oh no, will you look at that.'

A hairline crack in the plaster above the lift had grown into a fracture double in size. 'Wasn't like that a week ago.'

'Wasn't it?' he asked.

'I need a photo of that.'

'What's the point?'

'It's going on all the time. Even while we sleep. Think about that.'

As they waited for the lift, waiting for it to come, they stared at the crack as if expecting it to grow before their eyes.

'Lots of things are going on while we sleep,' Eric finally noted. 'But everything needs repairing. There's nothing on earth that doesn't need repairing from time to time.'

'Replacing, you mean.'

'No, repairing.'

'There I disagree,' Monica said. 'There we have to agree to disagree.'

Sam drove his parents to the airport.

Scolding them for their lack of support, their divisiveness, their rigid point of view while he suffered huge setbacks, he kissed them on both cheeks in the departure area. Their opinion of his life so closely resembled that of the family court that he had taken out his frustration on them all week. Both parents and son knew it was time for a return home.

His mother's cheeks were wet with salty tears as she made one last plea. Now that his adult life had been cleared up, his proper wife reinstated, he should return soon to Iran. A mood of political tolerance was in the air. He owed it to himself to participate in the new debate. The future was being shaped at this minute. To stay away was cowardly. The new Iran needed him. In his absence people spoke of him as a dissident, an atheist, and yet she knew how he loved his country, retained deep links to his faith and missed his own people. It was time to return, she begged her son, pressing her hands together.

With a kiss on the forehead he gave her a gentle push, smiling at her familiar zest, her tireless mothering energies which even old age could not confiscate. 'Enough. Go. Take her.' He embraced his father next, felt the tickle of beard on his neck. Even through the layers of cotton Sam could feel the old ribs, the smooth corrugations under his hands. As he released him, his father turned away, depriving the son of visual proof that they indeed loved each other.

From the velvet rope Sam waved goodbye and smiled as they passed through the immigration barrier, managing to hold up several other passengers in a minor dispute over papers.

Sam shook his head at the two small figures wandering off into the void of the international machine: he couldn't be sure he'd see them again. He loved them deeply, but if he was honest, their criticisms exhausted him. And yet they still had many things to teach him, not least about growing old. Perhaps they were right. Now that his marriages had been deconstructed, perhaps it was time to go back.

But driving back to town in the dark, flanked by black cabs with bubbly tourists craning to take their first looks at London, he changed his mind. He had been away too long to return. He would expect certain things of the society that it could not deliver. And his mother was on the money about one thing. In Tehran they would look at him sideways now. He couldn't tolerate such righteous looks. His years as an émigré, a traitor, a fly-by-nighter, would mark him out. And he refused to explain over and over again to strangers that he had not slipped out of his country to protect his cash. Not guilty! Money is easily scattered. No, his rationale for leaving, and also for staying away, was pure. Simply put, he was a lost soul.

Tracy, Yvette and Firouzeh met at one of their regular places, on the grass in a secluded part of Battersea Park.

The breeze was stiff, and delivered to them across the lawn the odour of freshly turned soil set free by an old bearded gardener whose tiny trident dug spring marigolds into the earth.

The women's sunhats had to be regularly retrieved as they cartwheeled across the lawn. Sun flecks and lacy shadows skimmed their exposed legs, sunning them — in Tracy's case — to the mid-thigh, in Yvette's to the knicker-line, with a demi-tuck of skirt under elastic, but in chaste Firouzeh's case only to the knee, her ancestral modesty impressing itself even in an English park on a sunny day.

They were arranged as an old-fashioned portrait photographer might set them: three milkmaids in a noonday tableau.

Hanging over their clandestine meetings was the forthcoming hearing. The judge had read it out without looking up from her notes. The children would be permitted to remain in the custody of their parents, under the scrutiny of the Social Services, so long as no attempt was made — 'none' — to return to the previous 'quasi-polygamous situation'. The wording was a triumph for Ridley. It was a triumph also for Sam's parents, who had returned to Iran, mission accomplished. It was a conditional reprieve for the children. But for the those at the centre of the marital drama it represented disaster.

Firouzeh had immediately offered to move out of the big house with the children, allowing at least Tracy to move back in with Sam, but Sam had ruled this out. It would be too hurtful for the children, the very ones they were aiming to protect. He was very much their father by now and he could not stand to be parted from them. Firouzeh would stay put: about this everyone was agreed. Yvette and Tracy would hang on in the hotel until the hearing and, spread between two addresses, try to preserve what had hitherto existed in one.

Initially distressed, defiant, then mournful, subdued and finally tearful, the women could not completely resist high jinx for long. Soon they were rolling about on the lawn in hysterics, letting off steam in their usual way.

Yvette had a story. Yesterday a man had approached her in the dark of a cinema — the place was full of lovers, *qu'on s'embrassait dans tout les coin*: she smacked fish-mouth kisses on the back of her hand, always the conscientious scene-setter — and asked if he could lick her ice cream.

271

'*Le nerve!* He wasn't even good looking,' she said, making a sour face. And so she let the creep have it. She spread her hand over her face to illustrate her crash-landing cone: '*Splooosh!*' She admitted another motive: she was glad of an opportunity to express her anger and frustration. 'And I feel much better after that.'

Tracy rotated the cap on the bottle of sparkling mineral water like a volume knob, keen to discuss what new initiatives could be undertaken. But before she could raise the matter, Yvette had an announcement of her own.

She had been in touch with her estranged parents. They wanted her to return to Paris. She couldn't live any longer with this feeling of official exile and punishment, of living in limbo. 'They have put us in . . . in a quarantine. They think we infect people with some bug, so that everybody will be living in fours and fives.'

She would go back to Paris in the meantime and wait for news of the court decision. Of course, she would return to their old life as soon as it became possible, but until then she wouldn't accept being treated like a 'citizen third-class'. Giving up her job at the restaurant at Sam's say-so, cutting that last link, was a last straw and had forced her to review everything.

'I think I need a holiday. We all do. So I telephone my family yesterday. After Guillaume died they think I am insane. Who would live with the man who had killed their husband? This they can never understand. Only a madwoman. But now they will talk with me again. Now we are broken up in their eyes, I am cured. *Tout est bien.*'

'Are we broken up?' Tracy asked.

'It is how it seems. So now they want to see me. So I think I must go back, if only for a small time. Then I will come back if we hear good news.'

Tracy shouted. All her hopes were pinned on preserving their solidarity against the bombardments of the social services. 'What if we do as Sam says? Maybe we need to go to a Human Rights court.'

Yvette shrugged. She had nothing left. She kissed Tracy on the cheek and held her hand. 'If anything changes I can come back. I will only be three hours away, *ma chérie.*'

'Then it's hopeless,' Tracy concluded. 'It's all falling apart, isn't it? The whole thing is coming apart.'

No one denied it. With Sam too paranoid — for the children's sake

— to be seen in any other company than Firouzeh's, living in constant fear of surveillance, the agreement between the four of them had effectively come to an end the day Tracy and Yvette moved out.

What could be said? Did anyone really think they could spend years like this: group meetings in the park, sunning their legs?

It was also no surprise that Yvette would be the first to question things. Lacking Firouzeh's connection to Sam through the children, or Tracy's romantic one, she had the least reason of the three to put up with prejudice and cruelty. Although Tracy might have argued with her, Yvette remained a mouthpiece for all the others' private thoughts.

'Perhaps we should all move to Paris?' Firouzeh suggested.

'I will organise it like ziss,' Yvette replied. She snapped her fingers. 'Ziss is a great idea. I will organise it.'

'We could,' Tracy added, looking avidly at them both, as if rabbits were begging to be pulled from hats.

But no one followed this up. They all knew that Sam couldn't be expected to relocate and restart his life for a third time. His heart wouldn't stand it. It would quite literally kill him.

Firouzeh stood and announced it time to pick up the children. 'We've got to talk again tonight and discuss all this properly.' Yvette had shopping to do as well.

Flicking away grass blades imbedded into the back of her legs, hiding emotion, Tracy felt obliged to say that she too had a few things to take care of.

They kissed one another on both cheeks and took three different paths out of the park.

As Yvette prepared for her departure, and as the date for the hearing approached, Tracy increasingly isolated herself in the hotel, crying herself to sleep every night.

But she also cried during the day now. She would cry when she was shopping. She would cry on the phone to her mother. She couldn't hold back tears when she and Yvette went out to a movie on her own and on the bus, in public, she suddenly had to hide her face.

Even at the Islamic Information Centre — a huge embarrassment — she needed tissues when she was told that they did not hold an address for Cat Stevens: she had decided to write him a letter. By now she was sure she was losing her grip.

She was also sleeping too much. Yvette accused her of trying to break a record, sleeping her days away with the curtains drawn, rising later and later until only the dimming of daylight in the crack of the fabric could compel her to her feet. Yvette eventually realised she had to intervene.

Returning from an excursion to Oxford Street at 4 p.m., she dragged open the curtains and shouted the time on the alarm clock. 'Enough! Ziss will stop now! You are going to die in your sleep!'

Hauling back the covers Yvette exposed a sea-horse figure beneath, curled up in denial. She seized an ankle and dragged her in three tugs off the bed. Tracy hit the ground with a thud.

'Ouch!' Tracy was splayed in her nightie, her hair a mess, blinking at her friend with half-shut eyes. 'That hurt. Fucking hell.' She massaged the ankle ringed with lethal fingernail marks.

'I hope so. Now get up. You are keeping zee hours of a whore.'

'Good.'

'*Oui*, a whore!'

'Good.'

But it pulled Tracy back from the brink. After this she made an effort. Over coffee she promised to keep up appearances and to hide her depression. In this way it might just go away.

Unable to watch Yvette pack up her belongings, however, she forced herself to go out. She invented things to do. She wandered the streets of London, stepping into shops that didn't interest her, turning merchandise over in her hands. She considered buying this rubbish, just to have something to show. But she was too lethargic even for that. In the big department stores on Oxford Street she read the labels on products, the countries of origin, and imagined the peasant workers responsible, bent in labour in China, in Bangladesh or Latin America, struck only by how little was made in Britain any more. London was a marketplace for everybody else. The English simply charged the world rent. Tracy moved through the gilded halls of the great stores in a distracted haze.

That is, until the time for a serious decision arrived.

On the day of Yvette's departure she ran out of excuses to shop and found herself watching Yvette fill her bags.

This French beauty, whom bereavement had not been able to age or tarnish, could not be discouraged from returning to Paris. She would go back to resurrect a family that could again acknowledge her. But she showed her frustration as she hurled unfolded garments into her bag. She had a sister on the Boulevard des États-Unis in a building out of which the Gestapo had operated. She would stay there initially and see what happened. Tracy could come and visit whenever she wanted. She would phone Burton Street when she arrived. Right now she should go. She would miss her plane.

But Tracy commandeered the case, sat on it. She wouldn't let Yvette go.

They wrestled for control of it until they began to laugh and collapsed on the ground. Tracy was too strong. They both sat there for some time, laughing at no single thing, until Yvette declared for a second time that it was time to go.

The hotel room, without Yvette, became a prison cell. It left Tracy on the point of screaming.

When Sam came that night it was only his fifth visit in three weeks. Tracy rushed into his arms in distress.

'Shhh,' he whispered into her ear, and then again, 'sshhh now.'

Creeping in like a bandit, denied even the satisfaction of knowing the extent to which his movements were being monitored, he admitted that he was on the verge of madness himself. Taking risks with the children's safety was not an option he could allow himself, but at the same time he wanted to be no other place but here. Then, even when he had navigated the streets and tunnels and byways, taken all the risks he could to get here, what pleasure were they both able to find? Meeting like an outlawed political faction, in a numbered room, cheered nobody up. Firouzeh had already refused to accept the humiliations imposed by this situation and told Tracy that she would meet her by day in the park. Anything else was insane.

Still puffing from the strain of eluding his perhaps non-existent and therefore tireless followers, Sam set down his jams, croissants, oranges, packets of julienned carrots, his antidotes to the poisons of hotel food. He picked up one of her course textbooks. 'Incredible. This is the reading schedule of a mullah. No moss growing around here, I see.'

But Tracy did not to smile. Not as fatalistic as Yvette had been, she was still to be convinced that defending their case in court was the right way to go. 'You don't seem to be worried about this risk to the children.'

'Not worried? Not worried? Do I look to you like I am not worried?' He most certainly did not. Dark hoops underscored his eyes.

'I simply cannot believe that we could lose. They have no basis for prosecution. So I am not about to abandon a life it took years to find on the basis of some wild official threat.'

Sam shook his head, sat on the single bed, bearing the burden of responsibility. He loosened his tie, unfastened his top button. He tried to break the mood. 'Why don't we get out of the city for a few days? Abdullah can manage.' As usual, in the face of problems, he suggested some new spending spree: a drive, taking up Yvette's offer of a weekend in Paris, a week perhaps in Cornwall out of the reach of the hypothetical snoops. But Tracy, whose despondency had by now outgrown her optimism, was past being excited by escapist ideas. Her nerves were undermined. She was actually at breaking point, she told him. 'So let's not do anything tonight. Maybe we can all meet up somewhere and do something tomorrow.'

He winced. Daylight posed great problems for him. She saw it at once. 'Well, tomorrow night then. We can meet somewhere and talk, all of us. Those who are left.'

'Stop it.' He sighed and picked up his coat. 'We will get through this, I promise you.'

She didn't reply.

He drove home in a depression, the smudge of Tracy's lipstick on his cheek for Firouzeh to wipe away as he came in the door half an hour later: only kisses on the cheek now for Saaman Sahar!

'Did anyone see you?' Firouzeh asked, obsessively worried as well.

'This is craziness. Tracy's right. This can't go on. I'll have to think of some bloody thing.' He stormed upstairs.

But the next night, at the back of his restaurant, his mind was still a blank. Struggling to control his new waitresses, a giggly twosome who had come in and offered themselves as a package, he lost his temper. Only the intervention of Abdullah stopped him sending them back out onto the street.

Sam phoned the hotel the next day only to be told that Tracy was too tired to see him. She was going to bed early. There was little point in him visiting. She told him to relax and have a night off.

As he said goodbye, adding that he missed her, he imagined her empty hotel room, Yvette's bed empty. He deserved the rebuff, he told himself. He was even proud that Tracy had put her foot down. The time had to come. He turned and crossed the kitchen to watch Abdullah stir a pot of heavy spinach sauce so green that it had almost become another colour, stepping over another plate recently broken by the incompetent new double act. 'How many plates is that tonight?'

Abdullah shrugged and looked curiously at his employer. Was the big, silent chef about to say something? Sam kept his eyes on the perfectly thickening sauce as his right arm lashed out and found a tower of saucepans. He swept them to the floor.

The new girls rushed back into the kitchen, by now instantly associating themselves with the din of falling objects.

Sam turned to his chef and received a reproachful look born out of a thousand years of nomadic hardship.

'I don't want to hear it,' Sam responded.

Unable to endure for another second the tropical heat and humidity of the kitchen he rushed past the dumb waitresses and entered the crowded restaurant.

Sitting right there, at the first table, he ran right into Richard Innes, in the company of a young woman.

'Hi,' Ricky announced. 'Me again.'

'Oh. Yes. How are you?' Sam tried to conceal how taken aback he was.

'Fine. Oh. Oh. This is Suze. Suzy, this is . . . Mr Sahar.' Ricky spoke with the lame enthusiasm of a man with a crushing headache.

'Pleased to meet you.' Sam struggled to remain focused on this young man. His thoughts were wildly scattered. 'This is good to see.'

'Yeah,' said Ricky.

'Are you two . . . you are — ?'

'Oh. Yeah.' Ricky tried to smile. 'Gotta move on, know what I mean.'

At this Suzy Ballantine blushed.

'Oh and thanks,' Ricky said. 'For all the help. Lot of help. Know what I mean?'

'No. Actually, I don't think I do. But it is good to see you have moved on.'

'Yeah,' replied Ricky unhappily, a touch defiant. 'Well, I have actually. It's brilliant actually. And this time it's the real thing. What's past is past. Funny. When the right thing comes along you just *know*, don't ya?' Ricky reached across and tried ineptly to paw his beloved's hair, an action she countered by pulling her head sharply aside.

'You most certainly do,' answered Sam. 'You most certainly do. Now if you'll excuse me.'

When Sam had gone, Ricky turned to Suzy. The woman had glazed over completely, most likely with shame and rage. 'What?' he asked, genuinely bemused.

What had he done now? Hadn't he just glorified her? What was the matter with her?

She looked away, out into the street, almost on the verge of tears.

'Never happy,' Ricky accused her bitterly. 'Never fucking happy.'

Against her instincts Tracy made herself attend lectures. Who knows, she thought, maybe she would hear something useful from the mystics. At the same time, ringing in her ears was Sam's two-edged epigram that a university education was the best way to come to terms with your own ignorance.

By sharing several lectures with a nervous young male student she inadvertently allowed this stranger to think that they had a lot in common.

Hector Robins's face, skin stretched taut like a tambourine, was the result of the conflicting pull of an unresolved childhood and an undiscovered adulthood: in other words a blank canvas.

Believing that ordinary-looking girls contained more secrets than 'stunners', he was drawn to Tracy's air of privacy. He decided to end his own long-distance turmoil and make himself known to her. In the bustling cafeteria at lunchtime he approached her, in one explosion of verbal diarrhoea describing the size and nature of his father's rural assets: a vast tract of land in Sussex, a house in Cannes.

She interrupted him. 'I'm married. I think that's what I'm trying to say.'

'Really?' He had not counted on this at all. She was younger than she looked from afar and more secretive than he had guessed.

She continued. 'I was, anyway.'

He brightened for a moment. 'Oh, so then you're *divorced*? Fantastic. Great.' He was at the age when a divorceé would be a great excitement. This was even more extraordinary than marriage.

'No, not really divorced either. I'm married. But . . . only kind of. It's a bit complicated.'

Hector nodded, looked away before framing his confusion. 'So, then, you don't know if you're married, or not? Is that the problem?'

She looked at him. He had just provided more insight than any of her lectures to date. She realised that her dilemma was exactly as he had said. 'Yeah. Actually, it is. Thanks. That's exactly it. See you round.'

She got up and went straight to a telephone.

Deep in draughtsman's papers Sam held his half-moons two inches from his nose to cope with the irresolvable focal distance: his eyes were on the way out.

He went over the plans for the new restaurant.

If it worked out it would be a triumph. Many of the best ideas had come straight from Tracy, who proved to have a fine eye, a creative bent. Taking a back seat at the meetings with the architect, Sam watched while Tracy waved her hands and suggested fixtures, columns, eastern cornices, a diorama on the ceiling. She had a fierce imagination.

'Have you done this sort of thing before?' the architect asked.

Tracy admitted she had arranged the odd display at Sainsbury's. 'I tried to do something a little different. People liked them.'

Tracy's master-stroke was to dispense with a formal seating plan and recreate a model desert containing a number of dining tents in the style of a ragtag Bedouin *caravanserai*. Each party would look out from their own camp at others, lit by flaming torches, all grouped under a twinkling planetarium-style night sky, a concave ceiling supporting an accurate eastern star system. It was an outrageous concept in a way, but if it worked out it would be a *coup de théâtre*.

Although Tracy's idea had come from her early efforts to imagine a desert nightscape that could unlock the Koran's encrypted poetics, she credited Sam with having given her the inspiration. 'Since you told me to imagine it I see it every night the second I close my eyes.'

The brave new menu, however, was pure Sam. The culinary style would be an even more radical fusion of east and west. The new chef, fortunately, was a magician. A vegetarian himself, Mahfouz was a fellow exile and brought with him his own groupies from the Savoy. It was said that the Michelin people had their on eye on him. The food would be edible art. All in all, not bad for a humble gourmand, Sam thought. He lacked only a name for the new place. He needed something big, not gimmicky, something with romance. 'Help me.'

Firouzeh looked up from the London edition of *Keyhan*.

'I need a name. For the new restaurant.'

She looked down again, as the phone began to ring. 'No. You need Tracy for that.'

Sam stared at her. Word-play was not Firouzeh's strongest suit. Nor was the sparing of his feelings. 'Thanks very much.'

Sam answered the phone, then quickly pulled on his jacket.

'What's happened?' Firouzeh asked.

In a tone calculated not to alarm her he told Firouzeh he was just popping out for a paper. He knew she wouldn't approve of a daylight meeting with Tracy but he was fed up. His fighting instincts were returning.

Only when he was gone did Firouzeh realise that he had long ago sworn never to read a paper again.

His diurnal route to the Hotel Metropole had become even more convoluted than his usual one, and in addition to the two-tube shuffle he had added a bus trip as well as an unnecessary taxi ride.

Today, Tracy wanted to meet in Battersea Park. He met her at their favourite bench under the trees. At the crunch of his footfalls on the gravel she looked up. She had prepared a statement.

'I don't know if I'm married or not,' she told him. 'That's basically it. I don't know any more whether I'm married or not. I feel more like your mistress actually. No Sam, let me finish. I've been doing a lot of thinking.'

'I thought you liked hotels?'

'Let me talk, okay?'

'You said you like them.'

'Sam!'

Sitting beside her he vowed not to speak.

'It doesn't feel right any more. Yvette was right. It's not working out.'

'Am I allowed to answer?'

'No. I think we have to face something. We'll never be able to make anyone else understand why we're all living under the same roof. People can't get their heads round it, and I don't think they ever will. Your parents, mine, the Social Services, everyone I know, it's hopeless!' Sam bit his tongue, but it was becoming harder to do so. 'And since the kiddies were grabbed like that the whole thing came kind of crashing down. Now maybe we can win this hearing, but maybe we can't, and I don't think we have the right to risk dragging the kids into this again. So we have to face it.'

'Face what?'

'Sam, don't be thick.' She recognised the look of anguish in his face, and his usual penitential willingness to throw himself in front of a train if that would help, but at the same time she realised that passion and willingness and regret wouldn't do any good now. She handed him the envelope. 'Okay? Don't be stupid. We've just gotta face it. Anyway, I put it all in there. Don't read it now. It took me ages. I rewrote it about a hundred times. Don't read it now.'

'Tracy, I — '

She put her gloved hand to his lips. He didn't try to speak through this web of suede. 'Just read it. Okay? I'm actually going now. I'll call you. Okay? I don't know what I'm going to do, but nothing immediately. So don't worry.'

She took her hand away and, doing well not to cry, leant across, kissed him on the lips, then rose and walked away from him. This time it was his turn to hear the tramp of footsteps on gravel.

He did finally leave the bench and make for the gate, but it was not until some time later. Dizzy with thoughts, stumbling as his hand slipped the letter into his hip pocket, he barely remembered where he had parked the car.

On the footpath ahead a mime artist busily imitated passers-by, exaggerating their gait with unflattering gestures. Sam at once left the path for the grass, hoping to skirt the mischievous performer and pass by without being lampooned, but the mime saw him. From the corner of Sam's eye he saw that the man had stuck out his belly, shortened his stride, cruelly puffed out his cheeks and wrenched back his hair. The theatrical expression hardened, became fierce, stern, pained: it revealed a sour individual.

Sam lowered his head and hurried to the gate, and in so doing, at last managed to escape his tormenting shadow.

He read the letter in his office at home, but the first lines took so much out of him that he had to put it away.

That night he made a second attempt at his little table in the restaurant kitchen which was so steamed up it could have been a bathhouse, his thumb nervously flicking the lid of the acquired Swedish Zippo, nibbling without interest his *zoolbeya bamieh*. He managed to get through the next two paragraphs and put it down again.

Then, at the new restaurant site the next day he felt suitably robust in his hard-hat and steel-capped shoes, momentarily a thick-skinned labourer, to try again. With his back to a stanchion, a jackhammer dinning in his ear, he raced workman-like through the remainder of the letter. But it was a non-reading, a quick scan for the word 'goodbye', protecting his heart.

At home, while Firouzeh picked up the children in the car, he finally set himself the task of reading the letter for real. This time he read and reread every sentence. He lowered his guard and put his future happiness on the line. When he had finished his eyes were flooded with tears and he leant back in his chair.

Dearest Sam, sweetheart.

My first letter to you. I'm sorry it's not hand-written but someone has leant me a laptop for my essays and this way I can spell-check it which is wise. My spelling was always gruesome (I would have got that wrong for a start — wouldn't have put an e in it.) But I don't want you thinking I'm dense. P.S. I got an A by the way for my last essay, it was on the life of Muhammad, not bad for an ex-checkout girl eh?

Anyway. You once told me that honesty made the whole thing work. But now, I can't feel that honesty any more. It feels like we are living in disgrace, which none of us can stand. And we need to be honest about the dangers the children face. I know this is your first concern, but I think you're just so angry that you're letting yourself take a risk with their happiness that you wouldn't normally take. I don't want you to do it for me. I really do not.

And that's why I'm writing this. I'm going to go my own way now. I blame myself. Otherwise, you would all still be happy as you were. When you married me people didn't like it, like Ridley said. That 'girl next-door' stuff.

So I'm not asking for anything like a divorce. I don't actually want to be 'set free' from what we had right away. So if it's OK, I'll just quietly jump ship for now. I'm so sorry. I've always been a bit mad. Sometimes I think this whole thing has been in my imagination actually. I loved the whole beautiful dream.

Love forever, Trace.

At times like this Sam could understand the inner drive of the criminal. A quaking heart made you capable of wildly untypical actions. He set down the letter and stared out the window at the overcast English sky. It had started to rain outside, a cold, weak, soul-destroying drizzle.

It dawned on him that this country, so generous at first, now wished to be paid back. It had not been an act of global generosity at all: just a steep loan. Damn their fine print! In fact, with the scales tipped, England offered him far less than his homeland. If he had lost Tracy to this crisis he could never forgive himself or this country. He had to face it: his east-west experiment was in tatters. A sudden, visceral revulsion for England arose within him. His parents were right, he decided. He could put everything on the market within days. Why not? Everything was possible. Ridley could tidy up the details. The entire kit and caboodle could be on a plane by Thursday if he really decided to leave. This exploding of his old life excited him. The gloom lifted slightly. It might be the rash idea of the criminal, one who sees the money in the bank and thinks to simply take it, but he didn't care. Everyone could be together if he went through with it. Who knows, in Tehran perhaps he could revolutionise the local restaurant trade.

In an instant he had decided. If he could persuade everyone to return with him to Iran, he would go.

He hurled his rolled draughts across the living-room floor.

'*Basteh*,' he shouted loudly, badly shaken for sure but exhilarated. He must phone Ridley at once, quickly lay out the plan, before he changed his mind.

But by the time Ridley's voice came on the other end to say 'Hello?' Sam had already had a better idea.

He fell silent, working through the logistics of his new plan, letting his attorney suffer the illusion that a crank had got through on his private line. 'Hello? Who is this? Who the hell is this?' Then the line went dead.

Seated behind a skyline of paperwork, his bald pate a pale, setting sun, Ridley's eyes searched his client's face for clues to prove that what he had just heard was a joke. 'Iran?'

'At what point could you assess whether we were going to win or not?'

'Assess?'

'You must get a feeling, a sense at some point, when you know which way it's going to go. Right?'

Ridley half nodded, half shrugged.

'Then that's when you lean over to me and show me a thumbs up or a thumbs down like a movie critic.'

'And what do you do?'

'I walk out of that hearing. Take my family with me. You ask for a recess and I walk out of there with Firouzeh. We have a car waiting. We go straight to the bloody airport. I'm serious. I know I haven't slept in forty-eight hours but I'm deadly serious. Could I rely on you tie everything up for me if I ran out on this?'

'Sam, you've got to settle down.'

'I know. It would mean selling the restaurants, the house. I've got some foreign exchange offshore. We would be fine for a while.' Sam needed the famous man as an ally. 'So tell me what you think?' As usual Sam would probably have to flatter the old trout whose face, year by year, was taking on the colour of calamine lotion. 'Just say you'll do it, then we can talk about something else which is on my mind.'

'Such as?'

'Like how you stay so slim, for one thing?' It wasn't easy to be flippant right now but Sam would do whatever it took.

Ridley leaned back, making his chair-springs creak, no doubt relieved at the break in mood, revealing his tight belly. He slapped it once the way a horse-buyer strikes the hind of a stallion. 'I play the stock market. Simple as that. The NASDAQ keeps the pounds off like nothing else on this earth. I rate it higher than divorce. In 2000 I lost a half a stone and half my value in a week.'

'It's not for me.'

'No. It's not spiritual enough for you. I thought vegetables would keep the weight down though?'

'Desserts.' Sam tapped his own belt-defying gut.

'Oh that's right. Your sweet tooth.'

'Everyone needs a vice.'

'Or three. Or three.'

Was this another jibe at his wives? Just like a lawyer to stick the knife in first, Sam thought.

'But this idea of yours is madness,' Ridley resumed. 'Pure lunacy. Let's come back to it. You're crazy to talk this way.'

284

'It's either that or I lose Tracy. Simple as that. Yvette has already gone, and I'm not sure she will come back. We're coming apart at the seams.'

'Sam!' Ridley gave him the *Oh come on* look.

'It's true. Firouzeh is a mess. Obsessively worried. The children aren't sleeping properly, their clocks are overwound ever since the bloody Night of the Long Knives, something I can never, *never* forgive this country for!'

'Okay, okay, okay. Have a glass of water. Settle down.' Ridley squeaked from his chair and went to his water fountain, an upturned plastic flagon. He filled a glass and placed it in Sam's hand. 'Now, let's look at this rationally.'

'That's the problem. That is what we have been doing.'

'And I don't want you to get a chip on your shoulder.'

'What chip?'

'Some idea that everybody is out to get you. I warned you. When you flaunt convention you could be in paradise and still wind up in shit creek with a concrete canoe. It has nothing to do with England. So let's not start a war with humanity.'

I have offended his patriotic sensibilities! I don't believe it! Sam thought, outraged that such a thing could be raised at such a time. Still, he needed Ridley. He glanced at the disassembled trout rod in the corner, the Home Counties photographs on the wall. 'Okay, Ridley, you're right. It could happen anywhere. But it didn't. It happened here, in this country which trumpets its own decency from the rooftops. And I have been first to join in, as you know.' Sam calmed himself 'Okay, you're right, let's put this aside, because you could never understand what it's like to be an immigrant. Of course not.'

But Ridley wasn't ready to let this go. They were now riding the line that divided them. 'A country isn't built for immigrants, Sam. It's built for its residents. Loving England won't protect you. Certain ideas simply cannot just be grafted on. The human body rejects certain transplants. I'm talking about three wives.'

'Okay, let's drop all this. This is another conversation. Let's get back to the issue. I need your help. Can I rely on you for two counts? For advance warning, so I can get prepared, and if it goes bad, to tidy everything up for me after I'm gone?' This was no time to draft a new charter for the British Isles: Sam had his family to protect.

'And what do you hope to achieve by leaving?'

'Peace. Harmony. Old concepts.'

285

'For yourself?'

'For my family. For it to function in the way it had been doing. I want all three women back under the same roof again, with no interference. And it's time it was officially sanctioned, endorsed and accepted. And if that means I have to go back to Iran, then fine.'

'I had a horrible feeling you were going to say that.'

'Will you do it?'

'No. Nice to see you. Now please get out of here. What do you mean will I do it?' Ridley had been losing his hair for years. He scratched the latest area of recession. His hairy nostrils whistled as he exhaled. He relaced his fingers in his lap.

'How much money will it take?' Sam asked.

'First I have to ask you something. And I want an honest answer.' Sam nodded. 'You'd really give it all up? Twenty years' work? Throw it away, the restaurants, your home, and go back to a country you've told me over and over again that you still have a lot of problems with? Just to keep hold of these other two wives? Come on. They're beautiful girls, Tracy, Yvette, very nice indeed, lovely women, delicious even, but man to man, are they worth throwing *everything* away for?' He raised his eyebrows. 'Especially when you've got a perfectly good wife there in Firouzeh, and all this other trouble? Come on. Isn't it easier for everyone to just walk away?'

This mutiny should have been the last straw but Sam found himself chuckling. It was absurd. Why had he never seen it before? Because it was too obvious. Ridley was jealous! It was quite clear now. He had been speaking about himself, all that claptrap about repressed fantasies, and liberals and film censors with hard-ons. He was the one with the hard-on! The man would simply feel more comfortable if Sam returned to the ranks of convention, back within the comfort margins of bourgeois aesthetics and class. The wifely arrangement ate away at him too. Under the smiles and the professional gloss lay a naked and laughable envy.

'Even you?'

'Even me? What?'

'Even you? I can't believe it. Even you can't get rid of this idea that I'm living a fantasy. Taking my fill of all three women, right? When and where I want to, some kind of sexual overlord.'

'Sam — '

'After all these years, you still don't understand.'

'Understand? Yes, what exactly?'

'*That I'm irrelevant*! Almost completely irrelevant, Ridley. The reason why these three beautiful women want to live under the same roof, barely has anything to do with me.'

'Oh come, come.'

'So save your jealousy for the kids in rock'n'roll bands who really are having all the fun.'

'I'm just trying to advise you.'

'I had always assumed you'd work this out, but you obviously haven't, so here it is. They are there for each other, the women. I don't even think they fully realise it themselves, but they're not so much married to me, as to each other.'

Ridley stared at him, hiding his reaction, but listening closely.

'And don't give that a lesbian twist either. It's a straight friendship, and me, I'm just the pussycat who they know won't throw his weight around and spoil the party.'

Ridley looked somewhat glazed and uninterested in this explanation. 'If that's true, then what's in it for you?'

'For me?' Sam took a second. 'Well, you've seen them. I am just happy to watch.'

A smile crept back onto Ridley's face at that. This bit made sense to him. 'Happy to watch, okay. Ah! Now I'm getting it.'

'Then I have satisfied your lurid imagination. Or perhaps not. But can you now get off my back and tell me if I can rely on you.'

'You know what your problem is, Sam? You don't know how unusual you are.'

Sam looked up from his lap, mock dejection in his eyes. 'Unusual? If I'm unusual that's only because it's unusual to help someone nowadays.'

Ridley sighed. 'You're a terrible client.'

'And you're a useless, overpaid ego-driven maniac.'

'You're not impotent, are you?'

'No. Why?'

'Just an idea. Would help your argument a lot. We just might have to have you castrated.'

Sam was in an exalted state. He pushed aside the suitcase and the clothes on the single bed and announced that he had found a solution.

He laid out his no-lose formula. 'Listen to this. Ridley has even agreed. So forget this breaking up nonsense.'

287

But Tracy was unimpressed.

'Wait,' he urged. He asked her not to be too hasty. Before she could say no a second time he began again. He used his usual tone, light, happy, even whimsical. He made leaving the country sound like a walk in the park, the massive relocation and uprooting of their lives like a taxi ride. He finished: 'Easy! So what do you think?'

She took her time. 'Live in Iran?'

'It might not come to that.'

'I think it might do.'

'And so?'

'No.'

'You couldn't live there?'

'I could. But you couldn't.'

'Well, obviously *I* could live there.'

'No. I don't think you could. Not happily.'

'Tracy — '

'Not, and be happy.'

'What's *happiness* got to do with it? Forget happiness!' He threw up his arms. 'What are you talking about happiness for?'

'Listen to yourself. Sam, no. No.'

'I'm serious. What has happiness got to do with this? That can be *arranged* any time. Happiness is just a matter of having three things to look forward to: a dinner invitation, a holiday, a roll in the hay: bingo, I assure you you'll be happy. That can *always* be organised.' He snapped his fingers. 'Like that.'

'No. No it can't. Not *lasting* happiness.'

'Ha! There's no such thing! You make it every day! It's like bread, it's got to be fresh!' He knew he was in a state but he was relying on his mouth to carry him through as he paced the floor. 'No one's happy all the time, except the insane. Like I say, it can be arranged. But never, never, let us base life-changing decisions on its pursuit. This is too trivial to discuss.'

'It would eat away at you. I know that. Leaving everything.'

'I don't care. It really doesn't bother me.'

'And if it's so easy to arrange, are you happy now?'

This stalled him. 'Of course not.'

'See!'

'*But I'm not trying to arrange it*! My God, woman!' He turned his back, took several breaths and then faced her again. 'I'm just trying to sort this bloody thing out because I love you and you won't stop bloody talking!'

Tracy stared at him. He slumped down on the bed.

Tracy shook her head. 'I don't care what you say, or how you say it. I'm not going to let you sacrifice everything just because of me.'

'What sacrifice?!' Sam put his head in the vice of his hands: his face contorted. '*Khoda ghovvat*! May I remember the words of the Blessed Prophet!'

Tracy added; 'May peace be upon him.'

He glanced at her. 'Yes. That's right. May peace. Be upon him.' He calmed down. 'Don't do this, Tracy. Let me try again.'

'I've already decided.'

'What are you going to do then, for God's sake? Where do you propose to go?'

'I'm going home,' she said. 'Mum and Dad's. For a bit.'

Monica crept home early, puffing as she reached the door. The lift was now permanently 'under repair'. It took her twenty minutes to climb the stairs, stopping many times to catch her breath, and each time cursing her foe, the local council.

Eric was not in and she wanted to have a quiet cup of coffee alone, undisturbed by Emily, who, as she knew, would be listening out for the thud of her door, and taking it as her cue to come over.

She eased the door closed. The lock made only the smallest click. Surely she had got away with it.

She put the kettle on quietly as well. Even in her own home she had to be careful, considerate to the neighbours. The walls were paper thin, the entire building an echo chamber. Monica hated such precautions. She had always loathed this forced intimacy, this false privacy. A stranger's cough three flats away — bronchitis? — was a semi-public event. The sound of some man's piss thudding into the toilet water in the neighbouring flat could be heard from her bedroom at night. The list went on: the untutored strum of a guitar; a child's scream in the night could enter her dreams; a smuggled dog barking its head off in a locked room or a heated domestic argument spoke of a drama she had no choice but to imagine. And all of it made gossip inevitable. Rancour was only a hair's breadth away in Melksham Towers. Two extra notches of volume on the TV at a late hour could generate resentment in four directions.

Monica had to get more than four names on her petition. That was certain, and time was running out. As it stood, the petition was a personal embarrassment, and sending it in like this to the council for their big meeting, convened a week from Monday to discuss the future of the building, was out of the question. Three hundred names — her target — would have said that The People had spoken and could not be ignored. Society had to listen to such pleas or else forfeit its egalitarian pretensions. Four names, on the other hand, said 'Take us, we're yours.'

Still, she planned to attend the packed meeting all the same and perhaps even speak if the chance arose. But there was no getting round it. The petition was a washout, a personal defeat.

With only the drone of a distant vacuum cleaner to break the silence, she sat in the armchair and picked up a new library book she had begun earlier that day. She folded open the dog-ear as the phone rang.

She couldn't believe her ears. 'You're on your way?' she said. 'What, right now? What do you mean to stay? Are you okay?' Tracy said she was fine. Monica's heart soared. Had she and Eric won? Had all their teachings over all the years paid off? 'Okay, look, we'll talk when you get here. That's great, that's great. So how are you coming? Do you want Eric to — no, okay, okay. Whatever.' Tracy would take a taxi. She would be there soon. As soon as she had checked out of her hotel. Monica promised she wouldn't go out as Tracy had lost her key. 'Okay, see you soon then. Yeah. See you soon, sweetheart. Come straight away.' Monica said. She then thought of an inconsequential detail. 'Oh, we've painted your room. Dad's just finished yesterday. Funny thing. Must've known something, eh? See you soon. I'll put the kettle on. Bye. Bye. See you soon.'

She put down the phone. She wished Eric had a mobile phone. She would have phoned him right away. Tell him the family would be together again. Unable to locate her handkerchief, Monica grabbed the lace coverlet on the arm of her chair, and wiped under her eyes. No longer would she have to lie awake questioning what it had all been for, the whole maternal-perpetuation-of-life rigmarole: the answer would be in the next room again.

In the lobby of Melksham Towers, catching her breath before the alpine climb, she passed a young white boy she had never seen before. Just then scrunching a sheet of yellow paper into a ball, he nodded then bumped open the door to the street with his shoulder, trotting away.

Passing the lift on the way to the stairs Tracy saw that the 'Out of order' sign had been taken down and so pushed the call button. She was happily surprised when the lift doors parted with their familiar *klink, ding, ker-lunk.*

Someone had fixed the thing at last. She threw her heavy case inside. She stepped in and pushed the button for the twenty-third floor.

Home.

When Eric came in, out of breath and perspiring heavily, having just taken the stairs two at a time in line with the yellow paper warning stuck to the lift doors that said the lift was out of order, he was told the news of Tracy's return. He shouted his joy, hugged his wife, then went to take a shower.

Monica meantime gave the lounge a quick tidy-up, plumping deflated cushions, lining up the edges of magazines. When Eric came out his hair was wet and combed and he had on a fresh shirt. Side by side they sat on the couch and waited for Tracy to come through the door.

How long did they sit there, quietly happy? It seemed at least an hour. They discussed hypothetical reasons for Tracy's return. Their daughter had missed them. And she had woken up to herself. At last.

'I'm gonna eat something,' Eric said.

They both ate and cleaned up a light meal. Soon, three hours had come and gone.

'I thought she was coming straight over?'

Monica shrugged. It would soon be evening.

'Call the hotel,' Eric finally suggested.

Monica tried but learnt that Tracy had checked out of the Metropole that afternoon. Monica next dialled the Sahars. She got Firouzeh on the line. Tracy had not been there. In fact, Firouzeh had tried to trace Tracy herself on her new mobile number, but could not get through. Monica should try Sam on his mobile phone. He was visiting the new restaurant site. Perhaps he and Tracy were together.

Sam's mobile must also have been switched off. Monica's call was diverted and she left a buoyant message, disguising her anxiety. The man must be crushed by Tracy's decision to return home. Then she phoned Firouzeh back, but by now she knew she was only going round in circles.

Eric asked for the address of the new restaurant. He would drive down there and talk to Sam in person, bring Tracy back personally if she was there. Under the circumstances he was prepared to speak with the Persian, now that the war was over.

'I hope nothing has happened,' Firouzeh told Monica.

'What do you mean?'

Eric pulled into traffic. Could he face Sam without animosity? *On second thoughts, I am probably the man for this job.* If Tracy was coming home, then it was time to make the peace. Sam wasn't such a bad guy and Eric wasn't without his own regrets. Sure, at first he'd wished the worst on the restaurateur, in the white heat of the wedding, but the trouble over the children had softened Eric, even making him feel guilt for his earlier behaviour.

I would sell my soul for a cigarette, he thought. A fair trade too. In its current condition.

He reached into his top pocket and pulled out the ungainly plastic tube that supplied a few micrograms of nicotine to his aching bloodstream. The contraption made it look as if he was sucking on a felt-tip pen in public. He didn't like it but he was desperate. At forty-six his lungs were already shot. A pack a day since the age of fifteen and the broken lift had graphically brought home to him the extent of his dereliction. He needed half an hour after the twenty-three storey climb before he could speak properly. At least he was aware of his body again, its capabilities or lack of them, and not just its ailments. He had begun to flex his muscles in the mirror, look at his nude body in the bathroom, a vivifying experience, correcting his posture and even doing six chinups hanging off the open door. It didn't all have to run downhill, his ego informed him. On the bath stool was a copy of *Men's Health*, which Monica was still to comment on.

He parked near the address and instantly saw Sam up ahead. The short, stocky man wearing a hard-hat, had a scroll of plans under his arm. His paunched body arched back inspecting the roof, his belly thrust out, he looked like some friar taking in a fresco. And this was his daughter's lover? he asked himself incredulously, recoiling from the thought. This guy was in far worse shape than he was, and yet, look at the young women he pulls!

Eric got out, started towards the man but slowed his pace. He wanted to prepare his ideas. The Persian was a quick-witted bastard, Eric had to grant him that, and he wanted to come out with a sharp few lines himself before he got embroiled in a tit for tat battle and lost his way. Get in, get out, make his point known, and take Tracy home, he told himself.

He had almost forgotten that he had come to take Tracy home.

Sam approved mightily of what he saw. It was exciting, he had to admit. Even in his depressed state it gave his heart a flutter. A new restaurant, and one as spectacular as this, would put him on the map in London's competitive dining scene. He had been prepared to walk away from it all, to turn his back even now, but this project was hard to forsake, especially now the architectural details were emerging. Tracy's ideas, he could now see, would culminate in a masterpiece.

That morning the twelve trefoil arches to line two walls had been raised into position. Fabric samples were passed under his nose and he had to make snap decisions. In Tracy's absence he had to be decisive. He continually tried to visualise the desert Bedouin, not as they were, but as Tracy imagined them.

He had seen enough. He unzipped the overalls thrown over his coat to keep off floating drips of wet plaster and the talcum dust thrown up by the floor sanders. He felt uplifted, buoyant, almost happy for the first time in weeks, though nothing could dislodge the pain he had felt since reading Tracy's letter which even now was in his pocket.

It was getting late. It was time he was on his way.

He turned to be confronted by a young man he had never seen before. His smile was not returned. He sensed immediately that something was wrong.

'Hello,' he said inanely to his destiny, though his weight was already moving away in subliminal retreat as the threatening man stepped forward.

Sam turned but felt the hoodlum's hand close on his collar, driving him forward. He barely kept to his feet as he was pushed towards a panel van where a second man, wearing a menacing balaclava, held open the rear door 'Stop!' Sam managed to shout.

Before Sam could shout a second word, a useless 'Please' half out of his mouth, his shins barked hard against the bumper and his upper body jackknifed forward. The bridge of his nose came down on the inside tray, splitting it. Sam heard the crack. It sounded like someone had hit a home a six in a distant cricket game. It had happened so quickly he had not thought of self-defence. His feet were thrown sideways and hurled inside the van as though his body were already a corpse. With the back doors slamming shut, all light was cut off. In darkness he heard the van's engine rev up. In his black hell he was thrown side to side as the vehicle pulled away at breakneck speed.

Peeling back his balaclava, Ricky Innes was not at all happy. He threw the van into gear and gunned it a short distance, while insulting his partner.

'You were meant to wear yours too! Now he's probably fucking seen you, you idiot!'

'Looks very natural, dunnit, standing on a street corner in a fucking balaclava!'

'You were meant to stay in the back and jump out at the last minute, you bollocks.'

'Couldn't see anything, could I! Dark as a cunt in there.'

'Okay, let's just get this done, all right? Let's just give him a fright. And put your balaclava back on. Bruce! I said put it on! Bruce, put it on!'

Ricky checked his mirrors, then hit the brakes and muscled the wheel heavily to the right as arranged, sending them into a dead-end service lane. He glanced left to see his companion rolling the balaclava over his face.

'All right,' Bruce grumbled, figuring to take out the cost of this inconvenience on the man in the back, 'but let's give this fucking Paki something to think about before we get on our merry way.'

'Iranian,' Ricky corrected.

'Whatever.'

'And don't go overboard. I mean it. He doesn't look too fit. Little roughing up is all.'

Jumping out together and each opening one of the back doors, Bruce barked, 'Right, you! Out!' Together the two men pulled the already groggy body from the back of the van. Blood flowed copiously from the victim's nose.

'Now hold him,' Bruce said, as he fumbled in his pockets. 'Just hold the bastard up against the wall here.'

'Please,' the victim again muttered without hope, held in a full-Nelson by Ricky.

'What are ya doing?' Ricky was reluctant to use his voice but had no choice.

Bruce had flipped open the cap from a tiny tube, grabbed Sam's left hand then shot the gelatinous contents into his palm.

294

'There!' Bruce cried, as he thrust the victim's palm flat against the brick wall, holding it there with heavy pressure, the glue setting already. 'Just hold him there for a few fucking seconds and Bob's your uncle.' As the vital seconds passed the incongruous textures of flesh and brick bonded and fused into one. Bruce grinned maniacally as he released the hand. 'Try that out for size then.'

Years earlier, Richard Innes had stood penitent before a judge. He had stolen a car, staved in one end against a power pole, ending a drunken joy-ride.

In letting Ricky off lightly with a heavy fine the magistrate summed up his opinion of the young offender. 'I fear that you are in grave danger of developing an entrenched and irremovable lawlessness in your character that bodes woefully on the rest of society.'

But Ricky had rejected this. He would prove the man wrong. And he had been doing very well until that morning when he had placed a mayday call to Bruce, a relic of his worst days, which set him tumbling again down that endless flight of stairs predicted for him by the old magistrate, a staircase which, Escher-like, would never lead anywhere.

Ricky did not mean to seriously hurt the restaurateur. He simply wanted to show him that certain deeds were unacceptable. In this way he viewed himself as a de facto arm of the judiciary.

He was also a Taurean. And this particular star sign did not let go of things easily. He had learnt of these divine destinies from his lover, Suzy Ballantine: Taurus was an earth sign, supposedly in need of developing intelligence, but he was not ruled by his emotions either. He lay somewhere in between. Reading his charts, Suzy told him he possessed native cunning. The zodiac could solve many of the riddles of his life, she said. She quoted intensely from her books as he lay on his bed, privately recovering from Tracy.

Late at night, with cat's piss reeking from the hall, she wittered on about Einstein's letters, Erasmus and Nostradamus, and returned to her principal subject: she loved him. Was he even listening to her? The charts said they were destined to be together. He grunted his response, seeing only Tracy.

'I'm hooked on you. Completely hooked,' she said. He would get over that other bitch. He had to open himself to new possibilities. Suzy was even sentimental about the chiselled crystals she plucked from his hair after their sullen bouts of lovemaking, the minerals blasted from the doors of the dead. But everything, even the highest human attraction, could be understood only if he first accepted the immense pull of the cosmos.

She did his head in. He eventually hid from her calls. The more Suzy talked, the more he longed for Tracy. He knew now that he wanted her back more than ever.

To escape Suzy he had decided to mend his ways and win Tracy back by a consistent demonstration of virtue. With his friend, Bruce, he spent two hundred pounds on drugs. He fantasised about a reunion, heating Brown in a Lucozade cap over a Zippo, taking an E, a line of MDMA, later valium and cannabis at sunrise, sinking into menacing reveries. He romanticised about a double suicide: pills, whisky, turning off the big light together. They had flown too close to the sun, he wanted to tell Tracy in some close darkness — badly paraphrasing Suzy! — just like that bloke Icarus. So why not do it together? A double headstone could unite them! The world would realise that two bright flames, two very beautiful lights, had gone out.

But it had not worked out that way. In the weeks since the fiasco of the poisoned sausage — he'd gone back and heard the healthy barks of both dogs — his frustration had got the better of him. So when Bruce had unveiled the drugs that morning, already on a bender some twenty-four hours old and crazy for action, a counter-measure was inevitable.

'You might wanna stick around here for a bit, old son.'

With a demonic grin Bruce tested Sam's Superglued hand and proved it was frozen solid to the wall. 'Know what I mean?'

Ricky, incredulous, stared as Sam tested for himself the hand that refused to leave the wall.

As Bruce howled with laughter Ricky put his face into his hands and rubbed his face. 'No, no, no, no,' he shouted. 'What are you doing? This is crazy. Okay, that's it. It's over. Let's go. Leave him. I'm out of here.'

'No you're not. We're sorting this geezer out.'

'We're going, I said. I'm in charge of this. We're going.'

Bruce frisked Sam. 'His money, remember.' The plan had been to make this look like a robbery. He found Sam's thick wallet and peered inside. 'Bingo.'

Resigned to his fate, Sam was still staring at the magic trick that was his hand. 'Amazing,' he muttered, suppressing rage and fear. 'The genius of the underclasses. Where do you people come up with such ideas?'

Bruce stared at him. 'It's mine.'

'Shut up,' Ricky counselled Sam.

But Sam, the lifelong talker, was not about to mend his ways now. 'You must lie around in your stinking bloody flats for days thinking up this kind of thing. Or do you people have courses? International muggers' conventions?'

'Shut up,' Bruce reiterated.

'Terrific. And all for what? Two hundred pounds? Don't you know I would have given you the money without a fight? I would have given it to you out of sheer bloody pity.'

'That's enough,' Ricky shouted, altering his accent slightly and cuffing Sam on the back of the head, trying to stop the situation degenerating further.

'Pity?' Bruce replied, taking offence, pushing his face close to Sam's.

'So buy your drugs. But I want you to know something. You have not scared me. I tell you that.'

This last statement made Bruce incoherent with rage. Normally at this stage he would deliver a head-butt right on the bridge of the nose but his intelligence had been impugned by the foreigner. And so to Plan B. He would not be underestimated.

Gripping Sam by the throat, he thrust him backward against the wall. The skin on the bonded hand stretched to breaking point. Then as if about to size him up for a humiliating kiss on the lips the mugger drew out the tube of Superglue once more.

Sam's eyes widened in horror as the man brought it towards his face. Unable to move, he felt the tip of the tube running cruelly along the line of his lower lip; the acrid smell of glue pierced his nostrils.

The man grinned. 'That's right, big boy, try to keeping talking now.' He was done. He dropped the tube, seized Sam's jaw and drove it upward. Sam's lips touched, adhered and sealed in seconds.

Bruce was able to release his victim. He wasn't going to say too much now. And it was time for some fun, the humorous pay-off. 'So let's hear you try and talk now?' He wheezed with laughter and clapped his hands. 'Come on, big boy, let's hear it now. This is fucking great!'

Out of dignity Sam did not test his cauterised lips as he had done his hand: he refused to give this man the satisfaction. Instead, and unable to speak his mind for the first time in his life, he delivered a lucid look that said what his mouth no longer could: *I am still unafraid. Now go. Go!*

This unspoken insult could not be overlooked. And even the protests of his accomplice behind him couldn't pursuade Bruce to walk away now. This mouthy foreigner deserved pain after such defiance.

The first punch to the stomach made Sam weak at the knees. He groaned through his sealed mouth, a muffled moan. His legs could not sustain him after that. Badly winded, he collapsed, fighting for breath through flaring nostrils. And as he dropped a tearing noise like Velcro accompanied his hand's detachment from the wall.

Blood leapt from his palm, pouring through his fingers, coating the three wedding bands, spreading onto the oily cobbles. He might now have cried out in pain, give his attacker what he craved, but incapable of doing so and on the verge of fainting, he was doomed to prolong his own suffering. And so a booted kick to the ribs followed. Sam, foetal, received it as though he couldn't have cared less, his face scrunching slightly, his stifled cries sent inward to echo unheard in his chest.

'Give it up,' Ricky beseeched his partner. 'Let's go, let's go.'

To the head, to the chest, then back to the head, the final blows came. Sam had stopped moving.

Eric had tried to make up the distance but he had not been close enough when it happened. By the time he started to jog, only half believing what he was seeing, the van's doors had been closed and the vehicle had sped away.

Incredulous, he watched for a few seconds, wondering what else he could do on foot. A telephone, he told himself. He needed to get to a telephone. But then he saw the van slow as the traffic light changed to red at the far end of the street. Would the van observe the red light? He started to jog. He would not reach it before the lights went back to green but he owed it to this man to try. It was everybody's duty, if only a gesture.

But then, when the van turned into an alley, he couldn't believe it. Did these kidnappers perhaps live just a few hundred yards from where they operated? He quickened his pace, felt his nerves rise. What was worse than not catching the van was catching it. What the hell was he expected to do? Unarmed, was he really prepared to throw himself into the fray? He was no hero, he thought, as he increased his pace, his broken ankle making its first complaints. 'Shit,' he began to repeat, as the ankle tried to do its share. His gut bounced and his gammy foot hurt him more with each step. It was a miracle he even had the muscle-memory to run. He began to really hope that he could not catch up with the van.

At the service lane, with his chest heaving, he rounded the corner. The van was parked right there. Its masked driver, seeing him, beat on the horn. A second man looked up at Eric. At his feet, in a defensive ball, was all that was left of Sam.

Eric heard himself calling 'Hey!' He was running on auto-pilot. It might end up being one of the more foolish things he'd ever done. Both men stared at him in surprise, neither sure of their next move. Instinct told Eric he had to either move forward now or else run away. To stand still would prove himself as no threat at all. Maybe these people had guns, he thought. He took several shaky steps forward into the unknown, holding wide his arms, making himself bigger, making himself look angry. He barked a second 'Hey!'

This did the trick. The other man dived head first into the passenger seat of the already moving van, his legs sticking out on Eric's side as it raced towards him.

Eric suddenly wanted to catch them. 'You fucking little pricks!' he shouted as they came closer. They were no more than kids. But the van was coming at speed towards him and the passenger's door held open by the hoodlum's legs spanked the wall, sending off sparks. Eric jumped back into the recess of a door as it passed, emerging to see an arm reach for the door handle as the car hit the road and swung to the right.

This was their undoing. In the sharpness of the turn, the passenger, overextended, was catapulted out onto the road, tumbling several times until he came to a standstill at the feet of a stunned workman.

Eric ran again. He glanced back at Sam who wasn't moving at all, while shouting ahead excitedly, 'Grab him, grab him, just hang on to him.'

The driver hadn't stopped for his accomplice and was lucky this time with the lights. The van was three streets away when Eric reached the road. Retributional anger flooded into him. 'Hold him!'. But his shouts confused the worker even more, and he did nothing to stop the fallen mugger from getting to his feet and limping across the road.

'There's been a mugging,' Eric quickly shouted, darting through traffic, half crossing the road. 'Get the police. There's a man back there.

Police!' He stopped for a truck to pass and shouted back again: 'Police!'

Eric now began his pursuit for real as the labourer turned and looked into the alley.

If Tracy's watch was right, and she had not rewound it since Greenwich, then she had been stuck in here for four hours. Unlike the other occasions, when the stop between floors had been brief, this hiatus was far past the point of being funny. She was already prey to weird thoughts.

The situation had taken on the qualities of an abduction. Unable to be heard, she could not help but let her mind go. Her thoughts were racing. And because with every hour that went by the possibility of never being rescued, of remaining lost to the world, increased, new fears began to flit through her mind. How many weeks until she wasted away? How many weeks until breathing seemed pointless, like skiers tossed under avalanches, like invalids who fell and couldn't reach a phone, their front doors releasing a thousand moths weeks later when it was finally kicked in. This was no joke. It happened all the time. Tracy was off the radar screen, and because she could not be heard — she had shouted out several times but got no response — and because the emergency phone was purely ornamental, there was nothing she could do. In this lift between floors, she was invisible to the real world.

She had to assume that her future was in her own hands. Her mobile phone gave a no-signal sign: it was useless, but she kept it in her hand. Her best chance was that her parents would narrow down the possibilities, trace her here, send someone down. Lucky for her she had phoned before leaving her hotel to say she was on her way over. Everyone would otherwise have assumed she had flown the coop, checked out and left town as she had toyed with doing. Yes, her parents would definitely work it out.

On the other hand, considering the lift's reputation, and her own terrible record of unreliability and erratic behaviour, wouldn't everyone be more likely to assume she had changed her mind about returning to her parents, left town after all or gone to stay with a friend? The lift, in that case, would be the last place they would think of! This could go on for a very long time.

Crouched in the corner, she opened her case. Taking out a magazine, she flicked through to the first decent photograph she could find and tore it out. Licking the back of it with her saliva she stuck the picture to the

300

wall of the elevator. A lonely lemon grew on the branch of a tree. It hung there like a human heart, waiting to be picked, or to fall.

The shouting had long since died down but no one had come down the alley. No one ventured to help the man on his back among the tyres and boxes, as spasms of pain died within him, each successive wave fortunately gentler than the last, as if some sedative was leading him down into a gentle, calming sleep.

He lay there, still. He listened to his own ragged breathing. He would soon be unable to feel a thing.

Above him, he dreamily took in a grey sky in which flocks of starlings banked above the South London houses. It was November already. They were assembling in their thousands to fly the trades to North Africa. Watching these migratory creatures form swirling towers in the air, his last concrete thought was that, unlike them, he had always lacked the instinct to be in the right place at the right time, heading in the right direction. Perhaps he had lacked the unanimity these birds enjoyed. He stared upward at them with a new admiration. He blinked at the sky. He could hear no sirens, no sounds of rescue. But he was not in a hurry for anything to happen. He was happy to be left there.

Eric's feet pounded the pavement. With each stride bolts of pain shot up from his bad foot. *Fucking Graeme, I don't care if he's dead*. Although Eric drew no closer to the bobbing villain ahead, he didn't lose him either.

As he gave chase he tried to clear the air passages clogged with phlegm. What a grim lozenge of sputum it was that hit the gutter: he was in terrible shape. He ran purely from memory, and held nothing back. *I'm gaining on him. I must be! Or am I kidding myself?* He wanted fervently to catch this arsehole kid.

But in reality, Eric's head was reeling. This was a joke. His heaving chest was already at breaking point, his foot was killing him and the little prick ahead, too far off to be identified, was clearly so confident of his escape now that he threw away his balaclava, a bravura flourish, and magically turned himself into just another kid coasting the streets in trainers, a fitness nut perhaps, while Eric behind took on all the insidious connotations of the mugger. With his mouth agape, his heavy body unable to run in a straight line, his shirt flapping, his felon's limp he looked far more dicey and dangerous than his quarry.

But giving up was out of the question. He owed it to Tracy to keep going, but he also owed a secret debt to the beaten restaurateur himself. He had been too hard on the foreigner and that debt would have to be paid sooner or later.

But just as the chase was about to turn into a fiasco, fitness deciding the issue, the young man dropped into the mouth of an underground station. Eric chased him down. Here, his cunning could play a part: it was the best thing that could have happened.

Painfully taking the steps three at a time, Eric could follow this punk down and corner him in some tunnel, settle the score and hold him until the police arrived. If he got that far he'd give the kid something to remember him by as well. Eric could call it self-defence. Payback for his suffering foot.

But below ground, temporarily lost, Eric searched wildly for signs. Arrows pointed to McDonald's outlets in three directions. Only a shout from an underground employee told him where to head next. He swung his legs over the unmanned turnstile, and soon overtook the official on the escalator who was less interested in giving chase than in getting his walkie-talkie working.

'Get some help!' Eric shouted back. 'Get some help!'.

The platforms were ahead. The end might be in sight. But if a train pulled up now it could be over as well. Or if the kid just merged with the crowd, Eric would have no hope. The tunnel ahead spilt into two choices offering services east and west. Eric popped his head quickly into the western platform — the waiting commuters were too relaxed — and he ran to the other platform: a hubbub ran along it, heads uniformly turned away from Eric.

He pushed his way down the channel carved for him by the fleeing young man. He ignored the looks of concern, the confusion, the people drawing back in fear. He called 'Stop!' but felt too self-conscious, and didn't do it again.

A 'No Entry' sign sat over the last pedestrian tunnel and it drew Eric inside. He was in agony now, his tanks empty, but round bend after bend he followed the sound of the young man's echoing footfalls. His desire to catch this crook had doubled since he had set out but his ability was receding fast. His pride was all that kept him going. And when the tunnel opened up into a tiled cavern, containing a single downhill escalator descending from the street, the sight of the kid

302

assailing it two uphill steps at a time, gave him renewed hope.

Eric screamed 'Gotcha!' as he mounted the moving flight, and now that the chase had been thrown into slow motion he was tantalisingly close! Against the opposing current of the escalator, Eric tried to match the younger man, but where the latter was able to make slow but steady progress against the flow, Eric's legs made less and less impression. After a promising start, he was soon only holding his own, merely treading water while the young man inched ever upward in a ridiculously protracted escape.

Still, Eric simply refused to give in, not after all this. With his legs gone and his whole body stinging with pain, he summoned non-existent forces and demanded that his body live up to the expectations he now had of it, even as the young man crested the top and disappeared.

Alone on the escalator, marooned on the spot, his speed dictated by a mechanical taskmaster, Eric still believed he could do it. A second wind would yet get him over the top: this might be on the edge of his abilities but not beyond them. He was a man. He could not give in. His life had seen too much of that.

But after a few more seconds he had no choice but to surrender. He let himself be carried back down and as he stepped off at the bottom of the escalator he collapsed against the wall, coughing his lungs clear. Self-disgust rose inside him. When a man of action such as he — he was allowed his own illusions — has been unable to *act*, then what use was he? When the best he could do was proven to be not good enough, what was left? *Failure*! The word hit him like a bullet. *Failure*!

Shoes belonging to the underground official appeared under Eric's nose. 'I will need to see your ticket, sir.'

Eric looked up into the provincial face of the youngster. *Tracy, I tried. And tell him, tell your husband too. But the kid could really run.*

'I need to see your ticket, sir. Right away.' Static snarled from the man's walkie-talkie.

'I don't have a ticket. Okay? I've been chasing someone. I'm *still* chasing him. Okay? A friend of mine was just assaulted. Assaulted!'

The young man regarded the collapsed individual before him with deep suspicion. Certain things didn't add up in his orderly brain. 'I'm sorry, but you'll have to accompany me. And I warn you against doing anything stupid. You have to have a ticket to travel on the underground.'

'You don't understand! Someone was attacked! You've got to help.

Use your walkie-talkie. Quick! We can stop him.'

Eric reached for the instrument on the man's hip. His arm was knocked aside, and the man's stance became aggressive. 'Keep your voice down, sir. And now please come with me.'

'No,' Eric told him. 'Tell security at street level! Your walkie-talkie! He'll be coming through without ticket!'

The official nodded. He had dealt with human trash like this before; but he picked up his handset as suggested, and barked into it: 'We've got trouble down here. Yeah. I'll need some help. Let's get some help down here.'

Dear Yusuf Islam, Tracy began, composing this letter in her head, *I'm writing to you in a situation you might appreciate. I'm stuck in a lift several hundred feet above the ground in my parents' block. It's my own fault. I shouldn't have come back here. I need to move on. It might even be a sign. Anyway, I may never escape this, in which case, I will be dead when you read this. I have been here for exactly four hours and thirteen minutes so far, with no end in sight. I've learnt my lesson. Anyway, I just wanted to say I liked your music when you were still Cat Stevens and I watched your new video and I remembered what happened to you at Malibu Beach. Well, I have also just asked God to save me as well, and if this happens, as it did with you, then I promise to do something awe-inspiring with my life. I haven't got a clue what that might be, though. Anyway, the deal still holds, which is more than I can say for this lift, which has started to make some very scary noises. I'm hanging on by a thin thread once again. But Yusuf, what did you mean when you said . . .*

But nobody found Tracy Pringle. Time elapsed and nothing alerted people that there was a young woman locked inside the lift. Two months later, after the exhaustion of all scenarios, when a repairman with a lamp-hat succeeded in lowering the lift, her dead body would be found, a fossil curled up on the floor. The traumatised man would face the cameras: 'The walls were plastered with magazine photos. It was bizarre. And the smell! Shocking, shocking. She obviously went mad long before the end.'

Something like that, Tracy thought as she contemplated possible outcomes. *It will go something like that, Yusuf.*

She broke off from her thoughts. She heard a human noise. Someone passing on the stairs? She listened and heard it again. A voice, a woman's. 'Help!' she called, for the umpteenth time, rising to her knees, moving towards the sealed steel doors, putting her mouth to the crack. 'Help, help, help, help!' She beat on the metal then listened again for answering sounds.

The voice came back, stronger, closer. Someone was saying one word, calling out. She finally recognised it. It was her own name.

Tracy started to cry and her heart released its trapped emotions. She screamed back. 'I'm here! I'm here! I'm in here!' Her fists hammered the door. Shouting at the top of her lungs, she emulated Sam: '*Help!*'

A fellow resident had been the first to hear Tracy's stifled cries. This woman notified the authorities. An hour later the fire brigade, police, representatives of the council and two technicians from the Schindler corporation combined to make up the rescue party which worked to free the trapped young woman.

A sudden crowd waited in the lobby for the gridlocked lift to be lowered. Galvanised by the idea that it could have been any of them inside there, they spoke rapidly to each other as an electrician tested for current by running his meters on rainbow-coloured wire with spilt from the prised-open call-button panel.

Monica, to one side, continued to try to contact Eric. He must still be out there somewhere, following some false lead.

As they waited, angry tenants approached her. They were quite willing to sign her petition now. They were all on her side. Despite the risks, they would put their name to her controversial proposal. They were ready to pledge support and demand firm action. Monica's general fears had now become immediate and personal, triggering the human instinct for self-protection. 'You were right. You were right,' they told her, their eyes wide. 'We'll make everyone sign up. Something's gotta give.'

'Okay, stand back, here it comes!' a fireman finally bellowed, relaying the message the Schindler man had just received over his walkie-talkie. 'Everybody. Stand back now! It's on its way. It's coming down now! Stand back!'

Several people objected to being manhandled out of the way, but all could hear the sound of the lift now and it hushed the crowd, and the sense of expectation built. 'Bloody disgrace,' one isolated voice shouted. 'Should be ashamed,' yelled another, shaking a head at the man from Schindler. Monica moved as close to the doors as she was allowed.

'Just get it open,' she said. 'Please just get it open!' A policeman held her back. Next a policewoman stepped forward and linked a much more gentle arm with hers. 'We've got her now,' the female officer told her. 'Looks like we've got her now.'

The lift was indeed heard to settle. A mixture of applause, protest and sighs of relief broke out. Monica chewed the edge of her finger-nail on one hand. The all-clear was then given and the electrician stepped forward again to play with the wires. A snarl of white electricity produced no reaction and a second, third and fourth attempt merely made him turn and summon the closest fireman. Monica watched as these experts discussed the situation. The fireman called over a colleague who was heard to say the word 'claw', turned and went out to the fire-truck. Two bulky men in luminous fire-resistant clothing then returned and inserted a huge bar into the crack of the doors. They heaved, the metal groaned and then it buckled while the electrician, joining wires in various permutations, and aided by the fireman's efforts, finally got the inner doors to separate.

A woman whose face bore the placidity of a saint was revealed. Her suitcase was drawn up against her legs as if she were on a train platform. The suddenly silent crowd stared back at her, startled by the decorations in the lift behind: several hundred skerricks of a magazine were plastered on the walls. Tracy raised her hand in a soft wave but did not speak. Like an actress whose curtain had risen unexpectedly, she had utterly forgotten her lines.

She looked back at the crowd and with what must have taken considerable fortitude, murmured 'Thanks', then collapsed to sit on her case.

Monica rushed to her and threw both arms around her neck, while behind them, spontaneous applause and cheers broke out.

20

Tunica Intima

Yvette caught the Eurostar back from Paris as soon as word reached her. A pale, exhausted, depleted delegation met her at Waterloo.

Twenty minutes later all three of Sam's wives were gathered in an arc around his hospital bed.

'So, Mr Britannia, what do you say about England now?'

'A one off,' was his slurred response. His lips felt like slabs of stapled cardboard: it would be several hours until someone was brave enough to hold up a mirror and show him the horrific picture, two surgically unzipped lips swollen to twice their normal size. As every movement cost him in units of pain, he was forced to limit his replies to short sentences. 'Wrong place.' Then, seconds later, 'Wrong time. More morphine.' He waved a bandaged finger at the empty IV bottle.

Tracy rang for the nurse. An abrupt stocky woman, with snooker-table legs, came in and consulted the clipboard on the foot of the bed, went away again then came back in with a full bottle.

Morphine soon corkscrewed its way down the tube into Sam's arm. 'Coleridge,' he slurred as his black-and-blue eyes closed. 'I can see now. In Xanadu. Da-de-dah. Kubla Khan. Stately pleasure-dome. *This* is the pleasure-dome. Not a damn castle. The morphine.' He winced: a throb of pain slipped by the advancing medicinal guards.

'Stop it,' Yvette reprimanded, upset by his dislocated thoughts. Fresh off the train, her face was still tear-stained, her mascara in blots under her eyes. 'He is just playing up now. His mouth was always zee big problem.'

The impact of seeing Sam in this state, ballooned by dressings, hooked up to taps, tubes, valves, had taken all their breaths away. Muttering in shock, they had all put their hands simultaneously to their mouths. He looked truly awful, much worse than a corpse: a corpse can boast a certain serenity.

The list of his injuries was enormous. Two ribs had been cracked, some teeth broken, as well as the bones in one wrist. His skull on the left side had been fractured by a kick, his left arm had been dislocated, and his lips were yet to recover from the surgeon's knife. The skin was torn right off one hand: a skin graft had been taken from his hip, meaning further bandaging there. In addition to generalised bruising, his entire body was a swollen bladder of white-cell fluid. He had ceased to look like a man and now bore a much stronger resemblance to a beached puffer-fish.

'I talk like. A bloody telegram,' Sam said, with the last of his energies. He smiled and his wives gasped at their first full sighting of his tombstone teeth. 'Stop,' he said.

Tracy leant into his ear. 'Rest now. Now rest.' She kissed his cheek.

But just when they thought he was asleep he confounded them. ''Tis sweet,' he muttered. 'To hear a brook. 'Tis sweet.' His wives waited for the rest: he was not one to leave a poem incomplete. 'To hear. The Sabbath bell.' His voice came as if from the grave. ''Tis sweet to hear. Both at once. Deep,' he said. 'Deep . . .' but then no more.

Sam then slept, in his private 'woody dell'.

Over his papers the consultant made a steeple of his fingers, a gesture so reminiscent of doctors everywhere it must surely be a prerequisite for the practice of medicine.

'His condition has stabilised but I have some unfortunate news. Which of you is Mrs Sahar?'

After an awkward moment, full of glances, shrugs, compromises and nods, which seriously confused the doctor, who had never drawn such a complex response from so simple a query, Firouzeh lifted her hand.

'I need to talk to Mrs Sahar in private,' he continued.

'But we're sisters . . . his sisters,' Yvette interjected.

The consultant looked suspiciously at Tracy then back at Firouzeh before continuing. His tone and facial expression were ill omens in themselves.

'It seems your husband, that he has sustained some cerebral damage that we didn't at first detect. The X-rays we did this morning have found a small aneurism in an artery on the left side of his brain.'

'Aneurism?'

'As a result of the blows he received to his head, an artery would seem to have been weakened. This has caused a thinning of its walls, what we call the *tunica intima*, at one point. From the pressure of the circulating blood, this vessel has ballooned outward, forming a sac.'

'But you can fix it, right?' Tracy asked.

'Usually we can, but right now your . . . um, brother isn't strong enough for that kind of operation. We are hoping that the size of the aneurism remains constant until we think he's strong enough to go ahead. As soon as it's possible we'll act, I can assure you, but for now we must all help him regain his strength.'

'And what if it doesn't remain constant? What if it gets bigger?'

The doctor took off his glasses and sucked on the stem. 'Then I will ask you to come in again and we'll have to take another look at this. But there's no need for alarm. He's in a stable condition. We'll monitor him very closely and as soon as his condition improves we'll get him into theatre.' The doctor smiled in an attempt to hearten the women. But, if anything, this professional offering only made them more desperate.

Outside his office Tracy, Yvette and Firouzeh hugged and took turns at calming each other. The children should not know about this. They would be better off with the story that Daddy had had an accident at the new restaurant. Naughty scaffolding had collapsed on his head. They should be spared the idea that real monsters walked abroad in the world.

Yvette came in the mornings while Firouzeh chose lunchtimes to bring the children to the hospital, letting them play quietly around Sam's bed until he could take no more and waved them away with a flick of his hand.

Tracy opted for the evenings, when he was temporarily free of his drugs. She wanted him coherent, even if they opted to spend the time in silence, just enjoying each other's presence.

With his eyes closed Sam liked to play a little hospital game, one at which he was increasingly adept. By smell alone he liked to identify the latest visitor to creep in and sit by his bed. Lately, he was batting a hundred percent. 'Yvette,' he announced, cocking an eye to see Tracy. 'Damn.'

'I thought I'd trick you. I'm wearing her Chanel.'

'And spoilt.' Pause. 'My record.' Pause. 'Damn.'

The great monologist was growing used to this verbal house arrest, the curfew on his words imposed by his damaged lips. 'You look,' he said, 'nice.'

He was suddenly a man of few words, and generally, he chose these words with more care than at any other time in his life. To Tracy these morsels seemed to contain much more meaning than their many predecessors, and she gained the impression that this tragedy had created for her a much wiser husband. At his bedside she was quite happy with the smallest exchanges, and was refreshed by the absence of talk. His illness had removed the last barrier between them, and they prematurely enjoyed the level of serenity that is normally the preserve of the very old.

For hours she watched him drift in and out of natural sleep and when he opened his eyes she was proud to be the first thing that he saw.

'Isis and Osiris. That's who you two remind me of,' Firouzeh told her, after observing them united in their silence.

'Thanks.'

Later, Tracy read her new book on Egyptian mythology, and learnt that the God Osiris had been cut into pieces by his brother, and that he had been revived by Isis, his sister and wife.

Sam's recovery was Tracy's sole mission now. No court case and no tiny blood vessel would jeopardise the plan each women had secretly approved: to exchange England for the desert landscapes of Persia, thereby granting his wishes.

The announcement that they were all now prepared to return to Iran with him and start a fresh chapter would have to wait until Sam was back on his feet.

Yvette, sitting cross-legged, sipping from a miniature wine bottle, tried to fathom one of Tracy's textbooks. 'I can hardly understand a single word of ziss stuff.'

'That's okay. Neither can I.' Tracy's studies were on the back burner for now.

'Perhaps I should start to study too,' the French woman said, closing the book, 'if we are all going to live there.'

She sighed and admitted, by way of her look, that she was very worried. Her main concern was the extent to which she would have to wear *hijab*. To what backward regime were they sacrificing themselves? Tracy had been unable to console her. To this glamorous woman, the loss of individuality was a great threat. All her life she had employed her beauty to smooth her way. Firouzeh had put the fear of God into her as well. She needed to know the worst. Iran wouldn't be a walk in the park. The term 'women's rights' was virtually an oxymoron there. Shari'ahic laws, the fear of western women, allowed for more feminine diversity than outside views suggested but there would be aggravations, insults, daily offences to their sense of right and wrong. They shouldn't kid themselves.

'Someone told me women aren't allowed to drive!' Her eyes were wide: she didn't drive anyway.

'No. That's Saudi Arabia.'

'Zey even cut off z'head for smoking marijuana!'

'Wrong country, I think. Not in Iran.'

'But aren't you worried?'

Tracy lied. 'We'll all be together. And if we don't like it we can go somewhere else.'

Yvette calmed down. '*Oui*. It is true.'

They had all agreed to go, to give it a try, but none of them were without serious reservations.

'So, how was he tonight then?' Yvette asked.

Tracy undid the buttons of her dress. 'A little better. I think he's getting stronger.'

'Soon they will operate then?'

Tracy nodded. This remained the plan. 'They are going to do another X-ray tomorrow. To check on the size of the aneurism again. That'll tell us a bit more.'

They got ready for bed and then lay in the darkness posing and reposing questions that had, as yet, no answers.

During the course of the next week the morphine doses often left Sam incapable of speech altogether. At such times a crude sign language began to evolve in which Firouzeh proved herself a most expert interpreter.

A hand straight up meant he did not wish to speak with anyone. An outstretched arm meant he needed to sit up to belch and so desired assistance. A backward movement of the wrist meant that he was tired now and wanted the room cleared of visitors. Two fingers tapped twice on his lips — a request for a clandestine cigarette — went unheeded. These gestures Firouzeh associated with the tyrannical patriarchs of her father's family, not with mild-mannered Sam, but a man in his condition must be afforded every indulgence that the world possessed.

Later, however, when a nun on her 3 p.m. rounds of the infirm found Sam on his own and took the chance to fill an empty picture hook with the Sistine Madonna, she badly misinterpreted the belching gesture, and tracing the direction of his outstretched arm intoned triumphantly: 'The Virgin! He points! He longs for the Madonna!'

As the days passed, and Sam's vigour and wits returned, his wives not only maintained the same strict rota of visits but intensified them so that soon there was hardly a moment when Sam was left unattended. It wasn't, however, a sense of duty that motivated such heightened ministrations. Rather, all three women were simply in the process of falling more in love with their own husband.

Looking after a seriously sick person so resembled the rites of courtship — gifts, tendernesses plus the sense of triumph this tenderness inspires — that it began to have this effect on the Sahar women. It was a revelation: the closer to death the beloved, the more love solidifies.

Under such care, Sam began his return to life. From Tracy, he requested his mobile phone. Forbidden by the nurses to use it in the ward he kept it under his pillow, making a flurry of calls whenever the coast was clear. He had not lost hope of winning the court case and he proposed to manage the trial from his room.

He was also progressively lured from his bed. Daily a nurse materialised from the shadows to coax him to the day room where half-baked classes in the fine arts were being held.

Propped in a wheelchair with a long brush like Monet, he began and completed a series of still lives of assorted vegetables and fruit.

'I've rarely felt so good,' he told his third wife. 'The doctor said I've turned the corner. By the end of next week I should be strong enough for surgery.'

Tracy watched him, stroke by stroke, develop a new fruit she had never seen on any tree.

'I hope so.' The doctors had endorsed this view to Tracy.

'And you know why I feel so good? Because you have made my life a playground. A sun-filled playground. You know what my life is like with you? When I was eight I had my first big birthday party. My friends

312

all came over, I was surrounded by warmth for a day. Such indulgence. You expect such days never to come again.'

'Stop talking so much. The nurse said your talking is slowing down your recovery.'

'Did she now? Then I will have a few words with her immediately.' He steadied his hand to paint the fruit's stem. 'I'm tired now.' He set down his brush. His bursts of stamina were fleeting.

Tracy wheeled him back to his room, the linoleum so shiny that it would have suited ice-skaters. Over it the rubber wheels were fantastically silent: a sole squeak sounded as she swung him left.

As she helped him to his bed he told Tracy that he was experiencing moments of 'fantastic contentment', and gave warning of another development: his sexual appetite was once again sending back a signal like a space probe lost in deep space.

'It's time for your wash, I think.'

The prospect of a cold towelling by a usually hostile nurse finally silenced this braggadocio. 'Don't push the button,' he entreated.

'I've pushed it.' Tracy raised her hand.

'Bugger,' he said.

The small, red light over his head blinked on and off as his spirits fell.

Tracy packed her shoulder bag. She prepared to leave as they awaited the nurse with her kidney-shaped basin of water.

21

Recriminations

After the lift incident Sam didn't want Tracy to stay in that building ever again. The Marilyn suite was inhabited once more.

Monica and Tracy had been shopping. Their nerves were raw by the time they re-entered the tower block. Monica said she could handle the bags herself. Tracy should go back to her hotel.

'Twenty-three floors? Come on, Mum. You can't carry all these bags on your own. Anyway, you still haven't answered my question.'

'Discussion closed. I'm not talking to you. I don't know where you got so opinionated. And they're not even heavy.'

'Come on. Do me good.' She pulled three of the six plastic bags out of her mother's grip and headed up the stairs. 'Let's go.'

Monica had to concede. She caught up with her daughter and side by side they began to scale the very real mountain.

They climbed to the first floor without saying a word.

Between the first and second, Monica said, 'Need oxygen already. This is mad.'

Stopping on the third landing, just to get a better grip on the bags, Monica panted: 'I just don't think you can blame society for all the problems, that's all.'

'Have a look around.'

They set off for the fourth floor. Their progress slowed down. The going was harder. 'A few people go off the rails,' Monica said. 'That's all it takes. Those lads, who beat up Sam, they don't represent anybody. They're a tiny minority.'

'Mum! That's not true!'

''Tis true.'

'Mum — '

They stopped.

'Then, Mum, then look around. *Look*! Ask yourself. Open the paper. Then go and take a look at Sam. People are murdering, raping, abusing children left right and centre, living their whole life on drugs, drinking themselves to death, dying alone. And what does society say? Just like you. It says it's not society's fault, they're just deviant people. There will always be a few deviants. They just had a bad childhood or something, but they're nothing to do with society, they're not a reflection of it.' They started towards the fifth. 'Then how about the Jamie Bulger case?'

'What's that got to do with anything?'

'A two-year-old gets killed by two ten-year-olds — you've gotta face it, don't ya? Society is producing these children, children who are going to go on and do all these things. And what does the government do? Locks them up, and the church says they're freaks and is just grateful when they're locked away. And still, we don't stop and realise that we mass-produce these people.'

'People are actually nice, Tracy.'

'Yeah, they're nice. But why? So people will be nice to them back. That's the only reason why. Most people are hard with a nice coating. Every man for himself.'

Someone Monica had never seen before was coming down the stairs and she politely stood aside to let him pass. 'Thanks,' the guy said.

'Hi,' Monica replied automatically.

They resumed the trek upward. 'And that's not all. Videotape was taken of those children while they were hurting that two-year-old. And people were just standing around. They did nothing because there's this mentality being produced now: do nothing, don't get involved if it's not in your interest. That is western materialism in action. Just like with Sam.'

'I don't *believe* this is you talking.'

'Why?'

'Where's all this coming from? Up until a few weeks ago you'd never used the word society in your life and now it features in every bloomin' sentence!'

'It's obvious, that's all.'

315

'Classes are one thing — '

'And what about Dad? He sees Sam hurt in that alley, asks this guy to go and take care of him while he goes after the attacker, and what does this guy do?'

'A little knowledge is a dangerous thing.'

'He walks off! Just walks off.'

'We're not absolutely sure that's what happened —'

'That doesn't *disgust* you? Well, it disgusts me.'

They stopped on the fifth floor, catching their breath. Monica was too winded already to instantly reply. 'Course. Course it's not good. Not good at all. But . . . '

A door opened. An old woman put out a plastic bag of rubbish, then spotted Monica and in embarrassment, remembering her own civic inaction on the petition issue, retreated back inside.

'So?' Monica said. 'So society is bad. It's evil. Fine. But what can you do? You have to work with it.'

'Look at your petition. No one wanted to sign it. Even though this place is a death-trap.'

'In the end quite a lot signed.'

'How many?' Tracy asked, picking up her bag, pushing on in the lead.

'Twenty-three.'

'Out of? And only after I got stuck in the lift and they thought you might win. But till then they were *exactly* like that guy Dad asked to help Sam.' Tracy stopped and let her mother catch her up. 'Our lecturer says that since people stopped being afraid of divine punishment society has jumped off the rails.'

Monica arrived at her side. 'So when are you moving to Iran then?'

Tracy was shocked. 'Who told you that? How did you know?'

It was Monica's turn to be shocked: 'I was only joking. You're going to *Iran*?'

'It's only a possibility, Mum.'

'You've gotta be kidding me, Tracy. Tell me you're not bloody going to live in Iran now! Oh my God!'

'Only if it looks like we're not gonna win the case.'

'But you're not gonna win it, are you?'

'It doesn't look great, no.'

'No. Then you're bloody going.'

Tracy shrugged.

'Oh my God.' Monica slumped to the ground. She tried to visualise her daughter half the world away, but could not. It was like a death.

'Don't sit down, Mum. You'll never make it this way.'

Monica then considered the word Iran, the many connotations it held for her: distance, strangeness, danger. 'This just gets worse and worse,' she said. 'Worse and worse.'

Tracy went back down, put down her bags and sat beside her mother.

'It's not the end of the world, Mum.'

'I watch the news, you know.'

'I know.'

'So don't tell me it's not the end of the world. It's completely the other end of the world.'

'Six hours on a plane.'

'So when were you gonna tell me?'

'When we know about the case.'

'It's gonna kill your father.'

'He'll cope. You can both come and visit me.'

'Ha! In Iran? Got to be bloody joking. Can't get him to Brighton.'

They sat in silence for some time, two mountain climbers waiting for a helicopter.

They sat on the step beside their groceries until Tracy said, 'Oh, I could phone Dad.' And she pulled out her mobile phone.

'When did you get that?'

'Sam gave it me.' She dialled the telephone on the twenty-third floor. 'Here's my number if you want.' Tracy gave her a business card with the new number on it. Monica turned it in her hands. Her daughter had Sahar as a surname. It was the first time she had seen it written down. 'Tracy Sahar,' she said.

'Yeah. That's me now, Mum.'

Monica could hear the phone ring and her husband answer. When Tracy explained the situation Eric said he would be right down.

Neither women spoke after that as they listened to Eric's noisy descent growing louder.

'Bloody hell,' Monica said when he finally appeared, puffing heavily. 'don't break too many records.'

He grinned. The sight of the two waylaid women amused him. 'Right then, let's be having ya.'

Tracy picked up two of the bags, leaving four for her father, and instructed her mother to go ahead, but Monica said she could take one and so took a light one from Eric before starting up. Eric laughed as he stood with Tracy and watched his wife climb. 'See you on the South Col,' he called.

'What's that?'

'Everest.'

Bang, bang, bang went Monica's feet, as Tracy and Eric started up after her.

On just the next floor, Eric signalled silently that they should take a cigarette break. They heard the sounds of Monica going on; a real Edmund Hillary, heart set on the top.

Tracy set down her bags again and took out her cigarettes. 'You started again?' she asked.

'Yeah, since the selectors overlooked me for the Olympics I figured what's the point in training so hard.'

She lit it then handed it to him. 'Great,' he said, taking a puff and handing it back.

'I wanted to say thanks,' she said.

'Just watching the telly anyway.'

'No, not for this. I mean for Sam. For running like that, with your bad foot'n everything. Especially when you didn't like him much.'

'Oh that. Oh, that was the least I could do.' His heavy head was trained on the burning end of the cigarette which he waggled from side to side, playing with the wispy smoke. 'Believe me.'

'No, you were brilliant. And he wants to thank you as well. You have to go and see him. He wants to thank you himself.'

Eric shook his head, becoming stern, the anger muscles in his face flexing. 'No. I'm not having him thank me. I don't want that. Tell him not to do that, okay?'

'Why?'

'Because.'

'Because why?'

He delayed his explanation. 'Because there's something I haven't told you, Trace. There are things I haven't told you.'

She waited, querulous, trying to find clues in his shifting expressions. 'What do you mean?'

318

'Been looking for the right time to tell you actually. Looks like this might be it.'

'Dad, what is it?'

'I didn't mean it to turn out how it did, that's all. That's all you've gotta know. It all got out of hand. I never wanted anything to happen to the kids. I just wanted you back.'

'Dad? What have you done?'

'You were right all along, Trace.'

'What? What have you done?'

He rubbed his chin and finally plucked up the courage to face her. 'Told no one. Not even your mother. It was me. I done it. I phoned the Social Services.'

'You? Don't be joking with me, Dad.'

'You're gonna hate me now. And I don't blame ya, but I had no idea what would happen. Was all I could think of to stop you making a big mistake. I was out of my head with worry, Trace, out of my head. But when they took the kids like that, I felt sick, all that trouble, and now Sam in hospital, I didn't want any of that, but I was just trying to protect you, to protect you from him. Like any father would. I thought he was the worst thing that could have happened to you.'

She had turned away from him. 'You're making this up.'

He could feel his daughter hardening against him, could sense her pain and confusion and anger, but he wouldn't try to derail any of this. He deserved what he got now. 'So don't ask him to thank me for running, that's all I'm saying. After what I'd done, how could I stop running? I should be bloody running for the rest of me life.'

'Dad. Please don't let it be you.'

Her tone sounded terminal, as if something was about to be broken for good, but she needed to make absolutely sure of his crime before she cut the cord forever.

'Was me darlin'.' He dropped his head. He was shaking himself, the cigarette unsteady in his hand. 'Was your old Dad. Miserable shithouse, isn't he. Piece of rubbish, but now you know. You can hate me for the rest of your days now. No excuses necessary.'

She took some time to find her voice. 'Why? Why did you . . . did you even tell me?'

'Couldn't live with it any more, could I. It's been churning around, eating away at me till I'm not good for anything. And I'm not good for much anyway. Still I was hoping for a miracle. Like that you'd forgive me. So now I've told ya. You're the first that knows. Your old man's a rotten bastard.'

They stood in silence.

No one came up and no one went down. No one came to help. Eventually, Tracy's mobile rang.

Monica wanted to know how far they'd got. She had got home and sounded triumphant.

Tracy made up a number and hung up.

'I can't tell anyone,' Tracy said. 'I'm too ashamed.'

Eric used his hand like a cloth to wipe his sweaty face. 'Don't blame ya.'

Leaving the bags there and with no farewell she started down the stairs. He listened. After a few steps she stopped. 'And the mugging. Did you have anything to do with that?'

'What do you take me for?'

'Not very much.'

Back in her hotel room, Tracy was in turmoil. She needed to make a phone call but could not find the nerve. It was clear that she needed to call Partridge to officially report her father, but family loyalties either died hard or did not die at all. What kind of daughter turned in her father, opened him to ridicule? Her new loyalties were to her new family now, and she owed it to them to follow through on the news that Eric had betrayed them all, sold them down the river, plunging the happiness and stability of innocent people into chaos, but her fingers couldn't dial the number.

She managed to phone Ridley.

He could give her one minute, he was between meetings, 'Your father? Well, that's a shock I must say. Et tu, pater.' But the old lawyer didn't sound shocked: duplicity was his métier after all. Ridley knew better than anyone how to work both sides of the street.

'So what should we do now?'

'My advice? Your father has got what's coming to him, that's my advice. And you're unlikely to land him in any serious trouble by reporting him. He made a nuisance of himself, that's all. But make the call. I'm just not sure it's going to make much difference.'

'Why not? He can retract the whole thing.'

'It feels significant, but look at it. Yes, your father started this thing rolling but the Social Services didn't act solely on his recommendation. They checked it out, sent in their own people and now they believe they have the evidence they need.'

Tracy had a better idea. 'Then what if I get Partridge to help us?'

'Partridge? Who?'

'The one who came to the house, who asked the questions. Would it help?'

There was a brief silence on the other end of the line, then she heard him whispering to a secretary before his voice returned. 'Help? Sure. Perhaps. I don't know. But how could you do that? And what could he say? That he'd changed his mind? And why do you think this? Do you have a relationship with him or something? I don't understand.'

'A relationship?'

'What makes you think he'd help you? He's on the other side. He's the one feeding the enemy ammunition, Tracy.'

'I just have a feeling.'

'Well, I'll always bow to feminine intuition, and it's better than anything I've got right now, so go ahead.'

'So I should try then, should I?'

'It never hurts to talk, Tracy, so long as he talks and you say nothing at all.'

She changed into tarty clothes, an out-of-date and revealing outfit — *I look like a hooker again*, she thought — and went into the hallway.

With only a glance at her sexy reflection in the steel lift doors she chose the staircase and went down to the hotel lobby. Dressed to kill, she hit the street. A black man roasted chestnuts on an oil-drum bonfire. She raised her arm, hailed a cab. The taxi drew her into the serpentine traffic.

Three-quarters of an hour later she stood at the Social Services counter where an officious woman wanted her name.

'Tracy Pringle. But I'd like to see him in person. He'll know what it's about. Actually, tell him it's Tracy Sahar.'

'Sahar?'

'Yes.'

Before calling Partridge, this votary glanced disapprovingly at Tracy's exposed cleavage and figure-hugging top.

The open-plan office was filled with the drone of formal conversation. As the silent public waited their turn, the boothed-in workers vetted the badly filled out forms of those lucky enough to be served. Claims were triple-checked, pruned, reduced. The needy would never have all they asked for. Exasperated ex-wives, absentee husbands, step-parents, wayward guardians and those who simply needed stop-gap support shifted on their haunches at the counter. In the background, a dozen lower-order officials at their desks pinned receivers to their ears with their shoulders, pecking at their pads with ballpoints as Tracy refined her thoughts, checking her make-up in her compact, plotting her strategy.

When Mr Partridge appeared he looked embarrassed to see her.

His eyes darted up and down. *Click clack*, she thought.

'Fantastic,' he stammered with a tone that suggested he, and not she, had called for this meeting. He wanted immediately to get her off the premises and away from the eyes of nosy colleagues. She agreed at once to his offer of a coffee.

She might have protested taking the lift down but before she could do so he had walked inside and waved her forward. She smiled courteously as stepped inside. The doors closed and without event they descended to the ground.

'Very good to see you again,' he added as they passed through the lobby. 'Quite a surprise.'

She did not reply.

The coffee shop was nearby. He crossed the road ahead of her.

She asked for milk in her coffee and then faced him across the small table but before she could speak he had pressed his hands together, held them prayer-like to his lips and then launched into a pre-emptive confession.

'I want to speak off the record, okay? Let me just start.'

She nodded. She could wait.

'This is actually my last week on the job. I've resigned already but what I have to say must still be off the record.'

She nodded again.

'Personal reasons. Lot of things. In my spare time I do a little bit of stand-up comedy, believe it or not. It sounds absolutely daft but I really want to give it my best shot. You never know till you try.'

A nod, depriving him of the surprise she felt: this nincompoop on a stage?

'But I'd had enough anyway, and that had a little bit to do with you actually.'

322

He wished, he said, to explain how he had been shocked at the measures his superiors had taken in her case. He could not say how much the removal of the children from the family house had upset and appalled him. 'It wasn't what I wanted. That's why I'm talking to you now.'

There were a couple of things he wanted her to understand. 'I tried to warn you but your husband wouldn't listen. The department has a system for detecting dangerous situations. A set of five priorities. I won't name them. Some cases have one or two of them. Yours had all five. I knew you were heading for trouble.'

A spate of recent cases involving young European women of mixed ethnicity, robbed of passports and trapped in Britain by sex-slave traders and put to work on the streets of London for a pittance, in bondage to their corrupt overlords, had resulted in ministerial calls for departmental vigilance. The phone call they had received came while this crackdown was under way. 'Your case rang all the alarm bells. I hate to tell you this but it seems there was the belief, it seems ridiculous now,' his speech faltered, 'that your husband was fronting one of these *operations*.'

Tracy had to laugh.

'I know, I know,' he said.

'And you . . . you let them think this?'

He shrugged his shoulders. 'The department is designed to be suspicious. That's how social policy works. It has to gear itself towards worst case scenarios. It's officially overreactive and pessimistic. Better to temporarily inconvenience the innocent than to miss exposing the guilty. The lesser of two evils. Let's just say it prefers to be relieved when it's proved wrong. Anyway, look at it through our eyes: an older man, three younger women, all under this man's *special care,* under his control. We thought we'd hit the jackpot! I could be sued for telling you all this, but the restaurant was viewed as a possible cover. I know it sounds farcical, paranoid, but you wouldn't believe what we see on a daily basis. Under the surface horrendous things are going on. You learn the keep an open mind. You imagine the worst and half the time reality still floors you.'

Colour rose in her face. Her anger had reached boiling point. 'So you let them think we were . . . *that*?'

'Not me. I gave an impartial report. But you've got to admit, from a distance it all weirdly fits the picture.'

She stared at him.

He sidestepped the blame at once. 'You hate me now. But let me finish. And so once the department people got this idea in their head then they were simply looking for evidence. The children couldn't be left at risk. The situation boiled over. My pathetic recommendation for further enquiry wasn't enough to stop the children's removal.' *Sotto voce*, even though they were the coffee shop's only customers, he continued. He was deep in confidential territory now. He was at pains to impress upon her that he was taking a great risk. 'You have to understand that all the social agencies are so terrified of screwing up, of *not* reacting to a situation, and thereby permitting some atrocity to occur, and then finding themselves hung out to dry on the front pages of a newspaper, that the opposite happens. Also, and I think especially in your case, some people . . . well they might have got just a little bit . . . shall we say, obsessed. Me . . . ,' he allowed himself a smile, ' . . . included.'

'Obsessed?' She hid her fury. She needed to see what he meant by this. She even gave him a slightly better view of her breasts. 'With what?'

Holding her in his level gaze he went on. 'The whole situation.' He stared into her flaming eyes, perhaps hoping they burnt for him. 'I couldn't work it out. Your part in it especially. Yours was the most mystifying. To me anyway. What you got out of it. Three women, one man. I can accept that he loves you, but what did *you* get out of it, you most of all . . . ' His words trailed away. He was lost in a sharp spiral of conjecture, trying to imagine the inner workings of a run-of-the-mill harem. 'But anyway, that's all I've got to say. What did you want to talk to me about?'

The nerve, she thought, her coffee untouched. *I really just want to scream! Claw his eyes out!* But she held back. 'I know who it was that phoned you. That's what I came to tell you. The anonymous caller. I know who it was who made the report that started it all. He's come forward. Admitted it was all a hoax. He'll talk to you.'

'Great. But it's no good talking to me. Like I told you, I've resigned.'

'All the better.'

He looked confused by this. 'Tracy, I'm no lawyer but I really think your best bet in this case it to spring all this on everybody in the courtroom.' He smiled. 'It works on TV. "Excuse me your honour, I'd like to call so-and-so", gasps around the room, heads turning to see who it is.' He grinned. 'The surprise witness.'

'Exactly.'

'Right.' He laughed. 'I sincerely hope it helps you.'

'We'd like to call you.'

His laughter evaporated. 'Me?' His good humour vanished. He shifted uncomfortably, became awkward, all elbows and knees again. 'I'd like to help you. But I really . . . I don't see how . . . '

'Help us. I'm asking you. Please.' He had run out of words. 'Please,' she begged. 'I'm asking you. Just say in court what you just told me. The whole sex-slave thing. It's such crap that everyone will laugh at it. If you know we're innocent, like you say, then you have to do something. Jesus, you're quitting anyway!'

He was already shaking his head. He laughed nervously, his every gesture a red light signal. 'No, no. Come on. What made you come down here, Tracy?'

'You need to help us, Sebastian. Sam is in hospital. I'm on my own.'

'I know. Horrible. I heard through the channels. Terrible. I felt awful. Actually, that why I've said as much as I have. But that's all I can do.'

'No it's not.'

'Tracy, I'm the bad guy, remember? As you say, I'm responsible.' he held up his arms theatrically. 'What makes you think for a second I would help you?'

It was her turn now to stare at him. 'It's just something about you.'

He squirmed under this returned fire.

'I don't quite understand it yet,' she said, 'but I think. . . that maybe . . . ' She calibrated her words with extreme care: In this critical game of darts she needed a bull's-eye to go out on. 'I think that I might be just a little bit obsessed by you as well.'

She didn't blink.

Her blue eyes dove into his, causing a leap of Adam's apple, a nervous inclination of his head, a rapid conjoining of fingers; this constituted his reply.

S for Sebastian, S for Seb, S for just S, Partridge was pierced at the heart, pierced clean through, and nothing, thereafter, could really save him.

When Sam awoke he found that Tracy's father had materialised at the foot of his bed. Neither spoke. Both seemed to be trying to decide in whose hallucination the other was appearing.

'Just wanted . . . ' Eric said, his thoughts draining away. He held a mop of flowers.

'Sit. Just the person, Eric. Just the person.'

Eric looked around for a seat. All the chairs held gifts and he didn't want the forced intimacy of sitting on his nemesis's bed. He waved his hand. 'No thanks.' The patient was fed like a machine with tubes and meters and wires, one monitor giving off the sonic *bleep* of a submarine from time to time. 'Just a flying visit. Just came to say hello. Bought some flowers as well.' He laid them on the foot of the bed.

Sam tried to smile at his foe, the forger of his troubles, then nodded.

'Anyway. And there's just a couple of things you need to know, that I wanted to tell you. Then I'll get out of your hair.' Sam nodded, so Eric went on. 'Just about me and Tracy really. I thought you should know, if you don't already. You may know already, in which case you get a free bunch of flowers.'

Sam smiled. He was hardly going anywhere.

'Right then. Well, I'm not too good . . . too good at these kinds of things but anyway. You'll have to bear with me.'

Eric gathered himself. He beheld the ravaged man before him in the raised orthopaedic bed. Had Eric's telephone call in some way contributed to this? *If that's the case then it deserves to be me in that bed. It ought to be me that's in traction.* 'You're such a cool customer. You are. Now I don't know about you but I wear things pretty much on my sleeve. And I'm feeling pretty guilty right now, so I guess it shows. And it goes back to when Tracy hooked up with you. I went a bit crazy. As you know. And I need to get something off my chest.'

Sam nodded patiently.

'Now I don't know if she's told you this yet, but about six years ago. We had to run Tracy into hospital.'

'Tracy?'

'Yeah. She was fourteen. Had a lot going on.'

'Eric — '

'Let me just get this out, then I'll go. She'd always been the most talkative little kid then overnight she stops communicating with us. We didn't know what was going on. But we weren't the sort of parents to get too worried by every little hiccup. Well, that's how we were then. If you can believe that. Then one day I come home, I knock on her door, and go in and she's lying on her bed. There's something wrong. I can't wake her up. I get scared. Anyway, we get her to hospital, thinking something's wrong with her and the doctor tells us she's tried an overdose.'

Sam stared at Eric.

'Do you know this? She told you about this?'

Sam finally shook his head. 'No. I do not know this.'

'Do you want me to go on?'

'Perhaps she wishes it to be a secret.'

'It's over to you.'

Sam eventually nodded. 'Go on.'

'So anyway, the doctor tells us this. Well, it was like a bomb going off. We didn't know what had hit us. We found out that a lot of teenagers go through a patch, and that no one should read too much into it, but as a parent, how can you do that?'

Sam shook his head. 'She said nothing.'

'It's just the background to what I'm gonna say.'

'Background?'

'So she comes home, right, from the hospital and we try to go on like normal. Except now I'm a nervous wreck. Monica too, but I'm the worst. I can't stop worrying about her. She goes out, I wanna know where she's going, with who, when she'll be back. I offer to drive her, pick her up, stay with her. I'm going right over the top. But I can't help it. I keep thinking that the minute I turn my back it'll happen again. I get offers of work but I don't take any of them. I need to be on hand in case anything happens. Then Tracy asks if she can have a lock on her bedroom door. A lock. What for? What does she want a lock for? Well, all her other girlfriends have got one, she says. She just wants one too. You can imagine how we feel about that. But we've gotta show we trust her. I've gotta get a grip, right. I mean, what's her life gonna be if her parents show they can't trust her?

'So I put a lock on her door. It kills me, but I put a lock on her door. And she goes in there and locks it. I can still hear the click. And the first night I couldn't fucking sleep. I was up three hours before she came out for breakfast. She looked at me, in her pyjamas, sleepy, and just said, "Chill." That's what she said. I must've looked like a madman. "Chill."'

Eric shook his head as Sam managed a smile. 'Yes,' he said, nodding, meaning that yes, this was Tracy to a T, the woman they both knew.

'And from then on Monica and I made an effort never to go in. Point of principle kinda thing. Know what I mean? We left it to her. It's her space. We respected her privacy. I'm a nervous friggin' wreck every day but we show her we trust her. And that we know she's not gonna go and do anything stupid. And she doesn't. Course she doesn't. Never does anything like it again. Perfect kid. And I love her to bits.

'Then she hooks up with this Ricky character . . . and he's not perfect, but I've got a memory of what I was like at his age so I don't get too worried. And then hey-ho she meets you, dun't she. And it's not the fact you're a foreigner. I want that clear. Or old enough to be her father. And it's not just the screwy set-up you're involving her in either. But I'm in the habit of looking out for her now, of worrying about her. And I can't stop. I've tried, but I can't. So one day I just find myself picking up the phone to the authorities and making a complaint.'

Eric paused, as if the rest should be self-evident. He rubbed his face. His fixer's hands were shaking, now the whole story was out. 'But what happened I never intended. I felt sick when I heard the kids were taken away. There was no way I could have known they would do that. That was all wrong. And that's why I'm here. To apologise for that. I just hope it hasn't done your kiddies any long-term harm.'

Sam stared back at his scourge, the seed of his troubles. But still he did not become overheated, from what Eric could tell. True to form, his real feelings remained indiscernible.

'You must hate me. I know Tracy does.'

'You've hurt a lot of people Eric, but you have to make it up to her.'

Eric accepted this with a nod of his own.

Sam studied Eric. The visitor was bowed forward, tensely gripping the railing at the foot of the bed. Of similar age, Eric was paying the higher annual levy. Where Sam's hair still sprouted black, youthful and plentiful, Eric's was grey at the temples, wearing thin. Years of sleeping on his nerves — Sam now knew — worrying for his daughter, had visibly taken their toll.

'Eric, you must not permit life to become a life sentence.'

Eric looked up, caught off guard; less by this statement than by the priestly, emotive tone. 'Life sentence? Howd'ya mean?

'Tracy has moved on. I assure you. You must also move on. Free yourself.'

Free himself? What was this foreigner banging on about?

'This fortress mentality, it is no good. I see you locking yourself and others in. But the world is far bigger than three people, Eric. Let your feelings flow outward as well. Let go. Outward.' Sam, even in his state, moved his hands out from his chest, demonstrating how Eric's

328

soul should move, outward, incorporating great spaces.

Outrageous! Eric blinked in the face of this patronising sermon. He was being preached to. Only his guilt kept him listening and nervousness made him chuckle. It was all too much. He had not come here for an examination of his own condition. 'What are you trying to say?'

Sam's shoulders rose and fell. 'Simply that there are times when, I think, we should all be prepared to be our brother's keeper.'

Ah ha! Eric understood what Sam was referring to. It was radiantly clear. While Sam had taken over full responsibility of his brother's large brood, a whole wandering tribe plus an extra grieving widow for good measure, providing all with shelter from the storm, what had Eric done? Well, fuck him, Eric thought. I have raised a child. This was enough. Adopting dead men's widows, plus their children, was absurd. He was just a family man, like a billion others, perhaps ungenerous with his time, his affections, his money, his *heart,* shielding out all the invasions of the world, locked within his cultural limitations, asking only to be left alone. But he was an Englishman and made no apology for that.

'That's all I came to say,' Eric stammered weakly.

'One last thing.'

'Well?'

'Don't worry yourself. About my children. All the years of good work cannot be undone by the darkness of a single night.'

Eric gave this his fullest attention. His guilt gave him no option.

Sam went on: 'But you are a father yourself, so you know this. Children have their own destinies. Their own resources. And their own survival instincts, are more sophisticated than our desire to protect. They're racing to be adults but they reserve the right to revert to being babies without warning, and in which case we're expected to be there.'

The broken-toothed smile told Eric it was time to go. High time.

'Now would you like to stay for lunch? I cannot recommend the menu. The term *al dente* is unknown to these people. I've offered to help, but they refuse to take advice.'

'You're an unusual guy.' Eric shook his head. He offered Sam a look of grudging respect, of tentative thanks.

'Go home. I am fine. And talk to Tracy. She needs you. Just in different ways. Talk to her. Oh, and we intend to give you grandchildren by the way. So stay off the cigarettes. Tracy tells me you're giving up.'

'Trying.' *Grandchildren*? Eric's mind was in free fall. His low-level racism, vestigial as an appendix, throbbed once. 'I'll look forward to that,' he managed.

'Good. But in the meantime, you couldn't lend me one, could you? A cigarette?'

Eric reached into his breast pocket. 'Are you allowed?'

'This place is like being kept in quarantine.'

Eric stared at Sam. How this Persian was able to remain so balanced in view of everything Eric had just told him was a mystery. Reduced to a piece of human wreckage, bandaged, propped in a hydraulic bed, Sam, and not Eric, acted like the one who should go out to the carpark and drive away from here.

Eric lit the sick man's cigarette and eased it between almost lifeless fingers.

22

For Crooked Feet, Crooked Shoes

On the eve of both the court appeal and the council meeting about Monica's petition, the famously noisy Pringle washing machine broke down.

Emily was glad to help. She brought their freshly laundered clothes through from her flat, chipped in with the ironing and adjudicated over the row that seemed to be raging between Monica and her husband.

She had never seen Monica this angry before, but she did not want to enquire as to the reasons. At the same time she had never seen Eric so sheepish, so deferential, so humbled. She hoped only to get both parties to their respective engagements in time.

As Monica prepared for her meeting, Emily pressed her blouse. Eric chose to spend the hours before his court appearance taking wire wool to a motorbike part on the kitchen table. 'Should come up nice,' he said to anyone who was listening, the water turning purple.

'If she loses she's going to Tehran,' Monica finally confessed to Emily. 'I'll never forgive him.'

'Forgive who?'

'Eric,' Monica said, without further explanation.

Emily was happy to wait for further details on Eric's role and took the iron to a curled collar, giving it a squirt of steam. She tried to imagine Tehran, tried to visualise 'Arabia' as she ironed, and also Tracy standing there in the burning heat of a desert with her suitcase. Had this been her daughter, she would have been worried sick.

When the doorbell rang Monica answered it. Mrs Cochrane from the fifteenth floor hoped she wasn't too late to put her name down on the petition. 'Someone told me it goes in today.' Monica said the pink box of papers wasn't yet sealed and one more name could be added.

'Twenty-three,' Monica said to Emily, shutting the pink box. 'Getting there. One for each floor. Not too bad.'

'Ooh, that's right,' Emily replied, as if this coincidence guaranteed victory.

Half an hour later Monica was ready to do battle. She smiled nervously as Emily held open the front door for her. 'I think I've got everything.'

'Petition? Photos? Documents?'

Monica adjusted the large file-box under her arm. 'All set.' She grinned and looked towards Eric.

Eric waved from his chair. 'Good luck.'

Monica turned back to Emily without a reply.

'You look fantastic,' Emily said, kissing her on the cheek. 'Very executive. Powerful.'

'Do I? Good. Don't feel powerful.' The smart serge suit made Monica pull her shoulders back. 'My flight attendant outfit.' She adopted a posh voice. 'Leave your seat-belts fastened and your tray-table folded away. The life-belts are located underneath the seat in front of you.'

They both laughed. 'You look great. Knock 'em dead.'

'Hate it,' Monica called back from the hall, heading for the stairs. 'Make sure he wears a suit and tie, will ya? I've laid it all out on the bed. Wish me luck.'

'Charge!' Emily shouted back, making a megaphone of her hands.

Back inside, Emily went to stand over Eric's shoulder. She was dressed up to the nines herself: a white satin blouse, a tight skirt, heavily perfumed. It was difficult to resist dressing up when another woman was doing so. And there was a degree to which she was vicariously living a lot of what the Pringles were going through. 'You have to wear a suit and tie. Monica told me to tell you.'

'I know.'

'Sounds official.'

'Mon will tell you about it some time.'

'Mystery man.'

'Not really.'

Emily's eyes were on the set. 'So what's this then?'

'Third division.'

A football game was in progress. 'Oh.' Emily watched for a moment: a promising forward attack dwindled into a debasing return of the ball to the keeper, the oceanic crowd booed. 'You interested in this one, then?'

'No. Rubbish. Next one. But won't get to see it.'

Emily nodded. 'Better be off soon myself.'

'Right you are then.'

She sat on the couch, however, staring at the screen. 'Can I get you a cup of tea? Eric?'

'Mmm?'

'Cup of tea?'

'No thanks.' He then glanced over at her. He caught her fine-tuning her breasts inside her bra, the cleavage wrinkling slightly as she hoisted them into a better position. He glanced lower. From a short skirt her triangulated legs splayed girlishly outward to two pigeon-toed feet. Not bad, he thought. He hadn't seen her dressed up like this before. She was a very different woman in these clothes and with her make-up on. Perhaps this was how Graeme had seen her. For a second he looked at her with Graeme's eyes, momentarily saw her as a husband would, then snapped his eyes back to the set, but a second too late.

She had caught him looking. He couldn't look back to check on how she had taken it, or how long she looked at him, or how reproachful her expression, but he wasn't too bothered. He had much darker subjects on his mind.

What was an admiring glance anyway: they were neighbours after all.

The public gallery was crowded. Monica had no idea that these meetings would be so well attended. It reminded her, in the push to find a seat, of attending a comedy night: all she needed now was a strong drink.

The councillors were up and down on their feet, red with emotion, two of them loudly scotching a rubbish relocation scheme and at least three more reading newspapers and whispering to colleagues. Interest in the gallery also waxed and waned and the crowd replaced itself continually.

Monica's remit was next on the agenda. When would she catch the clerk's eye? The man seemed to yo-yo between this chamber and the next one, and he paid no heed to the public, who so far had had no input at all. She would give it another five minutes and then intercept him, plant the petition on him, secure her right to speak.

The public agenda was two inches thick. Monica flipped through it. She finally found the engineer's report on Melksham Towers. The fine print on pink paper told her that excessive settlement had resulted from the 'seasonal drying out and shrinkage of deeply stratified layers of sedimentary clay'. She had thought as much, *felt* as much, lying in bed awake at night, worrying, until Eric told her not to be ridiculous.

Some signs of structural stress were also apparent, the report said. *Some? Ha!* She would set them straight on this, if nothing else. *Ha!* Over the page she then found two quite opposing proposals.

One proposed the building be underpinned. Owing to recent interest by the National Trust in listing it a Grade Two building of some architectural interest, this could be viable. Monica was alarmed. Clearly this was a ploy on the part of the crowd campaigning for the status quo. Architectural interest? She might have believed archaeological.

The other proposal was that the building be demolished and replaced by a compound of terrace-style houses: it could be done quite cheaply. She turned the page to a picture of the modular units, between which, idealised multi-ethnic citizens came and went with dogs and prams between lollypop trees and ranks of hypothetical bicycles herring-boned in the sun-filled forecourt. Not a job for Eric here, she thought, nothing for Eric with his screwdrivers and spirit-levels and sash-planes.

Although nervous, she was bursting to speak. She had all the facts at her fingertips, the real ones, not these fairy statistics: just how impossible Mrs Rawlins found the heating on the fourth floor; how the generator kept the ground floor awake at night, how the windows leaked in most west-facing rooms and so badly that towels had to be laid permanently along the sill. Three floors with no sign of a fire extinguisher! God, what would happen in an emergency! God forbid what should happen in an emergency. Four photos of Eric's spirit-level measuring skills on the top floor, the bubble hard to the left or the right. And then Tracy in that lift for over four hours. It was lucky she was a young person. Mrs Chatterjee wouldn't have made it. She was a diabetic and needed her insulin . . .

The preceding matter on the agenda reached a climax of dissent, and yet, when it was put to the vote, the motion was passed entirely unopposed. Monica was flabbergasted. The entire debate seemed to be a vast exercise in egotism.

Suddenly, her very real petition felt weightless in her hands.

Emily was nervous. She adjusted the strap on her high heels as if prepping herself for some big personal moment, then checked to make sure she hadn't scratched the varnish on her nails. 'Monica could be talking at this very minute. She could be on her feet presenting her petition right now.'

Eric asked, 'What time do you make it?'

She looked at her watch. 'Two fifteen. And Tracy must be on her way to the court by now as well. You'd better start getting ready soon too.'

'Plenty of time yet.'

'I think it's so important that you're going along to support Tracy. It'll mean a lot to her just that you're there.'

'Mmm,' he said. Eric was growing nervous himself. Within two and a half-hours he would be standing in a public forum, admitting to the Great and the Good that he had misled a government department, misled them, and, even worse, betrayed his own daughter in the process. In fact, a headwater of bile was now rising in his stomach. He had seldom felt so alone. The TV was still on but he had completely lost interest in it and skipped between channels with maddening speed.

'Making me feel a bit sick, that is,' Emily said.

'Sorry.' He slowed down the changes for her sake, but his thumb remained heavy on the controls. 'I'm dying for a cigarette as well.'

Emily hadn't smoked for years but she had an idea. 'Do you really want one?

'You got one?'

'Cos I think I have an old packet of Graeme's still left over.'

'Still left over?'

'I can pop over and see.'

'Nah, nah, don't worry.'

'I can. No, I will. I'll just pop over.'

'Of Graeme's?'

'I think so, yeah. Should still be there.'

'No. Shouldn't do that. Should I? Know what I mean?' He screwed up his nose.

'Why not? Why not? Not as if he needs them, is it? And got quite enough smoke where he is I should think.' She forced a laugh.

'Ha!' Eric said. 'Ha.'

'Awful thing to say.'

'Still . . . would feel funny, y'know, a man's last cigarette'n all that.'

'Not one of those taboos though, is it?'

'Taboo? No. well, no. It's just a bit . . . y'know, off.'

'I'll have a look. It's okay. You stay.'

Good woman, Eric thought. Mightily good woman. He still felt sick. Tracy could well be in court right now. He should have told her the truth right away. *Failure! Failure!* Guilt and remorse tossed around in the foam inside him. *And lighting it up won't be easy either. History there too. Bad relations towards the end. But why should he worry about this as well, he shouldn't, that prick fucking someone on the side like that.* The problem was that Eric always knew Graeme had been doing the dirty on Emily. And Graeme knew he knew. Eric had been replacing a boiler thermostat alone in their flat and had answered the phone. The woman on the other end must have thought he was Graeme. The rest was history. Even if there was very little similarity, she asked: 'Is that you?' Three words on their own weren't much but when coupled with a steamy voice, plus the fact that when Eric replied 'Graeme's not here,' and she hung up in a flash, he had the beginnings of a theory. Still, he did not define it as an 'affair' until he reported the call to Graeme when he came in, wheezing from the stairs, which he had taken not because the lift was out but because he was always trying to stay fit, to improve himself, even though he was already on the downhill run into cancer. When Eric reported the call Graeme looked at him flat in the face and blushed. The blush did it.

From that moment everything else became strained between the two men. Keeping their thoughts to themselves, fear from one quarter collided with loss of respect from the other. *So he's hardly gonna to be too pleased seeing me smoke his last fags in the whole world.*

He flicked the channels with ferocity as he waited for a dead man's final legacy.

In the recess that followed, and as the secretary rose and left the room, Monica threaded her way out of the chamber, shadowing the clerk through the padded swing-door, stopping him in the hall, her pink box under her arm.

336

'Sorry I'm late. Hi. But this is the petition from the MTRC. Sorry it's a bit late, but better late than never, right?'

'MTRC?'

'Oh, Melksham Tower Residents Committee. I phoned up about it. A lot of support came in at the last minute actually. Usual story.' She grinned.

He looked down at the pink box, confused, which made her thrust it further forward, causing him to take a step back. 'Wrote to you about it several times. The council knows it's coming. Talked to someone yesterday. Twenty-three names. But I think that shows how up in arms we all are.'

Still he didn't take the box from her. 'Don't know anything about it, I'm sorry. Perhaps you could try the front desk.'

'No, I was supposed to give it to you.'

'To me? No, not me.'

'It's for presentation at the meeting. It's next. Melksham Towers.'

'You were supposed to give it to me?'

'Well, someone, and you look like the guy.'

'Of course. Fine. Let me take it.' He suddenly took it from her. 'Thank you for bringing it in. I'll talk to someone about what to do with it. Now, if you'll excuse me.'

And with that the man disappeared into an interior room, the pink file-box put to the bottom of the papers in the crook of his arm. The door swung shut.

Monica wondered what was happening to her pink box. She hoped the machinery was jumping into overdrive. She imagined secretaries being called away from what they were doing to handle this. In the light of the petition everything would have to be reviewed.

'Damn,' she said. She had forgotten to ask if she could speak. Surely the public would be invited to tender their comments. Surely the clerk would open it up. She hoped she had not just blown her one chance. Suddenly worried, she pushed her way back towards the chamber. The door's pneumatic return valve sucked air heavily as she slipped back inside.

Eric raised the disposable lighter and held it near the end of the cigarette. It was the third to last in the old, mashed pack. Age had stained them the colour of weak tea.

'I don't feel too good about this.'

'Don't be silly.'

'Know what I mean?'

Watched by Emily, he flicked the lighter. The end of the cigarette went red. He inhaled tentatively. The smoke went into his lungs. It gave him a merciful rush. 'Mmmm,' he murmured. He held it in, this smoke from Graeme's last packet of cigarettes, then let it out slow and nodded. They had lost most of their flavour from being in a dark drawer for two years. They weren't his own brand either — Graeme liked them lighter — but they were still okay.

'How are they?' Emily asked, fascinated by something more than just the act of Eric smoking.

'I hope you're sure about this.'

'Don't.'

'Okay. Not another word.' He looked at Emily, then rattled the packet, looked up and said, 'Two to go Graeme!'

It made Emily's hand jump to her mouth.

'Oh, sorry. Em. You okay? Didn't mean . . . '

From nowhere she was on the verge of tears. 'It's okay,' she said, trying to recover, already burying her feelings.

'Oh shit.'

'It's okay. Have them all.'

'Feel terrible now.'

She looked indomitable again. 'No. You finish them.'

Eric shook his head. 'Poor old Graeme, eh.' *Is that you?* the sexy voice on the phone had said. Eric heard it again. *Is that you, Graeme?* A timeless question. But now Graeme was dead, and it was Emily sitting there watching him.

'You enjoy them.'

He smiled at her, and she smiled back. She looked like a million quid compared to how she normally looked, he thought. *Tracy!* Betrayal was a dirty word. The image of Graeme fucking his mistress flashed through Eric's mind but he dispersed it with an exceptionally heavy draw on the cigarette.

'You know,' she said, 'just seeing you there . . . smoking . . . '

'I know,' he said, 'I know', guessing what she was about to say, but not wanting to hear it.

She then laughed again, back to herself, until she stopped, her face creased, and she began to cry.

338

'Oh, not again,' Eric said. 'Em? Come on. Jesus, come on.' He was concerned to help her but he didn't want to go to her. He couldn't get bogged down in her affairs any more than he already was.

'Seeing you, there, for a minute . . . ' She sniffed. 'Just reminds me, that's all.'

'I bet,' he said. This was what Eric had feared. He should never have smoked this. It brought back all sorts of demons and horrors. He wanted to put it out at once but he had no ashtray. Smoking another man's cigarettes, a dead man's, was no incidental thing. And when those cigarettes were smoked in front of that man's still tormented widow, it was suicidal. *Betrayal!*

'Em?'

'It's hopeless,' she said. 'It's just so . . . hopeless.'

'What is? Come on now.'

'I'm so sick of it.'

'I bet you are.' He didn't know what else to say.

'I'm so tired.'

When she didn't recover he went into the kitchen and tore off two segments of kitchen roll.

She accepted one, dabbing her eyes with it. 'Thanks, Eric,' she said.

'All right?' he said, as if a paper towel made a huge difference to everyone in the overall scheme of things. He held out the second one. 'It's my fault. It's all my fault,' he said. 'It's all my fucking fault, isn't it.'

'I'm so sorry,' was all she replied. She looked up into his face as he waited to give her the second napkin. She stood to receive it.

'Gimme that one,' he said, referring to the wet napkin.

'Oh Eric,' she breathed. It was a fragile murmur, but there was more to it.

'It's my fault,' he said.

Before he could retreat she wrapped her arms around his neck and kissed him on the mouth. And with her mouth on him her fingers spread out through his hair. Her lips were hot with sadness, salty with emotion, suffocating him at first. His nose filled with the shock of perfume at close quarters. He couldn't breathe until she released him.

With eyes as close as only lovers' are, they examined each other's faces. Eric saw two mascara-stained eyes, smeared by tears. Emily was a real woman: he couldn't look past it. Here she was, all of her, in his hands. He had once seen through a crack in a door her black lace underwear. Was she wearing this now?

'Don't tell me off,' she whispered.

'We'd better . . . stop . . . '

'I know, I know, I know, I know, I know.'

'Em?'

'Don't know what's going on. You're lovely. You are. You really are.' Her emotions again became too much for her. 'Oh — ' She pressed forward with her mouth, caught him on the side of his own, even more desperately laid her kisses upon him, until she moved to his neck and peppered it with machine-gun smacks above the collar, leaving a necklace there of vermilion. She was hot now, hot in his arms. She spoke between kisses: 'Monica. Wouldn't. Eric, she wouldn't. Mind. I know. Mind. Oh Eric.' She hugged him, hard, strongly, encircling him, tugging at his shirt for a response, for reciprocal kisses, wringing him like a sponge for emotion.

'Em, Em, steady on. Em, Em, okay, come on. Ha! Ha! Easy, easy.' But Eric was too stunned to extricate himself. Fireworks were going off in his own head. He saw Graeme in his mistress's room and fended this image off only to have a sudden vision of Emily supine on the carpet, he over her, he and not Graeme moving, about to explode: for God's sake, stop! But his hand accidentally found her buttock — was he out of his mind? — and she squirmed under it, willing the hand to grab, squeeze, to go to work. Yes! They were seconds away from commitment to the act when he broke free. 'Em!' He pushed her back. 'Okay, Jesus, that's enough!' He gripped her shoulders and with brute force kept her at arm's length. 'Wait! Em! Slow down.'

But she was finished anyway and she sagged. Defeat already showed in her face. The tears ran as he watched. She let out a sigh and caved in, her shoulders slumping.

She stared at him. Her eyes now asked only for understanding. Her voice was breathless. 'I'm so unhappy, Eric.'

The words reared up between them. For a few seconds he didn't even attempt a reply. *Unhappy?* What could another person do about that? She was falling to pieces in front of him. The lure of her lacy black underwear dissolved. 'I know, Em. But it's not my business, darlin', is it? Know what I mean? It can't be.'

She nodded. She knew as much. Who knew better than her that in private rooms right across the land we were all on our own. 'I know. But it's funny, innit. If I'd had my leg blown off or something, people'd be more interested.'

'We've all got our hands full. Simple as that. Everybody has.'

'I know.'

'Come on. Okay?' He squeezed the jutting bones of her shoulders.

'I know. I *know*. I'm so stupid. I'm just being silly. I'll be all right in a minute. I just needed to tell someone.' She wiped her eyes and tried to smile. 'I'm so embarrassing.'

'I'll make us a cuppa, or something. How's that? You just sit down there.' He stopped at the door. 'Told you I shouldn't have touched that cigarette.'

She nodded and shrugged, tried to smile. He escaped into the kitchen, made her a cup of tea in record time, barely dipping the tea-bag in the piping water, and hurried back to her, relieved that the worst was over, but a little deflated that life was again no more than it usually was. She looked up, and smiled weakly. 'I'll tell Monica. Don't worry. It's my fault.'

Eric's brows crossed. 'About what?'

'About this,' she sniffed. 'It's okay. I'll sort it out.'

He became alarmed. 'Tell her what?' He simulated a smile. 'Tell her what?' He was on thin ice with Monica already. Since his confession his whole marriage was up for grabs. Would Emily say he had grabbed her ass? Panic replaced the last remnants of desire.

She smiled and sipped her tea, calm again. 'About this. She'll understand. She needs to know about it. No secrets. And you were wonderful. Letting me do that.'

Eric's tone quickly became hostile. 'Em, listen, okay? There isn't a secret. Okay?'

'No, Eric. I want to tell her.' Her voice was also firmer, more implacable, a principle now at stake. 'It was my doing, not yours.'

'Em. Listen to me.' He got angry. 'There's nothing to tell. Now I'd appreciate it if you stay out of this. I'll tell her. Now I've got to get ready now. I can't be late. So you sit there as long as you want but I really hope you're not gonna mention this to her.'

Eric was already halfway to his bedroom. 'I'll see ya, okay, and I'll tell her myself.' His shirt was half off.

Emily gently settled her cup in its saucer on the couch, looking like a woman on a train who had gone one station past her own.

On TV the game remained goalless.

In his bedroom Eric angrily pulled on the shirt his wife's friend had just ironed for him, the cloth still warm.

And balanced on the armrest, forgotten, a dead friend's cigarette quietly began to burn a hole in Eric's precious Naugehyde.

'Yes, that's right,' the witness replied.

'Then would you care to clarify that for us?' Ridley's voice rang out with excessive volume and his delight at the coup of having secured this man's testimony played devilishly on his face.

'I just mean that the Burton Street situation, as we called it around the office, seemed to be a more than respectable one to me. In fact, it seemed actually, well, actually quite an enviable one.'

Partridge was enjoying himself already. He turned his eyes to where there might have been a public gallery, the source of imaginary laughter. It encouraged him to go further. The ex-public official looked over the heads of his former colleagues in the front row, indeed his superiors, happy to play to his phantom audience.

'And this "Burton Street situation", I gather it became something of a *cause célèbre* around your office.'

'Everyone wanted to know about it. Everyone was speculating and had theories. It was the big coffee-time conversation. What did the women look like, how it worked and so forth. Was the husband a pimp? Should someone be put on the house to see if male customers could be seen going in and coming out? There was a lot of spec . . . a lot of talk. Women were as interested as the men. A couple of guys even hassled me to take some pictures.'

'Quite a prurient atmosphere, in other words?'

'But that wasn't the official line. This was just people chatting.'

'And your own personal conclusion about the Sahars?'

'Like I said. The real atmosphere wasn't sensational at all. Somehow these four adults seemed to me to have found a way to live together. And what's more, in a way which seems so miraculously devoid of jealousy, and of envy, and I suppose boredom and infidelity that it defies our actual notion of marriage.'

He grinned. Once again he fed his invisible crowd, who now fell off their seats, stamped the floor, applauded with rapture his impromptus

342

and goaded him onwards. He was very near to experiencing what the psychologists call 'a defining moment'.

'And did this satisfy your colleagues around the coffee machine?'

Partridge shook his head. 'They preferred their own ideas, I think. They thought there had to be more to it.'

'I see. *They preferred their own ideas.*' Ridley turned to face the Social Services representatives. 'Preferred. Their *own*.' Ridley laid his argument like an explosive expert, placing his little charges, weakening his opponents at all the load-bearing points. 'And so what was your eventual recommendation, to your superiors?'

'My recommendation?' Here Partridge rose to his full height. Clearly it was the question he had been waiting for and he projected his voice into the gods. 'Well, they chose to overlook it, simple as that.' He was shouting now. 'In fact, they chose to go one hundred and eighty degrees in the opposite direction. One hundred and eighty!' A darts scorekeeper could not have belted out the figure more clearly. 'My report was basically buried. And I was never given a satisfactory reason why.'

'Buried?' Ridley turned again to the underpaid repairers of social harm, redrawn suddenly as con men and reprobates.

'They ignored it. Totally ignored it, and went ahead with the criminal action of removing the kids from the family home.'

The assembled lawyers, social workers, psychologists and witnesses stared back at the man in the dock with bleached faces. This accusation was far more forcefully expressed than anyone had imagined and the volume level he employed made him seem vaguely unhinged.

'It was mind-boggling,' Partridge went on, following the old vaudeville credo: if it works do it again. 'But it was *always* my impression, after several visits to their house, and I made this very clear in my report, that despite the unusual nature of the whole set-up, that this family should not only be permitted to go on functioning as one, but should also be called upon to deliver seminars.' The applause in his mind was stirring; a string of encores was on its way.

The judge leant forward, gestured at Ridley who nodded in agreement. Ridley approached his own witness to whisper, 'Just a little lower. The voice.'

Partridge nodded. He was overexcited.

'And can you recall the contents of this official report?'

'Yes I can. In detail.'

'How can you be so sure?'

'Because I have a copy right here with me.' He drew out a photocopy of his ignored report and raised it in the air, giving Ridley another opportunity to leer at the prosecution.

The report was quickly inducted as evidence and passed to the judge, who stabbed on his glasses. 'Very well,' the judge mumbled after a cursory reading. 'Let's go on.'

'Could you perhaps summarise this report for us?' Ridley asked.

Partridge was happy to do so. Without requesting to have his notes back he stated that he had found no evidence whatsoever that the children were in any way damaged or in danger, or that the adult's sex lives were a negative influence on the children, or that in themselves they were improper.

'Do you have anything else to add?'

'Just that my department, in my opinion, seems to have either unwittingly or otherwise affected the lives of several decent and respectable people.'

'Thank you, sir. That will be all.'

Partridge was dismissed. He almost bowed but began to step down.

The Social Services team stared at a point somewhere on the wall in front them.

Ridley found his seat and squeezed Tracy's hand. 'We'll call your father now. Though we hardly bloody need him.'

Ridley retook the floor as Partridge, passing Tracy, fired her a look. Tracy gave him a thumbs-up sign.

Ridley next called Eric Pringle.

A bailiff escorted Eric into the room, and he made his slow, limping way to the box. To a choice of the Bible or the Koran he said, 'I'm a Christian.' Under pain of divine retribution he then pledged to tell the truth.

This witness was unforeseen by the Social Services barristers, and they shoved their heads together like budgerigars.

Eric stated his full name and address while staring about him, overwhelmed. One minute he was in his car, the next he was in a witness box and about to reveal his innermost secrets to a public hearing.

Deep in his own thoughts he missed his first question. 'Mr Pringle?'

'Mmm?'

Ridley repeated it.

'Yes, that's right,' Eric replied, listening to his own words. 'I'm Tracy's father.'

Tracy slipped into the courthouse hallway. She pulled out her mobile and phoned Sam's mobile to update him. Hopefully he'd be alert enough to sense the pulsing under his pillow. To avoid detection she had switched off the ringer.

'Answer, answer,' she said aloud.

She wanted to tell him that her father had gone a long way toward making amends for his crimes. She also wanted to quote a few of Partridge's life-saving phrases, describe their impact, recreate the mood of optimism on their side. *Sam*, she'd say, *Partridge showed up, spoke against his own people, admitted what they did. He's got another job now, you should've been here.*

Her spirits were soaring. But still he didn't answer. She had inadvertently pushed her new family into the centre of a storm but she had found a way out for them as well.

Passing her by, on the way into a second courtroom, a son supported an ageing mother to the door. Tracy nodded her encouragement when the son gave her a *What can you do* shrug. Someone else was going to face their crisis. *The world is the evil person's paradise.* This was the Persian proverb she had in mind. If that was right, then it was lucky for us that paradise was flawed. The good still got a look in from time to time. *Be patient with little, God will give you much.* She'd memorised dozens of these from her lectures and reading. *The best women are those who ride on camels.* What was the modern equivalent? Her father's Ducati 750 perhaps. *Hospitality is for three days.* Fatima should heed that one.

A recorded voice told her that the party she had called was either unavailable or that their phone was switched off. She dialled again. She would give it one more go.

As she waited the same young man held open the heavy courtroom door with one arm, forming an arch through which, with his other hand, he drew the sway-backed old woman. The woman dipped as she passed underneath, a sweet gesture. The moment looked like a little dance.

23

Internal Complications

Perhaps it was the pressure being exerted on the brain by the elasticising bubbles in his skull, or the drugs coursing through the highways of his body, or the frustration felt by a talker with damaged lips and with a hand that longed to caress but was bound in bandages, but whatever the case, Sam's initially placid mood began to give way to tempers, mood swings and bouts of excessive behaviour as the days of his convalescence expired.

While Tracy tried to preserve the calm and tranquillity that had marked the first few days of his hospitalisation, he seemed equally determined to engage in some kind of personal metamorphosis.

Demanding things he only fleetingly desired, from a margarita he couldn't possibly drink to ordering Tracy to phone an art dealer to buy paintings to conceal the terrifying white of the walls, he taxed everyone's patience to the limit.

Increasingly wakeful, as the doses of morphine were scaled down, he criticised everything from the food he couldn't eat to the weather that didn't affect him. From Tracy, he requested a new Mastercard to replace the one stolen by 'those vigilantes', and began a campaign of demented purchases.

Although Tracy and the others noticed a change in him — he was like a concentrate of himself — he was so full of life and determination to overcome his setbacks that they welcomed every eccentricity as an improvement.

And then, when he had wound himself up like a spring, so that Tracy began to visualise the straining bubbles of blood in his head and feared for his safety, the clamorous mood would pass like the noisy tea trolleys outside his door, and calm would be restored again. He would become a lamb, tenderly holding Tracy's hand long into the night.

His doctor told her not to worry unduly. This hypomania, caused by phases of high toxicity in the brain, was a by-product of both the blood-pressure drugs and delayed reaction to the trauma of the assault. The old Sam would return soon enough, he promised.

In the meantime the whole family decided to go along with his moods, avoid argument where possible, humour his wishes, no matter how irrational, and do everything they could to pacify him, lest the straining vessels give out and his condition worsen.

Love and attention would pay dividends, the consultant told them.

This last prescription, at least, seemed to have a positive effect. Although the latest batch of X-rays showed no decrease in the size of the aneurism, the sick man's vitality and outward appearance began to improve immensely. His ribs and left hand healed and a proper sense of the man returned as the mummy began to unwind.

Working carefully on his lips, a nurse peeled away the last scales of dead skin, revealing pink, new skin beneath, flesh softer and two tones lighter than before.

It gave his mouth a youthful, new-born quality and Tracy was the first to test it with a kiss.

'Bit like snogging a girl,' she concluded.

He squinted in suspicion. 'And what would you know about that? What have you women been up to? While I've been in here?'

'Wouldn't you like to know.'

'Yes I would. Wouldn't want to miss out on that!'

Tracy shook her head. 'Dirty old man.' She hoped this was the morphine talking.

'You think I'm joking? That's my whole trouble.'

'Stop talking now.' She didn't want to excite him but she didn't want to deny him anything either.

'What kind of man has three wives and doesn't make use of them all? When I get home, quite a few things are going to change.' His waved his finger decisively.

'Come off it.'

'This rough stuff has helped me rediscover my masculine charge.

What a dunce! Three sexy women at my fingertips. What a flop!'

'Stop now.'

'You don't want to know what I've decided?'

This got her attention. 'No,' she said. 'I don't. Now stop talking.'

Tracy convened an emergency session in Hyde Park, a safe place to discuss Sam's state with her fellow wives while the children took rides in the Princess Diana Memorial Playground.

She needed to air her concerns and had a list of 'incidents'. Yesterday, at bath time, he had flaunted his injuries to the nurses who washed him. 'I've never seen him like that. Almost *macho*.'

Next she reported that he had quashed her suggestion of having his broken teeth repaired as soon as possible. 'His smile is horrific, he'll need a plate, but I think in a weird way he's quite proud of them. He treats them like battle scars.'

And there was more. He had told Tracy, but not the others, that in some ways a beating might have been just what he needed. He had said he had been an observer of life for too long. The mugging was a lesson — 'a call to action' was the phrase he had used. Thinking his days away had got him nowhere. The world was for tasting, he had said.

'He kept saying he now wanted to sample everything on the menu. Everything on the menu, he said.'

They contemplated the meanings of all this.

Firouzeh was the first to offer an explanation. 'Because he can't talk and can't move properly he's compensating. Like a thirsty man in a desert, what does he think about? He craves what he can't have. I saw it right away. It's nothing. Nothing at all.'

'And ze drugs,' added Yvette. 'Of course he will say crazy sings with all ziss stuff in his veins. I told you I caught him ordering sings with his credit card. Gifts for the children. Jewellery. A horse.'

Yvette had failed to mention this. 'A horse?'

'Oh, didn't I say? Yes, he said he always wanted a white palomino. A white Arabian.'

The women looked to Sam's first wife for confirmation. She gravely shook her head.

'Of course I phoned z'jewellers and z'toy shops back. Zey refunded the purchases luckily.'

'And *the horse*?' Firouzeh asked.

'I am sure I didn't need to. And I didn't know who he talked to anyway. But they can't just deliver a horse, can they?'

'Oh my God,' Tracy said.

The women agreed that they would all have to keep a much closer eye on him, and definitely take his credit card away.

'There's something else as well,' Tracy said. She had saved this bit for last. 'He told me that when he got out of hospital, that when he's better again, he wants to start availing himself of his conjugal rights, right across the board.'

A sharp look of apprehension fell over Yvette and Firouzeh.

'What!'

'That's what he said. Right across the board.'

'He is not serious,' Yvette said. 'Ziss is a joke. Now he is just joking with you.'

'Yes,' Firouzeh agreed. 'He's just joking.'

Tracy was unable to smile. 'He asked if I would mind.'

'Mind?'

'If we all slept in the same bed. With him. Together. Once we win the court case.'

Firouzeh was slower to see the joke this time. 'The same bed?'

Yvette stared at Tracy. 'And what did you say to him?'

'What did I say?'

'Yes.'

'I told him it was fine with me. I did what you told me. I went along with him.'

'So you told him . . . ?'

'I said it was fine with me.' She blushed. 'He wants to make love to all three of us together.'

At this point Firouzeh and Yvette's powers of speech escaped them.

'I did what you told me,' Tracy said, seeing the disfavour on their faces and waiting for their approval, waiting longer still, until she realised it would not come. 'I did the right thing, didn't I?'

Firouzeh drove the children home. A large removal van was waiting for her in the driveway when she arrived. The driver, a bald man with Popeye forearms, had a dispatch form he needed signed before he unloaded the item. The children assembled like a committee on the footpath as the back doors of the van were opened.

The colossal bed, big enough to sleep an entire family and far wider than it was long, was slowly drawn out. Two men groaned under the load.

'Big one, innit. So where's the bedroom, missus?' the burly man grunted.

'The bedroom?'

'The boys have got orders to set it up in the master bedroom, so if you can show us the way.'

Firouzeh, whose husband could suffer no rejection, no setback, no contradiction, directed the men towards the house. Little Mostafa ran ahead to open the door, standing sideways as the great sedan past him by. Firouzeh herded the men quickly inside, eager to have the doors shut but shooting one last look up and down the street to ensure that no one had seen the arrival of this stupendous bed which alone would sink forever any hopes of public absolution for the Sahars and their irregular arrangement.

As the police inquiry into the beating continued, it was inevitable that a newspaper would eventually track down the Sahars for comment. A journalist visited Burton Street that morning but Firouzeh sent him away without comment. Undeterred, the man visited Sam in his hospital bed, and found the patient coherent and quite willing to talk.

Airing his views officially for the first time to the national press, Sam spoke torrentially, sometimes incoherently, but at other times he was eloquent, informed, even elegiac. It was a stunningly rosy defence of the city he had come so far to embrace.

The journalist, taken aback, simply wanted Sam's views on the motive for the vicious attack, and pointed to the Superglue as a clue of racist hatred.

But Sam doubted that it was racially inspired. He didn't believe people looked at him as a foreigner in the first instance. 'There are other levels of compulsion to consider before we reach for race. These muggers were depleted of spirit. I spoke with them. These kids crave celebrity, even if it is the criminal variety. That was where the Superglue came in. It was their brilliant low-life idea. Their piece of cinema, and they were *proud* of it. To them I looked wealthy, someone high up to drag down, a vessel to assist them in becoming famous, if only in their own sad, little circle. I even doubt money as a motive. You can bet these young men are pretty high right now.'

The journalist dutifully filled his pad with shorthand, but when the item appeared that night, edited to a morsel, the public were given only the bare details, in three short paragraphs: Persian man attacked in bizarre circumstances last week; masked youths employ Superglue to restrict, and then silence the victim; social organisations outraged; a comment, even, from a spokesman from the Race Relations Board.

Tracy took a taxi to St George's Hospital, passed the mini-shop, buoyed by helium Get Well balloons and stocked with tabloid newspapers carrying the story, and made her way to Sam's ward. There were no nurses in reception and going straight to Sam's door she was shocked to find an empty bed.

Immediately, terrible thoughts raced through her brain. She raised the alarm at once, running in several directions down the halls before she tracked down a nurse who told her that Sam had been taken down to X-ray.

An hour earlier Sam had gone briefly into a coma. Oxygen had brought him around again. Attempts had been made to contact her. The X-ray unit was one floor below and Tracy was welcome to go down and be with her husband.

Her heart began to pound; she felt feverish. She went back into the hall and got into the staff elevator, making room before the door closed for a transferring patient in a serious condition, this man's eyes closed, concentrating on his disorder. The hospital porter in green smiled at her but no one spoke as they descended. Tracy slipped by them as the doors opened.

Taking directions from two different nurses, she pushed open the swing doors of the X-ray unit. Children's pictures and colourful posters baffled her before a distant sign across a series of glass cubicles told her that entry was prohibited. A small red light confirmed that the X-ray was already in progress.

'Can I help you?' a new nurse asked.

Tracy turned. The woman had a watch clipped over her breast. 'My husband. He's . . . I think he's having his X-ray done, right now, I think. Mr Sahar. Is he in there now?'

'It's okay. That's fine. Yes, he's in there now.' The nurse's tone was calming. 'And you are?'

'His . . . his wife.' Yes, she was.

'Okay, fine. He's in there now. Would you like to observe? You could observe if you like.'

Before she could decide she had replied, 'Can I?'

The nurse led her at once into the restricted area, gave her a lead apron and left her alone.

Through the heavy safety window Tracy viewed Sam on a stretcher, his arms bare at his sides, plastic ID tag on his wrist, eyes shut, a passed-away colour to his skin as the large X-ray machine crept up his body towards his damaged head, scanning as it went. The London Aquarium offered these same views of unseen worlds, and Tracy peered in at her husband from the bathysphere. She had slipped the heavy apron over her head and fastened the ribbons behind her.

Sam on his back, sedated, immobile, was alone in the X-ray room, prey for the creeping machine, which had moved up to his head, taking its deepest soundings there. With no emanation of light, it gathered its data, feeding it via streaming machines to a TV monitor that Tracy could narrowly view. A cross-section was building up on the screen.

She was shocked by this glimpse of her husband's brain, a white-on-black fossil that she couldn't associate with the man she loved. Here was the centre of this thinker's life but looking no more than the segmented pulp of an orange. When the image on the screen abruptly flicked to a side view, his skull was revealed in profile; it was even more shocking: the bare bones were quite unrecognisable, a snapshot of his death: rays bombarded him from two directions now. This was hard on her. She took in air like a diver, holding her breath. Sam, who had a contempt for new technology and a phobia about rays, a reluctant twenty-first-century man, was here at its mercy. She searched the monitor but could infer nothing, seeing no sac of blood, no damage done. Of course, she thought, he had made an astonishing recovery. Like Isis, their talks had entered him, radiated his skull and restored the damage. Any second he would sit up and smile at her.

Then the process clicked off. Lights on the machine went out. The radiologist, unaware of her, sleeves rolled up, pulled Sam's trolley out of the steel bay. The procedure was over and Tracy watched as Sam was wheeled away, lifeless, the crown of his balding head the last sight as the swing-doors swallowed him.

A second aneurism had suddenly developed near the first, and this had also increased in size overnight, briefly cutting off the supply of oxygen to the left side of Sam's brain and putting him into a coma from which he soon recovered. The patient was oblivious to this missing segment in his life and opened his mouth to say that he was feeling 'vaguely hungry'.

Unable to get a signal on her mobile, Tracy relayed the news to Firouzeh and Yvette by pay-phone, driving 20-pence coins into the slot, her eyes damp. Sam's situation was now officially critical.

The doctor wanted to know what the wives — he now knew of their status — wanted to do now. The news was bad.

'He may live for months, years, it's quite impossible to say,' the consultant told the graven women, the latest X-rays on the table between them. 'He could live longer than any of us, who knows, if the size of the aneurisms suddenly stabilised. On the other hand, you have to know that those arteries could give out tomorrow in the shower when he bends over to pick up the soap. Just like that. We simply cannot predict the day, the time, the hour.'

Sam was now at the disorder's mercy, the condition inoperable. The ballooned condition of two tiny arteries ruled his life. The chances of his survival if a surgeon were to operate were below five percent, unacceptably low.

'He's dying then,' Tracy said. 'So he's dying?'

The doctor, a sudden amateur, made no reply.

This kind of news couldn't be contested. Anger had no place in anyone's response. The facts had simply to be absorbed. But this would take time. Right now all they could offer each other was their silences.

'How are we supposed to live with *that*?' Firouzeh asked, fighting this *fait accompli*, still leaning towards the possibility of an operation.

Tracy spoke up. What should they tell Sam? What could Sam possibly be told?

'That's a good question. It's really up to you. But it's my feeling that the stress of knowing would be the biggest stress we could place on him right now.' The women considered this and eventually nodded, fighting back tears. There was no doubt that this was the right thing to do. 'And what I would like to see happen, as soon as possible, is for him to go home.'

Everyone knew what this meant: despite the doctor's bedside talk that Sam might still have years in front of him, time was, in fact, short. The word *home*, with its connotations of cure, resonated around the room, stirring them. 'I think it's time for you to have him home again.' Except there would not be a cure.

The women stared at him. Even at times like this, even in the striking of life deals, you deferred to the professionals. But he was right: every means possible had to be used to stretch out Sam's life, and there was no cure in the whole world that rivalled the ignorance of bad news.

Tracy rose and announced she had to go. Sam would wake up soon and she wanted to be there when he did.

The meeting was over.

'Still here,' Sam said, opening his right eye. The left oddly remaining half closed, as though he had suddenly suffered a stroke.

'Still here,' she managed, hiding a lot of emotion.

'Groggy again today. Don't know why. Mysterious.'

'The doctor said you might be able to come home soon.'

'What did he say?'

'He said you're getting better.'

'Did he?'

'Yeah.'

Sam pondered this. Did he detect a lie? 'You see? Worrying about nothing. Tell them to get me that surgery date. Will you do that?'

She nodded.

Sam was sick of waiting. He was ready to go, ready to fight. He had a new restaurant to open. But then he sighed. 'Don't know what's wrong with me today. They're gonna teach me. Did I say? To paint?' He seemed to have forgotten his half dozen lessons so far. He turned and looked at her. 'What are you bloody. Crying for, woman?'

'Just happy. You're getting better. That's all.'

'You're starting. You know. To talk like me.'

'Sorry?'

'Watch it. Everybody does. All the visitors. End up talking. Like bloody halfwits?'

'It's contagious. That's why.' She smiled. 'Now shush.'

'Smart aleck. What are you crying for?'

'Hold my hand.'

He held her hand, unaware of the dangers lurking in his head.

Tracy, Yvette and Firouzeh prepared for Sam's return home, determined to make it positive, a triumph.

After the victorious ruling of the family court — who found no reason why the family should not be allowed to live together, chiding the

354

government agency for 'hyperactivity' — Tracy and Yvette had settled their bill at the Metropole and come home themselves.

A fanfare greeted them. A surprise party of guests shouted congratulations as the two exiles came through the front door with their mountains of luggage. Ridley led the toasts with a summing up of the successful legal strategy: 'If you can't beat them, enlist them'.

As an act of exorcism, clearing away the bad spirits of the court case, Firouzeh began to redecorate the house. In the same vein, Yvette overhauled the restaurant menus, adding new dishes and altering the table plans. Meanwhile, Tracy handled the opening of the new restaurant, named The Zahir after her.

When all this was happily reported to Sam he cocked his good eye and muttered through his drugs: 'Just as I thought. I am irrelevant.'

To cover his increasingly bad eye, forced shut by the arterial pressure, he had ordered an extraordinarily piratical eye-patch. When he first pulled it on his wives refused to look at him.

'Take it off,' Firouzeh demanded.

'My new image,' he said. 'This will make me feared and respected in the same breath. Just like Moshe Dayan!'

At the same time he was still so weak that he needed to be helped in and out of his wheelchair. His verbal audacity was in stark contrast to his worrying infirmity. 'Has the house been made ready for me?'

'What do you want to be ready?'

'You know what. The big bed.'

'We all hope you're not serious' Tracy replied.

'Then they don't know the new me. Oh, and I ordered new lingerie for you all this morning.'

'New *what* ?'

'Did it arrive?'

Tracy didn't answer. Her mind had turned to the job of explaining to Sam why he was about to be released from hospital when a date for corrective surgery had not been set.

'Friday,' she announced.

'Friday?'

'Afternoon. They're letting us take you home. They think that's the best way now to prepare you for the operation.'

'At last! But it's just what I've been saying. A bit of home cooking. I can't wait to get back in a kitchen!'

Despite his setbacks, despite the tragic half-mast eye, the visible loss of weight, the endless headaches, Sam had lost none of his high spirits. In fact, they seemed to have returned in full force. Not for one second had he stopped plotting grandiose schemes, undimmed by the ward sister's commandeering of his mobile phone. This only drove him out into the hall, walking shakily to the lobby, small change for the pay-phone held in his palm. He was still in business.

'Tell me what you thought about,' he asked. 'All those hours. In that lift.'

'In the lift?'

'All those hours. Stuck. Trapped.'

He seemed to want an insight into his own predicament.

'Nothing really. I just waited and daydreamed.'

The nurse came in, smiled, checked the cardiograph, the meters, the drips. At the morphine bottle she inspected the tubes and twisted the tap. In a second she was gone again.

Sam rested his eyes for a second, focusing on the drug's opening fanfare.

'You have the mind of an artist. You have all the qualities of a great artist.'

'Such as?'

'Lack of interest in the real world. You have worlds in you, entirely thought-out worlds. Everything in place. And I think you will one day do something. Very special.'

She shook her head and reworked this statement in her mind so that it meant simply that he loved her.

'But I have no illusions. Not about you at least,' he said, resting his eyes. 'Why you are with me. I know very well. With two wives I fitted into. An imaginary landscape of yours. A world unreal enough to attract you.'

He sighed at the first impact of the morphine. He opened his eyes again. 'That lift. Terrible. Terrible.'

'A mind of its own.'

'Like you. Oh!' He waved his arm at his bedside table. 'Top drawer.' He was going under. He had to speak quickly. 'Photo. Meant to give it to you. Had it developed. Remember that time?' But she couldn't follow this. 'I pulled you out of the shower? Overcome I was. By your youth, your frightening beauty, your wet body. I couldn't stand it. So I pulled you, remember, down on the tiles. And made love. To you.' He fought his delirium. Running against the clock he spoke in compressed bursts. She didn't recall this event at all. 'Well, what you didn't see was what you left behind. Your wet imprint. On those tiles, your shadow, exaggerated lines but your body all the same. I took a photo of it. Before it evaporated. It was one of those moments. I knew it couldn't be captured. On a photograph, what it did to my heart, and it doesn't show, you'll see, in the drawer there . . . '

Tracy opened the drawer. His eyes had closed. There wasn't a photograph in the drawer.

'I can see it,' she said.

'Take it. That's just. A bad photograph. But it jogs the memory. And *that* photograph,' he raised his arm, tapped his head, a monumental effort, 'my mental one . . . well I wish . . . I could show you . . . that one.'

She was crying. But he had gone under and as usual didn't see her tears.

The house was ready. Bedroom doors had been widened by carpenters to allow a wheelchair to pass, long-term ramps built. The children painted and erected a banner. And a huge welcome home party was planned; invitations had gone out, delighted RSVPs had been received. Only his wives were aware that Sam was coming home to die.

The day itself was cold, inhospitable. The ambulance that brought Sam crawled up the street and into the driveway at the speed of a hearse and dampened everyone's spirits. Sam had planned to walk proudly up the path on his own but he was easily dissuaded by the two medics.

His family crowded around him and all the children found a way of exerting some pressure on his wheelchair, spinning their father up the path towards Tracy at the front door.

'Welcome home, General.'

'Bloody ambulance got lost.'

'That eye-patch looks ridiculous.'

'Nonsense,' he adjusted it. 'I rather like it now.' He reached and squeezed her hand. 'Good to be home. Let's go in.'

The gathering of close friends quickly exhausted him, and by 9 p.m. the house was quiet.

Tweaking his eye-patch again he asked, 'So where is this bed?'

357

A second bedroom had been established for him downstairs in the library, since there had not been time to install a wheelchair lift, and he was shown to it.

'Now that is what I call a bed!' he said, clapping his hands, and lifting himself out of the wheelchair onto the super-king, swinging his feet. 'Fantastic! Now I can get to work.'

As Tracy and Yvette helped him off with his smoking jacket, two of his three wedding rings, now too loose for his emaciated finger, fell onto the floor and rolled under the bed, where they had to be retrieved. In his silk striped pyjamas he then rolled into the middle of the bed and lay there too tired to move, an eccentric monarch drained by affairs of state, his fragile head sunk on the pillow. 'Come on, I want you all in here too,' he said, waving at his three wives. 'And where's that new lingerie?'

'It never came,' Firouzeh replied in all honesty, throwing doubt on the fact that he had ever ordered any.

'Shame. Never mind, lie by me. I want all my wives to lie by me. From now on you all need to understand a few new things.' He spoke with fading energies. 'Number one. The lion is the king of the jungle.'

Yvette and Firouzeh on one side and Tracy on the other slipped onto the bed beside him, their three heads pillowed on his outstretched arms, their bodies curling into him, arms draped over each other.

'King of the jungle,' Yvette repeated dutifully. She tried to hide the fact that she was crying.

'That's right. King of the jungle.' Sam's good eye was closing, fighting sleep. 'Number two. A lion has needs. Needs not necessarily satisfied. By one woman. This is Nature. His appetites are avaricious. And Tracy understands this.' The good eye had closed. 'Firouzeh?'

'Avaricious. I'm here.'

'Number three. I am like that lion. So you must not be jealous of each other. Who I choose. How often I choose her. Tracy?'

'I promise,' Tracy said, stroking his brow.

'Good. Then. That's settled.'

Sam's wives agreed that it was.

24

Life is a Quarantine for Paradise

On an overcast day in mid December, Saaman Wahid Akram Sahar was buried in the last of the dual ceremonies that characterised his life.

A friend from his Oxford days, the smarmy Viscount Romy Merchant, wrote the obituary notice for the *Daily Telegraph*. 'Sam, a classic opsimath, so long in thrall to vegetables, learnt late the joys of romantic love, and passed away in the bosoms, *sic* plural, of his large, devoted family, and peacefully in his sleep.'

A surprisingly large outpouring of sorrow also reached the Sahar house. Flowers arrived that had been sent from Iran, Egypt, Turkey, the United States. How word had travelled so far no one could trace. But due to the irregularities of the London postal service, condolences were mixed with distressing get well cards for some days to come.

The church service was well attended, which would have surprised Sam more than anyone. His beloved choir sang. His taste, by the end more Anglican than Muslim, meant that his wives let the English clergy have him one more time: he would be interred by the customs of his country of choice. His parents, arriving that day, supported each other in the front aisle. Fatima registered her disappointment that a Muslim burial had not been conducted earlier in accordance with the *sunna*, while Mostafa senior extended to the wives the apologies of their last surviving son, Sassan, who had been delayed by an army manoeuvre in the remote western deserts. Both parents were grief-stricken. To have lost one son prematurely was enough to sour life beyond repair. To have lost a second was to remove one's interest in it altogether.

Ridley provided the eulogy and steered clear of the court case, focusing on Sam's long-time love affair with two foreign countries: England and Women.

Following the catafalque out of the church, Tracy spotted Partridge in the back pew and even the furtive figure of Ricky Innes who had offered to cut the stone at no cost. She turned away.

In an unfortunate scene, Sam did not slide easily into the back of the hearse. The rollers stuck and he had to be waggled inside, the strain showing upon the pall-bearers' faces stooping to slide him home. Tracy looked away, and steered herself towards the follow-up car.

The cortege then made its sullen way to the cemetery.

On the clipped lawn the party gathered in arcs of diminishing emotion. As at most funerals the mourners appeared to be dressed in other people's clothes. Tracy was flanked by Yvette and Firouzeh, forming a wall of loss against which the four children nestled their backs. None of the other mourners dared approach them until long after the formalities had ended.

The stonemason, for his part, must have laboured long hours because the grave was surmounted by a near-cenotaph richly decorated with Persian calligraphy. Supported by a scaffold — the concrete still wet — the headstone carried Sam's favourite English proverb, both in English and Farsi translation:

Endure. Abstain. And remember to die.

Beneath came his details, the names of his wives, his children, the obligatory RIP.

Taxis finally ferried the family back to Burton Street where at last a tiny percentage of a cooking bonanza found mouths. The dogs became obese in the frenzied consumption of leftovers and groaned like oxen at the garden door. The children played soccer with a fang-punctured ball in the garden or else fed handfuls of grass to the last of Sam's purchases to have slipped by his wives' blockade. The previous night, the women had returned from the mortuary to find a haulage truck in the drive. 'Oh no,' Tracy had said aloud, guessing what it might contain. But the palomino had already been led into the Roman garden by the children, and the truck pulled away before anything could be decided.

Leashed to the fig tree, standing calmly among the marble busts, the creature resembled something from classical literature, the white stallion of Antioch. Clearly, it would have to go right back to the farm from

360

where it came, but the children's wishes were heeded until after the funeral. It could stay on for a couple of days more, it was agreed, shitting bucket-sized turds on the lawn and eating up everything in sight.

Aisha was the only child to have stubbornly refused to sit on the animal. She couldn't rid herself of the idea that its arrival was mysteriously connected to her father's death.

Inside the house after the burial the wake was in trouble. Lacking topics in common, many of Sam's old customers spoke only of their favourite dishes or the weather. The mood was stiff and the sectarian divide which Sam had so calmly spanned now lacked a footbridge. But when someone dropped a punch glass and screamed as it shattered, it became the excuse everyone needed to raise their voices above a sepulchral whisper. Instantly, the wake gained momentum, the division of groups fragmented and the whole affair became a much more fitting tribute to a lifelong polyphylete.

With Eric acting as barman, the assembled Christians were soon drunk. The Muslims remained fervently sober.

'All right, Father? Eric asked the mullah, who arrived at his table with an empty tumbler. 'What can I get you?' Eric snapped his fingers and clapped his hands in a performance intended to create a thirst.

The mullah surveyed the beverages. 'A drink. Non-alcoholic. Thank you.'

Eric cocked his head playfully. 'Come on. Sure about that, Father? Got quite a bit of stuff here. Caught a little note of hesitation in your voice there. Can't tempt you with something stronger?' He winked. 'Little something?' Eric laughed. 'No, no. Just kidding. Whatever you like. What do you fancy then? Fanta all right?' He held up the last of the kids' soft drink.

The mullah nodded and Eric poured a glass. 'Nice big one, eh? Must have a bit of a thirst on ya, under all that? Liked what you said by the way. About not letting . . . what was it? . . . death put "fetters on the feet", on the feet, of those left behind? Excellent.'

The cleric didn't reply and only watched the glass fill.

'There you go. That'll be three pounds.'

'Three pounds?'

Eric laughed again. 'Pulling ya leg. Just having you on, Father, you get into it. Plenty more where that came from . . . well, there's isn't actually, but I'm sending the kids out for some more. Drink that stuff like fish. Mind you, fish don't actually drink do they. Just squirt it back out again for propulsion. Think that's right any how. So . . .'

Over the rim of his Fanta the cleric stared at Eric.

'So . . . how's it going then? Your end? How's it going? The Muslim thing, in Britain and that, generally? S'all right, is it?'

Perhaps confused by the question's breadth the mullah looked taken aback. 'Going . . . ? I don't . . . I don't — '

'Catching on, innit. Well, seems to be anyway. Obviously you're doing a good job there. Our Tracy's a bit caught up in it actually. Had us worried for a bit there. But it's interesting, innit?'

'You are interested?'

'Yeah. Well, no, I'm just saying, it's interesting. Growing like wild fire, innit.'

'Then come. You should.'

'*Me*? No, no.'

'We have classes.'

Eric topped up the Persian's Fanta. 'No, no. No offence, but I couldn't keep up with your rules. Bit on the lazy side, me.'

'Thank you — '

Eric stopped pouring. 'Sure?'

'No. No more.'

'Mind you, a bit more discipline generally wouldn't go amiss round our place. Not sure about the old hands business though. Chop-chop.' He mimed chopping over his wrists. 'Now you see 'em, now you don't, but anyway, I'm not changing now. I like my singing too much. Actually, lovely bit of it today, wan't it. Sam's old choir. Beautiful. Got the hankies out, that did.'

The cleric finished his drink and looked about the room.

'Very sad, this whole business,' Eric said.

They both stood reflecting on this.

'Yes,' the mullah said.

'Terrible. Want the rest of this then? Finish it off? Last of it? Might as well. Go on. Yeah, go on.'

The cleric sighed, shrugged, nodded and held up his glass.

'That's the spirit.' Eric emptied the bottle.

Elsewhere, Monica confided quietly in Emily.

'Sorry, Em.'

'What for?'

'For not understanding what you were going through all this time.'

'No, you were wonderful.'

'No, I used to switch off actually. I used to switch off, Emily. I was terrible. Sometimes you'd knock and I wouldn't even answer the door. I couldn't handle it, y'see. And I'm so sorry about that.'

'Oh well. It's not your concern, is it. You've got your hands full.' Monica's eyes fell on her friend's daughter, Christina, richly dressed, childhood friends, jokily talking with Tracy about something, certainly not death. *The internet? Whatever it is, don't let her be trying to interest Tracy in it.* Though nothing would surprise Monica now.

'It's hard to know what to do,' Emily sighed.

Monica looked at her, then pulled out the black notebook. She opened it. 'Love is not to be learnt from men,' she read.

Emily thought about this. 'Is that one of Tracy's?'

'Mmm.'

Emily thought about it some more. 'Cheers,' she finally said, then raised her glass approvingly. 'I like that.'

'Cheers,' Monica replied.

'Got another one then?'

'You want to hear another one?'

Emily did. And so Monica began to search the notebook for further quotes previously dismissed as outrages but now dispensed liberally.

Abdullah had put an awning over the door to the garden to handle the spill-over if it rained. Underneath it, the three widows looked across the garden full of chatting mourners, the fat dogs lolling on the ground in their midst, their distended bellies inviting the scratch of a shoe. 'I wonder if they will still call it a harem now?' Firouzeh asked.

'No,' said Tracy. 'Probably a convent.'

'So what are we going to do now?' Yvette asked. No one had an answer to that. 'Well? We've got to discuss it sooner or later.'

The others nodded, it was true, but none made an effort to do so.

To mourn him in private over the next few weeks, Tracy went up to her room. The sound of her crying set everyone else off, carrying from the master bedroom to all the other rooms of the house. Eventually, and for everyone else's benefit, she decided to get out of the house.

She also thought that the privacy of some wide-open spaces would do her good. What she really needed to do was to walk, to exercise away the immovable pain, dissolving it on the pebbled paths of London's parks.

But first she would have to get past the front door.

'Going out?' Yvette asked with surprise.

'Just for an hour or so.' She pulled on her coat. 'Need a walk.

Tracy caught the bus on the corner, rode in the back seat, hidden among strangers, just like old times.

She watched grey London through the window. Beads of rain on the steamed glass were drawn horizontally as the bus pulled away. She tried to understand why Sam had allowed himself to surface from unconsciousness only to vanish permanently a few weeks later. What was the point of such a temporary return? She tried to remember all the things he had said to her during her last visits, turning them over for clues. His three unfinished canvases now sat in her bedroom. She had studied them from her canopied bed, scouring these abstractions for meaning. But mainly, she simply worried a single question: what the hell was she going to do now?

The global positioning system still lay beside her alarm clock. She had never learnt to use it. The day she had finally picked it up and pushed the power button the small digital screen illuminated with the words: 'WAITING FOR SIGNAL'. She had stared at it for ages, as it blinked on and off and on in front of her, but it failed to come up with anything further.

She disembarked at Baker Street, and against a light drizzle wove through the tourists heading to Madame Tussaud's. The park came as a relief.

Walking its familiar paths she remembered Sam at every bend. She could see him walking towards her, inviting her aside, curling his index finger, luring her into the trees. She saw the places where they had left the path. She walked by them, denying their significance.

The cupola of the Regents Park mosque appeared over the tree tops, a chunk of Arabia dropped directly into London clay. She wiped rain off her face and followed two veiled women up to one of the high wooden doors. Perhaps no-one would be offended if she went inside. She would ask for permission as soon as she saw someone in charge. Copying her guides she took off her shoes.

She was visiting at a quiet time. The line for the believer's shoes — which could accommodate hundreds — housed only six pairs. Leaving hers at the door, and seeing no-one with whom she could discuss

364

protocol, she stepped inside and right away found herself in the domed citadel, a vast space, the marble cold on her naked feet, the air cool as it rose toward a high blue apse, the aroma of hyacinth inconsistent with December. She held down a deep breath.

Luckily for her, a muezzin had yet to call the noonday prayers and but for three or four devotees, she was alone.

Disorientated at first by the lack of an altar she moved to a central space in the vast domed hall. The carpet was checkered with small rectangles in prayer-mat shapes and over one of these she dropped to her knees, an impostor in a foreign place. She wouldn't stay long. She simply needed some peace, some time out. She centred herself on one of the small rectangles, the great vault of air unstirred above her as she adjusted the scarf on her head.

She only vaguely knew what to do next. Though she had no right to pray here she was determined to begin her experiment and so she assumed the correct posture and bowed forward. Her eyes closed automatically, like a baby doll with lead-weighted eyes. Her forehead reached the mat and the floor's coolness passed into her damp, heated brow. What were the other faithful feeling, bent like this? She could guess. They were saying to God, instruct me, tell me what to do. She was weighed down by the same question, and asked the same thing.

Sam, where do the dead go? A serious question. She would never be able to work out on her own what it had all been for. What was she meant to have learnt? She had tried in vain to make herself a receptor for his afterlife messages but had so far received nothing back. What was the phrase? WAITING FOR SIGNAL. Yes, that was true now. The soul sent out its messages, on its strange wavelengths, but to no avail. Unable to blame the dead, the living blamed themselves.

She had married a talker. So where was he now? And weren't churches, mosques, temples the airports of the spirit, the take-off places, the departure terminals where the dead could still be paged? Then that's what she was going to do now. She needed Sam's guidance, his steady advice. Should she just pack up her bags and go back to her old life? If not, then what? The whole family was lost. Who would bind them together? Were there alternatives that she and the others couln't see? Perhaps in this mosque he could end this Superglued silence.

In this unauthorised place, with her head on cold stone, all the strength she'd shown up till now went out of her. Her heart burst its banks, fanning out in all directions, and she mourned a dead husband as a desert nomad might when swallowed up by sand. Opening the sadness floodgates, she shook with sobs, even as she tried to stifle them. She had no right to come here and cut loose her feelings. But now she had begun it was not easy to turn off the taps.

When she raised her pale face after her feelings had petered out, her cheeks were wet, her eyes streaming, and she caught her breath, taking in air deeply. Her eyes wandered up into the great, sea-blue apse yawning hundreds of feet above her. What was it she had learnt in her classes? *To love is religious*. That was it. Well then, perhaps this was her excuse in being here now. A widow had honorary status in any church. And if this was so, then maybe to mourn was sufficiently close to prayer to pass for the real thing. As the pagans brought baskets of bread-fruit, gold-leaf, incense for their stone Gods, so Tracy Pringle would set down her tears.

On an impulse, a dormant Anglican reflex, she brought her hands together and she closed her eyes, offering up her sorrow-gifts in a way she was familiar with. What did she feel? Aware of her own breath, a certain calm circulated up from an interior spring. It wasn't joy or condolence, not censure or perjoration, something more subtle and nondescript. She tried to press herself for more emotion, hoping to identify it, but in so doing she staunched it, cut off the supply. The analytical approach was wrong. The moment was gone. But when she opened her eyes she did feel a little better.

Yes Sam, you were right when you quoted that ancient rabbi. You had to be over 37 to qualify for divine help. By a quick calculation — yes, some supermarket was waiting right now for such skills — she worked out that she would have to grope in the dark for another seventeen years.

She looked around her. The numbers of the faithful had swollen greatly. Several dozen Muslims had materialised on mats patterned like the back of playing cards and were already deeply engaged, eyes sealed, rocking to and fro. These were the serious professionals, she thought as she watched, able to dispel the world's troubles with a few incantations, flood the desert plains of the human heart with life-giving waters, all in the twenty minutes allotted them for lunch.

Kneeling there, with her hands pressed together like a nun, she turned to see that she had come to the attentions of an official. 'Salaam Aleikum.'

She looked around. The robed elderly cleric, tall, with a flat circular hat, a heavy beard, a benign tilt to his head, nodded to her.

'Aleikum-al-salaam,' she remembered.

'Are you a visitor, sister?'

'I hope it's all right?' Her tears were still in evidence. She wiped the last of them away.

'Of course. Only ... I'm afraid you are in the men's section.'

'The men's? There's a men's? Am I? Oh. I'm not a Muslim y'see.' She lowered her pressed hands, a give-away.

'The women's section is just through there. You're welcome to go through.'

She rose to her feet with difficulty. her legs were cramped. 'I'm finished now anyway, thanks very much. I hope this was all right. Just coming in here.'

'Of course. Stay longer. Don't rush. Stay. Find peace.'

Did her distress show that much? 'No, I'm finished now. Thank you,'

She smiled and then hurried past the man, making for daylight.

Outside she stopped on the white stone steps. The square was almost empty now. She had to admit that she felt slightly better. For whatever reason her crisis had receded. Luckily, pain had a life-span too: it knew fatigue and petered out like everything else.

It had stopped raining. Standing there a scrap of sunlight fell on her face. She angled her head to better mop up its warmth. A shiver passed the length of her body and caused her to smile before she started down the steps again, heading back toward the trees, a small smile preserved on her face, the fetters loos'd, perhaps — for a brief few seconds — from her feet.

25

Smithereens

On the opening night of the new restaurant Monica and Emily splashed out on a visit to a beauty salon.

'Oh, I didn't tell you about the lottery,' Monica said as they waited for service.

'What lottery?'

'Councils apparently do it a lot now when they demolish these old tower blocks. They do a draw to see which resident gets to push the old plunger.'

'No!'

'Never guess who won it.'

'Not — '

'Old Mr Alexander on five.'

'Which one is he?'

'The one with the zimmer, y'know, and the little whoosiewhatsit.' Her hands described something in the air the size of a pumpkin. 'Y'know, the little chihuahua thingy.'

'Oh, I hate that dog. Horrible little thing. He's never gonna manage that, is he? It'll kill 'im. His ticker won't handle it.'

'He's still gonna give it a go anyway. Apparently he's still got a bit of shell-shock, the old buzzard, after the blitz'n'that. Hope it doesn't send him off again.'

'Nice to let one of us blow it up, though.'

'Yeah. It is. Sky-high. Least they could do, I say.'

'Yeah. It is.'

The salon was an integrated exercise area and arts and crafts gallery, all under the trendy title of healing centre.

'So have you settled into your new place yet?' Emily asked. 'I haven't. Feels weird.'

'No. We're still living out of cardboard boxes.'

'Nice to have a bit of garden, though.'

'Yeah, that's nice. No view, though.'

'Put a few spring bulbs down and everything.'

'Place for his highness to store more of his rusty motorbike parts.'

'Oh yeah. That's right.' Emily picked up a bottle of shampoo on the counter. 'Eighteen quid.'

'Criminal,' Monica replied without looking.

The big move had taken place ten days before. A tremendous stockpile of furnishings was assembled on every floor as the lift yo-yoed continuously, processing and setting at ground level the entire human store of the tower's several hundred residents, their million hand-picked possessions, lamps, couches, pictures, cracked cups, mementos of every kind, a colony uprooted and turned into nomads, refugees. Monica and Eric had bided their time, fighting nostalgia, drinking tea on the balcony, in no hurry to rush for the life-boats. Consequently they were one of the last evacuees to walk away.

On the footpath they had looked up wistfully one last time. Eric had said something rueful to the effect that the place where they had raised their child would soon no longer exist and what a shame that was. Monica had read this as an insensitive criticism of her years of hard lobbying and walked away from him. 'Thanks very much,' she had said.

'Two please,' Monica told the attendant when the girl arrived.

The girl in pink took their names. 'Which programme?'

'Programme? Blimey, sounds scientific, doesn't it?' Monica said.

'We have a list of therapies,' the girl replied tersely.

'Then we'll just have the lot, won't we, Em?'

'Yeah,' replied Emily, happily. 'How much is the lot?'

'Passing on the boob jobs for now,' Monica concluded.

The pink girl added up the cost, and reported that the complete makeover came to £475 per person.

Monica and Emily looked at each other.

The girl said, 'We take credit cards.'

'What about IOUs?' Monica replied, staring at her friend. 'Shit! Up to you, Em. What you wanna do?'

'We'd better . . . just . . . only do a couple of things then.'

'Yeah. Two nice ones.' They looked at the board again. 'Which ones then?'

'Don't know. Hard to chose.'

'What's the best one?' Monica asked the pink girl.

'They're all good,' she said, bored by their naiveté.

'Oh don't say that. Okay . . . what's vibration therapy then? Sounds a bit rude, dunnit.'

'A form of acupuncture. The therapist vibrates the needles.'

'Oh no, y'mean *twangs* them?'

'Ugh,' said Emily.

'No, no. Not having that. Sorry,' said Monica, squinting at the list. 'What about the . . . what about epidermal peel then? What's that then?'

'Slowly peels off your top layer of skin with a chemical wash.'

'Oh no, don't! You're joking me! People never pay for that, do they? I don't believe that!'

'Just the very top layer,' the girl explained with a sigh.

'Don't matter which layer, still a layer. No, I'll try something else. Who wrote this list then? The Gestapo?'

'My stomach's all of a go now,' said Emily.

'Putting me off n'all.'

The pink girl gave an unamused smile.

As Monica looked afresh at the treatments menu, Emily asked: 'What about we just go somewhere else and have a haircut?'

'Not chickening out now. We're here now. Okay, what's in the ginseng bath, a crocodile?'

The girl was slow to reply. 'Ginseng.'

'Em?'

Emily shrugged. 'I suppose. Yeah. Could do that.'

'Right then, we'll have two of them then, and Em, you choose the last one.'

With a short-sighted squint Emily studied the board. 'Umm . . . mud? The mud facial?'

'Yeah,' Monica interrupted, 'but the body scrub looks good too. All over with a loofah after the bath?' She faced the girl. ' You don't use sandpaper, do ya?'

The girl looked away.

'Yeah. Sounds nice,' Emily agreed. 'Go on then.'

'Right then. We'll have two of them as well. And a big burly Swede with hairy arms to toss me about.'

The total came to £75 each. Monica had to borrow some cash off Emily. They followed the pink girl towards the cubicled rooms.

'New women when we come out,' Monica said.

'Sue if we're not,' Emily replied.

Tracy delayed The Zahir's ribbon-cutting ceremony as long as she could for her parents to show up but she could wait no longer.

With Firouzeh and Yvette gripping her forearm on either side she snapped the big scissors shut. The tape fell. A cheer circulated. Tracy then led them all inside towards the staff waiting with flutes of champagne.

Eric arrived late. 'Amazing,' he said, looking around him at the replica desert landscape at night. 'Like Disneyland.'

'Where's Mum? You're so late.'

'Trace, your mother's not coming.' His tone was serious. 'That's how come I'm late. More bad news. Bloody awful.'

Eric sank into a chair. Tracy saw that he was actually in a sweat, his shirt darkened under the arms. He looked drained. During some part of his journey he must have run. Tracy had no stomach for further bad news and had learnt not to cultivate it with questions. 'It's her Cambodian kids. She ever mention them?'

Tracy nodded. They had come up in a phone call.

'Seems the two littl'uns she had in her play-group, they didn't show up on Friday for class, did they. So Monica makes a few calls last night and finds out the father has been refused asylum. They were all gonna be sent back. Well, I shouldn't tell ya, but they've just found them all this morning, didn't they.'

'What?'

'Whole family.'

'What?'

'Gassed themselves in their car.'

Tracy didn't speak.

'What can you do, eh?'

Tracy didn't speak.

Eric rubbed his brow. 'Hmm? About something like that? Bloody terrible.'

The awful image flooded both their heads: a dead family, a car, just waiting to be found, parked somewhere, the driver's head resting against the glass, the children in the back leaning against each other, frozen on a perpetual Sunday drive. What had been their last thoughts? Perhaps the children wanted to ask their father how long it would be until they all arrived at the place he had said they were going to, a nice place, a warm place, a better place than this, don't worry.

Tracy didn't move.

'Anyway, so, your mum's not coming down obviously. Knocked her for six. Bit of a mess. Fucking terrible.'

Someone tried to put a champagne glass into Tracy's hand. She waved the young man away. Eric also shook his head. She turned to her father, and her face was twisted with emotion. 'What are we gonna do, Daddy?'

He turned to look into his daughter's face: her young, clear features still giving off a childish fragrance as she looked to him for answers. 'How do you mean, love?' She hadn't called him Daddy in years.

'I mean, what are we gonna do?'

'We'll be okay, hon.'

'No we won't.'

'Yeah. We'll be fine.' He was hugely touched that she would still come to him like this, after all his crimes.

'Will we?' she asked, innocent belief in her voice, innocent faith.

Eric paused. He knew what he wanted to say, to distil his view of the world and gift it to her, be a true father. But he wasn't sure he had a view of the world! He felt himself grow desperate. He was often like this, at a loss for words at the most crucial times, struggling not only to find the right things to say but also the right things to *feel*, resorting to physical gestures, an awkward hand movement, a knowing wink, when actually some *insight* was needed! All he could think of saying was, 'We'll just have to get through it somehow.'

'Yeah?' Her eyes brimmed with tears. She waited for more.

'That's all,' he said. He shrugged. 'What else can you do?' He reached for her hand. 'We'll just have to . . . stick together,' he offered. 'Just . . . look out . . . for each other, I s'pose. I know I let you down.'

'Oh Dad.'

His own heart was breaking. 'Y'know?'

She needed more. 'I know, but what shall I do *now*?' she asked. 'I don't know what to do any more. I feel so alone.'

All her walls were down and Eric again saw Tracy as she once had been, pony-tail and hair band, running towards him, the skips and songs of her stick-trailing youth, well before the door-locks and the secrecy. He fought the desire to just grab her, to hug his feelings into her, to sidestep the verbal completely. But he had a grander sense of this moment. She sought advice of lasting value. But he was dry. No wonder she had turned away from him years before in frustration and married a talker. But all he could think of was 'You're not alone, Trace.'

She nodded, and looked away, accepting the fact that she was on her own.

But Eric tried to prolong the moment: Sam was his invisible competition now. 'It's all been said before. Sounds a bit stupid but we've all just got to take it . . . one day at a time.'

'It's okay,' she said. She smiled sweetly at him, letting him off the hook.

He wasn't finished yet. 'Sounds stupid but it's true: one door closes, another opens. It's silly stuff but it's all actually true. Rome wasn't built in a day, that's true too.' Men like Eric had no intellectual role models. He was carving his own nuggets out of bedrock, took help from no one.

'It's okay,' she replied. 'It's okay, Dad. Thanks.' She really wanted him to know that she'd be all right and for him not to worry.

He squeezed her hand even tighter, wanting to hear her say again Dad, Dad, Dad, to have the child back. 'You'll be all right, I'm dead serious. Cos you've got it in here!' He tapped his heart. 'You're strong.'

'Have some champagne, Dad. I'll phone Mum in a minute. Poor Mum.' She looked around for the young waiter. Her mind had returned to the party.

'Trace, listen to me . . . look at me.' But her father still needed to nail down this thing for himself, the uncreated meaning of his own life. Surely every father had one original thought to impart, a lesson that could raise her above human folly. 'I've got hundreds of things to tell you.'

'It's okay. Dad, let's get you a drink.'

'You just don't know what's ahead, Trace. Round the next corner. You don't. You think I know? I'm lost. I am. Completely *lost*. You're not looking at one of the world's great achievers, ask your mother.'

Tracy smiled but couldn't help looking distracted. She waved and caught the waiter's eye across the room.

'We, we . . . we all find . . . cos we all find ourselves tied up in funny little arrangements. And if people, if people even knew the half, Jesus, even *half* of what we did to make them work, on a daily basis, then they'd think we were all bonkers. Like I told you once, remember, after we had that little bit of bother . . . we're all putting together a jigsaw puzzle in the dark. Remember that? And it's a tough bugger too, one of the five thousand-piece jobs, the ones with three thousand bits of sky — almost impossible.'

Tracy looked back at him and smiled. She had heard this before. A man like Eric did not coin gold everyday. Gems had to be recycled. She nodded.

But he still wasn't happy. An old platitude, was that all he could come up with? He milked himself again for a wisdom he didn't possess. 'And these pieces, Trace, every day we get a different one, right? And you think, Jesus, where the hell does this one fit in? No way does this fit in. But in time you realise . . . well, actually . . . it's just a bit of the . . . ' Tracy drew up her eyebrows: she was trying to follow this. ' . . . of the barn,' he said. 'Or the wagon wheel.'

Tracy was lost for words. The waiter's arrival rescued them both. 'Thanks,' Tracy said, reaching for two glasses of champagne. 'Just what we needed. Here you go, Dad.' She put a flute in his thick hand. 'Cheers.'

They raised their glasses and drank.

'Nice,' he said, with a small pucker.

'I'd better go now. Talk to people.'

'Right. Yeah, yeah.'

'I'll call Mum in a while. That's so terrible. I can't believe it. Horrible. About that family.' She kissed him on the cheek.

She was gone.

On his chair Eric sipped at the flute of champagne. No, he didn't really like the taste, too bitter-sweet, neither beast nor fowl. His mind was still worrying a thought. He had failed to hit the nail on the head. He had not even told her his belief that in all probability he and Monica would be splitting up. There had been no decision but he felt the split to be imminent. Monica could not, it seemed, forgive him for his betrayal of their daughter.

He looked about the room. Most people were laughing now, communing, taking in the murals or looking up at the magnificent ceiling of stars. And far too late, looking upward himself at some constellation, it struck him: the thing he should have told Tracy. It was so exactly what he tried to say that he thought to go after her, call her back. In its economy and profundity it was worthy of a father rescuing a daughter; a unique message that he alone, in all humanity, was born to impart to his daughter; it was his legacy.

Don't expect too much. And you won't be disappointed.

The day was sunlit. Perfect. Even the wind played its part. It dropped away as the big moment approached, reducing the risk that a noxious cloud would shroud the suburbs in dust for miles around.

In the build-up, a crowd of officials mingled with newspaper reporters, ex-tenants and the general public. The lure for these spectators was the miracle of razing to the ground something so huge that it seemed an immovable piece of history.

The big prize, drawn by lottery, of who would have the privilege of pushing the actual plunger on the detonator, had moved to Monica Pringle in acknowledgement of her tireless efforts to bring this day about. The actual winner had been happy to pass on the chore. Mr Todd Alexander, too old by his own assessment for such 'ballyhoo', had decided it would be much better for his precarious health to avoid such excitement.

It was Monica then who would have the pleasure of bringing down the twenty-three-story tower and up on the makeshift stage, erected to set her in the public view, she adjusted the overlarge hard-hat on her head. The overseer of safety wanted to carefully explain the detonation procedure.

'Go ahead,' she said.

She was privately disappointed with the plunger itself. Just a twistable handle, it looked more suited to a garage door. A short wrist-snap was all that was necessary to set it off. She had hoped for a T-shaped affair, a full-blooded heave needed to drive it down: she had played out the scenario a hundred times in her head. She would have to make do, hope that in the explosion itself she would experience the watershed of emotions she still wanted to feel. She turned to look for her family. Held back by safety ropes some distance behind, they stood at the cordon manned by police officers. Poor Eric, all his plastering and shaved doors and eased windows would soon dematerialise.

'That's all you do,' the munitions expert told her. 'Are you listening?'

'Got it.'

'Little jog to the right, up she goes.'

She had it. She felt butterflies and the first twinge of a headache.

'Any second now,' the official said. 'Just waiting for the all-clear.'

She turned back to look at her supporters. Eric and Emily waved. Tracy and the Sahar wives and children had shown up as well, plus a contingent of her play-group colleagues. She saw that most of them were taking pictures of her. She put her hand on her hip and posed quickly like a movie star.

The expert's walkie-talkie snarled the okay. It was time. He moved her up to the spot. 'Are you okay?' She nodded gravely. He adjusted the hard-hat for her. 'Shall we do it then?' She nodded, pale already. 'All right then. Nothing to it. Let's get it on.' He put a key into the detonator, and a red light went off, a green one came on. 'All yours, love. In your own time.'

Monica gathered herself. She was at liberty to twist the handle any time she liked. She sucked in air to relax herself and looked up at the building. Birds flew across the space between and she paused to ask the official if she could wait a second until they had dispersed. The expert sighed but agreed. The entire crowd waited for the squadron of starlings to wheel and disperse.

Monica was then asked to proceed. She gripped the cold metal. 'Here goes,' she said.

'Take it away.'

'Blimey,' she said.

'Now.'

'Okay.' Her right hand rested on the business end of several tons of explosives.

The munitions expert was becoming urgent. 'Mrs Pringle?'

'I can't.'

'Go!' The entire area had been brought to a halt for this event. Time was crucial.

'Oh hell,' Monica said, her hand frozen.

'For God's sake, go!'

She looked up at the tower which, by her hand, would soon be rubble, and compressed into the next few seconds, as her hand turned, all the accumulated years of her memories: her marriage, the raising of a loving child, the lobby stench no one ever took responsibility for, the barren hallways off which everyone had their nearly identical key, her own hours of door knocking, the hundred-fold rejections and the impossibility of getting people to be of one mind. All these vertically stacked lives. External order, internal chaos. Enough. All gone. Whoosh. She twisted the handle. Abracadabra.

The explosives ploughed through the building. A building that couldn't decide which way to lean at last found a consensus. It was phenomenal. The vast tower came down vertically.

In a crisp sequence, like the crack of a sheet being snapped over a bed, followed by a mounting roll of thunder you might associate with an earthquake or avalanche, the tower gave in at the middle and blew out from the bottom, ignition jets of dust spewing from the base in the manner of a rocket launch, allowing the floors to crumple neatly and concertina downwards, allowing brief glimpses of opened-out rooms, a falling dolls' house, whole lives cross-sectioned and in free fall.

In that suspended second, Monica threw up her fists with a thrill that surprised her. 'Yes!' she shouted. 'Yes!' She spun round to look at her family. Her face was jubilant, shining. The last of the building hadn't even sunk into its own mushroom cloud before she had begun to celebrate.

But her family were not looking at her. Their jaws had all fallen open. She could make out their expressions, even from this distance. They were lost in the awesome spectacle, in the mystery of great destruction. They were stunned, dwarfed, staring at the sudden absence of all that had been there just a second before, while Monica could think only of all that she had cleared the way for.

She turned back to the scene of destruction, a shipwreck slipping into its own waters.

'Just like that,' shouted the official, whom the sight clearly never failed to humble. 'Just like that.'

26

Dead Men's Wives

A grave tended by one loving widow is usually immaculate. One tended by three is a work of art.

Wreathed in orchids, decked in chrysanthemums, Sam's grave had no equal in that part of the graveyard, if not the borough. And apart from the family it drew many visitors curious to read the polygamous inscription. 'Lovely,' the toiling Sahar women were often told, as the visitors stepped back from a close inspection, folding spectacles and resuming their tours of the cemetery, their hands behind their backs.

The children added their own touch. Twice rendered fatherless, they set twin photographs of both brothers in plaster of Paris and laid this on the body of the grave as a heart-breaking *memento mori*.

A visitor arrived one morning by taxi. Dressed in the clothes of a traveller, wearing a new straw hat, cargo shirt and trousers, almost every square inch of his clothes decked with a pocket, he made his way to the location by consulting the co-ordinates written on a crinkled piece of paper.

Like the others he read the inscription but then paused to undo the buttons of his tunic, he took off his hat and removed from around his neck a crested medallion which he laid amid the flowers and beside the children's pictures of the fallen brothers. He looked a moment longer, then returned to his taxi.

Half an hour later, the same taxi pulled up to the Sahar driveway. The same improbable figure alighted, paid the driver well, then, with a suitcase in tow, walked up to the front door to press the bell.

Tracy was home.

'Hello?'

'Hello. Hello. You must be Tracy. Hello.'

'Can I help you?'

'Yes. I think so. Yes. I must introduce myself. I am Sassan.'

'Do I — '

'Sam's brother.'

Sassan wished to apologise, and not once but a thousand and one times. He had to be stopped from literally doing so.

His leave had been delayed. By the time it had come down it was too late for him to attend. He had been on a train, riding alone in first-class, when the funeral had taken place, his own brother in the ground as he rose over the Zagros Mountains. Crossing a rail-bridge over a ravine he threw his sidearm out of the window in a last tribute and it fell to the 'centre of the earth'. He announced that at this moment he had decided to resign his commission. By the time he had reached Tehran central he had penned his letter of resignation, but it had taken until yesterday to complete the formalities. Still, the guilt of having missed the funeral would hound him forever. Such guilt would 'never find a home'.

Ten years younger than Sam, slim and soundly built, and at least six inches taller, bronzed under a desert sun from eleven years of military service and now combat ready, this breathtakingly robust younger brother sat opposite the three widows, regarding them with the same mix of curiosity, admiration and caution just then being directed at him. The pungency of his sweat had already overwhelmed their collective perfume.

Tracy and Yvette had to wait some time for the translation as a fierce debate broke out in Farsi between Fatima, her son and Firouzeh. When it ended a red-faced Fatima signalled to Firouzeh to proceed with a downward bat of her hand. But Sam's first wife delayed the English trans-lation Sassan himself could have made, having a working grasp of English. He thought it better, however, to leave it to his sister-in-law, who preferred to fidget a good deal instead of opening her mouth. Only when Fatima clapped her hands twice and barked a new command, so that the dogs barked and Yvette and Tracy jumped, did Firouzeh find a voice:

'Can't you guess?' was all she said.

Tracy and Yvette stared back at her, jaws agape.

'We don't have to decide right away,' Firouzeh said, finessing the foreign offer and attempting a diplomatic smile. 'He is merely, I think his phrase is, offering his services.'

'Yes,' ratified Sassan with short military nods and a firm voice. 'Exactly so.'

Yvette and Tracy's eyes bounced between him, Firouzeh and each other, incapable of a clear response.

Firouzeh went on. 'As our joint brother-in-law he, I think this is right, he offers to fill the shoes left empty by his departed brother. I mean, it is, I must say, a very nice offer.'

Yvette and Tracy stared at this witheringly handsome pretender, who didn't blink.

'And under tradition, it's . . . well, it's actually quite common . . . ' The old mother nodded, restless, wanting urgent confirmation, insisting that her daughter-in-law continue. Her hands were ready to clap again at any second.

' . . . but he . . . well, he . . . wouldn't expect to be our husband in every respect. Unless . . . well . . . ' Firouzeh then blushed.

'Oh my God,' whispered Yvette, as though to her conscience.

'You're kidding me,' said Tracy.

'I mean, at least, not immediately, or not necessarily at all. Whatever. Not unless someone . . . wished. But that would be our choice, he says. If we wanted that.' Firouzeh was gabbling now. 'And only when we got to know him. If things went that way. That would be up to us. As . . . as individuals.' Her closing smile was one of total innocence. 'Phew,' she said, and fanned herself superfluously with her hand.

All the women then united to stare at Sassan. He did not relax his proud mien or flinch in the face of the intense scrutiny. Perhaps the parade ground had prepared him. Seated on the extreme edge of his seat he had the look of a man asked to pose for a photograph but permanently denied the releasing sound of the shutter.

Old Fatima had seen enough. 'Good,' she barked, firing off a last salvo with her hands, deducing from the blood-drained faces that the correct news had been relayed satisfactorily. 'Good.'

'He asks our permission,' Firouzeh said. 'But I don't think we have to decide right now.'

Sassan then smiled. It was a shame he didn't do this more often.

Where he had been handsome before, a perfect and albeit serious specimen, he was transformed with this shameless display of perfect teeth into a heart-throb. 'If I can now speak now,' he said in excellent English. 'Thank you, Firouzeh. Yes, I would consider it a great honour if you would allow me to do my duty to both you and my family and to the memory of my two departed brothers. I ask your permission for this. Certainly, the children will at times need a man in their lives. The restaurants will also need hands and minds and many energies. Also, I have a degree in business, not a fancy English one, but a worthy one. And I think, I hope, *in shala*, that I can help in all these areas. I bring no family life of my own to complicate this arrangement. I bring only myself, and my suitcase. And of course, these hands.' He offered them. 'And this heart also. But please take your time. You don't need to decide right now. I'm not in a hurry to return to the desert.' His black eyes dazzled with a look of dark conviction.

Business concluded for now, Fatima placed her hand on Tracy's shoulder as she rose. This was the first time the mother-in-law had ever in fact touched her daughter-in-law, a conspicuous acknowledgement, made more so by the fact that Fatima kept the hand there a few seconds more than was strictly necessary. The other wives broke from their trance to acknowledge the momentous gesture. Tracy herself was stunned as the hand remained in place.

Fatima had a parting message. She spoke in short bursts, ensuring that Firouzeh made no mistakes.

'Sam was a philosopher,' Firouzeh translated, then waited for the next sound-bite, 'but this one, Sassan. He is a warrior.' At this, Sassan dutifully raised his chin to an even more regal angle: he lacked only a pedestal. 'He will look after you. Even better. Than Sam. Now I leave you. So you young people. Get to know each other. Better.'

Releasing Tracy's shoulder, Fatima left the room. As she intended, the young people were left to get to know each other, but for the time being could do no better than stare.

'Well then,' said Firouzeh, clapping her hands together in unconscious imitation of her mother-in-law, 'who would like some tea?'

Eric was incredibly weary. He had never been so tired. He had felt for some weeks that he was doing no more than move between emergencies.

In his new garage that adjoined the Pringle's temporary flat, and to the light of a single light-bulb, he had been extremely busy this last fortnight. He had put in huge hours. The move from Melksham Towers and the fury he now continually felt from his wife had asked of him a bold move. He had responded. The luxury of his own garage gave him the chance he needed. He would rebuild the motorbike of their courtship years.

The Ducati now stood on blocks, a shining miracle, the processes of decay and decrepitude remarkably reversed, and now the big moment had arrived. The engine was ready to be turned over.

Two dozen jars full of copper slime sat around him. The acids that had retrieved the bulk of the working parts from the grip of rust had done their job. Shiny metal had been unmasked. Other bits, gaskets, fuel jets, wiring, hoses, had to be purchased new. The gas tank was once again a vivid metallic red. Duck-tape cauterised the wounds in the seat.

He slid the key into the ignition still reeking of WD40, then nervously hit the starter motor. A million tiny acts of conveyance and combustion had to work at this moment. Had he got it right? A million acts also of nearly blind assembly. He had refused, as usual, to work from a manual. He was a professional. As a matter of principle he had pitted himself against the challenges of memory.

The engine didn't even turn. His thumb released the starter button. It was not yet a disaster. He had a checklist to carry out. Nothing in this world ever worked on the first attempt. He fiddled with the wires to the battery, waggled cables optimistically, made his way around the bike, tweaking and tightening, happy to find anything loose, grabbing his spanner off the seat, his heart rate rising.

This time when he pressed the button he heard an orchestra, a beautiful sound! The starter motor squealed, turned, whirred, whining out of extinction. The engine of his youth kicked over. Maintaining the starter, he waggled the throttle, waiting, gauging fuel flow, not wanting to flood the carbs, muttering *Come on, come on, come on baby* until the 900cc creature climbed back into beautiful life. Eric feasted on the sound of the famous Ducati grumble as he wrung the throttle for revs, shaking the walls, shimmying jars to the edge of shelves. Twin geysers of oily smoke flew out of the exhausts so that soon he couldn't even see the other side of the garage. But he didn't much care. If he collapsed of monoxide poisoning right now then this was okay with him. He could die like a man. Goddamn it if he wasn't back in business.

But he could seriously die like this. His sanity returned. He sputtered, released the throttle, threw open a window. It was hard to breathe. The engine idled perfectly. Going back to the enlivened bike he affectionately slapped the petrol tank which was now, God bless it, as warm as a liveried horse. He stared at his old comrade for some time until his joy settled. Finally, when he'd had his fill of success, he could turn off the workshop light. There was a lot left to do before he could take Monica for a ride but the back of the work had been broken.

Under the night stars he climbed the path. The temporary terraced council flat, a bolt-hole until something permanent came up, was on the ground floor: quite a change. His mates at the pub had a new name for him: 'Ground Level'. 'Here comes Ground Level Pringle!' But he didn't mind. There was no thinning of blood as he mounted the three neat steps to his front door, no agony in his legs, and he was spared the dizzying nausea of the lift ride. And when this ordinary door opened there would be his wife, whom he could now hear talking, and the sea-level certainty of a hostile, icy reception.

Still unforgiven for his wrongs and perhaps years away from a pardon, he paused before opening the door. Monica was not on the phone, as he'd first thought. He could hear a second voice. Yes it was Emily. No longer a neighbour, she was housed so far away that she was a prisoner of bus and train timetables. Visits were more rare but longer. As he applied the key he knew that his hope of slipping into bed beside Monica, of pulling sleep over him like a blanket, was doomed. 'Shit,' he cursed.

Emily's laugh reached him. They were having a good time in there. He knew what that meant: a long evening of feminine humour, philosophising and wound-licking from which he could only eventually detach himself. By then he would be exhausted, but unable to sleep, too afraid of what he would overhear from the next room, the fatal words — no doubt — that Monica was leaving him. Emily was certain to be told the news before he was. His wife would need to shore up her feminine support network before pushing the plunger. The nerve to make the final break, to destroy their twenty-three year marriage would come on a night exactly like this one. Was this the night then? Was the calendar of their marriage to solidify on this day, turn into a frozen tablet of stone?

Inside, when he opened the front door, he caught the two women laughing, sitting on bar-stools, obviously drunk. Monica closed, as if guilty, the infamous black journal in her lap.

It was deeply ironic to Eric that this record of Tracy's most extreme statements of recent months was now being used by his wife as a source of comfort and meditation. What a bizarre turnaround, to add to the others. Well then, what inspirations had she drawn from those extremist ravings now, he wondered? What witchcraft had been summoned? Was his old armchair, beer-drinking world never to return?

'Eric, come and have a drink,' Emily announced with more volume than usual and more gaiety as well.

He was slow to respond. 'I got it started. Did you hear it? The Ducati. I got it going.'

The women answered in unison: 'Happy Birthday'.

He scowled. 'Birthday?'

Monica then leant over the kitchen counter and produced from under the counter a cake whose unlit candles equalled his age.

He had forgotten about his birthday. It was insignificant anyway. 'Is it?' he asked, dumbly. In his terror of dates, afraid of what they might augur, he had blanked out all significant occasions. What was a birthday to a refugee like him, an asylum seeker in his own home? 'Forgot. That's a bit of a worry, innit.' He tried to laugh.

'Surprise,' they called, with minimal enthusiasm before producing, just as magically, a bottle of champagne.

'Oh great. Champagne.'

'And that's not all. Is it, Em?'

'No,' said Em, betraying some nervousness.

'We've been talking. That's not all.'

Emily shook her head gravely.

'And no smart cracks. And don't you mess this up,' Monica instructed severely.

'I didn't say anything!' Eric replied. 'I just wanna go to sleep, actually. If anyone cares what I think on my birthday.'

'You've got the rest of your life to sleep.'

He warily fluffed his pillow and sat back. 'If only that was true.'

In their pyjamas they sat side by side in the brand-new four-poster bed that Monica had gone out and ordered. It was a catalogue purchase. As soon as she had seen it she phoned up and Eric had assembled it from a kitset. It took hours. Monica loved the result.

The two of them stared up now into the poled canopy above them.

'She missed the last bus,' she said.

'I could have just dropped her home.'

'Oh shut up.' Monica then turned and called toward the bathroom, 'All right in there?'

'Thanks,' came the reply as the door opened. Emily Powell, in a nightie came out and stood before them, shaking head to toe with nervousness. 'Had a bit of trouble finding the light.' She tried to smile. 'I really don't mind sleeping on the couch.'

'Don't be silly. Get in.' Monica shifted a little.

'Okay. Is this side all right?' Emily got in on the other side of Eric, who shifted a little to let her in. When they were all in Monica said, 'See? Loads of room.'

'It's lovely, innit.'

'Ikea,' Monica said.

'It's lovely.'

'Eric put it up.'

'Ooh, good man.'

Eric, riding bodkin, piggy in the middle, the meat in the sandwich, smiled wanly.

Emily folded her arms in a buttress under her breasts. 'Are you sure this is a good idea?'

'Well, as long as Eric takes manly control we'll be fine,' Monica replied, making clear on whom she believed the success of this venture rested.

'I hope you're joking,' Eric said, not amused.

'Wouldn't mind one of these meself,' Emily finally commented. 'For me and my many lovers.'

Monica leant forward to talk with her friend. 'They're quite afford-able actually. Coming right down in price.'

'Are they?'

'Yeah. Get yaself one. Lovely to sleep under. S'like camping.' Monica then turned to her husband, to whom she had not shown an iota of affection in weeks. 'Well, Eric, here's your big moment. Birthday boy. How's it feel to be in bed with two women after all these years of fanta-sising, eh? What's reality like?'

Eric thought carefully before giving his reply. His marriage was on thin ice and he had concluded that this was all an elaborate test of his limits. He was determined not to fail. He would prove himself a better human being. 'If you wanna know the truth, it's a bit much actually. Not my sort of thing.'

Emily was more sensitive to Eric's embarrassment than his wife. 'We can all just go to sleep if you want.'

But Monica was disappointed. 'But we were kind of hoping, weren't we, Em, that you'd look after both of us, like a mighty sultan. Weren't we, Em?'

Emily blushed. She hadn't meant for this to be repeated. It had only been a joke.

Surprised, Eric turned to Emily. 'Yeah?'

Monica followed it up. 'That's what you said, wasn't it, Em?'

It had only been a joke. 'Monica!'

Eric lowered his voice in suspicion, 'You both haven't got a camera set up somewhere, have ya?'

'Course we have,' Monica replied. 'We fancy a little zippy Porsche ourselves, don't we, Em, so put your arms around us before we run out of film! Right, Em?'

Emily nodded gingerly.

Convinced that he was stationed on the borderlands between reason and chaos, Eric didn't move. This was a perilous situation. He wanted to placate his wife, make amends for his sins, but was he being lured into a trap? If he made a move towards Emily would she leap out of bed and declare him a pervert?

'Oh, for goodness sake!' Monica shouted. 'I thought guys'd be into this like a rat up a drainpipe.'

He reluctantly played the gamble of his life and put his arm around both of them. Roulette had nothing on this.

To make this easier for him the women leant forward. In a second his arms were around both of them, entwining their waists.

Monica said, 'How hard was that?'

'It's fine,' he said, his heart agallop.

'See?'

'Not bad.'

'See?'

'No worries.'

'Em?'

'Mmm. Nice,' Emily agreed.

'All right?'

'Yeah. It's nice.'

Eric then turned to Emily, surprised by this green light, almost encouraged. 'Yeah?'

'Yeah. It's nice,' this woman — *this widow!* — of his best friend replied.

'Easy, innit?' Monica concluded.

'Been a long time,' Emily agreed, suddenly smiling. Her eyes showed some moisture at the edges.

'See, Eric. She likes it. See?'

'He's nice,' Emily said. 'I told him before. He's lovely.'

Monica grumpily conceded. 'Yeah. He's all right. Cute when he was younger anyway.' She elbowed him. 'Well, give us your big squeeze then.'

'My what?' He'd forgotten about this.

'Go on. Your big squeeze.'

'Oh that.' He gave them both the big squeeze, holding both women tight for a few seconds. 'UK Squeeze,' he said. This was one of his oldest lines: it dated back years.

'I actually dunno what all the fuss is about,' Monica observed. 'It's not perverted, is it?'

'It's nice,' Emily agreed.

'Just looking after each other. That's all it is.'

Eric had a thought on this subject. 'Gotta be prepared to be our brother's keeper sometimes, dun't we.'

'What brother?'

'Our brother's keeper, that's all.'

'He means Graeme,' Monica said.

For a second the ghost of a dead man was invoked, a phantom's consent petitioned.

Monica was the first to speak again. 'That's what it's all about. Graeme'd know that now.'

Eric nodded. 'That's it.'

Monica prodded Eric, and winked at Emily. 'Eric's harem.'

Eric blushed. 'Fine. Just so long as the cops don't bust in.'

The women slid into his embrace, laughing across his chest at each other. Monica winked. Emily winked back. When Monica put an arm across his big stomach, over his hairy, middle-aged pot, Emily did the same. They were all getting on. Ageing together. There was not so much to lose as one might first have thought.

387

Lean from his desert patrols along the Iran-Iraq border, Sassan made himself semi-ubiquitous at the Zahir.

Every time Tracy turned around he would be standing there, puff-chested in his broad vertical stance, asking for his next assignment, another responsibility, and then another. He wanted to make himself indispensable.

Tracy went to the cash register and tore off the figures for the previous night. It was hot in the restaurant today. She adjusted the air-conditioner. She was feeling a little faint.

Going to sit in one of the caravan tents, she began to tabulate figures on a calculator and as her fingers raced over the keys, her eyes barely skimmed each receipt before she flipped to the next. She was a pro. *Tap . . . tap . . . tap . . . tap . . . tap . . .*

Sassan appeared without warning in the mouth of the tent. In a heavy sweat from moving barrels, he had poured himself a pint of water and held it to his chest, still puffing. 'Finished,' he announced.

Her heart jumped out of her chest. She turned to face him. Standing there he looked exactly like a character from one of her distant super-market day-dreams.

'Sorry.' He realised he had made a soldierly mistake. 'Creeping up silently is a habit. Used to stealing up on the enemy. I tend to forget that people are on my side.' He grinned, his teeth a lunar crescent. 'Plus it is very hard to knock on a tent.'

'Thanks Sassan.'

'Now I will take the rubbish out.'

Before she could tell him to relax she was alone again.

She resumed her adding as she heard him bump around in the kitchen. She felt light-headed now. She wasn't herself. And it was more than the muggy heat. She felt heavy, as though on the brink of sleep, either waking from it or falling into it. In the heat and in her fatigue she let the sound of the calculator lull her into her first day-dream in months.

Tap . . . tap . . . tap . . .
Blip . . . blip . . . blip . . .

She was back in the supermarket again, and nothing had changed. She was at her seat at the checkout and lost in some gigantic scenario where far-fetched characters were ensnared by some tragic but ultimately beautiful arrangement. She was at its centre, naturally, and by her actions eventually its heroine. The fiction as always seemed destined to end on a happy note. But an outside voice entered the dream. It was distant, but it called out her name, asking her if she was all right, reviving her. She didn't want to respond to it, now or ever. She didn't ever want to say goodbye to these characters. But the voice didn't give up and she eventually realised that it was time for her to shake her head and find a path back to daylight.

'I'm fine,' she replied, starting to work again. 'I'm fine.'

And with this effort, and at that precise moment, Tracy Pringle awoke from the great dream of her life.